diane's

Prai... ...
of Lori Aus...

An Outlaw in Wonderland

"A fast-paced Civil War–era romance between Ethan Walsh, a Union doctor spying in a Confederate hospital in Virginia, and Annabeth Phelan, the nurse who helps capture him. . . . The romance starts out sweet and tender, but rapidly becomes dangerous . . . a nail-biting tale of love lost and regained." —*Publishers Weekly*

"It didn't take me long to fall headlong into the story. . . . Very well written, and I can't wait for the next installment of this series." —Southern Musings

"Does not disappoint! . . . A captivating story of love, betrayal, and redemption . . . this story has it all." —My Book Addiction Reviews

"By the end of chapter six . . . I had to buy the previous book in the series, and it's even better." —Dear Author . . .

"A compelling story told by a writer with heart." —*RT Book Reviews*

Beauty and the Bounty Hunter

"Riveting, poignant, and unforgettable, *Beauty and the Bounty Hunter* by Lori Austin is a page-turner that reminded me why I love Westerns. I adored the unique characters and the depth of their story lines. Lori Austin is a brilliant and talented storyteller who doesn't disappoint." —Lorraine Heath, *USA Today* bestselling author of *Lord of Wicked Temptations*

continued . . .

Also by Lori Austin

Beauty and the Bounty Hunter
An Outlaw in Wonderland

THE LONE WARRIOR

ONCE UPON A TIME IN THE WEST

LORI AUSTIN

A SIGNET ECLIPSE BOOK

SIGNET ECLIPSE
Published by the Penguin Group
Penguin Group (USA) LLC, 375 Hudson Street,
New York, New York 10014

USA | Canada | UK | Ireland | Australia | New Zealand | India | South Africa | China
penguin.com
A Penguin Random House Company

First published by Signet Eclipse, an imprint of New American Library,
a division of Penguin Group (USA) LLC

First Printing, January 2014

ISBN 978-0-451-24232-7

Printed in the United States of America
10 9 8 7 6 5 4 3 2 1

For my moms, Beverley Miller and Judy Handeland,
who still like the Westerns the best.

PROLOGUE

Kansas, 1865

"Only good Injun is a dead Injun." The soldier—maybe Will, or perhaps Bill, even Phil—spat a stream of tobacco juice from the side of his mouth. "Let's just shoot 'em all and be done with it."

Luke Phelan stood on the top of a hill along with the hundred or so other men in his army company overlooking a peaceful Cheyenne village by the river. "If we shoot them *all*, it's gonna be damn hard to bring back live captives."

The man scowled. "I don't take your meanin', Reb."

Luke was a Southerner, that was true, but he'd been captured and incarcerated in the Confederate prison at Rock Island, Illinois. He'd gone half-mad there, and had always felt as if the walls were closing in. The Yankees had offered him a deal he couldn't turn down: if he swore allegiance to the Union, he could go west to fight Indians. When the war was over, he could return home.

As Luke rode a horse nearly as well as an Indian, and he thrived in the sun and the wind and the wide-open spaces but died inch by inch while locked away, the offer seemed like a godsend.

He'd been assigned to the 2nd U.S. Volunteers. Known as the Galvanized Yankees—a company mostly of Confederates who'd agreed to the same deal Luke had—they'd been transferred from Rock Island to Fort Leavenworth, then to Fort Riley. For the first time since he'd been captured, Luke saw the sky for more than a minute, and he was glad.

But Kansas wasn't Virginia; the Yankees were not the Rebs. Everything felt foreign and not quite right. While most of the regiment were Southerners like Luke, there were several like Maybe Will—Yankees who'd been sent west as punishment for dereliction. That the Rebs were better soldiers than they were did not sit well with their Northern comrades.

Now that the war was over, Luke just wanted to go home. However, a promise was a promise. A vow was a vow. He'd stay as he'd agreed to do until they released him. They couldn't keep him in the West forever.

"If we ride in shooting everything that moves," Luke said now, "we'll most likely shoot a captive."

"Ya think I can't tell the difference 'tween a white woman and a squaw?" Perhaps Bill objected.

Luke had been there only a few months, but even he knew that "squaw" was an insult. He also knew that very few of the soldiers cared. "I don't think you can tell the difference between your ass and your face."

Perhaps Bill blinked. Everyone else glanced back and forth between the two men, then toward their captain, who stood in conference with the Pawnee scouts who had led them to the Cheyenne encampment. The man's hands curled into fists. "Why, you—you—"

"What's going on, Private?" Captain Murdoch joined them.

As both Luke and Maybe Will were privates, along with nearly everyone surrounding them, no one answered.

"Fight the Indians," the captain continued, "not each other."

Even Phil cast a triumphant smirk in Luke's direction. "You orderin' a charge, sir?"

Before Captain Murdoch could answer, Luke spoke. "Looks like it's mostly women and children down there." Everyone glanced at him blankly, and he stifled a sigh.

"The Cheyenne have been troublesome for the past several months because of the massacre at Sand Creek."

"Massacre." Perhaps Bill snorted. "That weren't no massacre. It was a victory, plain and simple."

How the murder of hundreds of Cheyenne and Arapaho women, children, and old folks by a troop of armed and mounted soldiers could be touted as a victory, Luke never had figured out. Once the Cheyenne had begun to murder innocents in retaliation, folks conveniently forgot why and devoted themselves to making them stop.

So instead of killing the settlers, the Cheyenne had begun stealing the settlers. Which was how Luke's troop had gotten here—wherever here was. They'd started at Fort Riley, but they might be in Colorado Territory by now. Who knew?

"If we notch another 'victory' like Sand Creek," Luke said, "it'll only make things worse."

"You think you can give the captain advice since *y'all* did so good in the war?"

The sneer in "y'all" was not lost on Luke. Nevertheless, he refrained from pointing out that the Confederates had been winning that war for most of the war. The losses had begun only when Lee started to run out of bullets, food, guns, and men. They'd had nothing to do with the caliber of the army or the command.

Luke had been a member of the 43rd Battalion, Mosby's infamous Rangers—a band of partisan cavalry labeled guerrillas by the enemy and known for their quick strikes on Union communication and supply lines. Then treachery had resulted in Luke's capture and imprisonment. He still didn't know who was responsible for that. But if he ever found out . . .

Hell was going to be a relief for the bastard.

"Phelan!" Captain Murdoch snapped.

"Yes, sir." Luke discovered he was the only one who had not mounted up.

"You planning to join us?"

Luke glanced at the peaceful Cheyenne camp, which wasn't going to stay peaceful much longer. Why had he thought fighting Indians would be just like fighting Yankees?

The sound of a pistol being cocked brought his eyes back to Murdoch, who'd aimed his Colt in Luke's direction. "Get on that horse."

Maybe Will grinned. "Shoot 'im, Cap'n. It's what they shoulda done right off."

General Grant *had* ordered immediate execution for captured partisans. That Luke was still alive was either a miracle or an accident. Luke had never been quite sure of the difference.

He got on his horse.

The captain shoved his Colt back into its holster. "Slow and easy. Scouts go first. They'll ask for the captives. Then we'll see what we'll see."

They rode toward the river. At least Murdoch had the sense not to thunder down upon the Indians like the apocalypse. The Cheyenne didn't appear happy to see them, but at least they didn't scatter. Luke had been hunting often enough to know that if the prey ran, the predators chased them. Nothing good ever came of that.

A wizened, white-haired Cheyenne man waited in the center of the circle of tepees. His dark gaze remained on the soldiers; he ignored the hated Pawnee scouts.

The traditional enemy of the Cheyenne, Sioux, and Arapaho, the Pawnee now worked with the U.S. Army. Luke couldn't blame the old fellow for pretending such traitors were invisible.

"Tell him that Black Kettle has ordered the release of all white captives," the captain told his scout translator.

Black Kettle had released captives of his own before Sand Creek. As that had gone so well, Luke wondered if the chief had truly demanded the release of any others.

The Pawnee translated Murdoch's words, but the Cheyenne elder continued to stare at the soldiers as if he hadn't heard the scout speak. He almost seemed to be waiting for something, or perhaps someone.

Luke let his gaze wander over the camp. As before, all he saw were women, children, and old people. Where were all the fighting men? He lifted his eyes, saw nothing but swaying prairie grass all the way to the horizon.

"Search the tepees," the captain ordered.

Luke glanced at the prairie again. He'd heard tales of the Indians training their horses to lie on their sides, silent and still, hidden by the tall grass until an ambush was set. He'd always thought the stories nonsense, but now he wasn't so sure.

"Captain," he began. "We should probably—"

"Do it!" Murdoch ordered.

Luke bit back a retort and got off his horse. The sooner they followed orders, the sooner they could return to the fort.

A handful of soldiers scattered, ducking into tepees, coming back out. Within moments, they'd retrieved the two women and three children who had been captured from a settlement near the Colorado-Kansas border.

The sudden thunder of approaching hooves nearly drowned out a high-pitched whoop. Luke spun, hand to his gun, as dozens of Cheyenne warriors surrounded them. Most held rifles; those who didn't had drawn their bows. His gaze went to their headdresses—feathers sticking straight up instead of cascading down their backs.

Dog Soldiers. Hell.

The most elite of Cheyenne warriors, the Dog Soldiers had separated from the other bands after the Sand Creek massacre. While many of the Cheyenne leaders had preached peace, the Dog Soldiers wanted only war. Both vicious and fearless, they'd been known to picket themselves to the ground by a tether known as a dog rope, then defend that circle of land to the death.

Had the army known that Dog Soldiers had taken the captives? If so, they should have sent more men. Perhaps all of them.

"Tell the Dog Soldiers to stand down," Murdoch ordered.

The Pawnee scout released a guttural stream, the only result of which was the movement of the Cheyenne women and children behind the mounted Dog Soldiers. The captives remained where they were—huddled together between the two armies.

"Let us take them." The captain pointed at the white women and children. "We'll return to the fort. They won't see us again."

The Pawnee translated. This time the Cheyenne with the best headdress—the snarling head of a coyote— whose horse stood slightly in front of all the rest, the only man who had not drawn a weapon, lifted a finger. An arrow buried itself in the chest of the Pawnee. He slumped to the ground, the lifeblood pouring out of him like grain through a hole in a burlap sack.

The warrior's gaze flicked to Luke, and interest lightened the ebony eyes. Only then did Luke realize he'd stepped in front of the captives.

"I think he wants yer pretty red hair on his scalp pole." Maybe Will's voice sounded delighted.

Luke lifted his hand and encountered his head rather than his hat. He'd moved so fast it must have flown off, revealing his Phelan red hair, a shade as bright and brilliant as the dying sun. Mosby had taken one look and ordered Luke to cut it as close to his scalp as possible; as soon as he had, the colonel handed him a hat so tight the wind never once tugged it off. But in prison, and out here, there was a dearth of scissors, razors, and mirrors, as well as hats that fit, so his hair had grown well past his ears and his hat lay on the ground.

"Godammit," the captain muttered. "That was the only scout who spoke both Cheyenne and English."

"Life for life," the leader said, his gaze still on Luke's hair.

The captain, Luke, and everyone else in a blue uniform

stared at the man as if one of the horses had suddenly opened its mouth and spoken.

When no one responded, the Cheyenne's lips tightened. "You take them." He pointed at the captives.

"Yes!" Murdoch's agreement was so sudden and sharp, several of the army horses skittered. The Indian ponies did not.

"Many lives we give you. You must give us just one."

"No," the captain said.

Again, the Cheyenne's finger lifted and an arrow pierced the dirt only inches from the nearest captive. She shrieked and threw her arms around Luke's knees, nearly knocking him over.

"Keep them," Murdoch said hurriedly. "We'll go."

The white women began to keen; the children joined in.

"You will return," the Cheyenne continued more loudly so he could be heard over their cries. "You or others just the same. Take them now, or we will kill them and leave them here. It is the only way to have peace."

"You think you'll have peace if you kill them?" Murdoch asked.

"More peace than I have right now," the Indian muttered, casting an irritated glance at the shrieking captives.

Luke swallowed a sudden urge to laugh.

"I can't just give you one of my men," the captain said.

"Then go."

Every Cheyenne weapon—arrows, rifles, a few revolvers—shifted to the captives. Luke remained exactly where he was—between the cowering women and children and the Indians.

"Get the hell out of the way, Phelan," Murdoch ordered. "Get on your horse."

"No, sir." Luke's gaze met that of the Cheyenne leader. "I'll stay."

CHAPTER 1

Six years later

Rose Varner needed a man. And not just any man, but the one the Cheyenne called the White Ghost with Hair of Fire.

"Folks go into the Smoky Hills," said a barkeep in one of the endless supply of tiny towns in north-central Kansas, "and none of 'em come out." He lowered his voice as if imparting a secret. "He done killed 'em and buried 'em up there."

"Why would he do that?"

"He lived with the Cheyenne once. Crazy, murderin' bastards. Done turned the ghost plumb crazy. They say he talks to the spirits."

"If everyone who's ever gone into the hills hasn't come back, then who's saying this?"

The barkeep's forehead furrowed. "Huh?"

Rose gave up and moved on. Everywhere she went she heard tales of the White Ghost. He was tall; he was strong; he was brave, bold, and daring. Everyone agreed he'd been a soldier, but some insisted he'd worn blue, while others swore he'd worn gray. He *had* lived with the Indians. However, opinions varied as to whether he'd been captured and enslaved or joined them willingly.

She tried to hire a guide to take her into the Smoky Hills, an area of strange, chalk-shaded rock formations that folks had started to call "badlands," but she could not entice a single soul to accompany her there. The legends terrified everyone.

Except Rose. She was too terrified of what would happen if she didn't go.

The Smoky Hills were visible for miles. She couldn't miss them if she tried. She didn't need a guide. She would ride to them alone. Once she was there, she wouldn't leave until she found him.

As her funds were dwindling, Rose purchased a small number of provisions. She wasn't certain what she would do when she ran out. Her split riding skirt and loose man's shirt had been torn and mended and washed so many times they appeared older than she was. Her boots and her slouch hat were the same. She should have brought her coat, but she hadn't thought she'd still be riding when winter came round again. She'd been forced to buy another from an undertaker several months back. Hadn't wanted to—the garment had previously belonged to a dead woman—but the price was right and the snow had been falling.

She reached the hills about midafternoon and urged her horse through the brush and scrub, then into the shade of the towering rock formations. Shadows flickered, cool and navy blue. Spring in Kansas could go either way. She'd seen patches of snow on the prairie and ice floating on the rivers, which had made the sunshine today seem like pure heaven.

The rumors of precisely where the White Ghost lived had been as plentiful as the rumors of his origins. Another amazing wealth of information considering that no one had ever returned from the region alive.

Rose patted her mare's neck. "Do you think he resides in a cave on the east side or a dugout near the western creek?"

The horse blew air through loose lips. The sound echoed through a sudden stillness, and Rose bit her own lip, held her breath, listened. Nothing answered but the wind across the plains.

She found the creek, but no dugouts, no caves, no ghost, unless she counted the bones of a buffalo that decorated the bank. As night hovered, she made camp. The flames of her fire danced with the shadows, making it seem as if a hundred devils approached. But no matter how hard or how long she looked, she didn't see a single ghost.

He came silently, knife drawn. The mare snored, nose nearly brushing the ground. She never sensed his approach.

Neither did the woman. He was upon her, blade to her throat, before she drew breath to cry out. Not that crying out would have helped her.

For an instant the perfection of her cheek—smooth and white—distracted him. He caught the scent of lilies. Her hair, which she'd kept stuffed beneath a man's hat all day, would have glowed like the sun if she'd set it free. It was free now, shimmering silver beneath the moon. A lock brushed the back of his hand as she stirred.

He jerked in surprise and blood welled under his blade. He expected her to buck and scream. Instead her eyes opened—blue, like his—and she smiled.

"I found you," she said, as if he weren't straddling her waist in the dead of night, blade to her throat, a trickle of blood tracing the long, graceful column of her throat.

Something equally sharp pressed against the inside of his thigh, high up and far too close to parts he'd had no use for in years but still did not wish to lose. His breath caught as he realized she hadn't been asleep; she'd merely been waiting for him.

"Can you speak?" she asked.

He lifted an eyebrow, shifted his gaze to where her knife pricked his . . . prick.

"I'll remove mine if you remove yours," she murmured.

His treacherous body responded to the images that flickered through his treacherous mind at those words. As he straddled her waist, the weight of her breasts rested against his legs, warm and round, no doubt smooth and soft and white. He hadn't had a woman since . . .

He lifted the knife from her throat and rolled to his feet.

She sat up, eyeing his long hair—still Phelan red, but now shot through with silver. "I see the hair of fire. But why do they call you White Ghost?"

"Né-néevá'eve?" he demanded. *Who are you?*

She didn't answer. Why would she? How could she?

The wind whispered, *Kill her*, and while the wind had been his only friend ever since he'd come here, this time he didn't listen.

The first men who'd crept close in the night had planned to capture him and put him on display—five cents to see the White Ghost. If he caused too much trouble, they would kill him and sell glimpses of his body until the smell got too bad.

The wind had told him just what to do.

The next group had been searching for the first; they had similar ideas. The wind's answer had not changed.

Next came the law—a sheriff, two marshals, a detective. A whisper warned that if they found him, he would have to go back. He was not going back.

After that, the bounty hunters trickled in. None of them were smarter than the wind.

So why did he now ignore those whispers that had been his only companion, his best counsel? Perhaps it was the way that she smelled.

Nevertheless, she had to go. If not from this earth, at least from these hills.

He clasped his knife tighter, lifted it higher, and gave her a menacing glare. She rolled her eyes, and he gaped. He'd dispatched all intruders, yet this woman—Yankee from the sound of her voice—not only pulled her own knife but mocked him with word and deed, invading his territory, alone, as if she had no fear of the White Ghost with Hair of Fire. Perhaps she was insane.

Like him.

She got to her feet; her head reached only to the middle of his chest. She was so tiny he stifled the ridiculous urge to ruffle her hair like a child.

"My name is Rose Varner." She offered her hand. He stared at it as if it were the mouth of a rattler open to strike.

She reached forward; he stepped back. Exasperation puffed between dewy lips, and she snatched his hand, pumped it up and down. On her palm, she had calluses. He wondered why.

"It's polite, when someone offers her name, to offer yours in return."

Polite? He snorted. Where did she think she was? A drawing room in New York City?

"I know that you understand me."

He was tempted to spin about and disappear into the rock formations. She'd never find him. Except she'd come this far; she'd hornswoggled him by pretending to sleep, and she didn't seem the type to leave without getting what she wanted.

Whatever the hell that was.

"Shall we try again?" she asked, sounding like his mother when she'd been trying to teach him his sums.

"I'm Rose Varner, and you are?"

He opened his mouth, shut it again, glanced to the left then to the right. *"Ná-néehove—"*

It was only when she said, "English" that he realized he'd spoken in Cheyenne. "And don't give me any of that White Ghost nonsense. Tell me the name your mother gave you."

Her words, coming so soon on the heels of the first time he'd thought of his mother in years, made his eyes burn.

His mother. What he wouldn't give to hear her voice once more.

"If you give me your name," she wheedled, "I'll tell you what I want."

He very nearly told her that he didn't care what she

wanted; he just wanted her to go. But he was curious, and as he hadn't been for nearly as long as he'd been here, he indulged both himself and her.

"Luke," he said, then cleared a throat as dry as the Smoky Hills. "Luke Phelan."

Her smile dazzled like the stars above. He had definitely been too long without a woman.

"Irish," she said, her gaze brushing his hair. "T' be sure."

He would have smiled himself, if he remembered how.

"What I want from you, Luke Phelan, is for you to take my daughter back from the Cheyenne."

And suddenly . . .

Luke couldn't stop laughing.

CHAPTER 2

The White Ghost had a laugh as rusty as her own.
Rose doubted it was for the same reason.

The laughter went on longer than most laughter did.
She waited patiently, a talent she'd perfected long ago.
Patience had proven more useful than she ever would
have guessed.

The White Ghost—Luke Phelan, Rose corrected
herself—was very tall and far too thin. His blue eyes
and red hair would have hinted at Irish even before he'd
said his name and made it true. Despite his coloring, he
was fortunate enough to have skin that didn't burn
beneath the western sun, but had toasted to a lovely
golden hue. She wished she were half as lucky. However,
since she'd come west, her luck—if she'd ever had any—
had deserted her.

His clothing—half soldier, half Indian—only made
him seem more Indian. Many of the warring plains
tribes took shirts, boots, trousers, and hats—as well as
the hair beneath—as trophies.

Phelan had either kept his yellow-striped, blue cavalry trousers, or taken someone else's. It would be common to ask which. His feet were bare—as if there were
no spring chill—and as thin as the rest of him. The slice
of chest and stomach revealed by the open deer hide
vest was smooth and rippling with as much muscle as
his bare arms. The silver that circled one biceps and
dangled from both ears should have made him effemi-
nate but didn't.

He had lines on his face—the sun and wind had seen to that. However, she still didn't think he'd reached thirty, despite the streaks of white in hair the shade of a maple in late autumn. Most ladies would disdain that long, curling, tangled red hair. But Rose was no longer a lady.

The sudden silence breached her senses. She tore her gaze from his hair, which brushed his too-sharp collarbone, to discover he had been studying her as she studied him.

The heat of the fire seemed to press on her flushed face. She was no lady; he was no gentleman. Which was fine with her. She had not come here to find more of what she'd had quite enough of already.

The wind ruffled his hair, but Rose was the one with goose bumps. "I'd appreciate an answer."

"Laughter wasn't answer enough?"

"No," she said shortly.

His lips tightened; he lifted his face to the stars and his hands to his head. She caught her breath as the moon poured over him, revealing ridged scars around both wrists.

"You were a prisoner." He lowered his hands, then his gaze. She pressed on. "How can you not want to help a child in the same predicament?"

"Predicament," he murmured, as if the word were fresh and new. Perhaps, for him, it was.

"Perilous situation," she said.

"I know what it means." His voice had a slightly Southern drawl. "Considering where you are and who you're with, I'd be more worried about my own predicament, if I were you."

"I'm not worried about anything but Lily."

He winced. "Don't tell me any more."

Rose hadn't gotten this far by listening to advice. "She's three years old." His fingers curled into a fist, but she hurried on. "She likes newborn calves and butterflies, the color yellow, and—" Her voice broke.

Luke turned away. "I can't help you."

"Please." Desperation deepened her voice. "She—"

He ran, disappearing into the darkness like the ghost he was. Most women would have given up then. But Rose Varner was not most women.

She didn't chase him; she knew she wouldn't find him that way. Instead she stared into the fire until the sun came up. Then she doused the flames and urged her horse in the direction Luke Phelan had run. She soon found that bare feet across dry land, with a prairie wind blowing, left very few tracks. The Smoky Hills were deceptive—one pale, dusty, twisted rock formation appeared a lot like another. But she kept going. Eventually she'd find him, or he'd, again, find her.

When darkness fell that night, she made camp alone. Again, she lay by the fire, closed her eyes, and listened to the night. This time she kept both her knife *and* her guns nearby.

She caught the whisper of an approach. Louder tonight. She heard him from much farther away. He didn't even try to keep quiet. He clumped about so much he sounded like two men. And their horses.

Rose sat up as the moon cast its ghostly light over just that.

Luke tipped the whiskey bottle to his lips, enjoying both the fire in his belly and the spread of warmth everywhere else. His pleasures in this world were few. Not that he deserved pleasure, but it was human nature to yearn.

The woman, Rose Varner, and the story of her lost child had brought back all he'd tried to forget. Only whiskey made the memories fade. But it seemed to take more and more whiskey these days to achieve the desired result.

What was it about the woman that made him remember? She looked nothing like—

Kiwidinok, the wind murmured.

Luke's fingers clenched on the glass as agony flared. He suckled from the bottle until both it and the whisper went away.

He had to make Rose Varner leave. He'd heard her floundering around his hills all day. Now he could smell her fire. Hell, he could smell her. He'd have no peace until she was gone.

He'd have no peace *ever*, but he didn't need an audience.

The scent of smoke, the flicker of flame drew him through the darkness. He hovered just out of sight around a rock formation twice his height. He fingered his knife, wondering what, exactly, he could do to encourage her departure that he hadn't done already. Then he heard voices.

At first he thought it was the wind again. But these voices said things the wind never had.

"Well, hello, pretty lady. Whatcha doin' out here all alone?"

"I'm not." She sounded more annoyed than afraid.

"Alone?"

"Pretty," she snapped.

"Here, now." A second voice, rougher than the first. Luke did not like that one at all, even before it finished speaking. "No need to fret. My papa always told me all women are the same with a bag over their head."

"And my mama told me about men like you."

"What did she say?"

The two gunshots were so loud that Luke, who'd had his cheek pressed to the sandstone monolith, jerked and banged his temple.

"She said if a man can't be a gentleman, he's better off dead."

Luke had thought *she* was dead, and he was so glad to be proved wrong he'd stepped out from behind the rock before considering that a spooked female just might shoot him, too.

Except she'd already holstered her guns—where had they been last night?—to stare at the dead men, fists planted on her hips, exactly the way his mother used to when she was beyond exasperated. "I suppose you would have stood there and let them do whatever they liked?" She flicked him a disgusted glance. "I didn't need your help. I've met their kind before."

"Kind?" he repeated, moving from moonlight to fire-light.

"Those who underestimated women." Her lip curled with disdain. "It was their downfall."

"They're dead; you killed them." He couldn't seem to get his mind around the fact, as well as her lack of concern over it. Most women would be shaking and crying. Then again, most women wouldn't have shot two men with two bullets before they even had time to draw their guns.

"They had worse planned for me. Bag over my head." She spat at the nearest body, hit him right in the face, then lifted her gaze to Luke's. "Are you going to run away again?"

The whiskey he'd drunk earlier seemed to have disappeared from his blood like the life from those bodies. He felt as sober as a priest before Mass. "Are you going to shoot me?"

"Do you plan on putting a bag over my head?"

"The man who does is the greatest kind of fool."

She glanced at him sharply. He kept his face impassive as he stepped over the bodies and joined her by the fire.

"What do you mean by that?"

Her voice hadn't quivered when she'd faced men who would have raped and then murdered her, but it quivered now and he wondered why. There were so many whys that he wondered about her.

"The eyes," he said, "hold every secret to the soul."

Their gaze met and held. The air crackled. Or was that the fire?

"If I put a bag over your head," he murmured, "I'd never know what you were planning."

"You'll never know that anyway."

She was right. She was like no woman he'd ever met.

"How did you learn to shoot like that?" His sister could have made those shots, but she'd been raised with five brothers and had always tried to best them in every way that she could. She wasn't stronger than them, couldn't be, but she could shoot as well, or better, if she practiced more. So she had.

"You think I'd ride around alone if I couldn't take care of myself?"

"I hope not." He paused. "That really wasn't an answer."

"I taught myself. I had to."

He didn't think he was going to get more of an answer from her than that. And what did it matter? She could shoot. He was glad. His gaze returned to the dead men. "They were probably here for me."

"They seemed to be here for me."

"Why would they come looking for you?"

"Why would they come looking for you?" she countered.

"You did."

"I have a very good reason."

"I'm sure they did, too." He scratched his chest. "I think there's a bounty on me." Which would explain the bounty hunters.

Her eyebrows lifted, but she didn't ask why. Which only meant that he was right.

"You could have told them how to find me and saved yourself."

"I did save myself. And if they had you, I wouldn't."

"You don't. You won't. I . . ." He paused to swallow the river of dust that had suddenly filled his throat. "I can't go back to the Cheyenne. I just . . . can't."

Her gaze brushed the scars on his wrists, and he shuddered as if a ghostly fingertip had trailed there. Disgust? Desperation? Desire? It had been so long since he'd felt any of them—it had been so long since he'd felt anything—he wasn't sure.

"I'm sorry they hurt you. But what if—" Her voice broke.

"They won't hurt her," he said.

"How do you know?"

"I know."

"You lived with them." As she wasn't asking, he didn't answer. "Why did you leave?"

"I couldn't stay."

"Because you were . . ." She waited for him to finish the sentence. He remained silent, though his mind offered suggestions.

Foolish. Selfish. Hated.

Lost.

"Crazy?"

He blinked. "What?"

"Did they make you leave because you were crazy?"

"No."

"You aren't crazy?"

"Oh, I'm definitely crazy." Had been for quite some time, perhaps even before he'd left the Cheyenne.

"Did you kill all the people they say you killed?"

"Probably."

"You don't know?"

"I don't care."

"I'm sure you had to kill them before they killed you."

"I killed them because the wind whispered."

"You what?"

His lips twitched. "I told you I was crazy."

"You don't seem crazy."

"And you don't seem stupid, yet here you are."

Now her lips twitched. "The wind speaks to you?"

His amusement faded. "Yes."

"What does it say?" She lifted her face to the eerily still night, baring the long, smooth white column of her throat.

Kill her.

He clenched his hands. Her gaze, as she lowered it to his, held not a trace of fear. "Did it tell you to kill me?"

He could only nod.

"You haven't."

Did that make him less crazy or more?

She was the biggest problem to come into these hills since he'd arrived. That he hadn't killed her worried him. If he didn't listen to the wind, the wind might stop speaking, and then what would he do?

"You smell like lilies," he said.

"I know."

She wasn't concerned in the least over his statement that the wind wanted her dead. He considered the blood dampening the dirt at her feet. He wasn't surprised.

"I was starting to forget." She drew in a deep breath, let it out slowly. "The shape of her face, the way that she smiled."

"Yes," he whispered.

"The scent of lilies helps me remember."

The wind made sure that Luke would never, ever forget.

"I bought some perfume, but now it's gone and I . . ." She blinked several times, then drew herself up. "What do you want? Money?"

"Money means nothing to me."

"What does?"

"Solitude."

She sniffed, and her nose wrinkled. "How about whiskey?"

"You're going to give me whiskey?" He doubted there was enough in the world to grant him the peace that he craved.

"I'll give you anything you want if you take me to the Cheyenne."

He let his gaze linger on the swell of her breasts that even the loose man's shirt could not disguise. "Anything?"

She laughed, the sound harsh and cold amid the quiet of the night and the warmth of fire. "You don't want me."

He tilted his head. "I don't?"

"No one does."

He frowned, but she continued before he could say anything else. "I would go myself."

The thought of this tiny, pale woman approaching a Cheyenne camp made his skin prickle.

"But I don't know the language, the customs, or where in creation they might be."

"You think I do?"

"I know you do."

"You shouldn't listen to rumors."

"If I'd listened to rumors, Mr. Phelan, I wouldn't be here. You're a killer."

"Pot. Kettle," he murmured, his gaze on the two bodies.

He thought he heard a burble of laughter, but when he looked back he saw nothing of the kind on her face. Instead she stared at him steadily. "I'd prefer that you go with me, but if you won't, I'm not going to just leave her there."

"You'll die."

"Better than living without her."

He'd once thought the same thing. Hell, he still did. But he hadn't the courage to die. He thought that Rose Varner probably did. Why that bothered him, he wasn't sure.

He still wasn't taking her to the Cheyenne.

"You've proven you can take care of yourself," he said.

"I always have. It's my daughter I wasn't able to take care of."

Which only made them two of a kind.

CHAPTER 3

As Rose saddled her horse the next morning, the wind blew south, which seemed as good a reason as any for her to blow south, too.

She hadn't planned to leave the Smoky Hills without the White Ghost, but short of knocking him over the head and lifting him onto her horse—neither of which she thought she could accomplish—she didn't see how she could turn that hope into a reality.

In truth, when he'd abruptly stood and left last night—no good-bye, he'd just stalked into the darkness—she'd been relieved. She'd done her best to pretend he didn't frighten her, but he did. There was something desperate about him. She recognized it, because there was something desperate about her. Desperate people had nothing to lose, which made them not only unpredictable but dangerous. Her being that was one thing; she had to be to retrieve her daughter. His being that way could ensure just the opposite.

Rose glanced over her shoulder and saw nothing. Still, she thought he was watching her. She didn't much like it.

Rose considered riding to another fort. She'd already been to several—Fort Dodge, Fort Harker, Fort Zarah, Fort Hays, and Camp Sherman, which she had been informed was now called Omaha Barracks.

Since that idiot Custer had massacred over a hundred women and children at the Washita River not three years ago, the Cheyenne had been troublesome.

The progress of the railroad across their hunting lands hadn't made them any happier. They attacked the work crews and supply trains; they destroyed the tracks wherever they could.

She hadn't needed a pretentious army colonel to tell her that the soldiers had all they could do keeping the Indians from obliterating everyone in Kansas, Colorado, and Nebraska. She'd lived it, thank you very much. As she'd known from the moment she'd started this quest, she was on her own.

Perhaps a larger town would provide greater possibilities. There had to be someone besides the great White Ghost who could take her to the Cheyenne. Or at least someone who could point her in the right direction. They were out there. One only had to know where to look.

Without warning, her mount shied. Rose tightened her legs, gripped the saddle, murmured nonsense. In response, the animal reared.

She kept her seat. It wasn't easy. The horse pawed the air, huffed, then slammed its hooves back onto the ground so firmly Rose's teeth nearly clipped off her tongue.

Snake, she thought, expecting her mount to bolt or stomp, then buck. She held on with all her strength. She could not afford to be thrown onto a rattler. Instead the horse stilled, nostrils flared, ears pricked, muscles beneath its sleek skin twitching.

The Indians rose as if they'd grown right out of the ground. Where had they been? She'd seen nothing in any direction but prairie grass—all the way to the horizon.

In her mind she reached for her gun; she shot them before they got anywhere near. *Bang. Bang. Bang.* Three bullets, three dead Indians.

In reality, the sight of them caused a jolt in her chest, in her blood. They were half naked, wearing only short breechclouts and moccasins, and their scalps were nearly shaved, the spike of a scalp lock trailing from the center.

Her head went light; she was unable to breathe. When they dragged her from her horse, the Rose that lived in her mind fought. She kicked and shrieked, cursed and bit; then she ran.

The Rose that lived on the earth hit the ground in a heap, then lay there as they gathered in a circle, their soulless eyes seeming to crawl all over her before one of them reached down. She tried to scream, to move, to run. Nothing came out but a moan. One leg twitched.

He flicked her hat from her head, and that circle of eyes lit on her long blond hair. He lifted several strands to the sun, the contrast between the gold and brown so stark. His other hand lifted; the knife glinted. She wanted to close her eyes, and she couldn't even manage that.

The blade descended, disappearing from view above her. Pain flared, brighter than the sky across her scalp. The air filled with the familiar sound of screams. But they weren't hers.

The Indians scrambled up. The one with the knife let go of her head, and it thumped to the earth so hard her ears rang. Or perhaps that was the thunder. The prairie shook with its force. How odd since the sky remained bright blue.

Three dull whacks sounded, similar to the thud her head had made against the dirt. She lifted her hand, touched her head. Her fingers came away painted red.

Her attackers staggered back. Rose sat up—the better to see past the tall grass—and a warm, wet flood doused her eyes. Impatient, she tore a strip of cloth from her shirt, swiped her face, then tied the band around her forehead so she could see.

A horse raced in their direction. No saddle, the only bridle a rope looped around the horse's jaw, but a rider clung low to its back; a long, thick stick swung from his hand. The sound she'd thought was screaming, but was more of a *whoop*, returned. The volume made her ears ache. As he rode past, he thumped the Indians on the head with the stick—*thunk, thunk, thunk*—and was gone.

A hysterical giggle threatened to break free, and Rose slapped a palm over her mouth. The Indians seemed to have forgotten her. Who wouldn't with that whooping, thumping maniac turning around for another pass? However, this time he leaped free several yards away. The horse continued on, making a wide curve and coming to a stop, his gaze fixed on his rider.

The man wore fringed buckskin leggings and a matching shirt, beaded and quilled. His features had been painted with black and white streaks; a headdress of dark feathers dotted with white tufts covered his head. She'd seen similar headdresses, similar paint, a similar shirt once before.

On the night she'd last seen her daughter.

He lifted his face to the sky and gave another long whoop, before he took the rope tied across his chest like a sash and drove the picket at one end into the ground, staking himself to the earth like a horse.

Her attackers raced in his direction. If Rose could have moved, she would have considered climbing onto her horse and fleeing. But she wasn't so foolish as to believe that she was not the prize in the coming battle. The idea of being ridden down and captured by the man wearing that headdress, or the three who had planned to take her hair, was too terrifying to contemplate. So she sat in the grass and watched, unable to move any more now than she'd been able to before.

The new arrival twisted and kicked the first warrior in the chest. The man smashed into the second and they both fell. The third leaped out of their way and practically ran into the knife the painted warrior had drawn. He fell to his knees, then onto his side and lay still.

Jab after jab opened cuts in all of them. The sun beat down, warmer than it should be, and the sweat painted their bodies, as well as the earth, crimson. A second died the same as the first, and the two that were left circled.

The staked man stumbled. The other moved in for the kill. The first drove upward with his knife. Not weak, not off balance, had he even tripped at all? The kill was a dance, graceful and sure. The final attacker fell backward without a sound.

The victor yanked the picket from the ground and stalked in her direction. Rose meant to meet his eyes, to face her death as bravely as he'd faced his. But as he approached, the streaked paint, the waving feathers shimmied. He became another man, in another place, on another night.

"Not night," she whispered, fighting against both confusion and unconsciousness. "It's *day*."

So why did the sun suddenly go dark? Why could she smell the house burning? Her daughter screaming?

There *was* no house. Just as there was no daughter.

Not here. Not now. Perhaps not ever again.

Rose toppled over as Luke approached. Considering the amount of blood on her face and clothes, in her hair—it now appeared nearly as red as his—he couldn't believe she hadn't fainted before.

Of course she wasn't the fainting type. She'd faced down two armed men, sparred with them, then shot them without a flicker. Hell, she'd spat on one seconds afterward. He admired that. So why were her guns still in their holsters? Why had she just lain there and let the Pawnee nearly scalp her? He had an idea, and he didn't much like it.

Luke knelt at her side, gazed on her wound. He'd need to stitch it; she'd probably have a scar. He doubted it was her first. And traveling alone as she was, it wouldn't be the last.

He retrieved all the water from the nearby horses, whistling sharply to his own. The animal returned, standing next to Rose's mount, avoiding the Pawnees' like the smart Cheyenne-trained horse that he was. All Cheyenne hated the Pawnee, even the horses.

Luke yanked off her gruesome bandage. The contrast between the pale skin beneath and the brownish red all around made her appear as if she'd been in the sun for days. Her eyes opened, then widened. Her breath caught and held. Panic washed over her face.

"It's me," he said, and she blinked, her gaze lowering from the top of his head to his eyes.

She let out her breath. "Mr. Phelan?"

"Who else?"

She waved weakly where she'd stared, then ran her fingertip down his cheek. He jerked back at her touch. She held up her hand. Her finger was covered in paint. He couldn't remember when he'd slapped it on. He'd felt uneasy, watched, stalked from the moment he'd woken. Which only made today the same as quite a few others.

"Could you—? Would you—?" She breathed in and out once more. "God, take it off!"

He removed his headdress, set the item carefully out of the way. His movements caused dried blood to flake off his neck and sprinkle the ground like salt. *That* didn't seem to bother her.

"You shot two men and didn't flinch, but some paint and a few feathers scare you?"

She sat up. "Yes."

"Well, at least something does."

"You surprised me is all. The only thing that truly frightens me is never seeing my daughter again."

"Liar."

She blinked; her mouth opened, but nothing came out.

"You were so scared of those Pawnee you didn't even draw your gun."

"I didn't have time."

He didn't bother to call her a liar again. They both knew that she was.

"That's a Dog Man headdress," he began.

Her gaze flicked to the feathers and quills, then to his face. "Dog Man?"

"It's what the Cheyenne call the Dog Soldiers. Dog Men. *Hotametaneo'o.*"

"You *did* ride with the Cheyenne." She sat up straighter. "You can find them."

Instead of answering, he took her left hand, rubbed his thumb along the mark on the third finger. There'd once been a ring there. Even though there was no longer, the sun and wind had darkened and roughened the skin on either side of where it had rested.

"When you said the Cheyenne took your daughter, you meant the Dog Men took your daughter."

"What difference does it make?"

"Comparing the Cheyenne and the Dog Men is like comparing a tomcat and a lion."

"The Dog Soldiers—Dog Men—*are* Cheyenne."

"Some are Sioux as well." The tribes that had warred in the past had now mingled, their warrior societies, too. "But all Cheyenne aren't Dog Men. Only the best fighters, best horsemen . . ." He paused, deciding to keep "best killers" to himself. She appeared frightened enough already. "It's a military society. There are several: Fox Soldiers, Elk Soldiers, Red Shields, Crazy Dogs, Bow Strings. But the Dog Men are the most deadly military society there is."

"I wouldn't mention that to the U.S. Army."

"I don't have to." He was pretty sure the U.S. Army already knew.

He rubbed the pale flesh that circled her finger again. "What about your husband?"

"He's . . ." She swallowed. "Gone."

"Mmm," he said, and continued rubbing. "What about you?"

"I'm *not* gone." She yanked her hand from his, placing it on the ground on the other side of her body.

"No?" He thought parts of her were not only gone, but they weren't ever coming back. Like certain parts of him.

"What are you trying to say?"

"You killed two bounty hunters."

"They *were* asking for it."

"But when three Pawnee try to scalp you, you leave your guns in the holsters."

"I was ambushed."

"I know." He tore a piece of the cloth he'd found tied to one of the Pawnee's saddles, along with a water jug. It looked like some poor farm wife's skirt; he hoped Rose didn't notice. He doused it with water and started to wipe the blood and dirt from her face.

She circled his wrist with her fingers, and his scars burned. "How do you know?"

He'd returned that morning to her campfire, only to discover it cold and her gone. He'd stripped the bounty hunters of whatever he could use, buried them, and led their horses back to his own camp. He'd trade them, as well as anything else he could, to a prospector who drifted through now and again. The fellow was crazier than Luke, didn't remember from one visit to the next that he'd met Luke before. Each time the old-timer traded his whiskey—and for some reason, he always had a lot of it—for whatever Luke had collected.

Despite his spending the night hoping she would be gone, once she was Luke could not shake his unease. He thought she might still be there, or maybe someone else was. He'd walked the boundaries of the Smoky Hills. The only trails he'd found were hers and the bounty hunters', yet the feeling persisted. Finally he'd climbed the highest peak. At the top, he could almost see Denver City. He'd peered west, east, north, and then—

"I saw them."

"I swore I could feel—" She bit her lip.

"Someone watching you?"

"It happens." She lifted her chin. "I've learned to listen."

"You should." Listening to feelings—and voices— had saved him on several occasions.

"How did you see them?" she asked. "I didn't." Her brow furrowed; her wound started bleeding again. "They rose right out of the ground."

"They were lying in the grass." He returned to cleaning her face, and this time she let him.

"But their horses—"

"Those, too. There isn't much cover. The tribes on the plains have adapted. I saw them from higher ground." He pointed to his hills. "You couldn't."

"Why were you watching me?"

"I felt . . ." He shook his head and more dried blood rained down.

She watched it sprinkle onto his legs through the gaps in his leggings. He didn't have much hair there. He'd plucked it when he lived with the Cheyenne. It was what a Cheyenne did. He must have done a good job, because not all of it had grown back. The hair on his chest was the same. In the white world, lack of body hair would be seen as an indication of youth; in the Cheyenne world it was one of the things that made a man.

She lifted her gaze from his legs to his face. "What did you feel?"

Since she'd arrived he'd felt so many things that he hadn't felt for so long. Curiosity. Lust. Fear. Anger. Admiration.

"Something was coming," he said.

"You were right."

Luke didn't answer, just continued to dab at the blood until she gave an impatient huff and snatched the cloth out of his hand to scrub at the mess herself.

He shifted his shoulders, trying to make the tickle between them go away. It should be gone. He knew what had put it there; he had killed them.

Turning, he let his gaze wander over of the seemingly empty prairie. But that feeling of eyes on his back did not go away.

CHAPTER 4

Rose gritted her teeth and refused to let a single gasp or moan escape as Luke Phelan used her needle to stitch up the gash in her head. His gaze kept coming back to hers.

"Quit looking at me," she said.

"It's going to be pretty hard to do this if I don't look at you."

"You aren't looking at what you're doing. Your stitches are going to be crooked."

"They are crooked," he said, but he returned his attention to her forehead.

"Doesn't matter." She pressed a cloth above her eyes to stanch the blood.

Silence settled over them, broken only by the snuffle of the horses and the murmurs of the prairie grass and the wind. He seemed better out here, away from the hills, and she had to wonder why.

"You never screamed."

She lifted the cloth so that her gaze met his. "What good would it do?"

"You were terrified."

"Was not."

He gave a huff—half snort, half laugh. "You sound like my sister."

"You have a sister?"

"Don't sound so surprised. I have brothers, too." He frowned. "Had."

"What happened to them?"

"The war."

"The war happened to a lot of people."

He peered at her wound as if it were the most fascinating thing on the earth. "Do you have a scissors?"

"Use your knife."

He gave a quick shake of his head. A lock of his long, curling hair flipped into her face and stuck there. She reached up to pull it free. The end was bloody. He didn't seem to notice.

"My knife is . . ." Luke shrugged, and Rose remembered where his knife had been. Stuck into and out of several Pawnees. "Hold still."

Before she could ask why, he leaned in so close her nose nearly brushed his neck. She jerked back. The thread in her forehead pulled tight, and she hissed.

"I said hold still! I can bite through the thread if you give me a second."

"Leave it."

"I am not going to leave thread trailing down the side of your face."

He leaned forward again. Blood traced his skin, just like hers. She caught a whiff, and ground her teeth against the nearly overwhelming urge to move—or be sick. In the promised second, he leaned back, spitting the soiled thread to the ground. He reached for the whiskey he'd used to clean everything he could, sipped, then held the bottle out to her.

The idea of putting her mouth where his had been caused an odd flutter in her stomach in the same place her stomach had fluttered the first time she'd seen him.

"No," she said. She was dizzy enough without whiskey. "Who taught you to do this?"

"This?" he repeated, gaze flicking to the dead Pawnees. She could figure *that* out for herself. However . . .

"The rope," she said.

"When a warrior stakes himself to the ground with a dog rope, he's saying he will defend that ground to the death. At the least, it's intimidating."

"At the least," she agreed. She wanted to ask more, but he peered at her stitches with a frown. "What?"

He shrugged. "I didn't do too badly for a first try."

"You've never done that before?" She wasn't sure she liked his practicing on her, but she'd liked bleeding even less.

"No, but I've had it done to me plenty of times. My sister always sewed anything that got torn when we were kids."

"She was a seamstress?"

"Not hardly. Her seams in flesh were much better than any she took in cloth."

"A nurse, then."

"She took care of everyone." His gaze went distant. "I wonder if she's still alive."

"You don't know?"

He spread his hands. "How would I?"

"How long have you been in those hills?"

"Not long enough," he muttered, and got to his feet.

"Where are you going?" The panic in Rose's voice mortified her, even before he cast her a quick, appraising glance.

"I'm going to bury them before the buzzards come."

"Let the buzzards have them."

"That would be a gift they don't deserve. Burial is an insult."

"Why?"

"The Cheyenne leave their comrades where they fall, in the open, beneath the sun, the moon, the stars. To nourish the earth and the animals is the greatest gift. To be buried—" He broke off, swallowed, seemed to shudder before he continued. "To be buried beneath the earth. Trapped forever away from all that's open and free. In the dark, with no air . . ." He drew in a deep, rattling breath as he dragged a shaking hand through his tangled hair.

"Mr. Phelan—"

He lowered his arm. "I've straddled you in the dark

of night. I've felt your breasts against my thighs. I've touched your face; I've saved your life."

Once upon a time, such crudity would have made her gasp and flee, cheeks flaming, heart pounding. But, as that was what he no doubt wanted, she merely got to her feet and said, "Your point?"

"My name is Luke."

"I thought it was White Ghost."

"Ve'ho'e Mestaa'e," he said.

She wasn't sure if that meant *Luke*, *White Ghost*, or *go away*. She didn't care. "Luke," she repeated. "Call me Rose."

"Do you have a shovel, Rose?"

"No."

He kicked the closest Pawnee, but since he was barefoot and the Pawnee was dead, the action was more about frustration than fury. "I'll have to get mine."

"Leave them." She raised her hand. "I know; they don't deserve it. But is it worth riding back to those hills for a shovel?"

He swung onto his horse—a smooth, graceful movement that made her breath catch. "You're just worried you'll never see me again."

"Will I?"

He grinned and she gaped. She'd thought his movements poetry? His smile was a sonnet.

Luke returned to the Smoky Hills more slowly than he'd ridden out of them.

He didn't like that he'd found the Pawnee so close. He especially didn't like that they'd been stripped to only their breechclouts and moccasins for war. The Pawnee were known as Wolf Men to the Cheyenne because they were both deadly and clever. Which might be why they'd aligned themselves with the army. What wasn't clever, and deadly, about that?

However, their presence here, their behavior toward Rose made him wonder. What was going on out there in the world? How soon before its troubles spread all over him?

"Already has," he murmured as he packed his shovel along with his saddlebags, dressed in his Kersey blue trousers with the yellow cavalry stripe and his vest. He scrubbed the paint from his face as best he could, then rooted about until he found his black-heeled boots, grimacing as he shoved his feet into them.

If Rose Varner wasn't trouble, he no longer recalled what trouble was.

He tethered the bounty hunters' horses in a row, then rode out of the Smoky Hills as fast as he dared considering how hard he'd pushed his mount already. But if any more Pawnee came searching for their friends and found Rose with their dead bodies instead, they'd do worse than scalp her.

The sun had reached its peak and started to descend by the time he arrived. The area appeared exactly the same as when he'd left it. Except for the buzzards.

Rose had spent the time he'd been gone attempting to cleanse every trace of blood from her person. She'd done an admirable job with her face and hands. She'd also changed her shirt—though the one she had on now appeared as old and worn as the last, at least it wasn't dyed red. However, the only way to get all that blood out of her hair would be to dunk her head below the surface of a river and scrub.

He probably should have taken her along to the Smoky Hills and tossed her into the creek. Except the prickly feeling he'd had this morning had now grown into such a sense of urgency to be gone from here that he could barely think. Therefore, Rose looked exactly like what she was—a too-white woman who'd nearly been scalped.

"Why did you bring those?" She indicated the line of horses.

"We'll exchange them for supplies."

"We?" Hope lit her voice.

He slid from his horse and drew the shovel from the saddle. "You can tell me that nothing frightens you, but I know better."

She lifted her chin and met his gaze. "Of course I'm frightened. I'm a defenseless woman."

"You're the least defenseless woman I've ever met. Unless you're confronted by a warrior."

"Is there a reason you like to hold my weaknesses up for ridicule?"

"Not ridicule. And not a weakness. Not being afraid doesn't make you strong, it makes you stupid."

"You're not afraid."

"Of course I am. Why do you think I've been in those hills for—" He stuck the shovel into the dirt. "What year is it?"

Her eyes widened. "What *year* is it?"

"Don't you know, either?"

She made a strangled sound of annoyance. "It's 1871."

"Huh," he said, and went back to digging.

"How long have you been here?"

The Cheyenne did not measure time in years or months but in seasons. He could probably count how many he'd been with them, but that would involve remembering and that was something he did not want to do.

"No idea," he said.

"You are the most exasperating man."

"I've been told that before." By every woman he'd ever loved. His mother. His sister. His wife.

The wind whispered, *Ve'ho'e Mestaa'e.*

He'd hoped the wind would stop speaking to him once he left the hills. He should have known a change of location wouldn't make a difference.

"Being unable to move, to breathe, to speak whenever I see—" Her voice broke, and she waved an impatient hand at the bodies. "How is that anything *but* weak?"

"Weren't you on your way to find the Cheyenne? Alone? In all your defenseless womanhood? You planned to ride straight into their camp when the very sight of one makes you shiver and shake, then freeze."

"I hadn't seen any since . . . I didn't know I'd—"

"And now that you do?"

She took a breath, let it out. "Doesn't make a damn bit of difference."

"You're still going to ride into a Cheyenne camp and demand your child?"

"Someone has to," she muttered, but her shoulders slumped.

"I guess that someone is going to be me."

Her head came up. "You changed your mind?"

"You changed it for me."

"Because I was foolish enough to nearly get scalped by the Pawnee?"

"Because courage matters." He shoved all three bodies into the hole and began to shovel the dirt on top. "It might be the only thing that does."

They rode toward Colorado Territory, trailing both the bounty hunters' horses and the Pawnees' ponies.

"The Cheyenne have mostly been harassing the Kansas settlers," Rose said. "Shouldn't we ride farther into Kansas?"

"The Cheyenne don't know Kansas from California."

"Meaning?"

Luke wasn't used to this much talking. The wind spoke in phrases, made demands, but rarely asked questions. "They raid in their territory. A lot of which is now Kansas. But not all of it."

"I thought they gave up their territory in a treaty."

"Some of the elders signed a paper, but that doesn't mean the Cheyenne gave up the land."

"The government thinks it does."

"Exactly." He sighed as she opened her mouth for more questions, then spoke before she could ask them. "The land belongs to all the people. All the people did not sign. Particularly the Dog Men."

She went quiet, but not for long. "Where are we going?"

"There's a town." He pointed west, where said town had just begun to darken the horizon. "We'll get rid of these horses and buy supplies."

"I have supplies."

"Not enough for where we're going."

"Where are we going?"

"I'm not sure."

Rose rubbed between her eyes as if her head hurt, and her bloody hair fell in disgusting hanks across her face.

"Where's your hat?"

"It fell off when they were . . ." She made a cutting gesture near her stitches. "I think you might have buried it."

Luke cursed, then yanked his own slouch hat free. "Put this on."

"I'll be fine. It isn't that far. I'll buy another in . . ." She flapped her hand at the town.

He reined in; she did, too. "Your hair is full of blood."

She touched the once golden length, winced at the texture, then wrinkled her nose at the slash of rust across her fingertips.

"At the least," he continued, "someone will want an explanation."

"I'll give them one."

"Depending on the sheriff, there'll be questions. He might wire the army." Luke really needed to avoid the army. "If they come, they'll want to return to where we were, backtrack those Pawnee." He lifted his gaze to the sky, then lowered it, took a gander to their rear, saw nothing behind now as he'd seen nothing there the last dozen times he'd looked, shifted his shoulders, and faced front. "Time's a-wastin'."

Her lips tightened, and she snatched his hat, slapping it onto her head. Her breath caught. The brim must have scraped her stitches.

"Shove your hair underneath," he ordered. "And don't let anyone see you without it, even after you order a bath and wash your hair. Those stitches are gonna cause comment."

"You said yourself time's a-wastin'. Let's get the supplies and get gone. Forget the bath. Forget my hair. I did."

"You don't mind riding for days like that?"

"I'll ride for weeks naked if it'll get me to my daughter faster."

The image intrigued him. Too much.

"Wash it," he snapped, and clucked to his horse.

Rogue, Colorado, was like many small towns in the territory. Both wild and tame, depending on where one had been and what one had been doing before entering it, Rogue was busy enough so they didn't cause a stir upon arrival and empty enough that they could conduct their business and be back on the trail before dark.

Luke definitely wanted to be out of town before nightfall. He already felt as if the buildings were closing in. They blocked out the sky on either side. The noise. The smell. People were everywhere.

He hated it.

"I'll sell the horses," Luke said as they dismounted in front of the stable. "You head to the hotel and make yourself pretty."

"There isn't enough water in the world for that."

He contemplated her in retreat. Certainly she wasn't a beauty. But there were more important things than pearly skin and pink lips, soft palms, and a soft voice. Out here courage and a strong back could be the most beautiful qualities on earth.

"Meet me at the mercantile," he called.

She lifted a hand to indicate she'd heard but did not glance his way again. He watched until she disappeared into the hotel.

"Help you?"

Luke tensed at the deep, booming voice so close to his ear but kept himself from spinning, ducking, kicking out with his foot, palming his knife. He was in the world now, and that kind of behavior would land him in a cell—or worse. Although, having been in a cell, he wasn't sure there *was* worse.

He withdrew a step as he turned, putting enough space between himself and the stable man so he did not feel crowded or trapped. It didn't help. He'd felt crowded and trapped since he'd left the Smoky Hills. One of the reasons he'd gone *into* the Smoky Hills.

Though he wanted to jump on his horse and go back where he'd come from, Luke couldn't. Not yet. Courage did matter. It should be rewarded. Besides, he'd promised. He'd broken too many promises in his life, always with disastrous results.

"I'd like to sell these horses," Luke said.

The fellow eyed the animals, eyebrows lifting at the Pawnee ponies. But he didn't ask where Luke had gotten them; he just nodded and offered a price. Luke offered another one. Ten minutes later, Luke left satisfied.

He strode down the boardwalk, ignoring the tempting scent of whiskey from the saloon and the "hello, sugar" from the whore outside the whorehouse. However, the man clad all in black from head to toe who stood in front of the batwing doors of the gambling hall stared at him so intently Luke stumbled.

"Ostorozhyny," the fellow murmured.

"What?" Luke righted himself, annoyed at his own lack of grace.

"Careful." The man lit a cigarette with incredibly long fingers, then blew smoke through his nose. "Your hair is an interesting shade, *moy drug.*"

"What language is that?"

Smiling, he tossed the match. The languid way he moved, the casual way he leaned against the building made Luke think of a wildcat in the weeds. He'd look like a gunfighter with those hands and black clothing, except he carried no weapon that Luke could see. Considering that he stood outside the gambling hall, his profession no doubt lay with the cards. Still, most gamblers carried guns. If they didn't, they often wound up dead.

"I apologize, *moy drug*." He dipped his head. "My friend. It is just . . ." He waved and smoke twirled. "Your hair is striking."

Luke had thought he'd walked past the whorehouse. He glanced in that direction, and the same whore who'd hailed him before waved. The two buildings stood right next to each other; perhaps one held women and the other men.

The strange man laughed. "I don't want to fuck you."

Luke frowned at the language. With every minute he spent in the world, he realized just how long he had been out of it.

"It is not that you aren't lovely, but my wife, she is—"

"Your wife is what?"

The woman who now appeared in the doorway was so heavily with child, Luke gaped. Once they could no longer disguise their pregnancies, most white women remained out of sight, as if the condition were an embarrassment. This one proudly set her hands atop the rolling mound of her belly. The smile she turned on her husband made her beautiful face shine as if lit from within.

"Well?" she prompted.

"She is *moya zhizn'*," he murmured.

The woman rolled her eyes. "That means *my life* for those of us who do not speak Russian."

The man put his arm around her shoulders, and she leaned into him as if he were the only sturdy tree in the midst of a hellish storm. Luke's chest went tight. He missed that.

"Might I ask your name, *moy drug*?"

The woman's gaze narrowed on the final words—she appeared to speak, or at least understand, more Russian than she pretended—and she peered at Luke with interest.

"You can ask," Luke said.

"But you will not tell." The man drew on his cigarette, blue eyes too intent on Luke for his comfort.

"Nice . . . uh . . . meeting you," Luke said. He reached up to tug his hat, then remembered he'd given it to Rose. He let his hand fall back to his side, nodded, and moved on to the mercantile.

He tried to dismiss the exchange as a chance encounter. He didn't know that fellow; he would have remembered. Perhaps the stranger had seen someone else with red hair recently and was reminded of it. Though Phelan red was a shade all its own.

He was so busy considering the Russian, who didn't seem all that Russian, that he didn't notice at first when the murmur and bustle of the mercantile died.

"Well, well, well." The sound of a gun being cocked cracked through the silence. "If it ain't the White Ghost."

CHAPTER 5

Rose had just rinsed her hair with cool water—she hadn't been willing to wait for a heated bath, much to the consternation of her hostess—and she was missing again her lily-scented perfume, when a ruckus erupted outside.

She doubted it was her concern; nevertheless, the continued shouts made her uneasy, and she hurried to finish. In truth, clean water felt heavenly no matter the temperature, though it *was* easier to cleanse away blood with warmer water. She'd had practice.

Someone tapped on the door. Hoping it was Luke, despite his admonition for her to meet him at the mercantile, she stepped behind the screen before calling, "Come in."

The owner of the hotel, a rotund German woman who had become much friendlier once Rose had given her name as *Varner*, entered with more water. The sight of Rose already clothed in her riding skirt, gun belt, and boots, drying her chest above what was left of a very worn chemise, caused a frown.

"Why are folks shouting?" Rose asked.

"They have caught a wanted man."

Rose's skin prickled and not from the breeze that blew through the window and across her still-damp skin. "Who?"

"He is called the White Ghost. He—"

The rest was lost as Rose dashed from the room,

pulling her shirt over her head as she raced down the stairs and out the door.

It wasn't difficult to find the source of the commotion. Most of the residents of Rogue had gathered in front of the mercantile. Rose pushed through the edges of the crowd, and heard the conversation at the front even before she got there.

"The pitcher on this here wanted poster looks like 'im." Paper crinkled. "How many folks got long red hair?"

Murmurs of agreement rose.

"He done killed the sheriff of Wanderin', Kansas. He should hang for that alone. 'Sides, we ain't had a good hangin' in pert near a year."

"Ye're just wastin' money if ya hang him without collectin' the ree-ward."

"I'll do it!"

"Me!"

"I done seen him first!"

Jostling and shouting commenced. Strangely, Rose did not hear Luke's voice. She hoped he hadn't been knocked unconscious. It would make it more difficult to get away. Though how, exactly, she might get him away at all, she had no idea. But she couldn't let him be hanged. She couldn't even let him be jailed. Once he was behind bars, everything would be that much harder.

"The gun won't help."

Rose hadn't realized she was stroking her thumb over the grip until a woman's voice drew her attention.

She stood outside a gambling hall, or at least Rose thought it was a gambling hall since the sign read TWO OF A KIND. However, the woman in the doorway appeared ready to give birth. Her gaze narrowed on Rose's forehead, and she frowned. "Did he do that?"

Rose lifted her hand, wincing when her fingers encountered the stitches. Hell, she'd left the damn hat in the room. "No! Never."

The woman peered into Rose's eyes for a moment,

then gave a sharp nod. "Tell them your *husband* can't be the man they're searching for."

"He's not—"

"Shhh." The woman pressed a fingertip to her lips. Her dark hair billowed about her face, making her green eyes shine like a cat's in the night. "If he's your husband, he can't be the White Ghost. If you're new here, he can't have been around long enough to have done what he's accused of. Understand?"

"Yes." Rose took a breath, let it out slowly. She'd never been very good at lies; she was even worse at pretending.

As if she'd heard Rose's thoughts, the woman stepped closer and spoke just above a whisper. "Believing you are who you say you are makes everyone else believe it, too."

Rose hoped she could do this. She *had* to do this.

"Kiss him right on the mouth, as if you mean it. That always works. If you had time, you could stuff a bag of clothes under your shirt." She rested her palm atop her burgeoning belly. "Pregnancy makes men foolish. But—" The woman tilted her head as the shouts became louder, and the crowd began to move away. "I don't think you have the time. He certainly doesn't."

Panicked, Rose hurried around the crowd. She had to run to reach the lead where two burly men held Luke by the arms. His hands had already been bound behind him. He walked between them as if they were escorting him to a throne and not a noose. At the sight of Rose he shook his head, his red and white hair flying around his face like a firestorm.

Rose planted herself directly in front of the group. The captors halted; several of the followers bumped into them. Rose stepped forward and cupped Luke's face between her hands. "Are you all right?" His eyebrows drew down in confusion. "Did they hurt you, sweetheart?" Now his eyebrows lifted as his eyes widened.

Kiss him right on the mouth, as if you mean it.

How did one mean a kiss? Wasn't the mere act of the kiss meaning enough?

Before he could say something that might ruin everything, Rose lifted herself onto her tiptoes and pressed her mouth to his.

His beard scraped her palms; his hair drifted over her wrists. Hard and soft, the sensations seduced; she was surprised to find she wanted more. She curled her hand around his neck and drew him closer. He tasted of licorice, dark and sweet. She licked his lips; he nipped hers back and she burned.

"Ma'am?"

Luke lifted his head. He stared at Rose as if she were a stranger. That kiss had made her feel like one in her own body. Or, maybe, it had made her feel at home in that body for the first time she could recall.

"Ma'am! May I ask what in Sam Hill you're doin'?"

What was she doing? Oh! Yes! *Saving Luke Phelan's life*.

She released him and turned to the dark-haired fellow with the unfortunately large nose on the right. "I might ask you the same thing."

"He's the White Ghost. Wanted in both Kansas State and Colorado Territory."

"He's my husband, and as we only arrived in the West a few weeks past, he certainly hasn't had an opportunity to become wanted in both a state and a territory."

"Husband," the man repeated. "I don't—"

"I do," Rose interrupted. "Untie him."

Luke's lip twitched. At least he had the sense not to speak.

"What's your name?" The man addressed Luke.

"What's yours?" Luke replied.

The fellow punched Luke in the stomach. Rose kicked the man in the shin. The crowd murmured; the tone was less riled than before. They sounded uncertain, so she pressed forward.

"I'm Rose Varner and he's Luke. He isn't a ghost. He's as alive as you are. He isn't wanted. Let him go."

The man on the left reached for the rope around Luke's wrists, but the one she'd kicked stopped hopping about and threw out a hand. "Wait."

Rose's eyes narrowed. Did she need to kick him again?

"If you're married, where's your ring?"

Her thumb went to her ring finger; the smooth empty skin caused her tongue to thicken. She couldn't think what to say.

"We had to sell it." Luke put just the right amount of chagrin into the words. "There's still a mark where the ring used to be."

The angry fellow snatched her wrist, yanking it so hard she stumbled forward. He squinted at her finger, then shoved her hand away as if it were dung. He turned and ran right into Luke.

"Touch her like that again," Luke murmured, "and I'll kill you."

Rose stifled a sigh. How was she supposed to convince people he was a greenhorn settler and not the dreaded White Ghost when he said things like that?

The man stepped back, startled, then glanced at the crowd and fled.

"Apology accepted!" Rose shouted.

Luke choked on what might have been laughter.

The guy on the other side cut Luke's bonds. "Uh, sorry," he said, and fled as well. Within moments, Rose and Luke stood alone on the street.

"Who taught you how to do that?" he asked.

"I was never very good at lying. But I suppose I never had to lie for such an important reason before."

"I meant the kiss," he said, and walked away.

Luke entered the mercantile and ducked down an aisle, focusing on the items stored there in an attempt to make his erection go away.

He'd thought he'd had trouble as he was being dragged to a noose. Then true trouble arrived in the form of his "wife."

"Holy hell," Luke muttered, and rubbed the back of his neck, which still tingled from her touch.

Her mouth had been both sweet and cool, her tongue along his lips like fire. Her breasts felt loose beneath that shirt; wet patches shone through. Thankfully none of them in places that revealed anything beyond the shade of her skin. If a damp spot had been over her nipple, the darker hue visible, the bud ripe and moist—

He swallowed and nearly choked on a throat as dry as Kansas. If that had been the case, being hanged would have been the least of his worries. He couldn't see how every man in the mob wouldn't have wanted her for himself. And Luke, with his hands bound and his guns still with his horse, would have been able to do nothing but watch.

When her tongue had tasted him, he'd forgotten they were surrounded by those who wanted to kill him. He'd reached for her, meaning to palm her hips, yank her close, and delve, but his bonds had scraped his wrists in the same way other bonds had once scarred them, and he'd remembered.

She wasn't his; she never could be.

Luke lifted his hands. His wrists were red, but not enough to worry about. They'd once been raw and bleeding.

The tap of her boots alerted him to her approach an instant before the scent of strong soap wafted over him. He wrinkled his nose; he didn't like it. He missed the scent of lilies, even though the knowledge of why she'd smelled like them saddened him. But he had been the one who'd told her to wash.

"Are you all right?" she asked.

His erection was gone. He wasn't surprised. Lack of use often made such things fleeting.

Her hair shimmered like gold beneath the late-afternoon sun slanting through the front windows. As he'd predicted, the wound on her forehead shone red and new. Only a blind man could miss it. He couldn't believe someone hadn't questioned them about the stitches already. They needed to get out of town.

He lowered his voice, leaned in close so only she could hear. "Why did you do that?"

"Save you or kiss you?"

"Yes."

"Did you really think I'd just run away and let you die?"

"You could have been hurt." Oddly, that disturbed him more than the noose. Too many people had gotten hurt, had gotten dead, because of him.

"I wasn't," she said.

"I'll go to the Cheyenne," he continued a bit desperately—hands shaky, throat like dirt again. "I'll bring her back to you . . ." He glanced around the store. "Somewhere else."

"No."

"Fine, I'll bring her here."

"No," she said again, and as if that had settled it, she picked up a new hat, tried it on, frowned, pulled it off, and handed it to him. "I'll keep yours." Her gaze wandered the store. Folks whispered and pointed. "We should probably get going before someone who knows you shows up."

"No one knows me," he said.

"Then how'd they get a wanted poster?"

The likeness hadn't been good—his nose was too big, his eyes too small, and was his hair really that wild?—but it had been good enough that Luke would be swinging by now if not for her.

He slapped the new hat on his head, then strode down the aisle, snatching coffee, beans, soap, bacon, razor, bullets. They both had their arms full by the time they reached the counter.

"I'll be right back," she said.

He snatched her arm before she got away. "You'll stay right here." He hadn't liked the way the man she'd kicked had looked at her. He hadn't liked that man very much at all.

"I'll get my things from the hotel."

"I'll go with you."

Her scowl almost made him smile. Her distaste for orders made him wonder how long her husband had been dead. Not long, considering the mark on her finger. Although perhaps she'd only removed the ring recently, choosing to remember her lost love every time she lifted her hand. Luke, however, had purged himself of everything that reminded him of his.

He paid for the items, picked up the sack, and followed Rose to the hotel. As they walked past the gambling hall, he glanced inside. The dark-clad man was nowhere to be seen, but his wife tended the bar. Her gaze met Luke's and he missed a step. There was something about both her and her husband that bothered him. But he hadn't seen the couple before; he would remember.

He wanted to ask them questions, but now that Rose had mentioned that damnable poster, his desire to get to the hotel and then get gone was overwhelming, and he couldn't make himself pause.

Who had made it out of the Smoky Hills without Luke knowing about it? Certainly there was the prospector, but Luke didn't think the old fellow could see straight most days, let alone describe the White Ghost well enough for anyone to draw a likeness. Then again, maybe he was wrong. Wouldn't be the first time.

"Mrs. Varner." The woman behind the desk smiled so widely her apple cheeks pushed her eyes to slits. Her thick German accent meant he had to listen very hard to everything she said. "I have not cleared yet the bath."

"Leave it," Luke said. "I'll wash."

"I will bring more—"

"No," he snapped.

"But, Mr. Varner—"

"I'm not—" He bit his lip. He was no good at lies. Never had been and living alone had not improved the ability. "I'm not in need of fresh water." All he really needed to do was shave.

"Thank you anyway," Rose said as if instructing a child in manners.

He hadn't had to use his in so long he wasn't much good with those, either. "Yes, thank you," he agreed, and followed his "wife" upstairs.

Inside the room, Luke set the sack on the still-made bed, rummaged through, and found the shaving soap and razor. "If you could pack whatever you can fit into your saddlebags," he said, then stepped behind the screen and opened the soap.

As soon as Luke disappeared, Rose sat on the bed. Her knees had gone wobbly, and her hands had begun to shake. She wasn't sure if her reaction was because of the danger, the lies, or that damnable kiss. She'd never experienced a kiss quite like it.

Rose was the youngest child of a once-well-to-do Boston family. The damp, cold weather of Boston had never suited her, and she was often ill. She was not pretty; she was too outspoken. She was smarter than most men, and she had never understood why she should hide that. As a result, even before the war took most of the boys away, returning them dead or forever broken, Rose was already on the shelf.

That would have been fine if she hadn't wanted children so badly. At church, she held the babies. At gatherings, she played with the toddlers. When her parents died, she would be alone—her two brothers and sister were much older and had families of their own—unless *she* did something about it.

She began to read the advertisements for wives placed in the *Heart and Hand* magazines. She wasn't sure what made her answer Jakob Varner's over all the others. Perhaps she'd just been getting desperate, and he hadn't sounded so bad.

The Homestead Act had been passed in 1862, allowing Jakob to file claim to one hundred and sixty acres in Kansas. By order of President Lincoln, if he lived on and farmed the land for five years it became his. Jakob worked hard, but what he really needed was a wife. Unfortunately women were as scarce in the West as men in the East. So he'd placed an advertisement, which Rose had answered. They had corresponded a bit, and then Rose had gone west.

They were married within an hour of Rose's arrival. Jakob was a good husband, as husbands went. He didn't hit; he rarely shouted. But the two of them were different. He was German and a Lutheran; she was Irish and a Catholic. He'd come to America to find prosperity; she'd been born to it. He had an accent, traditions she knew nothing of.

While Kansas couldn't make Rose prettier or taller, the dry air did heal her cough. She became stronger; she learned quickly. She made the farm a home; she was a good wife. In the bedroom she did her duty; she wanted a child. But theirs was not a love match.

Jakob had not seemed to care that she did not enjoy the marriage bed—or so she thought. For a long time, Rose believed *kalt wie eis* an endearment until he'd also muttered it at the snowdrifts that piled against the house all winter. She'd eventually deciphered their true meaning.

Cold as ice.

Rose lifted her fingers to her suddenly sensitive lips. Jakob had never kissed her with any warmth. But, to be fair, she'd never kissed him the way she'd kissed Luke Phelan.

As if she meant it.

Sometimes she felt guilty about Jakob, which she

supposed was better than feeling nothing at all. She should probably tell Luke the truth about her husband, but—

Water splashed behind the screen, drawing her free of the past. The scent of shaving soap drifted on the breeze. Rose imagined him just out of sight, his chest taut and smooth, water tracing a wet trail over the ridges of his stomach and disappearing beneath—

"Rose?"

Cheeks flaming, she began to stuff supplies into her saddlebags. "Yes?"

"I need your help."

Her hand curled around a tin of coffee. "Help?" she echoed.

"Would you come here?"

The coffee dropped to the bed. She should tell him no; she should leave this room. Instead she walked toward the screen.

Would he be submerged in the bath, naked, the water lapping against that exquisite skin, caressing him the way she wanted to? Or would he be standing on those long, strong, somehow smooth legs, droplets tracing downward, over every dip and curve, plopping into the water and causing gooseflesh-like ripples along the surface?

She licked her lips and tasted him—licorice and life. Her skin flushed; she was so thirsty. There was plenty of water nearby. Clenching her hands, she stepped around the screen.

His vest was off, his trousers still on. Muscles flowed across his shoulders as he lifted his hands. But she couldn't enjoy the view.

She was too shocked by what he had done.

CHAPTER 6

Luke had done his best with the shaving soap, the razor, and his knife. But he had no mirror. He needed help. There were still areas he hadn't reached. He turned and saw the horror in her eyes.

At first he thought she'd seen his scars, but he'd draped a towel around his neck, and the ends reached nearly to his waist, covered most of his chest, so that couldn't be the case. Not that scars had upset her before.

Then, suddenly, he understood, and called himself ten times a fool. Rose had nearly been scalped. Of course she would take one look at him and remember.

"I'm sorry," he murmured. "I wasn't thinking."

Her wide eyes narrowed; her gaze lowered to his hand. "Give me that."

He handed her the razor and then glanced about. "Is there a chair?"

"Do you feel faint?"

"I—" He glanced back. "What?"

"I understand despair," she said. "But you needn't hurt yourself."

His mouth opened, shut, opened again. "What?"

"I've heard of people tearing out their hair when agony overwhelms them. Do the Cheyenne cut theirs?"

"You think I cut off my hair because I'm sad?"

"Aren't you?"

He had been, but now . . .

The darkness that had been with him every moment since he had returned to the Washita River and seen what his selfishness had brought had lifted a bit. He had somewhere to go, someone to help, a purpose. The wind still whispered, but he had better things to do than listen.

"I cut off my hair so I don't resemble that damn wanted poster."

"Oh." She blinked. "But we told them you're my husband, and they believed us."

"There are more people in the world than those in Rogue, and I'm sure more wanted posters than the one we've seen. The next folks might not be so gullible." Although he wouldn't mind her *persuading* everyone again.

Just the thought of how she'd convinced the inhabitants here made him stir. He suddenly realized they were alone in a hotel room, and everyone believed they were married.

"But your hair," she murmured, and brushed her fingers over the hanks he'd set on the washstand. The gentleness in her touch made him stir even more. She seemed sad herself, but when hadn't she?

"Long red hair is too noticeable."

The white streaks that had crept in since he'd gone to the hills didn't help. He'd removed his earrings. Without hair they were too damn obvious. But he couldn't remove the armband. He just couldn't.

"There aren't a lot of men with hair like mine," he continued. The only ones he'd ever known were dead. "I should have done this before." Though he hadn't been moved to do much beyond breathe for a very long time. His hair was hot; it caught on things, became tangled and filthy; sometimes it smelled. "I doubt I'll miss it."

She met his eyes. "I will."

The air suddenly seemed thick and scalding. He wasn't sure what to say or do. So he said and did nothing as her gaze traveled over his face, his patchy head, then lowered to his throat and stuck there. Her tongue shot out; he could swear he felt it trace his skin. The stirring that had begun earlier continued. He had to turn away or she would notice.

"Would you finish what I started?" he asked.

Her breath caught.

"On my head," he blurted. "Use the razor. Shave me."

He needed to stop talking. He was only making things worse.

She moved away; he couldn't blame her. A woman like Rose . . . He was surprised she hadn't run.

Thuds and clunks had him spinning just as she dragged a chair around the edge of the screen. He leaped forward to help and ended up tangling their fingers together around the slats. They both pulled back, and the chair clattered, nearly tipping over.

"Let me," he said.

"I'm not incapable."

"No," he agreed. She was the most capable woman he'd ever met. Except for his sister. Which made him think that, perhaps, Annabeth was still alive.

Luke placed the chair near the bath and sat so his head was at a more manageable level. Water splashed; the scent of shaving soap surrounded him. He jumped as her hands, small and just a bit rough, spread the lather over his head. He had a brush for that, but he tightened his lips and didn't remind her.

As she scraped the remaining hair from his scalp, he caught again the scent of *her* beneath the soap. Why did it remind him of sun and wind, rain, and the moon? All those things that soothed him whenever he needed soothing, although her touch did anything but.

Her hip bumped his elbow, the material of her riding skirt sliding across his skin like sandpaper. Her wrist brushed his ear; he wanted to turn his head, press his mouth to the pulse that throbbed there, and suckle.

"Are you almost done?"

"I wouldn't rush me," she said. "I can count on one finger the times I've shaved someone's head, and I doubt I'll be able to stitch a cut as well as you did."

Right now he'd welcome a cut. It would give him something else to think about besides that bed, her breasts, and the way her mouth had warmed against his.

Soap plopped onto his neck and slid downward. He lifted his hand to brush it away. Hers got there first. Fingers scooped the white foam. At the scrape of her nails, he turned.

His mouth collided with her breasts. They jiggled beneath the no-longer-damp cotton. The razor clattered to the floor, and he lifted his gaze.

He expected to see her face gone pale, her eyes stark and scared. Instead her cheeks flushed and those eyes had gone heavy, the lids lowered, her head slightly thrown back.

He heard himself breathing—harsh, fast. Her shirt rippled with every exhale. She arched, as if warming herself before a flame. Her nipples peaked, pushing against the cotton. He wanted to taste her so damn badly he—

"Step back." His voice, low and hoarse, desperate, should have frightened her. Instead her eyes opened. She lifted an eyebrow and straightened but didn't move. His mouth was now inches from her stomach. Didn't matter. He wanted to taste that, too.

"Rose," he said.

"Luke," she answered, and reached for him.

He stood, knocking the chair to the floor, nearly falling on top of it, then grasped for his vest with hands that shook. He shrugged off the towel and put the garment on. When he turned, she stared, captivated, at the center of his chest. His own nipples beneath the covering of his vest were as hard as hers, as hard as him.

"Are you through?" he asked.

"No," she whispered, and licked her lips.

He felt her tongue lave every part of him that craved it. He clenched his hands to keep himself from tearing open her shirt and capturing her in his mouth. Then he would yank off that foolish riding skirt and take her against the wall.

"God," he muttered, turning away, kicking the chair, lifting his hand to run his fingers through hair that wasn't.

Her breath caught, and he remembered how she'd gone still and quiet at the sight of the Pawnee. How she'd shaken and stuttered, her gaze wide upon his Dog Man headdress.

The Cheyenne did not fight fair when fighting for their land and their lives. He knew what they did to anyone in their way, what they did to women, and he had to get out of here before he did it, too.

He had to do something about the need that gnawed at him like sharp teeth inside his belly, a war drum in his blood. If he didn't bury himself in someone, he would bury himself in her.

"Meet me at the stables." Luke snatched up his hat on the way out the door. The crown felt strange against his head, but he would get used to it.

A new hat was the least of his worries.

Rose rubbed at her eyes. She would not cry. She had learned the hard way that crying did no good.

She moved to the window and watched Luke hurry down the boardwalk. She didn't blame him for running away. He was a beautiful man; she was a painfully plain woman. He was sleek and strong and brave. She was . . . not.

She should have been petrified by his appearance. The last shaved head she'd seen had been on the man who had tried to scalp her.

Why, then, had the feel of Luke's scalp beneath her fingers, the scrape of the razor, the heat of his breath made her feel things she could not give a name to? Because she trusted him. In a way she had never trusted anyone else. Luke Phelan would never hurt her.

She nearly turned from the window, then hesitated when he stopped on the street below. His shoulders lifted, lowered, and then he opened the door he'd paused in front of and went inside. Rose's gaze lifted to the sign:

DOLLY'S SPORTING HOUSE

A burble of laughter escaped her lips. There were more ways to hurt than with hands. Right now she ached as badly as she had the morning after the Cheyenne had come to the farm. They had hit and kicked. Knocked her down, left her in the dirt. But the greatest pain had been in her heart.

She was a fool. She'd thought Luke wanted her, but he'd scrambled away from her touch so fast he'd nearly fallen, then covered his skin so she couldn't see, wouldn't touch. She'd believed he admired her, and then he'd fled the room without looking back. She'd hoped he cared for her, and then he'd gone to someone else. She understood. A man like him—any man really—did not want a woman who was *kalt wie eis*.

"Whatsa matter, honey?"

The buxom blonde who'd given her name as Delia trailed a fingernail over Luke's hand. He snatched it back, and she sighed.

"Ye're as jittery as a virgin." Her dark eyes narrowed. "Is ye?"

"No."

"Then what's the trouble?" She palmed his crotch; nothing happened. "Ye need a fella?"

"No," he repeated.

The room was neat as such rooms went. He'd been in a few. He'd never much enjoyed them. Not that he was enjoying this one, either.

The women gathered in the drawing room had been of all ages, sizes, shades, their gowns as garish as the decor. The blare of colors had made his eyes burn.

Choosing a blonde had been a mistake. All he could do was compare this woman's sand-shaded hanks to another's sunshine locks. Eyes the color of dirt did not compare to eyes that reflected the sky. Buxom was not to his taste.

"You want I should use my mouth?"

The shade of her lips reminded him of a wound. The idea of her wrapping them around any part of him made Luke shudder. "No."

"Well, ya ain't gettin' the job done with that." Delia lifted her hand from the front of his pants. "You'll have t' tell me whatcha want."

What he wanted was something he couldn't have. Rose's behavior today had confirmed his belief in the unspeakable outrage she had suffered at the hands of the warriors who had taken her child. He had come here to ensure that his sudden burst of lust would not be turned on her. But that lust had disappeared. How could he have been so hard he thought he might burst through his buttons less than a half hour before and now he couldn't manage so much as a twitch?

Delia shrugged, and her loose gown fell to the floor. She wore nothing beneath it. He supposed it saved time.

"Front?" She turned. "Rear? Bed? Floor? Wall?"

A sudden image of Rose came to him, flushed and moaning, her knees around his hips, her ankles pressed to the small of his back as she pulled him close, the rhythmic thumping of her spine against the wooden plank as he plunged into her again and again, until her moan became a scream he muffled with his tongue.

"Therrrrre," Delia purred.

His erection was back. The instant he looked at her it fled. This was stupid. *He* was stupid. "I have to go."

"I ain't givin' back the money."

Luke strode out the door, ran down the steps, past the room where the colorful women awaited. He burst from the whorehouse.

And ran directly into Rose.

She stumbled backward. He reached for her, and she cringed, staring at his hands as if they were covered in filth. Hell. Why had he run out now? Why had he ever gone in?

"Is she the reason?" Delia asked.

The whore lounged in the doorway. She'd thrown on her dress, but it was so loose nearly all of her right breast hung out. A bite marred the pale white skin. Her hair was tousled, her lip rouge smeared. Luke wanted to deny that he had touched her—he certainly hadn't left any mark—but protesting would only make things worse. Instead he closed his eyes, mortified.

Heat crept up his neck. The curse of a redhead, that tendency to flush. At least he didn't have freckles like his sister.

"R-r-reason?" Rose repeated.

Luke's eyes snapped open. The glare he leveled at Delia caused her to step inside and slam the door. He couldn't make himself turn. He couldn't walk; he couldn't talk. He couldn't do much today at all.

He cleared his throat. "I—"

"You don't have to explain. I understand."

"I doubt that."

Rose stalked away before he could say anything more. Though what he would say he had no idea. He could not tell her that he'd gone to a whore so he wouldn't take her like one, but then he'd been unable to perform, so his need still raged, worse than before. She'd sleep with one eye open, if she didn't already. She had been through enough; he could not add the fear of ravishment by him to all of her others.

Luke trailed behind Rose to the stable. He'd just finished saddling his horse when she mounted up and rode out. By the time he did, she was a good distance away, and he urged his animal into a trot. He did not want to gallop out of Rogue and make it appear as if they were fleeing town. Nothing good would come of that.

He pulled his hat low and his collar high. Undue speculation over his shaved head would only make the shaved head more noticeable than the red hair had been. He'd prefer no one knew about it at all. Since he hadn't taken anything off, including his hat, in front of Delia, he might just be able to manage that.

"You want to hold up?" he called.

In answer, her horse broke into a gallop. Luke cursed, glanced back, decided they were far enough from Rogue for it not to matter, and galloped, too.

He'd always thought his mount a good one, but the animal had been in the hills with Luke for years, and there had been very little running. He was not going to be able to catch Rose. He wasn't worried she might get so far ahead he would lose her. His gaze traveled over the flatland that stretched all the way to the dull blue of the Rockies on the horizon. Out here that was nearly impossible to do. However . . .

"You're going in the wrong direction!" At first Luke didn't think she'd heard, but after a few more yards, she reined in and then circled back.

"Which way?" she asked.

"Where was your farm?"

"Southeast of Hays."

She'd come a helluva long way to find him, which made him wonder . . .

"How did you hear about me?"

"You're a legend all over the damn state." At his frown she rolled her eyes. "You expected not to be?"

"I didn't want to be."

"Then you shouldn't have killed everyone who came near you."

"Not everyone," he muttered, thinking of the wanted poster.

And her.

"Bet you're sorry now."

He was sorry about many things. Not killing Rose wasn't one of them.

"What do they say about me?"

"What don't they?"

He tilted his head, waiting, and she let out an exasperated huff. "You were in the army—gray, blue—depends on who you're talking to. Though . . ." She eyed his cavalry pants, lifted an eyebrow. He said nothing, and she huffed again. "Either you lived with the Cheyenne and rode with the Dog Men. Or . . ." Her gaze brushed the scars on his wrists. "You were a captive, a slave. Some say you're crazy. Others believe you're just lost. Who's right?"

"All of them." Luke turned his horse south.

They continued for nearly a mile before she spoke again. "You don't seem crazy." Luke cast her a bland glance, and her lips twitched. "Anymore."

"Crazy doesn't go away."

"Which means you're still crazy? Or you never were?"

"Yes," he said.

"You're trying to make me crazy."

He'd told her the truth. Who he'd been, who he was, who he might become . . . He had no idea which Luke was the true one.

All of them? Or none?

"How long since your daughter was taken?"

"What difference does it make?" she asked.

"I can't find the Dog Men if I don't know where they were and when."

Her eyes went wide. "You don't know where to find them?"

"If anyone did, they'd all be dead."

She didn't speak. She seemed overwhelmed.

"Did you think this would be easy?" he asked softly.

"If it were easy, I wouldn't need you."

He stifled a sigh. "How long?"

"A year."

"Rose—" he began. A year with the Cheyenne meant the child was already one of them.

"I've been searching for her every second since they rode away," she blurted. "I've done everything, Luke. I'll *do* anything."

It was an entirely different matter to take back a child who was already calling another woman *Nahko'eehe* than to demand the return of one who was still crying for *Mother*.

"How old was she?"

"She *is* three."

She'd been taken at two, when children started to speak more than a few simple words. Which meant that Lily was speaking Cheyenne by now. Luke tried not to wince, but from Rose's expression he knew he hadn't quite managed it.

"Did they kill her? Is that why you said 'was'?"

"They wouldn't have taken her to hurt her." If they'd meant to kill the child, they'd have done so right away.

Rose's face paled; her lips seemed bloodless. "The Dog Men took a woman, Susanna Alderice, and one of her children near the Saline River. When the soldiers caught up to them at Summit Springs, the child was already dead. Before they could rescue the woman—" Her voice broke. "The Cheyenne killed her."

Luke frowned. That didn't sound like the Cheyenne. "What happened at Summit Springs?"

"I just told you—"

"I meant to the Cheyenne." They would not have behaved so violently without provocation.

"The Fifth Cavalry—Majors Carr and North, William Cody killed fifty-two warriors. Unknown numbers of women and children."

"Because they never bother to count what doesn't count," Luke muttered, hands clenching.

"They say they killed the leaders of the Dog Men. That the others fled north and joined the Cheyenne already there."

Except the Dog Men never ran away.

"But if that were the case," she continued, "then how could the Dog Men be at my farm?"

Exactly. "The army lies, Rose. A lot."

"Then there are still Dog Men in Kansas."

"Maybe," he said. *Probably,* he thought.

"Dog Men took Lily. So if we find Dog Men we'll find her."

Once, that might have been true, but now he wasn't so sure. "From what you told me, the Dog Men have scattered. They're no longer one soldier band. If there are any left in Kansas, they've joined other groups—a few of them here, another few over there."

"Dog Men took Lily," she insisted. "We have to find the Dog Men."

Well . . . it couldn't hurt.

No, that wasn't true. It *would* hurt. Him. But only for a little while.

However, she was right about one thing. If they found some Dog Men, they might find her daughter. If not, he would discover any whisper of captives. Rose would have more to go on than she had right now.

"Do you think the army lied about Susanna?" Rose asked.

"Maybe."

"They took her *and* her daughter. But they only took my daughter. Why?"

"The most common reason to take captives"—beyond their use as hostages—"is to replace a child who was lost."

"Lost," she repeated more quietly.

He met her gaze. "Killed." Probably by the damn cavalry. "They will love her, care for her. She's theirs now."

"She's mine. I'll never let her go. Never." She said the last word so loudly her horse shied, but she controlled it as well as any Cheyenne.

"Calm d—"

"Don't tell me I can have another. Children can't be exchanged like horses. One as good as the next. What's the difference as long as you have one?"

"I know," he soothed.

"Do you?"

He tightened his lips. There were certain questions he

would never answer, and that was one of them. Instead he asked her the question he needed an answer to. "What have you done, Rose?" She blinked. "You said you'd done everything. What is everything?"

She remained silent for so long, her gaze blank, empty, he worried that she'd retreated in her mind. He did the same often enough. Living anywhere but the present was often too appealing to resist.

"I rode after them in the dark."

He saw that night as if he'd been there. Dead husband, burning farm. Rose on a horse, clothes torn, face bruised, bleeding, half-mad—

"But they were gone. Like the wind."

He was silent, waiting for her to go on.

"I went to the army."

If the army had been any good at finding the Cheyenne, there wouldn't be any Cheyenne left to find.

"They wouldn't help. The 'hostiles,'" she mocked, "are on the warpath. They've been harassing settlers, attacking the railroad."

"They do that when provoked."

"*I* did not provoke them."

"So you say."

"So I know. President Lincoln gave Jakob that farm."

"Personally?"

Her eyes narrowed, and he held up a hand. "I know there were homestead allotments. But did you ever consider whose land it was before the government gave it away?"

"You sound as if you . . ." She contemplated Luke, brow furrowed. "How long were you with them?"

"Long enough."

"How did you leave?"

Another question he couldn't—wouldn't—answer.

"They hurt you," she said.

"It's the way of—"

"The Cheyenne," she finished at the same time he said, "Men."

Her lips parted as if she would pursue that; then she glanced at the horizon and didn't.

"Rose, what did they—"

"No," she said. "I can't talk about it. About them or my husband. I . . ." She took a deep breath, which shook. "No."

He understood the inability to talk about pain, death, the loss of those you held dear. Why did he think she would be any different?

He wasn't certain what to say, so he said nothing. After a few moments, in a voice grown strong again, she continued with the original topic. "If the Cheyenne were angry about the allotments, why didn't they protest when they started? Why wait?"

Luke swallowed; his throat was so dry he had to cough and swallow again before he could speak. "There were massacres. The Cheyenne lost a lot of people. Women." He coughed again. "Children. If they don't replace them, they won't survive."

"Replace?" she repeated. "They're as bad as—" She stopped. "Why don't the Cheyenne ever steal men? After Summit Springs, aren't they in need of more Dog Men? Or did they replace some after the Washita?"

Luke's hands tightened on the reins, and his horse slowed in response. Rose twisted, glancing over her shoulder to keep him in sight.

"The Dog Men weren't at the Washita." He clucked to his mount, which huffed in disgust at his indecision, but, nevertheless, followed the command and increased its speed. As Luke drew even with Rose, he murmured, "Which was why it became a massacre."

CHAPTER 7

The day waned and Luke no longer spoke to Rose. He seemed to have become again the man he'd been in the hills. There were a few times she swore he was listening to something she couldn't hear. A few other times, she heard him answer.

"Damn wind," she muttered. What in hell was it telling him to do now?

Darkness fell, and he continued to ride, though he kept looking over his shoulder. But his gaze always went to the horizon and not to her—searching left, right, left again—before turning forward and doing the same. The more he looked back, the more nervous she became.

"What is it?" she asked.

He kept riding.

When her horse stumbled, Rose reined in. "I'd rather not have to shoot my mount after it breaks a leg in a hole."

His shadow faded into the blue night.

"Then we'll have to ride on one horse or walk," she continued. "Which will slow us down more than stopping ever could." Rose had learned that the same way she'd learned most things.

The hard way.

She could still hear her horse squealing in agony, then the gunshot that had stopped the horrible sound, then the silence that had descended over the prairie afterward. She'd spent the rest of that night awake, holding her gun, waiting for someone—outlaw, critter,

Indian—to investigate the shot. When dawn lightened the horizon, she'd sworn never to spend another night like it.

What if Luke kept going? What if he never came back?

"He wouldn't," she murmured. Her horse snorted. She had no idea what Luke would do. She wasn't sure Luke even knew.

She started a fire with prairie oak—buffalo chips—at least they didn't spark. The sun had warmed her during the day to the point that she'd thrown off her coat. Now she was glad for it, as well as the fire. If Luke went too far, got lost, he'd be able to find her. Just like whatever, or whoever, had been following them. Unless it was only his ghosts.

She hadn't planned on sleeping, but in the middle of the night, she started up, ears ringing, fingers poised on the triggers of both guns. Her gaze flitted to the edge of the circle of light thrown by the campfire. Beyond it, shadows danced. They always did.

Had something screamed? Someone? Perhaps, even her? Sometimes, in her sleep, Rose shrieked.

Her heart pounded like the hooves of a horse. Her breath came equally fast. She set down one gun and placed her palm against the ground, afraid that the sound *like* hooves might actually *be* hooves. It wasn't. Nevertheless, something had woken her, and she had to discover what it was.

Rose snatched up the discarded gun as she climbed to her feet. She moved to the edge of the circle of light. Beyond it, night hovered like a cool blue fog. A scratch, perhaps a boot against rock, pulled her to the left. A rumble, similar to a growl, turned her to the right. She swore she saw yellow eyes, but when she blinked they were gone.

Had they been there? Or hadn't they?

No matter which way she turned, her back was exposed. What she wouldn't give for a nice rock, a single tree, a goddamn cave. Any place where she could put her back against something solid and feel safe, instead of like . . .

"Bait," she murmured, then gave a short, sharp laugh. "You son of a bitch."

Luke lay on his belly. His horse snored softly at his side. The flames flickered like a candle in the night.

Shadows scampered between him and that fire. One minute they appeared ethereal—smoke, nothing more— the next they curled into a coyote, a man, then something in between. He'd seen such things before. Usually right before he lost a helluva lot of time.

Coyote was a trickster, the maker of mischief. He was both imp and hero, a being that rebelled and broke taboos. Luke squinted into the night. Were those actual coyotes or a message from beyond?

Luke had thought that once he left the hills, his confusion about reality and dreams might lessen. He'd been wrong. Something was out there. But he wasn't any more sure now than he'd been then what it was or even *if* it was.

Coyote howled to the stars; the sound began low and mournful, then lifted in pitch until it became a shriek. Sharp. Terrified.

No longer Coyote at all.

His horse started up, but Luke was already running toward that fire where shadows mingled and merged. He slowed as he approached, crouched, crept. No need. The area lit by the flames was empty.

His knees hit the ground; his ear followed. If someone had taken her, he would hear a retreat. If she had left, he would hear that, too.

The earth remained silent.

He rose. On the other side of the flames, her horse pawed the dirt, staring into the darkness. Had that scream been hers? He had not been that far away; he had been watching, waiting for whoever was following them to appear. He had seen nothing but Coyote, unless—

Unless he'd lost an entire day or even two.

But the fire still burned. Lower, true. However, if it had been burning more than one night, it would not be burning at all.

He would walk the perimeter—round and round in larger and larger circles until he found whatever had screamed. He hoped it hadn't been her.

Luke turned to the right. The first thing he saw was the gun.

"Bang," Rose said.

Luke blinked.

"If I were whoever you think is out there, you'd be dead." She holstered the gun. "Who *do* you think is out there?"

He didn't answer. He didn't know.

"You used me as bait."

He hadn't meant to. But when she'd made camp and night had fallen, he'd been drawn to that flame—stark orange in the indigo night. Then, as he'd approached, he'd seen those shadows dancing, and he'd contemplated the possibilities.

"It was a good idea." She let her gaze meet the night. "Would have been an even better one if it had worked and they'd shown themselves."

He swallowed. "Did you see someone?"

Her gaze flicked back. "Did you?"

He hadn't actually seen. He'd felt. Just like the day she'd ridden out of the hills. He'd been twitchy, itchy. Something was watching. Someone was coming.

He'd been right then. But now?

"I see things that aren't there. Hear people that aren't . . ."

"Real?"

"Alive," he corrected.

She nodded as if he'd just said his shirt was blue and

not that he heard the dead speak. He *had* told her about the whispering wind before. She hadn't cared much then, either.

"Did you hear the scream?" she asked, and he nodded. "Might have been me."

"You don't know if you screamed?"

She stared at her boots. "Sometimes I do." Her gaze lifted. "In my sleep."

One more thing they had in common.

Rose woke to the acrid scent of smoke. She sat up, concerned the fire had sparked a prairie blaze. Considering the miles upon miles of dry brown grass, she wouldn't be surprised. Except buffalo chips didn't spark.

Her fire remained where it had been—the flame lower and dimmer than before. It could not be the cause of that smell. Her gaze went to the horizon. "Is that a fire?"

"Was." Luke sat exactly where he'd been when she fell asleep—back against his saddle, rifle across his lap, gaze fixed on the distance. "The wind shifted 'bout an hour ago. Started blowing this way."

"Are we going to blow that way?" She pointed toward the distant smoke.

He nodded, though he didn't look happy about it.

After a quick breakfast and an even quicker trip to the high grass followed by a wash of her face with chilly canteen water, they mounted up. They hadn't gone far when Luke dismounted, then went to his knees, squinting at the ground. The grass reached his shoulders. Rose couldn't see what he was staring at.

He straightened, peering north. Only then did she see the grass at his feet was stained red with blood. Horrible things went through her mind as she got down. All that was left was a bit of fur.

"I *did* see a coyote," he murmured.

"What did you think you saw?"

"A coyote," he said, and got back on his horse.

She stood for a moment contemplating what was left of the rabbit. Knowing that the scream hadn't been a woman, hadn't even been her, should have made Rose happy. Instead it made her uneasy. Were coyotes all that had been out here?

A few hours later they reached the smoldering remains of a homestead. Luke cast Rose an anxious glance.

"I'm fine," she said. If she retreated into herself every time she came upon a burned farm, she never would have gotten this far. She had learned to stave off panic by listing all the ways that *this* place differed from *her* place.

They have a larger barn.

"Had," she murmured, and was treated to another quick, anxious glance, which she ignored.

They had a shade tree.

Which was black now, like the house.

The scent isn't the same.

She sniffed, frowned. "What is that?" The smell was wrong somehow. She started toward the still-smoldering ruins.

"You shouldn't go there."

"Why?"

"Because that smell is . . ." He glanced away. His fingers clenched. "Meat."

Rose deposited her breakfast on the ground.

She was grateful he didn't fuss. Instead he left her to herself. It took her a while to settle her stomach because every time she breathed in, that scent caused everything to come out.

"There aren't any bodies."

Rose, who had just finished a bout of empty heaving, wiped her mouth with the back of her hand. "Then what is that . . ." She grimaced, gagged, and twirled her fingers through the stagnant air.

"I'll show you." He hoisted her to her feet.

"I don't think—"

"You'll feel better once you see." His grip gentled. "Trust me."

And because she did, she let him draw her toward the barn.

The structure was no more than a tumble of half-burned boards and stone. He'd pulled some of the debris aside to reveal a jumble of skulls and bones.

"Cattle." She was suddenly able to breathe without puking.

"I haven't found anything, or anyone, else."

"But there wouldn't be cattle without people. Where are the people?"

"I'm not sure."

"Who did this?"

He took her hand as if he'd done so a hundred times before, but it was the first time, and she wished it weren't here, like this. He led her away from the ruin of the barn toward the equally blackened house, stopping halfway between the two. Horse tracks crisscrossed one another all over the yard. He hunkered down, pointed at one set. "Unshod."

"Cheyenne?" she said.

"Can't tell by the tracks."

She stood there at a loss. The fire was out; the stock was dead. There weren't any people to bury. Should they just leave?

"Stay here," Luke said, then stalked into the swaying prairie grass. He stopped a hundred yards beyond the house and cursed. Rose hurried to join him. They stared at freshly turned mounds of earth, side by side.

"Husband and wife?" she asked.

"Only way to know for sure is to—"

"No," she said. The idea of digging up what had already been laid to rest made her ill again. "It doesn't matter." He remained silent, and she glanced at him. "Does it?" His contemplative expression drew into a frown. "What's wrong? Besides . . ." She waved at the graves, then the ruins.

"I don't like it."

"I doubt they did, either."

"Warriors wouldn't waste time on two graves. There's enough of an insult in one."

She saw his point. "Maybe someone else got here before us."

"Maybe," he agreed, though she could tell he didn't believe it. "Anyone who would bury them like this would be riding a shod horse, and there weren't any tracks like that. Except for ours."

This bothered him; Rose wasn't sure why. "What difference does it make who buried them? It saves us time. We need to follow the ones who did this."

"No."

"What do you mean 'no'? If these weren't the Cheyenne who took Lily, maybe they can direct us to the ones who did."

"You say that as if they'd be happy to help."

"We need to—"

"They weren't Cheyenne," he interrupted.

"I thought you couldn't tell from their tracks."

"I can't." His gaze flicked behind her. "But I know Sioux when I see them."

CHAPTER 8

A line of warriors approached, their horses parting the tall grass with little more than a whisper.

Luke didn't want to take his eyes off the Sioux, but he risked a quick glance at Rose. Her face was as pale as her hair, her blue eyes gone black with fear.

"Do not faint," he whispered. Weakness was not something the Sioux admired.

She set her jaw, but she still appeared ready to topple over in a strong wind, which could come up at any time out here on the prairie.

"Do not run," he continued. "They'll chase you, and they'll catch you." If possible she paled even more, so he didn't add that if they caught her, she would be theirs. He thought she already knew.

"Lean on me," he said, and faced the Sioux. He dared not let them out of his sight any longer.

For an instant he had hopes these Sioux had merely been riding nearby and smelled the smoke, that perhaps they hadn't been the ones who had caused it. But as they reined in and he got his first good look at them and their mounts, that hope was lost.

Each wore a feathered headdress, something the Sioux did not do when hunting or just riding across the prairie. Their faces had also been painted—red first, with different-colored markings that depicted their place in the band and their previous prowess. Their buckskin leggings and shirts were beaded and quilled, but the most telling feature was the scalps that decorated each one.

War shirts. War paint. War bonnets.

Clothed in their spoils—a straw hat on one, a strip of calico that could only have come from a white woman's dress held back the hair of another, a third had strung a fork from a thong around his neck—if they weren't responsible for the incident here, they were responsible for another somewhere else.

One of the warriors leaped off his horse and strode to theirs. Rose caught her breath as he inspected their things. She stepped closer, leaned against him as he'd ordered, but she trembled so badly he couldn't enjoy it. He tangled her fingers with his.

"Is that hair on his shirt?"

He didn't answer. Which was answer enough.

The warrior began to root through the saddlebags.

"What if they take something?" she whispered.

"What do we have that we can't do without?"

Besides our lives?

The Sioux let out a surprised "yee" and held up Luke's Dog Man headdress.

"Hell," Luke muttered. There went their lives.

The leader, marked as such by virtue of his many-feathered headdress, as well as the three black slashes of paint across his right cheek, scowled and motioned that the item be brought to him. He peered at the puff of black crow feathers, surrounded by brown turkey feathers. "Kill him," he said in Sioux.

"I am not who you think I am," Luke replied in the same language.

The warrior on the ground, who had drawn his knife and started toward them, paused, then glanced at the first, whose lips twitched once—the Sioux version of a smirk.

"You are not the one who has killed our brother Dog Man?"

"I am Ve'ho'e Mestaa'e."

From the sudden stillness of the Sioux, it was clear they had heard of him.

"Ve'ho'e Mestaa'e is dead," said the leader.

"Which is why they call me *mestaa'e*."

The Sioux was not amused. They so seldom were.

The Sioux and the Cheyenne had once battled fiercely over the same land. To be fair, the Cheyenne's home had originally been east and north of the plains—Minnesota and the Dakotas—where they'd been farmers. But once they discovered horses, and the whites began to push them west, they'd adapted and become hunters. Eventually they had joined with the Sioux and the Arapaho to become allies against one common enemy.

Ve'ho'e or white man.

In Cheyenne the word had once been used for a trickster, as well as the spider. Luke could see how it had come to mean white men as well. The *ve'ho'e* were clever and sly. They did not say what they meant, or do what they said. They spun webs to trap the unsuspecting.

"I had heard that Ve'ho'e Mestaa'e was a *ma'e-ve'ho'e*," the leader continued.

Luke removed his hat to reveal his bald head, then shrugged.

Literally the phrase meant *red white man* and was used to refer to Germans, many of whom had red hair. It was what the Cheyenne had called him when he first came to live with them.

Telling the Cheyenne he was Irish had done no good. Telling them that his name—Phelan—meant wolf only caused laughter, then disdain. Wolves were held in great esteem. White men were not. Therefore even if his name meant wolf, he would not be called such.

To the Cheyenne, every white man with red hair was German. Just as, to the whites, the only good Indian was a dead one. Still, they had begun to refer to him as *ho-esta-ve'ho'e* or *fire white man*, which he had considered an improvement.

A Cheyenne had many names throughout a lifetime. Children were at first called by pet names, such as *Potbelly* or *Busy Hands*. When they were five or six they were given a more formal name, usually one that had belonged to a father's relative. They kept this one until they distinguished themselves in battle, and then they were given another. That Luke had possessed several names while living with them was not unusual. The Cheyenne had eventually branded him *White Ghost* because they believed his spirit went out in the night and hovered over the white men while he learned all their secrets.

Luke hadn't had to listen or learn. He had already known.

"What is he saying?" Rose asked.

Luke tightened his fingers around hers. "Not now." The less attention she drew to herself, the better.

Too late. The leader's dark eyes lit on her. "Your woman?"

"Yes."

"They say Ve'ho'e Mestaa'e went to the spirits because he mourned the death of his wife."

Such a rumor would explain why the Cheyenne had not come looking for him.

Yet.

"A man may have more than one wife," Luke said. Some Cheyenne had several at a time, though wives were always of the same family—sisters, cousins. Less trouble that way.

The Sioux lowered his head in agreement, and his feathers fluttered in the spring breeze. He had done many brave things to wear such a large number of feathers. Those of a golden eagle were the most prized, as the eagle was believed to be a messenger of God. Only those who endured incredible hardship with courage and strength could wear a golden eagle feather. This man possessed at least two.

"Why do the Cheyenne believe that you are dead?"

Because one of them had tried to kill him. But Luke would not talk about that.

"The loss of my wife made me . . ."

When he paused too long, the Sioux finished for him. *"Witcko tko ke."* Crazy.

"Heehe'e," Luke agreed in Cheyenne, then repeated it in Sioux. *"Ha."*

"So you left the Cheyenne and you"—the Sioux's gaze went again to Rose and she caught her breath, tightening her fingers around Luke's—"found a new wife."

"A man must do what a man must do."

"Ha. I heard you were *wicasa wakan."*

The Cheyenne had named Luke a prophet because he knew what the soldiers would do next. Or at least he had until that day when he hadn't. He hadn't disabused them of the notion because being seen as a prophet had gotten the ropes taken off his wrists. However, if he said he was a prophet right now, he was going to have to prove it. If he said he wasn't . . .

His glance went to the knife that still rested in the nearest Sioux's hands. If he wasn't a prophet, he wasn't any good to them at all. Just like the Cheyenne.

While Luke wasn't afraid of death, he didn't need to be a prophet to know what would happen to Rose once he no longer stood in front of her.

"Ha," he agreed. "I am."

The leader's lips twitched again. The fellow was nearly chuckling. "Then you will have no trouble telling me what I do not know."

"I would be honored."

The Sioux waited expectantly. Luke racked his brain, trying to come up with something—anything—that might work. But he'd been in the hills too long. He knew very little about what was going on out here beyond a lot of . . .

His gaze flickered over the burned farm and the stark mounds of earth.

This.

"Why is he staring at you like that?" Rose whispered, and the Sioux muttered and shifted. Women were not allowed to speak during councils of war and of peace. They served the men and then went away.

"Forgive my wife," he said in Sioux. "She doesn't know the language of the people, or the proper ways. If I might explain so she stops her nagging."

"Wives," the man said in the same tone men had said the word since the ancients, then lifted one shoulder.

Luke turned. Rose was still too pale, but she seemed less likely to faint. Surprising considering that she'd thrown up everything she'd eaten since yesterday, and the sun was strong enough to make *his* head ache.

"They think I'm a prophet," he said.

Her gaze flicked from the Sioux back to him. "Why?"

"I told them so."

"Are you crazy?"

"Looking back," he murmured, "that would have been the better choice."

"You aren't making sense."

"If I'm crazy they—"

"Won't hurt you," she finished. "Tell them you're crazy."

"They won't hurt *me*, but that won't save you."

"So you told them you were a prophet?"

"I don't have time to explain. Do you know anything I might tell them that would make me appear as though I know the future?" Her continued confusion forced him into a quick explanation. "When I was with the Cheyenne I knew things. Which way the army might go, where they would camp, days they wouldn't be as alert as others."

Soldiers had a bad habit of drinking on paydays and holidays. It didn't take a prophet to know that if the warriors attacked the morning after, they would have a better chance of winning.

"You told the Cheyenne army secrets?" Her voice was horrified.

"Court-martial me later, Rose. Right now we need to tell the Sioux something that makes me seem like a seer and not a liar. Understand?"

She nodded. At least she didn't argue anymore, though she still stared at him as though he were Benedict Arnold.

"The railroad," she said.

"They know about the Union Pacific. It's a little hard to miss."

The Union Pacific had laid track west, headed for Colorado. The noise, the smoke, the increase of people had not only ruined the land but driven the buffalo away from the hunting grounds. The Sioux and the Cheyenne had responded by attacking the work crews and even the trains, but the "iron horse" just kept coming. A few times they'd attempted to pull up rail ties, but it wasn't that easy.

"It's the Kansas Pacific now," she said. "They drove in the last spike at Comanche Crossing last August."

Some prophet he was. The last he knew the *Union Pacific-Eastern Division* had stalled at Sheridan. Now their name had changed, and they were done.

"I heard the Atchison-Lincoln-Columbus Railroad is building from Atchison to Lincoln."

"Which explains the name," Luke murmured. Railroad owners weren't known for their originality. "Did they start yet?"

"I don't think so."

It wasn't the best information, but it was all the information that he had.

"Ve'ho'e Mestaa'e," the Sioux leader said. "If you have lost your ability to hear the voices of the spirits along with your hair, I understand. We have heard the tales of Samson."

The man's gaze went to Rose; from the way his lips tightened he considered her Delilah. Luke stepped more firmly in front of his "wife."

"Did he say 'Samson'?" she asked.

"Missionaries tell Bible stories at the reservation."

"If there's a reservation, why aren't they on it?"

"The agreement was that the Sioux could hunt in unoccupied territories."

"This seems occupied to me."

"Not anymore."

The Sioux, and the Cheyenne and any other tribe that had seen its favorite hunting grounds overrun by white men, their houses and cattle and barns and trains, often decided to make them unoccupied in the only way they knew how.

Luke returned his attention to the leader. "I still hear the spirits."

"What do they tell you?"

He made a good show of listening; he even heard a distant whisper. *Come back to us.* He just wasn't sure who was calling. The hills? The ghosts? Did it matter?

"Before long the iron horse will stretch north," he said.

"Paha Sapa?"

Luke spread his hands. He doubted the new railroad would reach the sacred Black Hills any time soon, but he wasn't going to tell them that. If they thought the hills were in danger, they would ride north without pause.

And those hills were far, far away.

"Paha Sapa was bestowed upon us in the treaty that ended the war of Red Cloud."

"If they are yours, then why did they need to be bestowed?" Luke asked.

The Sioux's scowl deepened. Luke had heard whispers of gold in those hills, which meant they wouldn't belong to the Sioux for long. He didn't have to be a prophet to know that white men digging in the sacred soil of Paha Sapa was going to cause another war.

"They give and then they take," the Sioux said. "It is their way."

Luke had to agree. The army had given him a second chance—twice. They'd taken it away twice, too.

"You would be a good man to make the talk at the next treaty."

"Perhaps." Luke doubted he'd live that long. "I am taking my new wife to meet my family. Have you seen the Dog Men?"

The leader tilted his head, and the huge headdress rustled. The feathers sounded as if a flock of birds had just taken flight. "The Dog Men no longer ride as one."

"So I have heard. I have also heard some still ride here. Is this true?"

The man's dark gaze held Luke's. "We met a *hoh-nohka* two days past. He said there were Dog Men riding south."

"Le mita pila," Luke said. *My thanks.*

"Hoka hey!" the leader shouted.

The warrior who had remained nearby, knife in hand, just in case Luke said or did anything foolish, leaped onto his pony shouting, *"Hoka hey"* as well. The exclamation was a general call to action, something the Sioux shouted to get everyone to come along.

"They're leaving," Luke said. The leader gave orders in rapid Sioux. "Riding toward Atchison to discover if my prophecy is true."

"Nake nula waun welo!" the leader called.

"I am ready for whatever comes," Luke translated. "It's what warriors cry as they ride into battle. They are willing to die." He kept his gaze on the Sioux as they rode away. "I hope you're right about the railroad in Atchison."

"There isn't an eastern connection." His confusion must have been obvious because she continued. "The railroad stretches west from Omaha. There's a river to the east. They need a bridge there." She let out an impatient huff. "What does it matter?"

"If the Sioux arrive in Atchison and they don't see rails going north, they'll think I lied. Then they'll come after us, and this time they won't be so friendly."

Rose glanced around the blackened land. "This was friendly?"

"This wasn't ours." He lifted his chin toward the graves. "Those aren't us."

"Yet."

"Exactly. Let's go before they decide they should have taken us along." He was kind of surprised they hadn't. He would have.

Rose's gaze flicked to the retreating line of warriors. "What are they going to do?"

"You know what they're going to do, Rose."

She bit her lip; he took her elbow and led her toward the horses. He helped her mount; her expression remained concerned. "Maybe we should have—"

"If we didn't give them something"—Luke mounted himself—"they would have killed us." Or at least tried.

He wondered why they hadn't shot an arrow at him just to see if he died. Ghosts didn't. Another reason he'd been given the name. He had not died, no matter what they had done to him.

"We just sent them to attack an innocent railroad camp to save ourselves."

"I have my doubts it's innocent." He'd seen those camps. There was a reason they were called *hell on wheels*. Gamblers, whores, sellers of whiskey and sin gravitated to wherever the money was, and right now it was with the railroad. Towns sprang up nearby, and when the railroad moved on, so did their hellish companions.

"Those workers aren't fighters; they're immigrants and Negroes and folks just trying to get along." She still stared at the Sioux, who were already far enough away to have become little more than large black dots on the horizon.

Luke probably should have felt bad about sending the Sioux after the railroad, but right now it was him and Rose out here alone—everything, everyone was the enemy. If they didn't fight hard and dirty, they wouldn't be fighting much longer at all.

"You said you'd do anything to get your daughter back."

She turned her gaze from the horizon. "I will."

"Consider this one more thing. They would have killed us. At the least they would have killed you." Or worse. He glanced again at the distant riders. "Hell, they still might."

He didn't trust them any more than he trusted any other strangers he came across on the prairie. Luke trusted no one. Most days he didn't even trust himself.

"How are we going to find the Dog Men?" she asked. "You said they could be anywhere."

"According to our golden-eagle-wearing friend, they met a *hohnohka* two days past who saw Dog Men riding south."

"Then why are we riding north?"

"Because a *hohnohka* is a contrary. One who lives his life in opposition. He says yes for no. He washes with sand, dries himself with water. He rides into battle backward."

"And they called you crazy," she muttered.

"Not at first." At first they had called him slave, then friend, then brother, husband, and finally . . .

Traitor.

"If you tell a contrary to go away, he comes closer. If you ask one 'where are the Dog Men?' and he says 'they have gone south . . . '"

Understanding spread across her face like dawn spread across the east. "Then you ride north."

"Yes."

"It was a test, their telling you about the contrary and what he said of the Dog Men?"

He nodded.

"But how will they know if you passed? They're gone."

"They aren't gone. Or at least they weren't until *after* we started north."

Her gaze went to the last place they'd seen the Sioux. "What if we hadn't gone north?"

He didn't answer. Didn't need to.

"Clever," she murmured.

"They haven't survived this long by being stupid." Or trusting anyone but themselves.

The tribes on the plains fought a losing battle. No matter how brave, how smart, how well versed in the land and its legends, they were facing too many white people. They would hold on awhile longer; they might even win a few large battles. However, with every victory, more soldiers would come. The U.S. Army was not going to give up. The U.S. government was not going to forget about the vast land west of the Mississippi.

Not when they had so many settlers and so little room, and so few Indians stood in the way of what they wanted.

CHAPTER 9

When they made camp that night, the darkness closed in all around them.

"Do you think anyone's following us?" Rose couldn't see past the flickers of light thrown by the fire, and it bothered her.

"I'm not sure."

The wind had picked up, tossing clouds over the moon and the stars like a navy blue shroud. In the distance a coyote howled, a second joined in, then a third and more. She'd heard coyotes before, a hundred times, and they always made her feel small, desperate, and lonely.

"I'd rather be alert over nothing than asleep when there's something," she continued.

His lips curved. He had the most beautiful mouth, and it did the most wondrous things. Things she'd never imagined a mouth could do. Rose ducked her head so the brim of his hat hid her blush.

She'd traveled west to avoid becoming a virgin old maid. She was no longer a virgin, which meant she'd never be an old maid. But she still felt like one. Who else would lust after a man who would rather pay a whore than lie with her?

Kalt wie eis, whispered the wind. Would it ever stop blowing? She'd heard of women left alone on the prairie too long who went mad because of that wind.

But she wasn't alone, and she would not go mad. Not while there was any chance of finding Lily.

"I'll keep watch," Luke said. "You nearly fell asleep in your beans."

"Maybe we should both watch." He looked as tired as she felt. "Four eyes are better than two."

He tossed her bedroll into her lap. "Get some sleep, Rose. I'll wake you in a few hours, and you can take over."

"Aren't you tired?"

"I'm always tired. But I don't like to sleep."

She didn't, either. While daydreams of late had been of him, her nightmares were the same as they'd ever been. Darkness lit by fire, tears brought by pain. "I might scream."

"I won't care."

She didn't think she'd sleep. Again, she was wrong.

She awoke to total darkness. The fire hissed. Had he doused it? As the only reason for that was a desire to remain unseen, she didn't start up. She didn't cry his name. She remained quiet and still, noting the changes all around her.

She was soaked and lying in a puddle, which explained the hissing fire. The earth shook. The air breathed thunder. She could see nothing. Even in her dreams the world wasn't this dark. In her dreams the world was always quite bright.

Which was what led to the screams.

She sat up, groping for her Colts, strapping them on as her gaze strained against the night. Could there be a stampede? Buffalo? Cattle? Horses? Didn't matter. She had to move or she was dead.

She stood, disoriented by the velvet darkness, the recurring thunder, the torrential rain. "Luke?"

The sky split, spilling white light from above. She was alone in the camp, except for their mounts. A crack shook the earth again, and the horses whinnied, reared. If not for their pickets, they would have galloped off.

They weren't the only ones. In that instant of illumination she'd caught sight of another figure, alone on the prairie. At least there wasn't a huge, rumbling herd of hooves. However, the shadow sped toward a solitary, not-quite-distant-enough tree.

Rose started to run. She'd lived on the prairie long enough to know that with storms like this trees were a very bad idea. She'd heard stories of cows, startled by the thunder, confused by the darkness, taking refuge beneath the only refuge they could find—a tree just like that one. When the storm fled and morning came, not only the tree would be black and dead, but also the prairie grass all around it, as well as the cows.

Lightning struck again, so close her hair hurt. Her fingertips buzzed. Rose unstrapped her gun belt and dropped the Colts to the ground. If she lived, she'd come back for them.

White jagged lines trailed from heaven to hell, illuminating the tree—craggy and stark—right before it burst into flames. She paused, searching for the figure she had seen before. For just a second, it was there. *He* was there.

Then, suddenly, he was gone.

Luke wasn't sure how he came to be running across the prairie in the middle of the worst storm he could remember.

He'd been sitting by the fire watching her sleep. The light of the flames had danced across her pale face, making her seem so young. Making him wonder how old she was, along with all sorts of other strange things. What would her neck taste like in the dark of the night? How might her breasts feel against his cheek? When he entered her, would she draw a breath in, or let one out?

His hands clenched so tightly they ached. To keep himself from moving closer, from reaching out to touch, he closed his eyes. And in that velvety darkness waited dreams. Those dreams had not been of her.

The fog over the river looks like smoke. The hooves of his horse sound like distant artillery. He shouts her

name and hears only wails that are so like the wind his
tears flow as cold as a winter rain.

He came awake as water dripped off his nose. At the
familiar rumble of guns he leaped to his feet, eyes wide
and seeking. Then mist as thick as smoke drifted across
his face, and the next thing he knew he was running.

Why was it so dark? Shouldn't everything be gray
and white?

Like her.

A streak of silver lit the sky. A tree blazed fire. The
finger of God. A burning bush.

"Luke!" his ghosts called to him.

He staggered as the earth trembled. He nearly fell,
righting himself only to have everything crumble.

"Hell," he muttered. No less than he deserved.

He didn't attempt to stop his descent. Now that the
devil had come for him at last in fire and ice and fury,
what would be the point?

When he hit bottom—not with a thud but more of a
squelch—he expected the flames to spring up—he'd
seen their flare, he still smelled the smoke. Eternal
damnation should commence. Instead he lay in a puddle of mud—wet and cold—as heaven wept all over him.

A silhouette appeared above—a woman framed in
the circle of night.

"Kiwidinok?" he whispered.

What greater hell than to know she would watch him
writhe where he belonged for all eternity, while she
remained up there where she did?

Earth tumbled over him, burying him alive. But not
before he saw one final thing.

True hell descended as she jumped.

Rose searched for a way to reach Luke, saw nothing but
the bank of mud sliding over his face.

The gaping crater was no more than six feet across,
perhaps the same distance wide, but several feet deeper.
However, the sides continued to slough away in the rain,

causing the hole to expand. Half of Luke's body had already disappeared as the earth slithered downward. He made no attempt to get out from beneath. Had he hit his head? Seeing no other choice, she jumped.

Her boots hit the bottom, slid forward. She saw them rising to eye level and clenched her teeth so she wouldn't clip off her tongue when she landed, but the impact wasn't as bad as she'd feared. The ground was mush. Dark flecks flicked up, then rained back down, pattering like sleet against a window. She tasted grit in her mouth and wondered how it had gotten there, considering that she still had her teeth clenched and her lips the same.

She suddenly remembered why she had jumped— had she hit *her* head?—that mud cascading over Luke's face. She had to get it off; she had to dig him out before he died. Why was he lying there as if he had already?

She rolled toward the body-shaped lump, clawing at the dirt. His mouth and nose emerged. Shoving the mud aside, she formed a halo around his head. His eyes remained closed. Perhaps his lashes were too full of dirt for him to lift. They were thick and long—dark brown with just a tinge of red at the tip—or at least they were when they weren't caked with slime. She used her fingertip to brush the last traces away.

Was he breathing? She set that finger beneath his nose, felt nothing. "Luke!"

Her palm went to his chest; she waited for it to rise and fall. When it didn't, she smacked him. Hard. "Breathe!"

A hand shot out of the filth, circled her wrist, yanked her forward. She sprawled atop his chest, and his eyes opened. They seemed unfocused, but perhaps that was just a trick of the light, which still flickered silver and white from above, as the world around them trembled and the rain continued to fall.

"Kiwidinok," he murmured.

"You're alive," she said.

"Hova'âhane."

"I don't underst—"

His kiss tasted like sun-warmed earth, and he smelled like blue sky. The hands that framed her face were damp and sticky, or perhaps that was just her face. His thumbs smoothed over her cheeks, and grit scraped her skin. She had never felt anything so delicious. She forgot they were both covered in mud. She was wet; he was cold. When he rolled out of the muck and onto her, she forgot everything except him.

A day in the sun and the wind had chapped her face, her hands, her neck. The mud was a balm, like his lips. Everywhere he kissed was cooled; everywhere he touched began to burn. His mouth traced a trail from her chin to the hollow of her throat and he worried a bit of skin with his teeth. Would that leave a mark? She didn't care. The combination of hot tongue, cool lips, gentle sucks, and sharp bites was one she had never experienced before, probably never would again; she should enjoy it.

When his head lowered and his tongue tasted the swell of her breast, for an instant she knew she was dreaming—she didn't own a shirt that dipped so low. Her disappointment caused a painful jolt. Why had she believed this was real? If Luke had been interested in her body, wouldn't he have taken it on a dry, clean bed in Rogue, rather than the bottom of a mud-ravaged sinkhole in hell only knew where?

However, when she looked down, her shirt gaped open to her waist. The leap into the hole had torn it. Oddly, her chemise—old, worn, thin as it was, she'd hacked it off at the hips after her first week on a horse—remained intact. Her hands itched to tear that material, too.

"Kiwidinok," he said again. "Sweetheart."

Kiwidinok must mean *sweetheart*. She hoped so.

Then his lips closed over a peak, taking both her and the chemise within, and she didn't care. He suckled, causing the cloth to slide back and forth, along with his tongue. She pressed his head closer, wishing again he had not cut his hair. Not only had it been beyond beautiful, but she wanted, needed something to hold on to.

He rolled again—*plotch*—landing in a puddle.

Squelch. The mud protested when he yanked her free and took her along.

Her undergarment tore down the center when he rent it in half, then gathered her freed breasts in his hands, kneading, stroking, tonguing her rain-hardened nipples until she groaned.

He was hard against her stomach, which was not where she wanted him to be. She wiggled upward. His head lifted, following the ascent of her breasts. She tightened and swelled.

"Rose," he murmured, flicking each nipple with the tip of his tongue. "So beautiful."

She was not beautiful. She knew that. She had eyes; so did he.

"You don't have to," she began.

His legs opened as he looped his boots around her calves. "Don't go. Don't leave."

His voice was so desperate she stayed.

Fool! It wasn't his voice that made her stay.

He tugged on her ruined shirt. She found it easy to shrug free and toss it away. His fingertips followed the rain across her skin. She wanted to do the same with his.

Clouds flitted over the sliver of moon, removing every vestige of light. Soon they were naked. She traced patterns of mud and rain along his arms, his back with her lips, her tongue, her teeth. His muscles fluttered and danced. Even when she spread her fingers over the rippling expanse of his chest and found scars there—bad ones—she merely touched them, kissed them, and moved on. Now was not the time to discover the origins of such a travesty.

His stomach was taut and flat, the jut of his hip so sharp. At times his hands were so smooth against her she sighed, at others just rough enough to make her tremble. The rain intensified, warmer somehow, and they stood in the center of their world as it washed everything away.

He took her wrist and drew it lower. Wrapped her palm around him and showed her a new rhythm. Her breasts heavy and tight, her skin tingled. She felt an emptiness inside different from any emptiness that had been there in the past. This emptiness could be filled, would be filled.

By him.

In her hand he thickened and grew. He pulled her to the ground. She started to lie back, but he murmured, *"Hova'âhane."* She didn't understand it any more now than she had then.

She couldn't see, but she could feel. Hear. Smell. Taste. Her senses were so full she thought she might burst.

He drew her onto his lap, setting her legs on either side of his hips as he filled her only emptiness. Surprise bloomed, along with the pleasure. She hadn't known two people could connect in this way.

He bucked, and she grasped his shoulders before she toppled off. Then he was thrusting up, pulling down, and that part of her that had been tingling, whimpering, needing something it wasn't getting, had never gotten, began to scream.

"More," she gasped.

He moved a hand from her hip to her breast, lifted the weight to his mouth, and latched on, sucking her in a rhythm identical to his thrusts. She answered those thrusts with movements of her own—a roll of her hips that reminded her of riding a horse. If she hadn't been completely captivated by what was happening between them, that thought might have made her blush. He wasn't an animal, even if his groans, and hers, sounded like one.

Deep inside he swelled and pulsed. Her own body answered; her hips echoed his strokes. He clasped her tighter. She rested her cheek against his head; he pressed his face to her breasts as those echoes went on and on.

When their bodies stilled, and their hearts slowed, they remained together, her legs wrapped around his hips, her arms wrapped around his neck, his around her waist. The rain had washed away most of the grit but not all. Until they got out of here and found a river, Rose would be rinsing gravel out of her teeth, her hair, and several other places where gravel had never been before.

She smoothed her palm over his head, imagined walking into the river with him, washing each other, doing the same thing in the water as they'd done in the rain. Perhaps she wasn't *kalt wie eis* after all. Or perhaps she just wasn't with him.

She kissed his temple. "We have to get out of here."

Though she doubted anyone else was on the prairie tonight, nevertheless the idea of climbing naked out of this pit was more than Rose could manage, so she rooted around in the slop, found her clothes and his, then put hers back on.

Luke sat in the mud, naked, his head resting against the movable walls as mud slid over his face, down his chest, into his ears and eyes and mouth, and over the clothes she'd tossed in his lap. Rose knelt as his side, flicking at the dirt. "Luke?"

He didn't speak, didn't move as more mud cascaded down. The sides of the hole continued to slither, making the area wider but less deep. If they waited long enough, perhaps they could walk out. Or perhaps the entire place would cave in and bury them forever.

"We have to get out." She stood, tugging him with her. He continued to stare, unblinking, at the walls all around. She didn't like it.

Releasing him, she crawled upward, but every time she got a handhold, then a foothold, the mud collapsed, and she slid all the way down.

"If I could climb high enough I could pull myself over the edge . . ." Then she would fetch a horse, some rope. Rose frowned. Did they have rope? One thing at a time.

Luke still hadn't moved, and the continual landslide had buried his feet to the ankles.

"Luke!"

He didn't react.

Panicked, she attempted to crawl upward again, this time nearly reaching the top, pulling until her head almost cleared the hole before her hold collapsed, tossing her back down. She landed on him. They fell in a tangle of legs and arms.

She sat up, took his icy hand. He did not seem to see her. He didn't seem to see anything. A prickle of unease skated over her. "What is wrong with you?"

She tightened her fingers around his, hoping to impart some warmth. Unfortunately his behavior had brought a cold ball of fear to her belly, and that fear, along with the soaked clothing, caused her to shiver as much as he was.

"Do you know who I am?"

Trembling, he crawled into her lap, arms circling her waist. She felt for his vest and drew it over his bare back. The thing was so muddy it probably did more harm than good, but she had no idea what else to do.

They weren't going to be able to climb out of here while the storm raged. Even then, they would have to wait until the sides of the hole dried enough so they wouldn't collapse and throw them back down.

Luke burrowed closer, hugged Rose tighter, murmured nonsense in two languages, and she stroked his cheek and did what her mother had done for her, and what she in turn had done for Lily, whenever the child had been ill, or tired, or scared.

"Hush a bye," she sang, "don't you cry. Go to sleep, my sweetheart; and when you wake, you shall have . . . all the pretty little ponies."

Rose lifted her gaze to the black sky. She hoped their pretty ponies were still there if they ever got out of this mess.

"Don't stop," he said.

She hadn't planned to, even before he'd spoken the first lucid words she'd heard from him in what seemed like hours. He'd leaned back a bit to stare at the sky; the silvery light cast him in the shades of night.

"Paint and bay, sorrel and gray, all the pretty little ponies. So hush a bye, don't you cry. Go to sleep, my baby."

Her fingers traced his chest, brushing the ridged scars just below his collarbone. She traced the twin marks that circled his wrists with her thumbs.

"What did they do to you?" she whispered.

CHAPTER 10

Threw me in a pit." *Dark. Deep. Damp. Like this.*

"I never thought I'd get out."

"How did you?"

That voice. Whose was it? Not his mother's, though it had just sung the same song she always sang whenever he—whenever any of them—had been sick. The sound had soothed him in the midst of torment.

Singing stripped away accents; he wasn't sure why. His mother's had been Irish, until she sang. This one was Yankee, once she was through. He wished he'd heard the song the last time he'd been in this place. Maybe if he had, they would have let him out sooner. Because hearing his dead mother's voice, or anyone else's, would have meant he was crazy.

Was he crazy now? When hadn't he been?

"How did you get out, Luke?"

Gentle fingers stroked his forehead. He waited for the light tug on his scalp as she brushed through his hair. When it didn't come, he reached up. His hair was gone. How many days, weeks, months had he lost this time?

"What year is it?"

"Same year it was the last time you asked."

When had he asked? Why had he? And what had she—whoever she was—answered?

"They captured me."

"I know." Her fingers were warm, and he was so cold. Sighing, he gave himself up to . . . whatever this was.

"I hid." He wasn't proud of that, but he'd had little choice.

Mosby had called the Rangers to Rectortown. They should have been able to meet and then disperse to carry out their orders. As Mosby's Rangers were partisans, their main occupation was harassment—cut a telegraph line, confiscate a supply wagon, as well as a few horses.

Though the Rangers were near one thousand strong, they divided into smaller bands of a dozen or so to carry out their missions. They moved behind enemy lines at will, then disappeared into the countryside, hiding in the brush, the hills, the houses of those who supported them.

But that day at Rectortown nearly one hundred and fifty Union soldiers were waiting for them. The meeting was secret. How had the enemy heard about it?

Despite the Rangers being surprised and outnumbered, they had triumphed. The Union lost one hundred and six men—twelve dead, thirty-seven wounded, and fifty-seven captured. Mosby lost six men. One of them was Luke.

Everyone had scattered. They knew the area. *He* knew the area. He should have been able to escape, but—

"They found me."

Treachery. Betrayal. Pain. And so much darkness. He had never really feared anything, until there'd been only the dark. Time lost all meaning. What had been so important faded away, along with any sense of yourself.

That slightly rough but exceedingly warm finger brushed the scars on his chest. "Did this hurt?"

"Yes," he whispered. But that was later. "I said I'd do anything."

The finger stopped moving. "What did you do?"

He'd denied all that he was, all that he'd believed, just to get out of that pit.

"It's all right," she said. But it wasn't.

"I killed her," he whispered.

It was only when the voice ordered, "English," that he understood he'd spoken in Cheyenne. Then he couldn't stop. He couldn't remember anything but the Cheyenne words for what he had done. So he babbled on, about blood and death, foolishness and youth. He'd been selfish and cowardly and wrong. He was outcast—from every place he'd known, from everyone he'd loved. If he went back, he was a dead man.

When he was in the pit he'd been so alone. It wasn't until after that he'd found a life, true love, any sort of happiness. He'd never dreamed of softness in that pit, never dreamed of her, never been comforted or tormented by ghosts because his ghosts, at that time, were not yet ghosts.

This night, this woman, this place made no sense. But what did?

"Nana'tose," he muttered. *I am cold.*

She drew him closer, held him tighter as he shivered and shuddered and moaned. She was warm, or at least warmer. Despite the night, she smelled of the sun and the wind and he was soothed. When she sang, she took him back to Virginia and the Phelan Farm on the outskirts of Richmond. The youngest of six children, Luke had led a charmed life. They had run and jumped and played. They had tormented their sister.

"Annie Beth Lou," he whispered. He had always called Annabeth that. She hadn't much liked it.

"Hush," that beautiful voice said.

Not Annabeth's voice. Was that good? Or was that bad? Did it mean she wasn't dead? Or, perhaps, that she was? Certainly he heard voices, but he had never yet heard hers.

How his sister had hated it when Luke called her Annie Beth Lou in a singsong, teasing tone. Annabeth had been raised with five brothers, and she had learned young to fight hard and fight dirty. It was the only way to survive.

She couldn't be dead. She just couldn't be.

When Luke thought of his sister, he saw her on the farm—alone—because everyone else had been killed.

"Abner. James. Hoyt. Saul."

They were dead. Moze had told him so.

Moses Farquhar and Luke had been raised together after Moze's mother died. Despite having plenty of children of her own, Luke's mother had just shrugged and taken in one more.

Moze and Luke were of an age and the two of them had done everything together, right up to and including their enlistment in the Confederate Army. Luke had gone with Mosby. Moze had gone . . . Luke was never quite sure. But his friend always turned up. Usually with bad news.

Luke's parents expired from illness; his sister had been left alone. Abner dead at Sharpsburg, James at Ball's Bluff, Hoyt at New Bern, and Saul at Shiloh. With Moze knowing so damn much about everyone else, Luke wondered what the fellow had discovered, then told, everyone else about him.

Luke had hoped and prayed while in that pit that Moze would come. Which was foolish. No Reb would walk into a Yankee prison. Not even for a man who was closer than a brother. Not if he ever wanted to get out. But as time passed, and other prisoners were exchanged, Luke had thought he might be. When he wasn't, he took the only way out that he had.

He had not realized how badly being incarcerated would feel, how shaky and sick he would become as the days upon weeks upon months stretched on in the same tiny space. He was weak; he knew that now. Anyone could ride and shoot and kill. But the truly strong survived anything.

"You're cold. Let me help with your clothes."

He fumbled and twisted and managed to put on his vest and pants. Everything was wet. He was wet. Had the guards thrown water on him again while he slept?

"Don't," he muttered. "No more."

"All right. We'll leave the boots."

He wiggled his toes. Also wet and cold, but they didn't burn as they had in the depths of an Illinois winter.

Had the cold broken him? Or had it been the silence? The solitude? The darkness? The despair? He would have done anything to be free of that pit.

The first offer they made, he took.

Luke finally slept as the storm died.

Rose hadn't understood a good portion of what he'd mumbled, the majority of it being in Cheyenne, but the names had been said in English.

Annie Beth Lou must be his sister. From the softness of his voice when he'd said it, Rose certainly hoped so. Then there'd been Abner, Saul, James, Hoyt, and Moze. Brothers? Comrades? A combination of the two? She had no idea because the rest had been Cheyenne, shudders, and gibberish.

Luke hadn't seemed feverish. Then again, how could she tell? They were both so damn cold. Even after she'd coaxed him into his clothes, he'd shaken like grass in the midst of a twister. It wasn't until the rain stopped that either one of them began to warm.

The sky above lightened to gray. Birds began to chirp. She hoped the new day would dawn clear. If another storm lurked nearby, they would have no chance of escaping this prison, and she wasn't certain what she would do, or what he would. When the slice of heaven above went from gray to pink, then yellow and finally blue, she breathed easier.

Luke still lay across her lap, arms around her waist, cheek pressed to her stomach, his head just beneath her breasts. She touched his temple, his cheek. The gentle strokes seemed to help whenever he tensed and murmured. She traced the muscles that fluttered beneath his skin, remembering how they had felt beneath her palms when he pulsed inside her.

Luke's languid, heavy weight lightened as he threw

off slumber. He frowned at his filthy clothes, then hers. Glancing upward, he grimaced before rubbing at his head as if it ached. "Where are we?"

At least he hadn't said, *Who are you?*

"Kansas," she answered. "Maybe Colorado."

"That much I—I—knew." The hand he ran over his mouth trembled.

"Luke?" She reached for his other hand, and he pulled it away. She let hers fall into her lap, curling her fingers inward and pressing her nails into her palm so she would not reach out again. "It's all right."

He laughed, the sound too high and not quite right. "We have to get out of here!"

"We will. As soon as the sides dry."

"Now." He leaped to his feet, raised his arms as high as he could reach, then dug a chunk of mud out of the nearest wall.

"I tried that," she said. "And I—"

He pulled himself up. The wall crumbled, and he sprawled at her feet.

"Did that." She knelt at his side, set a hand on his chest. Beneath her palm, his heart thundered like . . . thunder. "Calm yourself."

"I c-c-can't."

"We aren't in prison." His gaze flicked from its panicked perusal of the walls to hers. "We just fell in a hole."

"What's the difference?"

"When we climb out . . ." She took his hand. This time he let her. "No one will shoot us."

He sat up. "I told you about prison?"

"Yes."

"Don't you hate me?"

"Hate you," she repeated. "Why?"

"Did I tell you why I was in prison?"

"I don't care."

"Did I mention how I got here?"

"The ground gave way."

"Not *here*. I meant how I came west."

"I came on a train. Didn't you?"

"Yes. But I was in chains."

She let her thumb stroke his wrist. "Is that how this happened?"

He didn't answer. Did he need to? He was no longer trembling or stuttering. Remembering the past, as unpleasant as it was, had at least stopped him from remembering an equally unpleasant present. But the way he looked at her, even the way he touched her—mostly the way he didn't—made her think—

"What do you remember about last night?"

His forehead creased. "There was a storm, then . . ." He shook his head. "I was in the pit. But that was prison and this isn't, so—" He shrugged, and her heart clenched at the dismissal in the gesture. "Sorry."

Not as sorry as she was. The second most beautiful night of her life—the birth of Lily would always be the first—and she was the only one who remembered it. She wanted to die, or at least cry, but she couldn't. It was better that he never knew what had happened than that she admitted she'd thought he cared.

"Why were you in prison?" she asked.

"I rode with Mosby."

"That wasn't a crime."

"Tell it to the Yankees."

Yankees. Like her. Was that why he stared at her sometimes as if he hated her? Or was what she saw in his eyes, on his face, merely a reflection of how he hated them? Or perhaps himself?

The war had been over for six years. But Rose wondered if it would ever truly be done. A hundred years from now would folks from Virginia still say *Yank* in as derisive a way as those from Massachusetts said *Reb*?

"You were captured?" she asked.

"I was."

"Also not a crime."

"Yet I was sent to prison."

"A lot of men went to prison for little more than the color of their uniforms."

Nightmarish tales of starvation at Andersonville in Georgia and the brutality at Castle Thunder in Richmond had filtered north. No doubt as quickly as tales of the Fort Delaware Death Pen had gone south.

"Which prison?" she asked, dreading the answer.

"Rock Island, Illinois."

"They dragged you all the way to Illinois?"

"By the time I was captured the prisons were full."

Overcrowding had not only increased the deaths by disease but also decreased the amount of food available to the already starving masses. Rose had heard tell that more men had died in the prisons than had been lost on the battlefields.

"There was also the issue of Mosby," Luke continued. "The Yankees were afraid of him." Rose's eyebrows lifted, and he shrugged. "They called him *the gray ghost.* He could slip behind enemy lines, then out again, and no one ever knew he'd been there until they found their telegraph lines cut or their rail ties missing."

"So they sent you to Illinois, just in case Mosby wanted you back."

"As competent and loyal as the colonel is, even he wouldn't venture that far into enemy territory."

"And just in case he did, they threw you into a pit."

He blinked as if the thought had never occurred to him.

"Why did you think they did that?"

"Because it was there?"

"Because they *were* afraid of Mosby. If he came, he might have had a chance of getting you back if you were wandering free in the common yard. But if you were in a pit . . ."

He nodded slowly. "We were winning that war for a long time on the basis of leadership and grit. A successful operation like that could have lifted morale enough to push on longer. Maybe even long enough. But if Mosby had failed, been captured himself, the results would have been disastrous."

Rose didn't point out that by that stage of the war, everything was disastrous.

"Did they keep you in the pit the whole time?"

"Eventually I had my own tiny cell."

That didn't sound like any prison camp she'd ever heard of. Everyone was corralled together like animals. Inside a big warehouse at Castle Thunder, or outside, digging shelters into the dirt at Andersonville. Then again, she hadn't even known there was a prison at Rock Island until he told her, let alone what the conditions had been.

"Did everyone have their own tiny cell?"

"No."

"Then why did you?"

"I was weak."

"I doubt that."

"I didn't know. I'd never been confined. The place was so small and I was so large. The dark. The walls." He shuddered.

To be buried beneath the earth. Trapped forever away from all that's open and free. In the dark, with no air.

She remembered his voice, his face when he'd said those words to her on the prairie. Prison had to have been agony. And the pit . . .

Pure torture.

"What else do you call it but weak when I renounced all I held dear and pledged my allegiance to the enemy?"

"Survival?"

He snorted. "I agreed to come west and fight Indians if they'd only let me out of that hole."

"You weren't the only one who agreed, and the others had a lot less reason to do so." She hesitated, wondering if she should swallow any further questions about his past. But she was too curious. "Was Annie Beth Lou your sister?"

"Yes." He bit his lip. "What else did I say?"

"Not much." That she could she understand. "Names."

"What names?" His voice was hoarse. "Besides my sister's."

"Abner, James, Hoyt, Saul." The Moze he'd mentioned must have been Mosby, though she'd never heard the great man called anything so common. "Your brothers?"

He nodded, and his shoulders slumped. "What else?"

"Nothing."

His explanation of being released to come west to fight Indians explained how his legends labeled him both Yankee and Reb, along with his blue cavalry pants despite a south-of-the-Mason-Dixon drawl.

"I doubt I said nothing."

"Nothing I could understand." She still held his hand, continued to stroke his wrist, his palm with her thumb. It seemed to help, and he was letting her. "When the sides dry a bit, we'll get out. You'll see."

She should have kept her mouth shut. His gaze went to the walls, and he started to breathe fast and shallow again.

"Look at the sky," she said, and he did. "It's right there above us. You aren't buried. You aren't in a cell."

"He'amo'ome," he murmured.

"What does that mean?"

"Above world. Cheyenne heaven." His gaze lowered to the mud. "A place I will never see. I'm trapped."

"Not for long. Not forever. And you aren't alone." Her fingers tightened. "You have me."

He stiffened, pulling his hand away as he stood. "Did you . . . ?" He rubbed his head again.

"Did I what?" she murmured.

Did I touch you? Did you touch me? Did I discover for the first time in my life what all the whispers were about?

"I saw her watching me from *He'amo'ome*." His face had gone distant. "Then she jumped."

Had he confused Rose and his sister? Most likely.

"I jumped, Luke."

"Yes," he agreed, and she felt a bit better. He wasn't right while he was down here. As soon as they got out, he'd be better. Maybe he'd even remember her, remember them, and not run.

Rose winced. That wouldn't happen. Would it?

"Why did you do that?" His question drew her back.

"The mud slid over your face. You couldn't breathe. You didn't move. I—"

"You should have left me here."

"You know I wouldn't." She couldn't.

"We have no food, no water."

"The sun will dry the mud in a few hours. Then we'll climb out."

"This is a sinkhole. The surface collapsed because the area beneath is hollowed and weak."

She hadn't thought about why there was a hole. She'd only thought about how they might get out of the hole.

"The walls aren't going to hold, Rose. They'll just keep crumbling. We're going to die here." The eyes that met hers were resigned. "But I always knew that I would."

CHAPTER 11

"We aren't in Illinois," Rose said. "We're in Kansas. Maybe Colorado."

There was something different about her this morning. Something Luke couldn't put a name to. Something beyond the fact that she'd spent the night in a muddy hole with a crazy man.

"We aren't in prison, either," she continued.

"We might as well be."

He wished, not for the first time, that he had died in that pit in Rock Island. How many people would be alive now if he'd died back then?

"You give up too easily."

She was probably right. But that didn't change anything.

Rose plopped into the mud with her back against the wall, crossing her arms over her breasts as she set her jaw. "We will wait until the walls dry, and then we will climb out."

"Yes, ma'am." He'd learned that when a woman spoke like that—no matter the language—it was best to listen. She'd learn the truth soon enough.

He sat, too, on the opposite side, facing her, then frowned at his mud-encrusted toes. "Why are my boots off?"

"Why do you think?" she muttered.

He tried to remember, but last night was a jumble. Some of the flickers of memory were from Rock Island and not here, the past, and not now. His wife, his family,

the army—both blue and gray. Whispers of those he knew to be dead and those about whom he wasn't so sure. There'd been heat as well as cold. Loneliness and—
Her.

He remembered Rose. In ways that he shouldn't.

Because if he'd touched her—skin to skin, mouth to . . . everywhere—if he'd buried himself inside her over and over and—

Luke stifled a curse as his body responded to both thoughts and shady prophesies. If he'd done any of those things, she would not be sitting there like a prissy schoolmarm ready to smack her ruler onto the hand of a rowdy student. She would be crying and shaking, perhaps screaming, or even staring—pale and cold and silent.

But she wasn't.

Luke had always done his best to steer the Dog Men away from the settlers. There was game to hunt and there were other tribes to harass. Attacking the white men only brought trouble. But there had still been times when bad things happened.

Most women, after the warriors burned their homes and killed their families and did whatever else raiders had done since the dawn of time, shrieked whenever a man came near. If one reached out to touch them they reacted in one of two ways—either they fought like a black bear to get away, or they retreated into their minds, and they did not come back.

Rose had done neither. Therefore he had not touched her. Although in other respects she had not behaved in the same way as any other woman of Luke's acquaintance thus far, so perhaps in this, too, she was an exception.

With her daughter stolen and her husband dead, she chased after Cheyenne warriors in the dark. She spent a year traveling alone, asking for help and being denied. Did she give up then? No. She found him. When he refused to go with her, she continued on. When he relented, and was nearly hanged because of it, she saved him. When he fell into a sinkhole, she jumped in after him.

Who did that?

He had never known anyone—woman or man—so determined. As he'd considered before, courage such as that should be rewarded. He lifted his gaze to the blazing sky.

With something other than a slow and painful death.

The morning passed. Rose watched mud dry. He let her. He had enjoyed so few hours of silence in his life. The Phelan Farm had not been quiet, nor had the war. In prison the pit had been quieter than the common area, but the guards never left him alone for long. Neither the army nor the Cheyenne camp could ever be described as still. Even in the hills, the wind had whispered. But down here, with her, peace settled all around him. For the first time in a long while, he couldn't hear the wind, and he liked it.

Rose stood, set her hand on the westernmost surface, which, owing to the slant of the morning sun, had finally faded from deep mud brown to a pale dirt tan. "We'll try here first."

Luke climbed to his feet, happy to help. Not only would it give him something to do, but what man didn't enjoy being proven right? Though vindication usually involved something less dire than a death sentence.

"Should you give me a leg up?" Rose asked. "Or should I give you one?"

"You think you can lift me?"

"Yes. You're stronger, so you should be able to pull yourself up easier than I can."

Luke shrugged, and set his hand on her shoulder as she bent and made a cradle of her palms. She turned her head, and her hair flipped into his face.

He had a sudden image of a woman riding him— darkness all around, she was no more than a shadow in the night. His shoulders pressed into cool mud and sharp stones; she placed her hands on his chest as she leaned forward and her hair brushed his cheek . . .

It felt *exactly* the same.

He yanked back. She didn't seem to notice. She was too busy frowning at his feet. "Shouldn't you put on your boots?"

The idea of placing the arch of his foot in the palm of her hand caused him to quicken further in places he shouldn't have even started to. He turned away, lest she see, and took his time excavating his boots from the mud. Then he tossed them right where they'd been. "It's easier to climb if I can dig in my toes."

He'd tried to climb out of the prison pit often enough. That hadn't been a sinkhole, and the walls had been more stone than dirt. There'd also been guards with guns at the top. The single time he'd gotten his fingers over the edge, they'd broken three of them with the butts. He was lucky he hadn't broken his neck when he fell back down.

Turning, he set his hand on her shoulder, gritting his teeth against the impossible memory of touching her skin in the same place with both his fingers and his tongue. She had tasted like . . .

He licked his lips and stifled a sigh. He'd never known dirt tasted so good.

He'd thought he was crazy then? That was only because he hadn't yet gotten to now.

Luke put his foot into her palm, ignoring the warmth, the tingle at her touch. She lifted. He dug into the wall with both hands and then feet, scrambling higher as the dislodged earth rained down. He was digging his third set of handholds when the entire western wall shimmied. He had time to shout, "Watch out!" before it crumbled.

He hit the bottom on his back, and he couldn't catch a breath. He'd had brothers and he'd grown up riding horses, so as a boy he'd landed often and hard just like this. Eventually air would return to his lungs. It only *seemed* as if he were dying.

Rose fell to her knees. "Luke?" As he couldn't breathe, he couldn't speak, and the next time she said his name, she sounded panicked. "Luke!"

He blinked so she wouldn't think he was dead. Huge mistake. His eyeballs hurt, and he couldn't even moan. She slammed her palm into his chest. His eyes went wide. What in hell was she doing?

His lungs labored; she lifted her arm again. He wanted to grab her wrist to keep her from hitting him, but he hadn't the strength for anything but trying to live.

Without warning, his straining chest suddenly took in air. His gasp was louder than that of a floundering steer.

"Oh, thank God." Rose leaned over and kissed him— quick, hard, and right on the lips—as his mother, or his sister, would have done in the same situation. Relief, nothing more. So why did he want to grab her and bring her back so she could do it again?

"Are you all right?"

He wiggled his toes, his fingers, turned his head from side to side. Everything seemed to work, and nothing hurt any worse than it had before. "Yes."

"Can you get up?"

"I've found, in situations like these, that it's best not to get up right away."

Concern filled her eyes. "This has happened to you before?"

"Several times."

She sat on her heels. "During the war."

"No." If he'd fallen during the war, he would have been dead, or at least captured sooner than he was.

Not that there hadn't been ample opportunity for being thrown. He was a cavalryman. And while cavalry horses were the most well-trained mounts on hooves and rarely bucked, reared, or shied, even in the midst of artillery fire and a hail of bullets, rare did not mean never. Still, Luke had managed to keep his seat every time. Even on the day of his capture, Luke had not been tossed from his horse. He had been dragged.

"If not during the war," Rose murmured, "then when?"

He had to think for a moment what she was asking. He'd been at Rectortown, scattering as ordered, lying low, hiding awhile, before riding through the brush, across a creek, up the bank, and then . . .

There'd been Yankees everywhere.

He cleared his throat. The action caused a dull, painful throb between his shoulder blades and reminded him of what had just happened, along with the other times it had.

"I had brothers," he said.

There'd been tumbles from the hay mow, early bucks off a horse while learning to ride, and once—

"Once I fell out of a tree, nearly landed on Abner."

"He was watching, making sure you didn't fall?"

"He was trying to kill me. Why do you think I went up the tree in the first place?"

Her brow furrowed. "Your brother was trying to kill you?"

"Obviously you don't have any."

"Two."

"And they never tried to murder you?"

"I was the youngest."

"I was the youngest."

"And a girl."

"My sister was in that tree more than I was. Until she learned how to fight."

"Your sister fought?"

"Dirty," he agreed, resisting the urge to rub certain parts of his anatomy she had kicked. The shins had always been her favorite. Although, when desperate, she'd resorted to jabs much higher up. "She was raised with five brothers."

Six if she counted Moze. As Annabeth had broken

Moze's nose the single time he'd tried to kiss her, Luke thought she had.

"It was fight dirty or lose," he continued. "She didn't like losing."

"Your brother chased you?" she repeated. "Bent on murder?"

More than once, and more than one brother, but Luke thought that was beside the point, so he nodded.

"You climbed a tree and then you fell."

"To be fair, the branch broke. I was too heavy."

She considered the wall. He could almost hear her thoughts. If he'd been too heavy for the branch, he'd probably been too heavy for the wall.

"You're not trying it," he said.

Her eyebrows shot toward the still-reddened stitches on her forehead. "Why not?"

In a few days, he would have to cut them out, though he didn't have his knife. If they were still here by then it wouldn't matter.

"You could really hurt yourself," he said.

"You'll catch me."

She sounded so certain he frowned. What had he done to make her trust him that much?

"Hoyt tried to catch me once when I fell off a fence." His lips twitched at the memory. "I ended up with a black eye when I landed on his elbow."

He wasn't going to take the chance of her landing on anything that might hurt her, nor landing as he had. The idea of Rose lying on the ground, gasping for breath, believing she might die, almost wanting to, made him physically ill.

"What did your mother have to say about all this?"

"She never knew." At her incredulous glance, Luke continued. "We were trying *not* to die."

Her lips curved. He wanted to trace them with his tongue. What was *wrong* with him?

"How did you explain your black eye?"

The same way Moze had explained his broken nose.

"On a farm all sorts of injuries happen. A horse goes right when you think it's going left. A cow kicks when you least expect it. A door opens. A bucket falls."

"You told me your sister stitched you, not your mother."

"Usually in payment for us not telling our mother she put the holes in us in the first place."

"I think I might like your sister."

"I think my sister might like you." Too bad they would never find out.

"The other times you fell and weren't able to breathe, what made you start again?"

Luke thought back to the day he'd fallen out of the tree. Abner had leaned over, face panicked. If Luke died, he was in big trouble. Then his brother had—

"Lift my belt," he blurted.

"Excuse me?"

"Pull up on the belt, or the waistband of the trousers. So the body lifts, like this." He arched his hips to illustrate. It wasn't until she gasped, colored, and glanced away that he realized what he'd done. He let his ass fall back into the mud.

If he'd needed any further proof that what he had imagined between them wasn't real, her reaction to his scandalous movements would have been enough.

"I'm sorry," he said. "That was . . ."

"Enlightening." She met his gaze. Any mortification had passed, or perhaps never been there at all.

Women were so damn confusing. *She* was damn confusing. When he looked at her he felt things he shouldn't, remembered things he couldn't.

"Lifting your belt is better than hitting you in the chest."

He rubbed at the place where she had. "Why did you?"

"I had to do something, and it worked last night."

The mud slid over your face. You couldn't breathe. You didn't move.

"You hit me in the chest when I wasn't breathing and I started again?"

"Yes." She stared at her palms. "To be truthful, I was scared and angry, so I hit you. You started breathing. So, today, I did it again."

He sat up. They were so close their knees touched. He wanted to take her hands in his so she would stop wringing them. "Why were you angry?"

"I'd come so far. I'd found you. To lose you like that. I refused."

He wanted to laugh at the idea of refusing to let someone die—he should have tried that on the Washita—but her face was so stern and stark, her voice quite serious.

"I woke up, and it was dark and wet and the earth shook. I thought it was a stampede. You were gone."

Now he did take her hands. They were cold, despite the spread of daylight. He didn't think the warmth of the sun would ever reach this far. He unfurled her tight fingers, slowly, gently. He could picture how it had been. The dark. The rain. The thunder. The realization that she was alone. Although, out here, alone was often better than unexpected company.

"I'm sorry you were scared."

"The sky lit up," she continued as if he hadn't spoken. "You were running. Why would you run toward a tree in a lightning storm?"

"I don't remember."

"You're lying."

He both was and wasn't. He didn't remember running toward the tree because he hadn't seen the tree. He hadn't felt the rain or noticed the lightning. He'd thought the sound of the thunder was the roaring of guns, and that his wife was still alive, that she could be saved if he only ran fast enough. If he could just get there in time.

Falling into the sinkhole had been like falling into the past. The way the earth had crumbled, causing his stomach to jitter and drop, the way he'd hit the ground, the way he could not breathe had been exactly the same as that day long ago when he'd reached the top of the ridge and seen the smoking valley of death on the peaceful banks of the Washita River.

"How long have we been down here?" She reached out to feel his forehead. He grabbed her wrist before she could touch him. "Just tell me."

Despite wearing a hat—though where it was now, where his was, he had no idea—her nose had burned and started to peel. The dark circles from lack of sleep made her skin seem more pale and her eyes more blue. She wasn't pretty, but there was something about her that drew a man's gaze. Or at least this man's gaze.

"How long do you think we've been down here?" she asked.

"I don't know." He let go of her wrist so he could rub at the ache in his head. Not that it had ever helped before. "There've been occasions when I go into my past, and I stay there awhile."

He wasn't sure what he'd expected from her in response, but the snort that he got wasn't it. "Who doesn't? I wouldn't remember Lily's laughter, the weight of her in my lap, the scent of her hair, the pull of her arms around my neck if not for that."

"I don't mean memories. I mean living in the past, talking to the ghosts, hearing them answer. Hell, sometimes when I come to myself I wonder why there are three plates and cups set around the fire. Then I realize I not only talked to the ghosts, I made them breakfast."

She tilted her head, studying him. She didn't seem horrified or worried or scared; she seemed intrigued. "Does it help?"

"They never eat it," he said dryly. She lifted an eyebrow and waited. "No. They're still dead, and I'm not."

She reached for his hand. He put them both behind his back.

"Losing time means I have no idea what I've done for days, sometimes weeks."

"You lived alone in the Smoky Hills. What did you expect?"

He wasn't sure, but it hadn't been the confusion, the loss of not only time but a sense of himself.

"I've been alone for nearly a year." She lifted her gaze to the slice of blue sky. "Sometimes, when I ride into a town, I'm surprised at what day it is. Who pays attention when the only thing that matters is something that can't be measured? I'm never going to stop searching for Lily. What difference does it make if I've forgotten a few Wednesdays?"

Why did everything she said make so much more sense than everything he did?

She lowered her eyes from the sky to him. They were exactly the same shade, and they gave him the same sense of peace.

"When I lose time, Rose, there tend to be a lot of dead bodies lying about when I find it again."

CHAPTER 12

Rose took Luke's hands. Did he truly not remember killing those people? Would there come a time when he didn't remember killing Rose? There was already plenty he didn't remember about her.

"Things happen," she said. "People die."

"Around me, people die a lot."

"I'm not worried."

"You should be."

"I knew who you were when I went looking for you."

"No one knows who I am. Least of all me."

"You're Luke Phelan."

"I'm sure that, by now, Luke Phelan has been listed as dead."

"That doesn't make you dead."

"It doesn't make me Luke, either," he muttered.

He wasn't making any sense.

"*Ve'ho'e Mestaa'e,*" she said, and his head lifted sharply. "What does it mean?"

"White Man Ghost. The Cheyenne think I'm dead, too."

"That isn't why they called you that."

"No," he agreed. "It was because I knew things."

"Which you told to the Cheyenne." She'd been horrified by that revelation, seen it as traitorous and wrong. She wouldn't be the only one who reacted that way.

He sighed. "Not at first. At first I was a slave."

She touched the scars at his wrists. She'd thought

chains had made them. Maybe so. But ropes would've made them, too.

"Were you captured by the Cheyenne?" First the army, then the Cheyenne. Talk about bad luck.

"No. The army traded me."

"To the Cheyenne?" Her voice was incredulous; *she* was incredulous. "For what?" What could possibly be worth his life? Food, water, horses? Her hands clenched. She wanted to strangle someone.

"Captives," he answered. "Women and children. The Dog Men weren't going to give them up for nothing."

"So the army *traded* you?"

"I volunteered."

"You what?"

"What was I supposed to do, Rose? They were going to kill the captives."

"Who else volunteered?"

"The Dog Men only wanted one."

She felt again the ridges of scars beneath her fingertips in the night. "They tortured you."

His gaze fell on the walls of their prison. "Wasn't the first time. Eventually they accepted me. I became one of them."

"Because you told them things about the army?"

He shook his head. "I did that as soon as I saw what the army was doing."

"Their job?"

He cast her a glance. "If their job is to obliterate an entire population, then yes. I gladly offered my life to save women and children. That didn't change because the innocents spoke a different language and slept in a tepee. Murder is murder, Rose. Spilled blood always runs red."

Silence fell between them. Rose didn't know what to say. He thought she had courage? Only because he knew what true courage was.

"You're not safe here with me," he said.

"You aren't going to hurt me. I trust you."

"I never took you for a fool."

She ignored that. He'd also called her stupid. If she were easily insulted she would have gone back East years ago.

Kalt wie eis.

Rose could have sworn she heard the words on the wind. Who was crazy now?

"You seem fine this morning," she continued. "More yourself."

"Whoever that is."

"The beauty of the West," she murmured. "You can be whomever you like. Change your name, tell anyone anything about where you came from and what you've done. Out here, no one knows the truth. Most people don't care to."

"I know the truth," he said. "I'm dangerous. When night comes you need to hold your guns . . ." He frowned. "Where in hell are your guns?"

"I dropped them on the prairie."

"You what?" He put his hands to his head as if he wanted to tear out his hair. Except he had none.

"You don't have to shout. There was a lightning storm. I preferred not to die in it."

"So you'll die here."

"I am not going to die here, and neither are you."

He rubbed his forehead. "When night falls and I can't see the sky and the dark presses on me like a shroud, I don't know what I'll do."

"I do."

Luke lowered his arm; his gaze met hers and she smiled.

"You'll hold my hand, and you'll know you aren't alone."

He stared at her as if she'd said something beyond fascinating, and for an instant she thought: *He remembers!* Then he frowned, glanced up. The sunshine flickered and danced as several heads appeared around the edge of the sinkhole.

Luke cursed—or at least she thought they were curses; he spoke in Cheyenne—and scrambled to his feet. She followed, confused. Wasn't this what they'd been waiting for?

"Well, lookee here. I think we done found 'zactly what we's looking for, Cap'n."

Why would anyone be looking for them?

"Haul them out, Private."

"Yessir!"

Several heads retreated. The rest continued to stare into the hole. Rose couldn't see their faces as the sun blared from straight above and behind them. But she didn't like the way Luke had cursed—neither his tone nor the language. She thought he might be trembling, and that made her tremble, too.

She reached for his hand, but it wasn't there. He was already grabbing for the rope that unfurled from above, smacking against the wall on the way down and knocking dirt all over them again.

"Me first," he said.

She touched his arm. He wasn't trembling, exactly, but his skin twitched beneath her fingers, as if he were so tense he might jump out of it. "I know you can't bear being in a pit like this alone. That's all right. I understand."

"That's not why I'm going first," he said.

"What're you talkin' about down there? Send the lady up!"

"I don't think I will," he muttered, then leaned in close and spoke low. "Think, Rose. What if you're up there, and they leave me down here?"

"Why would they do that?" She kept her voice low, too.

His gaze wandered over her, and he lifted an eyebrow. "Once we're up there—or you are—they can do anything they like."

He made a good point. One she didn't like, but had to concede. Nodding, Rose stepped back and let him go first.

Luke was so nimble and quick he'd scrambled halfway up the wall before anyone could protest. "Hey, I said fer her to—"

Luke crawled over the edge and tossed the rope back down. "Your turn. Sweetheart."

She heard the warning in his voice. Better if they thought she was his. Rose wrapped her fingers around the rope and began to climb. The trip wasn't as easy as Luke had made it appear. It took her much longer than it had taken him. Rose used the wall for leverage, walked with her feet, pulled with all her strength. When she was nearly there, palms burning, legs aching, strange hands hauled her over the edge. She shoved them away, her gaze searching out Luke. He lay trussed on the ground in front of their horses.

She tried to run to him. The man on her right grabbed her arm. Rose elbowed him in the stomach so hard she left him retching. She narrowly avoided the rest of the grasping fingers.

Someone—probably the *cap'n*, considering that he had gold bars on the shoulders of his uniform and no one else did—stepped into her path. She thought about kicking him in the shin, or perhaps a place farther north, but decided against it.

"What is the meaning of this?" she demanded.

He held out his hand. One of her Colts lay in it. "Yours?"

"Yes." She snatched it. "Thank you." She cocked the gun, pointing it in his direction as she stepped out of his reach. "Let him go."

Luke choked. She thought it sounded like laughter, but, bound as he was, that couldn't be right.

The captain, an older fellow, perhaps her father's age or near enough, did not seem disturbed to face the business end of her gun. Only when he lifted his hand in a staying motion did she notice that several of the soldiers' weapons were trained on her. She didn't care. Without Luke, her chance of finding Lily was gone, and without that she might as well die.

The man removed his cavalry hat to reveal a shock of graying brown hair and narrowed blue eyes. He wasn't nervous about the Colt, but he obviously didn't like that she'd snatched the weapon. She supposed it had made him feel like a fool. "I'm Captain Weaver, ma'am. Give me the gun."

"Only if you let him go."

"I can't."

"Then neither can I."

Beneath an equally graying mustache, Weaver's lips tightened. "You have to understand our position."

"What position could there be for tying innocent men like calves for a branding?"

"He's hardly innocent."

Unease trickled over Rose like a chill spring breeze. "Why would you say that?"

"We heard him talkin' Injun when we come," one of the soldiers near the hole said.

Rose kept her gaze on the captain. "Is that a crime?"

The man didn't answer, merely lifted his chin to indicate Luke's mount. "Cheyenne pony."

"He likes good horseflesh."

Captain Weaver strolled to the pile of things near the animals. Rose recognized their saddlebags and bedrolls. How long had the army been wandering about, picking up their seemingly discarded belongings, before they saw the hole?

Leaning over, Weaver sorted through the jumble. When he straightened, Luke's Dog Man headdress trailed from one hand. He lifted a bushy eyebrow.

"We found it," Rose blurted.

"You *found* a Dog Soldier headdress?"

That thing had caused no end of trouble already. The Sioux had wanted to kill Luke over it. She would not give the army an excuse to want the same, so she remained silent.

"You sure there wasn't a Cheyenne attached to it at the time?"

"I'm sure."

The captain's gaze narrowed. "What's wrong with your head?"

"What's wrong with yours?" Rose muttered.

"I don't have a cut that looks as though someone tried to scalp me."

"Neither do I."

"You lie as well as I play piano."

"You must not play, then."

"Why?"

"Because I don't lie."

The mustache twitched again as his lips pulled into a frown. "What's your name, ma'am?"

"Varner. Rose Varner."

"And his?"

"My husband. Luke."

"Husband," he repeated. "Are you sure?"

"I think I know who my husband is, sir." Rose thought she put the perfect amount of outrage into her voice, but the captain did not back down.

"If you're married, where's your ring?"

She'd told this tale before, knew it by heart, almost believed it herself. The lie tripped off her tongue without a pause. "We had to sell it." She lifted her hand, pointed to the white line on her finger. "Not too long ago."

"Who tried to scalp you?"

"I fell. Hit my head on a rock."

The woman in Rogue had neglected to mention that the more one lied, the easier lying became.

"You must think I can't tell a skunk from a house cat," the man said in disgust. "I've been out here long enough to know a near scalping when I see one. I've also been out here long enough to know Cheyenne when I hear it."

"Just because he speaks Cheyenne doesn't make him Cheyenne."

The captain glanced at Luke. Rose had to admit that facedown on the ground with his head shaved, wearing tattered cavalry pants and a leather vest, he did not resemble a white man. He'd removed the earrings when he cut off his hair, but the armband remained.

Weaver flicked a finger, and two men hauled Luke to his feet. Luke's gaze went to Rose and stayed there.

"What Cheyenne has blue eyes?" she demanded.

The captain reached out and moved aside Luke's vest, revealing the scars on his chest. She fought not to flinch. She'd only felt them, never seen them. They looked even worse in the sun than they'd felt beneath the moon.

"What white man has danced the Sun Dance?" Weaver murmured.

"Sun Dance?"

"Barbaric ritual." The captain's lip curled. "The savages pierce themselves." He tapped one of the scars. Luke stared straight ahead, refusing to react. "Then they attach a lead from their chests or backs to a pole and dance for days."

"Is that true?" she asked Luke.

"Hova'âhane," he said.

She let out an exasperated hiss. "Do you want them to shoot you?"

He didn't answer.

"I've seen folks who were taken by Indians become one of them," the captain continued.

"He's with me."

"Seems like you're with him."

"What difference does it make who's with whom?"

"Fear makes folks do strange things."

She knew that better than anyone. So did Luke. His speaking in Cheyenne had her worried.

"Do I seem afraid?" She indicated the gun, which she still held on Weaver.

He lifted one shoulder. "I've taken back women and children who've lived with the Indians. They're never quite the same."

"How so?" The word came out sounding too high, and her voice trembled. The captain's mustache twitched upward, and she again wanted to kick him.

"They become attached to their captors. They've had to depend on them for their very lives. They don't know how to be who they were before. If they're taken away, they fight to go back."

She bit her lip. "What if they can't?"

"They die. Probably for the best."

Rose swayed. Luke stepped forward, but his hands were bound, and he growled in frustration. She laid her palm on his shoulder, patted it once, then placed herself in front of him so she could lean against him if she needed to. The position also put her between Luke and the majority of the guns. When she returned her attention to Weaver, he didn't appear so smug anymore. He appeared downright annoyed.

"You need to move out of the way, ma'am."

"No."

He gave a huff that blew the trailing ends of his mustache upward. "I'm at a loss for what to do here."

"Continue on with whatever you were doing before."

"We were trying to find our Pawnee scouts."

Luke stiffened. Thankfully, with her standing in front of him, no one noticed.

"I can understand why they might run off," she said.

"They didn't."

"How can you be so sure?" She'd only been in the captain's company a few moments and she wanted to run off.

"I'm sure. They were scouting, and they didn't come back."

"Good luck finding them." They'd be occupied with that for some time to come. It was a very big prairie.

"Oh, we found them."

Rose suddenly felt as if she might not be able to stand up. Luke inched closer, pressing his chest to her shoulders. She licked her lips, glanced at the soldiers, didn't like what she saw in their eyes any more now than she had before.

"They were buried," Weaver continued.

"I'm . . . sorry?"

Luke muttered in Cheyenne. She didn't blame him. The last word *had* sounded like a question.

Weaver's eyes seemed to crawl all over her face. "Why would you be sorry?"

"Why wouldn't I be?" she countered, refusing to bat at the annoying tickle his stare had brought to the tip of her nose.

He contemplated her for several seconds before moving on. "Odd thing was, they weren't shot."

"You dug them up?"

"How else would I know it was my scouts?" He shook his head as if she'd asked a fool question. "They were killed by a knife." He lifted Luke's weapon, which still had blood on it. "Look familiar?"

"It's mine," she said.

"Rose," Luke began, and she stepped on his foot. As his were still bare, and hers were not, his breath hissed in, which meant no more words could come out.

"They tried to scalp me. I killed them."

"All of them?"

"Were they all dead?" She certainly hoped they hadn't buried a live one.

"They were."

"Then, yes, all of them."

Weaver's gaze flicked to Luke's. "He didn't help?"

She used her other foot to step on Luke's other toes. "No."

"You killed three Pawnee by yourself?"

Rose refused to address again a question she'd already answered.

"Where was your husband?"

"Away."

The man lifted an eyebrow.

"If he'd been there, do you think they would have touched me?"

"I can't believe you killed them all by yourself."

"Believe whatever you like. May I have my knife?"

"I don't think so."

"Fine. Thank you for your help. We need to be on our way."

"Not so fast. You killed my scouts."

"They tried to kill me." She lifted her chin. "What kind of scouts do you employ?"

"The Pawnee and the Cheyenne are natural enemies. If they saw the Dog Soldier headdress, or even the Cheyenne pony, that might explain their behavior."

"They didn't."

Or at least they hadn't until after they'd tried to scalp her. She still had no idea why the Pawnee had attacked, especially if they were working for the army.

"They were dressed for war," Luke said.

Weaver tilted his head. "I thought you weren't there."

"He wasn't," Rose said. "He came after I killed them."

Now that Luke had decided to converse in English, the captain turned his attention to him. "How do you know anything about the Pawnee?"

Luke drew in a breath as if to speak, and she jabbed him in the stomach with her elbow. His gut wasn't as soft as the soldier's whom she'd jabbed earlier, but the movement did manage to quiet him.

"Did they wear paint?" Weaver asked.

"No," Rose said. "Should they have?"

"Most warriors use paint. The Pawnee don't. They strip for war. Cover their feet and their . . ." He cleared his throat.

Was the lack of paint on a warring Pawnee something no nonmilitary white man would know? The way the captain stared at Luke, she had to wonder.

Luke remained silent, and Weaver released an annoyed breath. "You owe me three scouts."

"You owe me a new forehead," Rose returned.

"I don't have one to spare."

"Which makes us even, since I don't have three scouts."

"One will do."

"No," Luke snapped.

"You speak Cheyenne," Weaver said.

"No."

"I heard you."

"If you understand Cheyenne so well," Luke murmured, "then speak it yourself."

"I know it when I hear it, but I don't understand a word."

"Just because I know a few words doesn't make me a scout."

"You're the closest thing we've got."

"I can't help you."

"I didn't ask you to."

"You did—" Rose began.

"I didn't *ask*," Weaver interrupted. "Because you don't have a choice. You killed my scouts. You'll need to go before a judge and answer for that."

"No court in this land is going to care about dead Indians," Luke said.

"We'll see. In the meantime, you're my prisoners. It would go a long way with the judge if you provided much-needed assistance in the field."

"He didn't do anything," Rose insisted. "Let him go."

"If you think I'm leaving you with them—" Luke began.

"You aren't going anywhere," the captain told him. "I only have her word that she killed my scouts. I don't believe her."

"Even if you did," Luke said, "it's me you want. Let her go."

"If you think *I'm* leaving you with them you're . . ." She paused. He'd already admitted he was crazy. At the moment, she felt a little insane herself.

Rose had begged the army to take her to the Cheyenne. Now she had the army waiting to accompany her there, and she didn't want to go. There was something about this situation that made her uneasy.

"We aren't going with you," she said.

"You are."

"I have a gun."

Weaver opened his hand. "I have the bullets."

CHAPTER 13

Which way?" the captain asked.

Luke didn't answer.

"Just because he knows some Cheyenne doesn't mean he *knows* the Cheyenne," Rose said.

"What does it mean?"

"He's good with languages."

"He didn't suddenly start speaking one without hearing it spoken. And the only way to do that is to spend time with the Cheyenne. So, where are they?"

Luke remained silent. As long as he was aboveground and not in that pit, there was very little they could do to him that would change his mind about talking.

Weaver backhanded Rose across the face. She stumbled and went to her knees. Luke lunged forward, but the rope around his hands, held by a now-guffawing soldier, prevented him from reaching her.

The only sound Rose made was a sharp intake of surprise. Slowly she got to her feet. Her lip had split. Blood ran off the end of her chin, dripping onto her already ruined, once-white shirt.

"You cowardly son of a bitch." Luke lunged at the end of his leash. "Hit me."

"You danced the Sun Dance. Hitting you won't do a damn thing but make my knuckles sore." He used his other hand to knock Rose to the ground again.

Luke glanced at the other men. "Are you going to stand there and let him hit a woman?" No one answered.

"Sheep," Luke muttered. He'd get no help from them. "What kind of soldiers are you?"

"Ones who've seen too many scalped women, missing children, and dead men." The captain opened and closed his fingers. Luke hoped he'd broken something other than Rose's face. "This is a war. One I aim to win."

"Don't tell him anything," Rose lisped, then spat blood on the captain's boot.

The man's lips tightened so far he appeared to be chewing on his mustache. He hauled back his foot.

"South," Luke said.

Rose muttered a word no lady should know.

Weaver set his foot on the ground. "That wasn't so hard, was it?"

When two soldiers attempted to take her by the arms, she jerked away, cursed some more, then got up on her own. Luke wanted to kiss her.

"Untie him," she said.

"Tie her," Weaver ordered.

"What did I do?"

"You're a murderer, Mrs. Varner."

Rose winced. Luke wanted to punch the man—with his knife. If only he had it.

One of the fellows tied Rose and shoved her in Luke's direction.

"Secure them in the wagon," the captain ordered. "Then mount up."

They tied the ends of the rope that trailed from both Luke's and Rose's bound wrists to a slat of the conveyance. There'd be no leaping off and running away.

Luke's gaze trailed over the flatland. As if that had ever been an option.

Weaver mounted his horse and trotted north. Rose glanced at Luke. He shook his head, and she shut her mouth.

"Scoot over here." The horses and the wagons made a lot of noise, but there were too many soldiers riding too close to them to speak freely. "Lay your head on my shoulder as if you're tired and hurt."

"I am."

"I'm sorry," he whispered.

"You didn't hit me."

"I may as well have."

"You'd never," she said.

She looked a fright. Jagged cut on her forehead. Split lip. Bloody chin. Ruined clothing. He thought she'd have at least one black eye.

His chest tightened. Before he realized what he was doing he pressed his lips to her temple, right next to her stitches. "I'll kill him."

"I'll let you." She laid her head against his shoulder. "Why did his scouts attack me in the first place?"

"The Pawnee have joined with the army; they lead the soldiers to the camps of other tribes. Maybe they just wanted to behave like Pawnee again."

"Why is the army going north when you said south?"

"The captain doesn't trust me. He thinks I've gone Injun."

"Dog Man headdress, Cheyenne pony, speaking Injun, can't imagine why." She paused for a moment, then blurted, "I don't like him."

"Can't imagine why."

She laughed as he repeated her own words in exactly the same tone she'd used, then gasped at the pain her laughter brought to her bruised face. If Luke hadn't already vowed to kill the man, he would have done so again.

Her laughter died. "Why do you think he's searching for the Cheyenne?"

"From the way he went about finding them, I doubt it's to say hello."

"He's going to kill them."

"He's going to try."

"And Lily?"

"You remember Susanna Alderice?"

She stiffened. "The Dog Men killed her when the army attacked."

"Someone did," he said.

"You think it was the army?"

"I don't think it matters." It certainly didn't matter to the dead Susanna Alderice.

"What should we do?"

"Escape."

Preferably before the army got anywhere near the Dog Men.

They traveled north throughout the day. The sun beat down mercilessly. They had both lost their hats—either running across the prairie in the rain and the wind in the night, or when they'd fallen into the sinkhole. Unfortunately there were no hats to spare—every one being perched upon a soldier's head. The captain allowed Rose to root through their things, but when she tugged a pair of sturdy moccasins from the saddlebags—Luke's boots were still in the hole—the soldiers glowered and muttered and Luke shook his head.

"You can't remain barefoot all the way to . . . wherever," she said.

"Can, too," he muttered, but he allowed her to put on the moccasins.

They were given water. However, Rose's request that Luke's hands to be tied in front rather than behind was denied.

"How is he supposed to drink with his hands behind his back?" she asked.

"That's what you're for." The man tossed a canteen in her lap.

She managed to raise the water to her lips and his, even with them being tethered to the slats of the wagon, but it wasn't easy. She couldn't recall the last time anything had been.

Rose slept on and off, head on Luke's shoulder. The

one time she'd begun to lie in his lap—her head aching, her lip throbbing—he'd murmured, "You shouldn't."

Flustered, she withdrew. She tried to sit next to him and not touch him, but it was impossible. The movements of the wagon continually threw her against him. She would jerk away, but within seconds she would be right back where she was.

"It's all right to lean against me," he said. "Lying flat will make your face swell up worse. It did mine."

The idea of his beautiful face all puffy and bruised made Rose want to cry. Or maybe that was just the pain from her own face—by no means beautiful—made even less so now. She laid her head back on his shoulder, but every jostle caused agony to flare across her cheekbone and jaw. Rose kept her eyes closed because the sunlight only made things worse. In that shadowed world of pain, two voices seemed very loud.

"Injuns don't stand a chance agin us. They can fight, but they ain't gonna win."

"Why'd the captain want someone who could talk their talk, then? If we're just gonna shoot 'em as soon as we sees 'em, we don't need no inter-pre-teer."

"Been a few times the savages done seen us comin'. They sent out a few old fellers to parlay. Cap'n's a cautious man. Wants to make certain there aren't five hundred Injuns just over the next ridge."

"Ya think that could happen?" The second man's voice wavered.

"Could but it wouldn't matter."

"How can five hundred Injuns not matter?"

"I was at Bear River in 'sixty-three with the California Volunteers. There were nearly that many Shoshoni. They run out of ammunition and we did not."

"How many was women and children?"

"Who cares? Bullet works the same for 'em all. 'Cept, if ye're runnin' low, ye can always use the butt of the pistol on the little 'uns."

Rose thought she might be sick, but the man wasn't finished.

"Like the cap'n says: Squaws only birth more braves. Tiny Injuns grow into big Injuns. Best to get rid of as many as you can right now so they don't sneak up on ya later."

"I heard tell there might be captives in them camps."

"And you heard the cap'n. They're better off dead. They're never right agin no how. And what white man wants a red man's leavin's?"

"True."

"Sure, some fellas come to the army and beg us to find their wives, but if'n we do, they're always sorry. Most of 'em don't bother to look. Once the Injuns ride away with their woman, she's as good as dead and they know it. They find themselves another wife."

"I heard about a woman who went from fort to fort beggin' the army to get her daughter back."

The first soldier made a sound of derision. "Kid's either kilt already or may as well be. It's Injun now. Ain't no point."

The men rode away. Rose lifted her head from Luke's shoulder and slowly opened her eyes. The brilliant sunshine nearly blinded her, but she met Luke's gaze. "They were talking about me, about Lily."

"Probably. I doubt there are many women who went from fort to fort."

"But why wouldn't they?" She couldn't imagine not doing everything she could, as long as she had to, to hold her child again in her arms.

"Most people feel the way those men do about captives."

"Not mothers." He didn't respond. Rose eyed the seemingly endless prairie. "We can't let them find the Dog Men."

"Believe me, the Dog Men aren't going to let themselves be found."

What happened when the army became frustrated at not finding the Cheyenne as they expected to? Rose didn't need to voice the question. The ache in her face was the answer.

"I won't let them hurt you," Luke murmured.

When Rose attempted to smile, the cut in her lip broke open and she tasted blood. "You won't have anything to say about it."

"I'll have plenty to say, but we won't be here for me to say it."

She lowered her lids so the sun did not blare into them so badly and assessed the situation. Dozens of mounted, armed soldiers. Luke's hands tied behind his back, then lashed to the wagon. Her hands tied in the front, tethered the same.

If any other man had told her what Luke had, she would have laughed—or perhaps cried with despair. But because Luke Phelan said they would escape, Rose simply murmured, "When?"

Clouds drifted in just before dusk, causing the sunset to mute from scarlet to mauve, orange to peach, buttercup to gold. The moon being new, darkness fell over the prairie like a blanket the shade of night.

They were untied to eat and relieve themselves, though a guard stood nearby the entire time. Rose was allowed to squat behind a wagon, out of sight. It wasn't as if she'd be able to run off and disappear on a prairie.

One of the soldiers—a yellow-haired, bucktoothed youth who should be pitching hay on his farm— approached with medical supplies. "Cap'n said I should take out them stitches."

"You ever done that before?" Luke asked.

"Yessir. I got the smallest and steadiest hands. I do most of the doctorin' outchere."

"You wash those hands?"

"What fer?"

"Can't hurt." Luke wasn't sure why, but it always bothered him to see filthy fingers touching the wounded. In the war, it had happened all the time. And most of the wounded had died. "Wash them," Luke ordered, and the boy sighed and turned away. "With soap!"

"You'd think you were in charge," Rose murmured.

"He listened." Thank goodness. Considering that Luke was still tied up, he wouldn't have been able to stop the kid from doing anything. But the stitches did need to come out. Leaving them in too long was nearly as bad as not putting them there in the first place.

When the soldier returned, his hands were clean all the way to his wrists. At least those were several inches away from Rose's head. He clipped the stitches with quick, practiced movements and went away.

"How does it look?" she asked.

A red line remained. "Not bad." It would eventually fade to white.

"I'll have my first scar."

"Not your first." Luke knew scars. "But the first one that shows."

They were left bound in the wagon to sleep. He had expected no less. Freeing them so they could lie down meant that a guard would have to stare at them all night. Being tied to a slat, having to sleep sitting up, meant there would be very little sleep, and what did it matter? The more exhausted the prisoners were, the less chance of an escape.

Rose set her cheek against his. "Tonight?"

The marriage lie had its uses. None of the soldiers gave them a second glance when they cuddled and murmured. Unfortunately her proximity, her gentle touch, the remnants of her scent aroused him. Fortunately the darkness prevented anyone but him from knowing it.

He kept having flashes of her, in ways that had never been. While he didn't feel as if he'd lost himself, he had to wonder how long until the confusion of dreams and reality took him to a place where he would be of no help. They had to get out of there before then.

He turned his eyes to the prairie again. There was something about it that bothered him. "Tonight," he agreed.

She lifted her bound hands and looped them behind his head. They rested lightly at the top of his spine. The movement pressed her breasts to his chest. He shuddered as images of those same breasts pressed to the same chest—with no clothes between them—shimmered.

"You're cold," she said, and snuggled against him.

He was far from cold, but he didn't correct her. Merely lowered his cheek to rest against her hair. "They'll sleep." His voice seemed too loud, so he shifted his mouth to her temple.

"Then?"

The word whispered along his skin like a feather, trailing gooseflesh in its wake. He ground his teeth, grateful that his hands were tied and he could not touch her. Although being unable to touch only made him want to all the more. The desire for what he could not have had made him harder than the wagon bed beneath him.

"We won't."

She lifted her head. Her lips, so close to his own, puckered on her *W*'s. He found himself staring at them as though captivated. "What will we do?"

Three *W*'s. He was lost.

He leaned closer. She tilted her head as if to listen. In that last instant before his lips brushed hers, she caught his intent, and her eyes widened. But she did not pull away. There was nowhere for her to go.

He was gentle. He had to be. Her lip was swollen. He pressed soft kisses all around it, yet still he tasted blood.

"Poor lip." He lifted his head, caught the shadow of a movement behind her. A guard paused to watch, perhaps listen. Her eyes were closed. She didn't see. She must not continue to question. Not now.

"Hush," he said, a bit louder. "Poor eye." He skimmed her bruised cheekbone with his mouth. His tongue might have eased out just a little.

Her breath caught; her breasts slid against him. He forgot the guard completely.

Her other cheek wasn't as bruised, but he hated for it

to feel neglected, so he kissed it, too. Her lips parted. Her eyes opened. "How's the nose?" he asked before she could speak, then pressed his mouth to the bridge and nibbled. "You don't taste broken."

"But I am."

Her words brought him back to the wagon, the prairie, himself. What was he doing?

He lifted his head, glanced over his shoulder. The guard still stood there watching. Luke's scowl only made him grin. Luke feared the man would remain there all night waiting for his own personal raree-show.

Despite the sweet taste of Rose's skin, her assertion that she was broken made him remember who she was and what she had endured. He found it difficult to believe she would submit to his touch without screaming, shaking, crying, or fighting. Then again, Rose had never behaved the way he expected her to.

Someone hailed the guard. His smirk became a scowl, but he moved off. From the lingering glance he gave Rose, he would return. They needed to be gone from here tonight for more reasons than one.

Luke leaned closer. Rose jerked back, but with her hands behind his head, her movement only served to pull him closer still. She lifted her arms and pulled her bound hands against her chest, hunching her shoulders over them as if they ached, as if she did.

He didn't ask what was the matter. He knew. Why she'd let him put his mouth all over her, he wasn't quite sure. A stranger's touch had to bring back terrible memories. Another reason he knew that what he dreamed had never occurred.

Luke would have liked to apologize, to offer an explanation, but he had none. He did not understand why he was drawn to her. Why the scent of her skin and the brush of her hair, the whisper of her breath, her very voice aroused him. Why he remembered things about her that he could not know was nearly as confusing as his response to her in the first place.

"We don't have much time." He spoke softly, and she drew near. "We'll pretend to sleep."

If they appeared all tangled up in each other, no one would look closely enough to determine what they were doing. Any guard wishing to watch would not want them to stop, so he would stay far enough away to make sure that didn't happen.

"You'll put your hands to my mouth." Her quick intake of breath made him click his teeth together—*tap, tap, tap*—and understanding spread across her face. He would pull free the knots binding her with his teeth; then she could untie him with her hands. They would sneak away beneath the darkness of the new moon and hide until—

She looped her arms around his neck once more. The movement was so surprising he stiffened, straightening and rearing back so hard and fast he lifted her right off the floor. Her lead, still attached to a side slat, yanked tight and rattled the wagon.

"Calm down," she murmured. "You'd think no one ever hugged you before. Rest against me." She tugged his head toward her breasts. No fool him, he went.

She settled against the side of the wagon and shifted her bound hands in front of his mouth. Clever girl. She was better at this than he was.

Leaning over, she pressed her lips to his temple as if saying good night. "I'll watch," she whispered. "You chew."

For what seemed like hours he picked and pulled and got nowhere. The knots were too well tied.

"Shh," Rose breathed as a guard wandered near.

He rested against her as if he were sleeping. She curled over him, effectively shading her bound hands. They stilled, but the guard did not come any closer.

Luke lifted his head. Oddly, he could still hear the thump of Rose's heart.

Movement in the night drew his gaze. It wasn't her heart he heard, but the approach of many horses.

CHAPTER 14

"Get down!"

Rose ducked at the urgency in Luke's voice. An arrow thunked into the wood where her head had been.

"Stay down," he ordered, then covered her body with his. "Dammit! I wanted to be gone before the Dog Men got here."

"You knew they were coming?"

He didn't answer. She didn't need him to. "You said south because you knew the army would go north." She shifted so she could see him. "And when they did, the Dog Men would be there."

"They asked for the Cheyenne." His face, stark in the light of the leaping fire, hardened. "They got them."

Once she would have been horrified at what was going on all around them. She *was* horrified, but she was also a bit glad. The soldiers had planned to do to the Cheyenne what the Cheyenne were doing right now to the soldiers. In truth, they would have done worse. They wouldn't have cared if there were women, children, or captives in their way.

Rose had said she would do anything to get Lily back, and she'd meant it. She just hadn't thought anything would mean throwing a U.S. cavalry company to the Dog Men, but . . .

"So be it," she murmured.

"Rose?" Luke moved so his face was directly in front of hers. "Are you all right?"

Unlike during her confrontation with the Pawnee,

she was still able to think, to move, to speak. She had been afraid when the Sioux came, but she had not disgraced herself. She hadn't fallen or fainted. She'd remained upright; she'd even spoken. Now, while her heart thundered and her hands were like ice, she thought she would be all right as long Luke was with her. They were so close to what she'd been searching for. Or at least closer than *she'd* ever been before. If these Dog Men didn't have Lily, perhaps they'd know who did.

"I'm fine. *You're* the man who just sacrificed the cavalry to the Cheyenne."

"They didn't leave me much choice."

"I know."

His gaze softened. "I said I'd kill him for hurting you."

"I don't think you'll have to."

The Cheyenne were going to do it for him.

Flames leaped. Men died. Time passed.

Luke placed himself between Rose and the end of the wagon, crowding her against the farthest wall. He doubted any of the soldiers would remember they were there. They were busy dying or trying not to. However, if they did, they might be inclined to shoot the prisoners to save them from dying by Indian. At the least, any soldier climbing into the wagon would draw the Cheyenne *to* the wagon. Luke wanted to avoid that as long as they could.

Who knew? Maybe the Dog Men would ride away without bothering to search for survivors. He doubted it. The Cheyenne were not known for their stupidity in warfare, the Dog Men even less so. But one could always hope.

"What should we do?" Rose yanked on her bonds. Whoever had tied her had done a very good job. His chewing on the knots had damped the rope. Instead of loosening, they'd only seemed to grow tighter. She stopped struggling with an impatient growl.

"We'll hope that our being tied marks us as an enemy of the bluecoats."

"Aren't we? We led them right into a trap."

"We didn't lead them anywhere."

"I doubt the army would agree."

"I doubt there'll be anyone left to argue the point."

"The army could win."

If that happened, Luke would probably hang—as soon as they found a tree. He doubted they'd do the same to Rose, though she might prefer it to what they would do if he was gone and they had no one to blame for the massacre but themselves.

"They won't."

"You're sure?"

Luke tightened his lips and nodded.

"If any enemy of the army is a friend of the Cheyenne," she said, "I guess we're lucky you weren't able to chew me loose."

Lucky would have been if they'd escaped before the Dog Men came. Lucky would have been never running into the army in the first place. Hell, lucky would have been dying a long time ago and never having to come back here.

Of course the only luck Luke had ever really had was bad.

Luke lost track of time, couldn't be sure if the lightening of the night sky was a result of the blazing tents or the approaching dawn. But the sounds of battle were dying away.

"Stay down," he repeated, even as he lifted his head so he could see through the slats. Rose peered through the slats right next to him. There were bodies everywhere. Most of them wore blue.

Luke didn't recognize any of the Dog Men. After what Rose had told him of Summit Springs, he thought that many of the warriors he had ridden with were either dead or gone north. But he doubted all of them were.

One of the nearby warriors, who'd been pulling the boots off a corpse, no doubt in preparation for confiscating its bloodstained, yellow-striped pants, suddenly glanced at the wagon. Both Luke and Rose ducked, then held their breath.

A shadow flickered above, as if a hawk had flown past the light. A face peered over the side for just an instant before the Cheyenne dropped to the ground. By the time the fellow reached the end of the wagon, Luke had gotten to his feet. He would not die lying down.

"Netonêševehe?" the Dog Man demanded. *What is your name?*

He was young. Luke had never seen him before. Perhaps they could still get out of this mess alive.

The Cheyenne glanced over his shoulder. "Haestôhe'-hame!"

"Shit," Luke muttered.

"What's wrong?"

"Everything."

Of all the Cheyenne to be here, it had to be Haestôhe'-hame. Luke should have known when he heard the approach of many horses that Many Horses was approaching. His old friend and greatest enemy was the leader of the Dog Men. Though countless of the band had died, Haestôhe'hame was almost as hard to kill as Luke. As there were very few Dog Men left on the plains, it would only follow that Luke would confront this one sooner rather than later.

The Dog Man appeared at the end of the wagon. He wore his sacred coyote headdress, his hair pipe breastplate, and a German silver pendant and armband. The blanket wrapped around his waist bore the morning star, reflective of the Dog Men's favorite time to attack— at dawn. He'd braided his hair with red cloth. Red was the color of war—the color of blood—and it both protected and strengthened.

Many Horses had blood all over his chest and hands. At least this time the blood wasn't Luke's.

The Dog Man squinted. Their end of the wagon lay in shadow. "Who are you?"

His perfect English caused Rose to gasp. Luke stepped in front of her.

"Why do they keep you tethered like a horse?" the Cheyenne continued. "What have you done?"

"He refused to tell them where you were," Rose said. Luke sighed and lowered his head.

"Yet here they are." Many Horses glanced at a few of the bodies. "Or were. Why would the bluecoats think a foolish white man knows how to find the Dog Men?"

"Shhh," Luke murmured, and Rose shushed.

Silence settled over them, broken only by the sound of Luke's—or was it Rose's?—harsh breathing. Haestôhe'-hame tilted his head, and the brightly wrapped braid swung across his face. Impatiently he shoved it back out. "Come closer. Let me see you."

Perhaps, if Luke kept his mouth shut, Many Horses wouldn't recognize him. Luke looked nothing like what he had, and the Cheyenne believed he was dead.

"We can't." Rose's silence hadn't lasted. The buckboard rattled as she tugged on her bonds to illustrate why.

Many Horses flicked a finger, and one of the warriors clambered over the side of the wagon with a knife in his teeth. At the sight of Luke, his mouth opened and the blade dropped. He caught the weapon before it hit the floor of the wagon, then stared at Luke wide-eyed.

Luke had been gone from the Dog Men for more than two years. Young men changed greatly in that amount of time. But just because he did not recognize this boy did not mean the boy had never seen him.

Many Horses released a stream of Cheyenne. It had been too long since Luke had heard so many of the words strung together. The only one he could decipher was *motšêške*. As that meant *knife*, and the man holding it reached forward to slice their bonds, Luke assumed the sentence had been something along the lines of *Quit dawdling and use the knife as if you own it.*

"Luke?" Rose murmured when he continued to stand in the shadows.

Many Horses stilled, and his head tilted in the opposite direction. He beckoned.

Luke didn't move, and Many Horses flicked his finger again. The man with the knife used it to prod Luke forward. Rose slapped the fellow's hand so hard the knife skittered away.

"Oops," she murmured.

"Netonêševehe?" Many Horses demanded. *What is your name?*

Luke stepped into the light.

The Dog Man's face did not change. "You are dead."

"Why do people keep saying that?" Rose asked.

Many Horses threw his knife.

Rose tried to shove Luke out of the way, but he refused to go. He deserved this, and he knew it. The blade buried itself in Luke's shoulder.

"He—he—he missed," Rose managed.

"He didn't." Luke held the man's gaze. "He doesn't want me to die quick or easy." Luke reached up and yanked the knife out. Rose swallowed audibly at the wet *slurk* the action made.

Which was no doubt why Luke was alive today. If Many Horses had just killed Luke the last time they'd seen each other, rather than playing with him, they wouldn't be here now.

"Who is he?" Rose asked.

"Haestôhe'hame."

"I mean who is he to you?"

"Many Horses," Luke translated, deliberately misunderstanding her. What man wanted to discuss a time when he had been enslaved? What slave wished to introduce his master to . . . anyone? "It means—"

"He has many horses."

"He does, but only the best warriors, the most daring raiders, the bravest of men possess the most horses."

"He's the leader. I knew that from the first moment I saw him."

Something in her voice made him turn. Loss of blood—or something else—made him stagger. "Was he at your farm?" he whispered.

"No."

Many Horses had never been one for rape, even before Luke had pointed out how furious such behavior made the white men. Many Horses loved his wife. He touched no one but her. But he wasn't the only warrior on the plains.

"I don't recognize any of them, but it was dark and I was—" Her voice broke.

He was surprised Rose was able to speak at all. The sight of the Pawnee had frozen her. The Sioux had made her shiver and shake. Now she stood tall in front of the Dog Men; she'd even slapped one. Her courage left him speechless.

"Ask him—" she began, and Luke yanked her to his chest.

"Shh," he murmured, running his hand over her hair as if soothing her, but really pressing her face into his uninjured shoulder hard enough to keep her from talking.

When she began to struggle, he realized he was holding her so tightly he was also keeping her from breathing. He loosened his grasp. She took a breath, then lifted her eyes. He narrowed his. Asking about Lily might cause someone to remember Rose and her farm. Just because she didn't recognize anyone didn't mean someone wouldn't—eventually—recognize her. Although what white woman who had been through what Rose had would go anywhere near the Cheyenne at all?

To be fair, while the army thought the only good Indian was a dead one, many of the Cheyenne felt the same way in reverse. They didn't pay much attention to the faces of those they killed. They killed them—or worse—and moved on.

Even if no one identified her, any hint that they were looking for a captive might get them both killed. At the least it would get Rose left behind. The Dog Men were warriors. While they hunted and fought together, their families—old ones, wives, children—remained wherever they had left them. Somewhere that was, hopefully, both safe and secret. The best way to reach those families was to stay with the Dog Men. To do that they needed to reach the Cheyenne encampment before either one of them caused too much suspicion by mentioning the child.

Lily might not even be there. The Dog Men had been decimated; they had scattered. They were no longer one band; they were many. Some had joined existing groups or made smaller ones of their own. Which meant that finding Dog Men might not produce Lily. Not that it had ever been a surety. Stolen children weren't horses, which were the property of whoever stole them. Children were given to the band that needed more children the most.

However, Dog Men were elite warriors. They would know where others of their kind had gone. As a leader, Many Horses should know better than most. The trick would be discovering the information.

Before the man killed him.

"You have replaced her." Many Horses spoke in Cheyenne, and for that Luke was grateful. Not only did he not wish to discuss his enslavement with Rose; he didn't relish her learning his greatest shame.

Because of him, everyone he'd loved was dead.

"There is no replacing her," Luke answered.

Many Horses snorted like one of his namesakes.

"I wouldn't say that all women are the same—at least not in English." Luke indicated Rose, whom he still held close to his bleeding chest, with a downward tilt of his chin. "She shot the last fool who dared."

Interest sparked in the Cheyenne's eyes. "She did?"

"Actually," Luke murmured, "she shot both of them."

"You're bleeding all over me," Rose said.

"Sorry." He stepped back, wavered, and nearly fell.

She grabbed his elbow. He gritted his teeth as the movement jerked his already beleaguered shoulder. A fresh wave of wet washed over his skin.

"I don't care about the blood," she snapped. "Well, I do care, but only because there *is* blood. I need to stitch that hole before you faint."

"I'm not going to faint," Luke said, and then . . .

He did.

Rose caught Luke as his eyes rolled up, and he fell down. He was so much taller and heavier than she was she fell down, too. By the time she was able to roll him onto his back, her shirt was soaked. She didn't care about it any more now than she had before. All she cared about was him.

"I need our saddlebags," she snapped. "Hot water. Whiskey."

She shoved his vest open, reached for the tail of her shirt, and yanked on the least filthy, unbloodied area, but it wouldn't tear free. She snatched up the nearest knife, which she had slapped out of the young man's hand, and hacked it off, then pressed the cloth against the wound.

None of the Cheyenne moved.

She met the stoic gaze of Many Horses. Though the attack on her farm had been made in the dark and the smoke had been thick, her terror even thicker, she was certain he had not been there that night. She would remember eyes so merciless. "If I don't stitch this now, he'll bleed out before he wakes up, which will not be the slow and difficult death you wanted for him."

The man's gaze switched to Luke's pale face. Then he lifted an arm encircled by a silver band she hadn't noticed before but now saw was exactly like the one

Luke wore. He said a few words she did not understand, and one of the others strode away.

Rose set a fingertip to the identical band on Luke's arm. "What does this mean?"

"We were brothers once."

"Brothers are forever."

"Until death."

"Death doesn't end the bonds of brotherhood."

"No," Many Horses agreed, then reached over and ripped the band off Luke's arm. "Only betrayal does."

CHAPTER 15

Rose stitched the hole in Luke's shoulder while the rest of the Cheyenne moved off to loot and pillage. He would have another scar. He probably wouldn't even notice.

The dark gaze of Many Horses remained upon her. Oddly, her hands didn't shake at his nearness, or that of any of the others. Though she *was* frightened, she wasn't terrified. Perhaps because those she'd thought would protect her had hurt her. And if that was the case, perhaps those she thought would hurt her would not.

Foolish thoughts. It was the way of men to hurt. If there was one thing she had learned in the West, it was that.

She touched Luke's face, but he did not stir and she returned to stitching his wound. The seam was crooked, but at least the bleeding had stopped.

"What is your name?" Many Horses asked.

"Rose Varner."

"You are his wife?"

"I . . ." She paused, uncertain if it was best that the Cheyenne thought so or not.

"I think no," he murmured, gaze still fixed on her face. "I do not recall his second name, but it was not Varner."

"How do you know that if we were married our names would be the same?" Rose used the knife to sever the thread.

"Is that not your way?"

"Yes, but is it the way of the Cheyenne?"

"No. When we marry we share our bodies, our lives, and our children. But we do not share our names."

Rose bit her lip to keep from asking about her child. Luke had crushed her against his chest until she thought her lungs might burst from lack of air to keep her from asking before. He had to have had a reason. Until she knew what it was, she would do as he wanted.

"Who hurt you?" he demanded. "Was it him?"

"Luke would never!"

"You would be surprised at what he has done."

"You would be surprised at how little I care."

The Cheyenne's eyebrows lifted, and he peered at her with more interest.

"He wouldn't tell them where you were."

"This you have said. So they hit you. More than once. And he happily gave them *tsitsistas*." At her frown he translated. "Our people."

"He gave them nothing. And he certainly wasn't happy. He told them the Cheyenne were in the south."

"I do not understand."

"Then the army went north, and you killed them."

"You are saying he knew this? That he led the soldiers into a trap?"

"Didn't he?"

His scowl deepened. "He had to have known that it was death for him to come here."

Rose blinked. He must have. Yet still he had come. For her. Because—

"Courage matters," she said.

Many Horses' lip curled. "You think he's courageous?"

"You think he isn't?"

"Stop." Luke sat up. He was still as white as a—

Rose stifled a hysterical giggle. Luke cast her a concerned glance. "Are you all right?"

"I'm not the one with the hole in my chest."

He glanced down. "Neither am I anymore."

"Come closer, Ve'ho'e Mestaa'e," Many Horses ordered, and Luke struggled to his feet.

"Are you crazy?" Rose snatched at his arm as he moved toward the end of the wagon. "He wants to kill you."

"Shh," Luke murmured, then sat down hard, legs trailing over the edge.

Rose followed. "Don't tell me to 'shh'!"

"And she said she was not your wife," Many Horses muttered.

Luke cast her an annoyed glance. "You said that?"

"No." She sat next to him. "He assumed."

"She said courage matters."

"It does."

"How would you know anything about courage?"

Luke traced a bloodied hand over Rose's bruised cheek. "I have seen it in her."

"Because they hit her so that you would speak?"

"Because she told me to tell them nothing, then lifted her face so they could hit her again." He traced his thumb over her scar. "Did she tell you how she came to have this?"

"Luke, I don't think—"

"The Pawnee tried to scalp her." He dropped his hand back to his lap and faced the Dog Man.

"Yet she survived."

"She still has her hair," Luke said simply.

"But you do not."

"I couldn't return to the white man's world with hair the shade of ice and fire. They would recognize me."

"What have you done?" Many Horses asked.

"What haven't I?"

Many Horses glanced from Luke to Rose and back again. "And the Pawnee?"

"They are dead."

Not by her hand, but from Luke's warning glare, Rose should not say so.

"The enemy of my enemy is a friend," Many Horses murmured, his gaze again on Rose.

"Heehe'e," Luke said.

Before Rose could ask what that meant—the word had been bandied about enough without her knowing— one of the Dog Men arrived and tapped his arm several times in a row.

"Soldiers," Luke murmured. "Coming fast."

Rose had once thought there weren't enough soldiers in the West. Now they were everywhere.

The Cheyenne leader let his gaze wander over the camp. The Dog Men could remain and fight, but so many arrows stuck out of the bodies they might not have enough left in their quivers to win. A few of them carried rifles; whether their own or taken from their victims, who knew? But considering how long the battle had gone on, their ammunition couldn't be any more plentiful than their arrows.

They mounted up. One of them trotted past, leading a second horse, which Many Horses leaped onto. He frowned at the heavy buckboard. They could not escape if they used it. However, if he set Luke and Rose on a horse, they could escape.

Many Horses snatched Rose around the waist, lifting her onto his horse.

"Luke!" was all she managed before the Dog Man rode away.

Luke jumped off the wagon, ignoring the thunder of pain in his head and the lightning slash of the same across his shoulder as he caught a horse—not his own; the Cheyenne had already ridden off with all the good ones—and mounted up.

He wondered for an instant if letting Many Horses ride away as if Rose meant nothing to him might be the best course. Would the Dog Man lose interest and let her go?

No. He might lose interest, but he probably wouldn't let her go. At least not alive. And Luke could not take that chance. While the Dog Man had torturous plans for the White Ghost, he might have equally torturous ones for Rose.

Luke had been unable to hide his admiration for her. He lusted for her almost as much as he lusted for death. He couldn't help it. He would do anything to keep her safe. She deserved that much from him and more.

Luke had a flash of Rose's breasts—smooth and white, with tips the shade of her name. They'd tasted of . . . dirt.

He lifted a hand to his head. What the hell was that? It had felt like memory. But it couldn't be.

Luke raced across the prairie in the wake of the Dog Men. For just an instant he felt as if he'd come home. Then the breeze brushed his head, not his hair. The horse beneath him shied for no damn reason at all, and he was able to keep his seat only because of the saddle— something no Cheyenne would ever place on his horse when he rode into battle.

As he struggled with his mount, his biceps flexed and his arm felt wrong. He glanced down and discovered the armband he'd been given when he was freed from slavery and welcomed as a Dog Man was gone. Had he lost it in the hole? On the prairie? To the soldiers? He felt naked without it. He desperately wanted to go back and search for it, but he could not leave Rose alone. He wouldn't.

The Dog Men rode hard. Though their scouts had detected the approaching force from far away and they had escaped before the army came close enough to see them, the instant the soldiers reached the destroyed camp, they would know the Cheyenne had been there. The troop would have scouts of its own that would follow. The Pawnee were hated not only because they tracked the Cheyenne at the army's request but because they could. Evasive maneuvers were required. But evasion was one of the Cheyenne's greatest gifts. Out on the prairie, with nowhere to hide, they did. Luke had forever been amazed.

They paused when darkness fell. Luke rode to the rear of the Dog Men; his horse was not good enough to keep up. From afar he saw Many Horses set Rose on the ground. He strode off with three of his men as, behind him, she crumbled.

Luke urged his tired horse into a run. When they were still several yards away, Luke slowed his mount, leaping off before it could completely stop and hurrying to her side. She sat on the ground, head tilted as if listening to the whispering prairie grass. Luke did his best not to. All day the wind had been telling him to run.

"Are you all right?" he asked, more loudly than he should have, but at least he drowned out the wind.

"Why wouldn't I be?"

His gaze wandered over her poor face. Her lip was bloodied and swollen; so was her nose. Her left eye was black, her right bloodshot. She had dirt on her neck, grass in her hair. And that wasn't even why he was so worried.

He sat, their knees just touching, ignoring the Dog Men as they set about making a cold camp. "You collapsed as if your legs couldn't hold you."

"They can't."

"Then you aren't all right."

She patted his hand. "Have you ever ridden for hours and hours without pause?" She gave a half laugh. "Of course you have. You just did, and you jumped off a horse and ran. But my legs aren't that strong. *I'm* not that strong."

"You're the strongest person I've ever known."

She frowned and lifted her palm to his forehead. "You don't have a fever."

He stood, afraid of what he might do if he didn't. "Why would I?"

She struggled to her feet. He reached for her, but she waved away his help. She pulled aside his vest, leaning in to squint at the stitches. Her breath puffed over his chest, and his nipples tightened. He ground his teeth to keep from grabbing her and—

She traced a fingertip beneath his wound. The sensation was so familiar he could have sworn she had touched him like that before. His breath hissed in. She snatched her finger away. "That must have hurt."

It had, but not for the reason she thought, and not in the place that she believed.

"I should have bandaged your shoulder. Your vest has been rubbing the stitches all day."

He had been too busy trying to keep up with the Dog Men, keep his eye on her, and ignore the wind to notice anything else.

She touched his face, and Luke resisted the urge to turn his cheek into her palm. "You shouldn't have come," she said.

"Where would I go?"

"Back to your hills."

For an instant he didn't even know what she meant. Then he remembered the Smoky Hills and the years he had spent there. They already seemed far away. Another life. Another man.

"You think I'd leave you with them?"

"I asked you to help me find the Cheyenne." She lifted her chin to indicate the milling Dog Men. "There they are."

Standing so close to her, their voices lowered, her pale, not-so-soft hands touching him, he'd almost forgotten them, too, and he couldn't. Shouldn't. They were dangerous.

Luke pressed his mouth to her temple so no one could hear him speak. "Do not mention your daughter." She started to pull away, and he held her in place. "We aren't sure she's even with this group of Dog Men. Do you recognize any of them?"

She shook her head. "Can't we ask if they know her? If they've heard of her?"

"If we ask, they'll leave us right here."

"Why?"

"She's someone else's child now."

"She's mine," Rose said fiercely.

He kissed her hair and she shuddered. She was such

an enticing combination of sweetness and fury. "If they leave us out here—" More likely they'd leave *her* out here—Many Horses had plans for Luke—and he couldn't let that happen. "—we'll never find them again. Not once they know that we're searching for a captive. But if we get to their camp, we can look for her." He didn't say what they would do if they found her. The Cheyenne weren't going to give them Lily just because they asked.

Payment would have to be made.

Rose lay on her bedroll and stared at the sparkling sky. Her legs screamed. Her face moaned. Her lower back wept. The thought of climbing onto a horse in the morning was almost more than she could bear.

The Cheyenne watered their mounts first, then themselves, then their prisoners. They followed the same order with the food. Luke was given nothing but stares and the occasional sneer. The Dog Men obviously considered food and water wasted on someone they planned to kill. They gave Rose squares of dried cakes that tasted of both berries and meat—what Luke had called *pemmican*. She offered him some.

He shoved it back in her direction. "You need to stay strong."

"And you don't?" He rubbed his arm where the armband had been.

Seeing the gesture, Rose explained, "Many Horses took it. He said you were once his brother."

"Once." He dropped his hand. "He thinks I killed his sister."

"But you didn't."

Luke's brow furrowed. "Why would you say that?"

"You said 'he thinks I killed his sister,' not 'I killed his sister.'"

"What difference does that make?"

"Quite a bit."

"Not to him. She's dead. I'm responsible."

Rose tilted her head. *That* he believed.

"I don't want to talk about it, Rose."

"If you won't talk"—she shoved the pemmican at him once more—"then eat."

He took the cake, put it in his mouth, chewed a few times, and swallowed. "Happy?"

She tossed him the water skin. "Not yet."

He scowled but he drank. Rose kept an eye on the Cheyenne. Everyone finished their meals, then promptly fell asleep.

"The soldiers are going to come after us," she murmured.

"Not us," he said. "Them."

"We both know that the army won't care who they kill after that massacre. If we're with them, we're dead, too."

"They won't find us."

"It's a prairie, Luke. There aren't a lot of places to disappear."

"If the Cheyenne were that easy to find, the army wouldn't need the Pawnee to do it."

"But they'll have some Pawnee. Won't they?"

"Not for long." At her frown, he continued. "Did you see the three Dog Men who spoke to Many Horses, then rode out?"

"I thought they went to hunt."

"They did. While the soldiers spent the day burying their dead, the Pawnee will have gone ahead, to scout. When they don't return—"

She caught her breath. "The Dog Men are hunting Pawnee."

"They can't let the scouts tell the army where we are."

"Won't more dead Pawnee make the soldiers angrier?" Dead Pawnee was how they'd gotten to this point in the first place.

"They can be as angry as they like while they wander across the prairie."

"I can't believe that trained soldiers wouldn't be able to find the enemy."

"They've depended on the Pawnee to track this

enemy. They've never learned how to do it for themselves." His lip curled in disdain. "Without their scouts, they'll flail about awhile, then go back to wherever it is they came from. The nearest fort, whichever one that is."

"So we'll head for the Cheyenne camp in the morning?" Her heart fluttered. As early as tomorrow evening she might hold Lily in her arms.

"No."

Her heart dropped.

"To make certain the army doesn't get lucky, or find a few more Pawnee, we'll stay out here for several days. We might even track them back to the fort. It's the only way to be sure, and after what's happened in the past . . ." He paused, looked away, swallowed.

She wanted to ask about that past, but there was something about his profile in the moonlight that made her stop.

"Why wouldn't the Cheyenne kill this troop, too? That's the only way to be completely sure. Then they could return to their families right away."

"Bloodthirsty, are you?" For some reason, the observation made his lips twitch, as if he were fighting a smile.

Rose considered herself practical. The Dog Men had ridden down on the last set of soldiers like the Apocalypse. Why should the new ones be any different?

"That many dead men might cause the army to send out an entire regiment."

"But only one troop won't?"

"Hard to say, but it's never a good idea to poke an angry, wounded bear with a stick." His gaze softened. "Get some sleep, Rose. Tomorrow isn't going to be easy."

She lay down again.

What tomorrow ever was?

CHAPTER 16

The three Dog Men returned with the dawn. They appeared no different from when they'd left. No wounds. No blood. No bodies.

"Did they—" she began.

"If they hadn't, they wouldn't have dared come back."

As far as Rose could tell, Luke hadn't slept. She had done so fitfully, waking every hour or two. Each time, Luke had been sitting nearby, staring at the night. Once she had murmured, "Come here," but if he heard her he gave no indication. He didn't move, didn't speak, didn't blink.

He'd been given no bedroll. She would have shared hers as she'd shared her food. They'd shared much more than that. Just because he didn't remember it didn't mean it hadn't happened.

Or did it?

For days they traveled from sunrise to well past sunset. First they rode west, then south, east, and north. A few times Rose could have sworn they crossed their own trail. The swaying grass looked the same no matter which horizon it spread to. But she assumed the Cheyenne knew what they were doing, or at least where they were going.

Every night was the same. She was given food and water, which she shared with Luke. He sat next to her and stared into the darkness. When she asked him to lie at her side, he either didn't hear her or pretended not to. At times she heard him whispering, though she could never make out what he said. He often stared at the land behind them as if he saw someone following. But no one was there.

As the days passed, he spoke to her less. He stopped arguing about sharing her food, just ate what she gave him, drank when she urged on him, and watched over her night after night.

Late on the seventh day the Dog Men's horses picked up their pace. Rose twisted, leaning sideways so she could see around the broad shoulders of Many Horses. As far as she could tell, no one was following them still. There was no reason to run.

As if the Cheyenne would ever run.

Many Horses made a guttural sound of annoyance and slammed his shoulder into hers. He did not like it when she wiggled or turned or did anything but stare forward and remain silent and still. Her movements caused his horse to slow, and Many Horses always rode in the lead.

Was that smoke on the horizon? Clouds? Perhaps both. She didn't bother to ask. Many Horses might speak perfect English, but he didn't like to waste it on her.

Though the prairie seemed to stretch endlessly to that smoky, cloudy horizon, as they neared, the ground dipped, revealing the uppermost branches of a few precious trees. She blinked, squinted.

There were people in them.

A movement to the side had Rose jerking her head in that direction. She ignored the grunt that became a growl at her movement. Her heart pounded; her breath caught as warriors rose from the grass all around them.

Sentries. In both the trees and on the prairie. They could warn of approaching intruders, or perhaps, in the case of the secret grass warriors, eliminate them before they came too close. If anyone managed to get past, the men in the trees, with the higher position, would be able to pick off the arrivals before they could do any damage.

The village lay concealed over the ridge, invisible

except to those with knowledge of its whereabouts. Rose was reminded of the tales her mother had told of fairies and leprechauns and sprites that had hidden in the rolling green hills of Ireland. However, the people who poured from the tepees were not the fey creatures of legend. They were solid and strong, windblown and sun bronzed; their voices rose in welcome as they surrounded the returning warriors.

Many Horses plopped Rose onto the ground. For the first time she did not crumple, and a flare of triumph blazed through her. The Cheyenne already cast her suspicious glances. She would prefer to meet them on her feet rather than wallowing in the dirt like a weakling. She waited for the fear, the dizziness that would follow her inability to breathe through the panic. She was surrounded by Cheyenne. She might not leave this place alive.

But she was so close to finding her daughter nothing else mattered now. She had no time for fear, no patience for panic. Besides, she'd been riding with these men for a week. If they wanted her dead, she'd have been dead by now.

Her gaze flicked from one small form to another, searching for one that she knew. Among the children, Lily's blond hair should shine like a star in the night. But it didn't.

Her daughter wasn't in the crowd around them. Luke wasn't, either. Rose searched desperately for him—he always appeared immediately at her side upon dismounting—but she did not see him in the camp. A single horse stood in silhouette on the ridge, the rider listing to the side.

She struggled up the incline, but while she had mastered standing after a day spent riding, climbing was too much. She fell, crawled, then managed to gain her feet again.

"Kiwidinok!" Luke shouted.

He slid from the animal's back, and she was too far

away, not fast enough to catch him. He landed on the ground with a sick, boneless thud and lay still.

"Luke!"

She stumbled to his side, collapsed to her knees—no longer caring if she appeared weak. She touched his face, expecting him to be both unconscious and on fire, but he was neither. He stared at the sky and muttered words she did not understand. His face shone pale beneath several days' stubble, as did his scalp, although the hair of his beard was a shade lighter—nearer her own gold than his bright red. She stroked his temple and missed his hair. It had been so damn beautiful.

He hadn't allowed her to examine his wound since the first day, insisting he was fine, that he'd suffered worse. Since she knew the latter was true, she had believed the former. What was she supposed to do? Wrestle him to the ground and force him to let her see? Now she didn't have to. Fearing what she would find, Rose shoved aside his vest.

Not red. Nearly healed. The cut looked better than hers had at this point in time. If she had a knife she could remove the stitches. So why was he raving?

She glanced at the village. No one had moved.

"Many Horses!" she shouted.

The Dog Man turned and disappeared into one of the tepees.

Rose struggled to her feet, cursing, then tugged on Luke's hand until he sat up. She continued to tug until he stood. He behaved like a sleepy child, mumbling, limbs clumsy and slow. Rose put her arm around his waist and together they descended the ridge, his horse trailing behind.

"Ve'ho'e Mestaa'e," the crowd muttered. The words lifted to the darkening sky like a prayer. Luke *had* said the Cheyenne considered him a prophet.

"He isn't well," she said. "Is there a . . ." Hell, why hadn't she made Luke teach her a few useful words in

Cheyenne? Though she doubted any of them would have been *Doctor*.

One of the women separated from the others, approaching with determination, as if she meant to help. Rose relaxed a bit, though she still held Luke tightly. He listed so far to the opposite direction, if she let him go, she feared he would fall.

The Cheyenne woman stopped with the toes of her beaded deerskin moccasins just brushing Luke's. She was tiny and plump, her black braids reaching to her hips, the ends wrapped in skin. Silver earrings similar to the ones Luke had worn until he'd cut his hair swayed from her ears.

For an instant Luke's face lost that distant expression; he seemed to see the woman, to know her. "Ominotago?" he murmured.

She spat in his face.

"Bitch!" Rose blurted, shoving the woman in the chest with her free hand. She fell back a step, her fingers curling into a fist.

"Nóxa'e!" The word was said in a quiet but commanding voice. The woman's fingers unfurled. Rose's did not.

A wizened old man, with braided gray hair that reached past his knees, stepped forward. His face resembled the skin of an apple after being left too long in the sun. His eyes were tiny, shiny black buttons.

"Ameohtsé," he said in the same no-nonsense tone. The woman turned and walked away.

Luke's gaze flicked from person to person in the crowd, and he muttered a word for each one as he shivered, despite the sweat that rolled down his cheeks and mixed with the spittle the woman had left there. Rose wanted to wipe his face, but she didn't dare let him go.

"Ve'ho'e Mestaa'e," the old man murmured. Luke continued to stare at the crowd and mutter.

The new arrival sighed, and his gaze turned to Rose. "What happened to his hair? Why is he . . ." The fellow went silent as if searching for the word, then shrugged and tapped his head. *"Oo'estseahe."*

For an instant, Rose believed that after a week in the company of the Dog Men she miraculously understood Cheyenne. Then, when the elder spoke the single foreign word amid the others, she realized that he spoke English as well as Many Horses.

"Oo'estseahe?" she repeated, and spread her hands. "Who has taken his hair?"

"Oh!" Considering the beautiful and distinctive shade of Luke's hair, she understood why the old man would ask after its absence. "No one. He shaved his head because—"

"Ah! Yes. Shaved head. That is what I meant." He peered at Luke again. "Why would he do such a thing?"

Rose wasn't certain she should explain about his being wanted. Did that matter here? She was spared the trouble of deciding when Many Horses returned. He held two spears. She liked that as little as she liked him.

"It is time." He tossed a spear at Luke. The weapon's long handle bounced off his chest and fell to the ground. Fury caused Many Horses' already dark face to burn darker. "Pick that up. We will fight. You will die. It is my right."

"No!" Rose said.

"No," the old man agreed.

"Ma'heonenahkohe," Many Horses began, and the elder lifted his hand.

"In English so his woman can understand."

Many Horses bared his teeth at Rose as the old man continued. "You will not fight today. Those who hear the spirits are protected."

"He hears the spirits of those who died because of him!" Many Horses threw his spear. It stuck in the ground between Luke's feet. He never moved.

"Nevertheless," the old man said, and walked away.

For an instant Rose thought that Many Horses might ignore the elder's orders. The Dog Man shook with fury. She wanted to put herself between him and Luke, but Luke still leaned on her too heavily for her to do anything but stay right where she was.

The joyous shout of a child caused Luke to jerk so violently she had to wrap both arms around his waist to keep him standing as a Cheyenne girl of about two ran up to Many Horses. His anger fled; his face softened. He leaned over and lifted her into his arms.

"Ayasha?" Luke whispered, horror and happiness at war upon his face. He reached out a trembling hand. Many Horses slapped it away, the crack of flesh on flesh ringing loudly in the silence.

Luke crumpled. Rose was so unprepared for his collapse she couldn't stop him from hitting the ground. She fell to her knees. "Luke?" His eyes were closed; he made no response. She patted his cheeks. "Luke!"

She lifted her gaze to Many Horses. "What did he say?"

That expression of anguish and hope had nearly undone her. It had certainly undone him. When the Dog Man did not answer, she shouted, "What did he say?"

The child buried her face in the man's neck. Rose felt bad about that, but she felt worse about Luke.

"Little One," Many Horses said. "It is what he called his daughter."

A chill whispered over her, though there wasn't any breeze. "He has a daughter?"

"No. Ayasha is one of the ghosts who speaks to him on the wind."

Luke tumbled into the past just as he'd tumbled into the pit.

"You are certain?" Many Horses' suspicious gaze remained on the waving white flag.

"Black Kettle's band is down the Washita," Luke said. *"He offered a truce and the commander of the soldier fort agreed. Even if soldiers come here who don't*

know of this promise, the white flag will keep our people safe."

After the Medicine Lodge Treaty of the year before, many of the young Cheyenne men had become angry. The elders had agreed the people would join the Arapaho, Kiowa, and Comanche on the reservations in Indian Territory, where they would give up hunting and become farmers. The warriors, especially the Dog Men, had expressed their outrage by raiding in Kansas. These raids had roused the army to action, and there had been several skirmishes.

But Black Kettle had preached peace, and he seemed to think they would have it. Still, Many Horses, whose wife had recently given birth, was understandably nervous about leaving the camp unprotected.

Luke desperately wanted to ride across the prairie, to feel the wind in his hair and on his face, smell the grass and the dirt, then walk freely upon it. Sometimes, especially when it became cold and the night arrived early, he remembered Rock Island—the damp, the chill, the dark—and he had to ride across the unending prairie or go mad. Now was one of those times.

He had recommended flying the white flag from the largest dwelling in camp. No bluecoat would attack while a white flag waved. But Many Horses continued to hold back.

"There are other warriors along the river," Luke said.

Even though the bands had made their winter camps out of sight of one another, they were within hearing distance. The gathering of Cheyenne was fairly large, another reason Luke didn't think the army would come. The recently appointed head of the Department of the Missouri—which was tasked with keeping peace from the Mississippi to the Rockies—was General Philip Sheridan, known to Confederates as Little Phil because of his short stature.

Once the leader of the cavalry of the Army of the Potomac, Sheridan had been a thorn in the Rebels' sides *during the latter days of the war. By then, Luke had been in prison, but every new inmate brought information. Most of it had been about Sheridan.*

He'd set fire to the lush farmlands of the Shenandoah Valley. By the time "the burning" was done, the place was nothing more than scorched earth. General Sherman thought that was a great idea and scorched the earth all the way to the sea.

After the war, Sheridan had been sent to supervise the rebuilding of the South. He'd been so brutal they sent him west to deal with the hostiles. Luke didn't have a good feeling about Sheridan, but the man was far from stupid. He would not attack a gathering of Cheyenne waving a white flag. Such behavior would only incite the tribes further.

"Other warriors are not Dog Men," Many Horses said.

Luke set his hand on his friend's arm. Their silver armbands were identical. They had been brothers even before Luke married the man's sister. "Everything will be all right."

Many Horses looked into Luke's eyes and nodded. Luke was Ve'ho'e Mestaa'e. The White Man Ghost. He knew things. If he said the white flag would protect the people while the Dog Men were away, it would. So far, everything he had ever said about the soldiers was the truth.

The Dog Men gathered their weapons and kissed their families good-bye.

CHAPTER 17

Luke continued to mutter in Cheyenne as though demented.

Those gathered around stared at him with curiosity, as if he were a show brought to camp for their amusement. But when he whispered, "Heova'ehe," several of them gasped and hurried away.

"What did he say?" Rose asked. No one answered.

When she dragged her gaze from Luke's pale, damp face, Many Horses was gone. Only the old man remained. He shook his head. Luke was delirious. Perhaps Heova'ehe meant nothing at all. But if it did, why had everyone run away as if the word *Satan* had spewed from his mouth?

"He needs . . ." she began, then paused. She wasn't sure.

The only doctoring Rose had ever done was bumps and bruises, small cuts, and the like. She'd given birth, but her confinement had been fairly simple. A lucky thing since at the first sign of labor, her husband had fled to fetch the nearest woman. However, near wasn't very near in Kansas, and by the time he'd returned, all that was left to do was wash the child and burn the bloody mattress.

"He shouldn't be lying out here." She waved at the tepees. "Which one is for guests?"

"Guests are those who are invited."

"Many Horses invited us."

The old man coughed.

"Perhaps *invited* isn't the right word."

What was? Kidnapped? Was it truly kidnapping if she wanted to come here? And would a Cheyenne elder even care if she had been kidnapped? Rose doubted it.

Luke had insisted she not say a word about Lily, and he was probably right. If she had seen her daughter among the children, she would have been unable to keep herself from crying out her name, snatching her up, and then running away. But since she hadn't seen Lily—yet—and Luke was unavailable for questions, she would continue to remain silent about why they were here.

"You are his new wife?"

"He has an old wife?"

The elder's lips twitched. "She was as young as you, but she is dead."

Rose lowered her head. She was sorry for that. Both his wife and his daughter gone. No wonder he had lived in the hills alone.

"Kiwidinok was her name."

Her head came up. Luke had whispered that word in the sinkhole, and she'd thought it a Cheyenne endearment. What a fool she'd been. He didn't remember what had happened between them because he'd lost time, returned to the past, whispered to a dead woman, and made love to a ghost.

"I'm not his wife," she said, her voice as cold and dead as Kiwidinok.

"Is it not forbidden for a woman to travel alone with a man who is not her husband?"

Forbidden was a strong word, but for the most part, accurate, and one of the reasons Luke kept telling people they were married.

"Yes," she answered.

"Then why are you?"

"He wanted to come back," she said. Not an answer to that particular question and also a lie, but she was becoming much better at them.

"To come back is death."

"I think he wants that, too."

The old man nodded sadly and lifted a hand. Two young men—not children but not quite adults yet, either—appeared and carried Luke into the nearest structure, which was the largest of them all.

Rose hurried after, entering as they lowered him onto one of the beds that lined the walls of the tepee. They turned and looked right through her. They would have walked right through her if she hadn't stepped quickly out of their way. She shuddered at the memory of similar faces staring right through her in the same manner on a long-ago night.

The Cheyenne pushed her aside as if she were nothing, and when she struggled to get up, they shoved her back down. She fought; she screamed. They hit. Then they took Lily anyway.

The world wavered for a moment. When it stopped, the young men were gone and she was alone with Luke.

The inside of the lodge wasn't round; the side opposite the door was shorter, making the back wall more straight than circular. A fire burned in a half-moon pit dug in the center. A painted buffalo skin stretched across the top, creating a ceiling that must keep the rain and the wind from reaching the inhabitants.

Luke lay on woven grass mats placed over a bed of willow rods and sinew, which held the sleeper several inches off the ground. Rose knelt at Luke's side, set her hand against his cheek. He was warm but not unnaturally so. She tugged one of the nearby buffalo robes to his waist.

She started as the old man appeared at her side and sat. She hadn't heard him enter. She waited for the chill, the terror to wash over her, but it didn't. He was so different from those who had hurt her. Ancient instead of young, frail instead of strong. Gray hair, not black. And while his eyes were dark, they were not angry.

Rose drew in a long, deep breath. She could do this. She *had to* do this. But first she needed to help Luke. Without him she was in very big trouble.

The old man leaned over, frowning at the stitches in Luke's chest. "Who did this?"

She didn't think he was asking about the crooked seam. "Many Horses."

He did not seem surprised. Why would he be? She'd only known the Dog Man for a week, but she could have chosen him from all the others within moments as the one most likely to stick a knife in Luke Phelan.

"Did he . . ." The elder waved a hand at her face.

For an instant Rose didn't understand; then she remembered her near-scalping scar, as well as her black eye, which should have faded to green or yellow by now but would still be noticeable. Her lip no longer pained her. She let her tongue slide over it. She could still feel where it had split.

"No," she said. "There were soldiers."

"Why would they do such a thing to one of their own?"

She indicated a still-unconscious Luke. "He wouldn't help them."

The old man muttered a word that needed no interpretation; then he handed her a knife. "Remove the sewing. If you leave it there too long, his body will . . ." He paused, mouth pursing as he tried to think of the word. *"Ema'o."* He let out an exasperated sound and spread his hands. "It will turn the color of his hair." His gaze flicked to Luke's stubbled head. "When he had hair."

"Red?" she asked, and the man nodded.

"The flesh will turn *ema'o*. Red. It will begin to . . ." He wrinkled his nose as if he had smelled something rotten. "He will become hot, then hotter. I am Ma'heonenahkohe. Medicine Bear. I know these things."

"You're a healer?"

"I spent time in the East learning from others."

"You learned medicine in the East?" She could not keep the surprise from her voice.

"And English."

"How? Why?"

He indicated that she should remove the stitches. "I would do so myself, but . . ." He held up hands that shook—not a lot, but enough that Rose tightened her grasp on the knife, leaned over, and did as he'd said. She did not want any sharp instrument held in hands that unsteady anywhere near Luke.

"My father believed the white men would come. Many, many white men."

"He was a prophet, too?"

"I did not think so at the time. At the time I thought him a fool."

"Yesterday's fool is tomorrow's genius," Rose muttered, her gaze on the next stitch.

"What is *genius*?"

"Very, very smart."

"Yes. My father was a genius. I was angry when he sent me to study with a white man. I wanted to ride and hunt like my friends." His gaze went distant. "But all of my friends are dead."

From the expression on his face Rose didn't think they had died peacefully by the fire of old age. Out here, who did?

She finished with the last stitch, pleased when the skin held together, the pink line beneath a much slimmer scar than any of his others.

Luke rested quietly—no mumbling or movement. She doubted it would last. She hadn't realized she'd set her fingers on the two gnarled white lumps just below his collarbone until Medicine Bear murmured, *"Hestôsanestôtse."*

She snatched her hands back as if burned. She should not be stroking him like that while he was unaware. Though she doubted he would let her do so when he was aware. The only time he'd ever let her touch him was when he thought she was someone else.

Rose ducked her head, praying the old man would not see the color that filled her cheeks at the thought. She hoped no one ever knew of her shame.

"*Hestôsanestôtse* is the dance of the earth's renewal," Medicine Bear continued. "He was very brave."

Rose twisted her fingers together in her lap to keep from touching Luke again. "He *is* very brave."

"Does he still hear the voice of Heammawihio?"

"Ghosts?" That wasn't the word Luke had used for them.

"The creator," he said. "The Wise One Above."

"You think Luke hears the voice of God?"

"He hears someone."

"He says the wind speaks to him."

"Perhaps it does. *Kiwidinok* means 'of the wind.'"

If so, then Luke's dead wife had been telling him to kill.

"Both his wife and his child are dead," Rose said. "What happened to them?"

"Heova'ehe." Luke had muttered that word while delirious. She still didn't know what it meant. "Yellow Hair," the old man translated. Rose lifted her hand to her own, but Medicine Bear shook his head. "It is what the Cheyenne call the man known as Custer."

"The Washita." Her hand dropped into her lap like a stone. "Luke said the Dog Men were away."

Which was why it became a massacre.

"He told you much."

He hadn't told her of his wife or his child. She had a pretty good idea why. "He blames himself for the deaths of many."

"He is not the only one."

The reason behind the Dog Man's hatred became clear. "Many Horses' sister died at the Washita, along with Luke's wife and . . ." Her voice broke at the thought of the small, still body of a child.

"Luke's wife and the sister of Many Horses are the same."

We were brothers once.

"He holds Luke responsible."

"Many people hold Ve'ho'e Mestaa'e responsible," the old man said.

"If he wasn't there, then how can it be his fault?" She wasn't sure how it could be his fault even if he *was* there.

Medicine Bear spread his hands. "He is Ve'ho'e Mestaa'e."

"A prophet can't see everything coming."

"I agree."

Rose released an exasperated huff. "Then tell Luke it wasn't his fault. Make Many Horses behave."

"Behave," the old man said. "I do not know this word."

"Neither does he," she muttered. "Luke has been in agony."

"Do you think he would be in any less agony because I told him something he already knows?"

"If he knows it wasn't his fault, then why is he in agony?"

"Have you ever lost a child?"

She flinched, and he nodded as his gaze sharpened on her face.

"Does the agony ever go away?"

It would when she found her, but they were discussing two different kinds of loss.

"It would help if people stopped spitting on him, calling him names, and trying to kill him."

"If he didn't believe he deserved such treatment, he would not have come back."

He came back for me, she thought. But had he? Perhaps he had returned for death after all.

She shouldn't care. But the time for not caring had ended in the sinkhole. Hell, it had ended long before that. Perhaps the first time she'd seen his face.

"He's been tortured enough for things that were never his fault. The army—" she began.

"I know about his time as a captive of the bluecoats."

"He was also a captive of the Cheyenne."

"At first," the old man agreed.

"And then?"

"We saw the man beneath." He tilted his head, bird-like. "I think you have seen him as well. I think you have done more than see."

"Are you a prophet, too, now?"

"It doesn't take a prophet to recognize love."

Rose cast a quick glance at Luke, who still slept, before returning her gaze to Medicine Bear. "He doesn't love me."

He still loved his wife.

Luke rode across the prairie. The wind tore at his hair, which reached past his shoulders. He should probably braid it as the others had, but when he felt like this— desperate to be free—he just couldn't.

Two eagle feathers tangled in the length. Silver earrings tugged at his lobes, a crescent-shaped silver naja *dangled from his hair pipe breastplate, the ends just brushing the scars he bore from* Hestôsanestôtse. *If it weren't for the color of his hair, and his eyes, he would be mistaken for a Cheyenne. In every other way, he was one of them.*

His horse was Cheyenne. Or at least he had become Cheyenne once Luke had stolen him from the Pawnee. He'd had to creep into their camp in the dead of night and creep out with their very best horse. For that he had earned his first eagle feather.

He had been with the tsitsistas *for over three years. Among them men were rewarded for what mattered. Courage. Strength. Sacrifice. The old were revered as wise. Beauty was found within. The Cheyenne way had become Luke's way. He would never go back to the man he had been or the life he had left. He belonged here.*

Always.

"Hotoao'o," the Dog Men shouted as a herd of buffalo appeared on the horizon and they gave chase.

Though it was winter and the meat would not spoil as quickly as it would in six months, nevertheless they killed only as much as they could carry. A Cheyenne would never waste a life. The buffalo were held in great respect. Every part of them was used. The skin for robes, for lodges, clothing, shoes; the bones for tools; the stomach for containers; the brains for tanning; even the tails were used for decorations, the hooves for rattles, the dung for fires. Nothing was left behind.

When the hunt was over, the Dog Men made camp—danced, sang, told stories of the chase as they feasted. Luke had once been a Confederate, the very meaning of which was "friend." And he'd had friends—good ones—back then. But that life seemed long ago and far away. Many, if not all, of those friends were dead. He had chosen this life and these men. They would die for him, and he would do no less for them.

In the morning they went home, still laughing and talking. They were young, strong Cheyenne males who feared nothing and no one. Very much like Mosby's Rangers, at least until they'd met disaster at the hands of a spy. But no Dog Man would ever betray his people.

Many Horses rode ahead of the rest, and Luke joined him. "You are that anxious to return to your wife?" Luke asked.

"Aren't you?"

"Of course."

"You are certain that the white flag has kept even soldiers such as Heova'ehe away."

Heova'ehe. Yellow Hair. What the Cheyenne called Custer. The Sioux called him Long Hair. The army just called him rash. He did not follow military protocol. He was unpredictable, impulsive, reckless. Which might be why he had been court-martialed for dereliction of duty and suspended for one year. The trial had been the talk of every troop that had traipsed across the plains. Luke had heard it discussed each time he had crept close and listened.

That year wasn't yet up. Luke doubted the army was inclined to be lenient to a man who'd left his post to ride *across Kansas to visit his wife. Then again, Sheridan liked men who got the job done. What if Little Phil had recalled Custer already?*

Unease trickled over him and he flicked a glance at the horizon. Those clouds looked a little like smoke.

The next thing he knew he was racing across the prairie in the wake of Many Horses, the rest of the Dog Men all around them. The thunder of hooves rose toward a brilliant winter blue sky. The first thing they saw when they were close enough to see were the bodies.

"God," Luke said. He wasn't sure if he was praying or cursing. Maybe both. There'd been close to eight hundred horses in camp. And now . . .

Every last one of them was dead.

His mount shied—probably the smell. Death hovered everywhere. Amid the horses lay the camp's dogs. What kind of men killed dogs and horses?

Luke reached the top of the bank that led down to the river.

The kind that had already killed all the people.

CHAPTER 18

Luke continued to speak, and while many of his words were Cheyenne, enough of them were English for Rose to relive the horror of the Washita through his eyes.

She tried to take his hand, but he would not let her, resisting comfort for his pain, still believing, even in his delirium, that he did not deserve it.

"You can go," Medicine Bear said. "I am here."

Rose shook her head. Luke had to have known that coming back would cause pain, yet still he had come. The least she could do was listen.

"You can go," she said. "I'm here."

The old man snorted. *"He'eo'o."*

"I don't like your tone," Rose muttered, and he snorted again.

"He will say things you will not want to hear. Ugly things. Bloody, horrible, evil things. What men do to one another and to . . ." Medicine Bear paused, and Rose lifted her gaze from Luke's pale, sweating face to his.

"You think I don't know what men can do?" While she had been spared such indignity—she still didn't know why—she had seen enough since, heard enough, to know the truth.

The elder peered into her eyes, seemed about to say something more, and then looked away.

"Maybe you *should* go," she said more gently.

It wouldn't be easy for him to hear Luke's tale, and

she didn't think either one of them was going to be able to make Luke stop. She wasn't certain she wanted to. The story of the Washita was what had set Luke on the path to becoming the man he was now. She needed to know it.

"I will not leave him," Medicine Bear said.

"Neither will I."

"Kiwidinok!" Luke shouted, startling them both.

Rose tensed, her hands fluttering, helpless, afraid he might begin to convulse, perhaps stop breathing. He seemed so very ill.

He whispered, *"Hova'âhane,"* in a voice so broken she wanted to sob.

"No," Medicine Bear echoed. "No."

The tracks of the soldiers trailed down the bank. They had to have been on the attack from the very beginning; otherwise the Cheyenne would not have run. But they had, and the only direction to retreat was through the water and up the opposite side.

Luke imagined how it would have been, running through snow, then icy water. The chill of the air like knives to the lungs. Climbing a hill under such conditions would have been difficult at the best of times. Doing so while being chased by cavalry, carrying babies, dragging children, herding old ones . . . the worst of times.

"Kiwidinok!" Luke shouted, though nothing moved in the camp but Dog Men.

They crept through the wreckage, weapons drawn, peering at each body, searching for any sign of life, finding none. Luke began to do the same. The river was sluggish with dead. The fifth body he touched was hers.

"Hova'âhane," he murmured. No.

She stared at the sky, and for an instant he had hope. Foolish, foolish hope. If she'd been alive she would not have been able to stare into He'amo'ome; *the sun was so bright that it hurt.*

Everything hurt.

Blood darkened the front of her deer hide dress, staining the creamy shells she had sewn there one night by the light of the fire. She was missing a moccasin. The sight of her tiny, bare foot floating just beneath the surface nearly undid him.

She had turned and faced the riders. He wasn't surprised. She had always faced every fear, every danger. She was so much braver than he.

Luke would have liked to sink into the icy water and pull her into his arms, but he still hadn't found Ayasha. He continued to search, to shout, with no sight of their child, no answer to his calls. This went on for so long he began to hope again. If his daughter was not here, perhaps she was not dead.

He should have known better. But hope was like that.

The calls of the Dog Men brought a few survivors—mostly children and those just a little older—from wherever the survivors had gone. Luke ran to them, crying his daughter's name, but none of them were her. He glanced about for Many Horses, but the Dog Man searched for his own loved ones. It was his duty as the leader of the soldier band to discover what had happened and then avenge it. But, like all the Dog Men, Many Horses seemed dazed, a bit crazed.

Luke watched him for several moments, waiting for his friend to remember his duty. Instead he continued downriver, disappearing around a bend, so Luke set aside his own concern for the good of the others. Someone had to.

He beckoned the survivors to gather around. "What happened?"

"The soldiers attacked." Morning Walker, a young woman of Black Kettle's band, fought back tears. "Our chief is dead."

It hardly seemed fair that Black Kettle had survived the massacre at Sand Creek only to die here. Luke stifled an inappropriate burst of laughter. When was the last time anything had been fair?

"His wife, too. Some of the warriors camped up and down the river heard the shots and ran to help. They died with the rest."

"The horses and dogs?"

"Heova'ehe ordered them shot."

"Why?"

She spread her hands. Luke wanted to take them in his to help her stop shaking. Except he was shaking, too.

"There are people missing," one of the Dog Men shouted as he turned in a circle atop the bluff, his gaze searching the horizon.

"They took them," Morning Walker whispered. "When the remaining warriors arrived, mounted and armed, they could do nothing for fear of killing Cheyenne, too."

For an instant Luke didn't understand what she meant. Then he spat on the ground. "Cowards." The soldiers had taken hostages as shields. No true warrior would ever do such a thing.

"Was Ayasha with them?" If his daughter was a prisoner, he would get her back. No one on earth would keep her from him.

"I don't know," she said.

"My wife?" Many Horses had returned. "My children?"

Morning Walker's forehead creased. "Yes," she said. "I saw them with the soldiers that rode . . ." She pointed where hundreds of tracks disappeared into the tall grass.

Many Horses sprinted toward his mount, vaulting onto its back and urging the pony to galloping pursuit. Several of the Dog Men followed. Luke would have. But he couldn't leave the people who stood all around him, helpless and horrified. He couldn't leave Kiwidinok.

His gaze returned to the river, and something about the sight of his wife from this angle disturbed him. He splashed into the icy water; droplets sprayed upward, soaking his clothes, his face, his hair. He was already so cold he barely felt them. He tugged on her arm, and she bobbed sideways.

Ayaysha appeared alive, too—eyes wide open, lips slightly parted—except she lay beneath the water and she did not breathe.

His child would never breathe again.

"Heova'ehe followed the tracks of the Dog Men," Medicine Bear said.

Luke had gone eerily silent after he recounted finding the body of his little girl beneath that of her mother. Tears had seeped from his closed eyelids and dripped onto the mat beneath. He didn't move; he barely breathed. He was so quiet he scared her. She took his hand, and this time he let her.

"If Custer followed the Dog Men, why didn't he find the Dog Men?"

That would have been a meeting Rose would love to see. She doubted Yellow Hair would have ridden away *with* hair if he'd had to face Dog Men instead of women, old folks, and children.

"He followed them *to* the camp."

Her hand tightened on Luke's. Because the Dog Men had left camp, there had been tracks *to* the camp. If they'd stayed, not only would there have been no tracks to follow, but the best fighters would have been there to protect the tribe.

"There had been trouble with the army. Ve'ho'e Mestaa'e insisted that a white flag would keep us safe. The others didn't want to go hunting, but he insisted. At times he just had to ride."

"Luke was kept in a pit once," she said. "Alone. In the dark. Cold. Hungry. Trapped. He—"

"You do not need to defend him to me," Medicine Bear murmured.

"Why is there a need to defend him at all? A young man wanted to hunt. He convinced his friends to go along. Bad things happened. It's a story as old as time."

Medicine Bear smiled sadly. "Most young men are not prophets."

"Luke isn't a prophet. He knew more about the white man than you did. That's all."

"He did not know enough."

"How could he know that Yellow Hair was near and that the man would be more concerned about his legend than the rules? Black Kettle was promised peace. Why is it Luke's fault he didn't get it?"

One of these days Custer's rash behavior was going to be the death of him, and where would his legend be then?

"Did Many Horses find his family?" she asked.

"You saw his wife."

"The one who spat?" Rose's lip curled. If she saw the woman again, Rose might do worse than spit.

"She endured much at the Camp of Supply." Rose frowned at the unfamiliar name. "The place the hostages were taken after the Washita—an area not far from the river where the army stored and gave out supplies. There they paraded the hostages before the soldiers. They took photographs to send east, showing the Cheyenne were vanquished."

Rose released a derisive puff of air from between her tight lips. If the Cheyenne had been vanquished, her daughter would be in her arms instead of God knew where. The Washita had only stirred up more trouble.

"The camp possessed supplies," Medicine Bear continued, "but not enough shelter for fifty more people. Many Horses' wife had two young children and a baby in her arms. They huddled together, but it was cold. By the time Many Horses reached them, the baby had gone to *He'amo'ome*."

Rose tried to push the sudden image of the woman rocking her dead, frozen child from her head, but she couldn't.

"How did Many Horses rescue them?" She needed something—anything—to focus on besides that imaginary still, blue face.

"From a young age, every Cheyenne boy practices

sneaking into a camp, then sneaking back out—usually with horses. Many Horses is our greatest warrior. If he could take the horses of the Pawnee or the Comanche without them knowing, he could take his own wife and children from the white men."

"He snuck into an army supply camp, took his family away, and no one ever knew?"

"One less woman and two less children." The old man wrinkled his nose and lifted one shoulder. "If they noticed they did not care."

"The rest?" she asked.

"To steal away one woman and two small children is easy. To steal over fifty is not."

Rose didn't think stealing one woman and two children was easy, either, but she didn't comment. "Where are the others now?"

She didn't think they were dead. Wouldn't that many deaths—even Cheyenne—have been reported? Perhaps not. The army, the government, the settlers considered Indian casualties irrelevant. As if the army merely swatted flies. A nuisance certainly, but nothing worth keeping count of.

Rose rubbed between her eyes. When had she begun to think like that?

"They were taken to the reservation," Medicine Bear said.

"And you?" Rose tilted her head. "You know too much about the Washita not to have been there."

"I was."

"Then why aren't you on the reservation?"

"I left," he said simply.

"You left prison?"

"A reservation is not a prison." Rose lifted an eyebrow and the old man continued. "There are no locks on the doors."

"There aren't any doors," Rose muttered.

"Hetómestôtse," he said. "This is true."

"Then how—?"

"I waited until the darkness. Then I walked away."

"If you were going to walk away, why did you go in the first place?"

"Leaving when the soldiers are taking is one thing. Leaving when the guards are old men or missionaries is quite another."

"No one came after you?" The thought of Medicine Bear shuffling across the prairie alone—no horse, no companions—both impressed and concerned her.

"They probably thought I slipped off to die." His lip curled. "Like an animal."

"You walked all the way from Indian Territory?"

"I am not so old that I cannot find a horse."

Rose smiled at the use of the word *find* for *steal*. His English was too good for him to have made a mistake. Instead she thought he had made a joke. That she found it funny was another indication of how much she had changed since meeting Luke Phelan.

"Some followed my lead and returned. Others decided to stay. The bands that had camped at the Washita were . . ." He flicked his fingers as if tossing them to the wind. "We gathered together what was left and began anew."

"And Luke?" she asked.

"To live he had to leave."

"I don't think he wanted to live."

"The Wise One had other plans."

"Did Many Horses try to kill him?"

"So they say. I was not here or I would have stopped it then as I did now."

"What happened?"

"I only know what I was told. Haestôhe'hame took Ve'ho'e Mestaa'e onto the prairie. They fought. One man came back."

"Which is why the Cheyenne thought Luke was dead."

The old fellow shrugged. "He is very hard to kill. He was protected."

"By whom? God? His ghosts? The wind?"

"Yes."

Rose wasn't sure if her head ached because of Medicine Bear's words, her suppressed tears over Luke's memories, or exhaustion. Her stomach cramped, and she set her hand on her belly. She couldn't recall the last time she'd eaten. Then she felt a damp, warm rush between her legs and understood the cause of both aches. She struggled to her feet. "I . . . uh . . ."

She wasn't certain what to ask for. Bushes were as scarce as trees out here, and the trees were full of Cheyenne. Besides, she needed more than a private area to relieve herself; she needed a cloth. Now.

Medicine Bear called out, and an equally ancient woman appeared in the doorway. When she beckoned, Rose gratefully hurried after.

Night had fallen while she listened to Luke and Medicine Bear. The sky had gone cool blue and silver; the air felt heavenly on her hot skin. Rose had no idea how to ask for cloth. She had no idea how to mime such a thing, either. In the end, she didn't need to.

The elderly woman's gaze lowered, and her breath caught. Rose glanced down, too.

Her boots sparkled wet with blood.

Luke's own voice, muttering, "Rose" woke him.

Medicine Bear smoked peacefully by his side. As the holy man had disappeared from the Washita and not been seen again, at least while Luke was still with the Cheyenne, everyone had assumed him either captured or dead.

The man appeared exactly the same as he had the last time Luke had seen him. He had not aged a day, while Luke now had white streaks in his hair, or at least he'd *had* white streaks when he still had hair. Maybe the old fellow *was* dead.

"You have awoken at last, Ve'ho'e Mestaa'e. I am glad."

"Have we gone to Heammawihio?"

"I am not a ghost." The old man drew on his pipe, let the smoke trickle out. "Yet."

"What happened to you at the Washita?"

"I was captured. By the time I returned, you had disappeared. I am sorry I was not here to help you."

"I did not deserve help."

"You did not deserve banishment."

He'd deserved death, but even that had been denied him. Though he did not think it would be denied him for very much longer.

"Where's Many Horses?"

"Gone."

Luke sat up. The world whirled. He waited until it stopped. "He brought me here." He frowned. "Didn't he?"

Things were kind of fuzzy in his head—the past, the ghosts, the present all jumbled together. Perhaps Many Horses was as much of a memory as a reality. Perhaps he was even one of the ghosts.

While that thought should cause relief, instead Luke felt a bit ill. He must have looked it, too, as the old man patted Luke's hand. "He did."

"Why would he leave without killing me?"

"I would not let him."

Medicine Bear was a holy man, a healer—in truth a doctor as well trained as any Luke had come across this side of the Mississippi—but he had not been a chief. With the loss of Black Kettle and many of the other elders at the Washita, he probably was now. However, Many Horses was the leader of the Dog Men. Though they were no longer a separate band but part of this one, his status should be equal to that of any chief. In matters of war, he would outrank them all. Was Luke considered a matter of war? He didn't think so.

"How did you stop him?"

"Those who hear the voice of the spirits are protected."

"What if I don't want to be protected?"

"The spirits choose, not you."

"And Many Horses?"

"He took his family away until his anger cools."

Which might be around the turn of the century. Or not. At least Luke didn't have to worry about dying in front of Rose. Not only would that be mortifying for him and upsetting for her, but she would try to protect him. She might be hurt or killed, and that he could not allow. That she wasn't here now worried him.

"Was I with a woman?" He hoped to God—any god, all the gods—that he hadn't imagined her. Or perhaps he should hope that he had.

"Pale as the moon, brave as the sun."

"Yes." He let out a long, relieved breath. "Where is she?"

"Safe."

"Did she find . . ." Luke paused, wondering how to broach the subject of Lily.

"She is at peace."

A chill went over Luke. "What kind of peace?"

"She fought well. But I could not let your woman come back."

"My woman is dead."

The flicker of sadness that came into the old man's eyes, the way he hung his head, caused Luke's heart to stutter. "Where's Rose?"

Medicine Bear got to his feet. "I will take you to her."

CHAPTER 19

"What happened? Is she ...?" Luke swallowed, unable to voice his fear.

Luke's panic lessened as the old man led him across the camp to the tepee that stood farthest from his own. The Cheyenne's fear of ghosts was so great they removed the dead from camp immediately, lest a lingering spirit take away with it the spirit of someone living. If Rose had died, she would not be here. She would already be on the prairie—bundled into a blanket, lashed tightly, resting upon a scaffold in a tree, or in the open, perhaps in a cave or a crevice, covered by a cairn of rocks.

People stared. They whispered, but no one stopped them. As Luke was the guest of Medicine Bear, and insane, no one would dare.

In front of the tepee, Medicine Bear paused. "You are no longer unwell?"

Luke hesitated. If he was well, Many Horses could take his revenge. And while Luke had come here knowing that, expecting it, embracing it, he realized now that until Lily rested in Rose's arms far away from this place, he could not allow it.

However, right now Many Horses wasn't here, and lying to Medicine Bear was not something Luke wanted to do. "I am not unwell," he said.

"I could not let her back into my lodge while you were ill," the old man explained. "Not until she was done."

"Done with what?" Luke was starting to wonder if Medicine Bear was crazier than he was.

The fellow drew aside the flap and indicated Luke should duck in. "You shall see."

Luke stepped inside. The flap flopped shut behind him. Though the interior was dim, the brightness of the morning sun through the smoke hole above lightened it enough to reveal Rose beneath a pile of blankets. Her face was so white he rushed to her side, calling her name.

Her eyes opened. The dark circles beneath made them shine very blue. Though her bruises had faded, the scar on her forehead blazed against her too-pale skin like a fresh wound.

She reached for his hand. He took hers and nearly cried out again at its chill. He caught the scent of blood, though he saw no indication that she had been hurt. Of course all he could see was her head and her arms, so he threw back the blankets.

She lay naked beneath, and the sight of her breasts, tipped with nipples the shade of her name, caused a flash of that dream again. The one where he had made her his.

He shook his head. Now was not the time to lose his mind. Any more than he already had.

"Where is it?" he demanded.

She snatched the blanket. "Stop that!"

"What did they do to you?"

Rose flushed and turned her face to the wall. "Go away."

"No." He tugged on the blankets once more. She held on tightly, and he was impressed with her strength. But he always had been. "Show me where you're hurt."

"Stop," she whispered. "Go away. Please."

He let go, but he didn't go. He couldn't. "Rose, just tell me where."

"Here." She laid her hand over her heart.

His mind shimmied again. He smelled dirt, tasted it, too, felt her skin both beneath his palms and against his own. "I don't understand."

Anything.

She faced him. At least some color had returned to

her cheeks, her lips. He felt both less panicked and, somehow, more. The one reason he could think of for her to be so pale, so cold was if she'd discovered her daughter pale and cold, too.

"Did you find Lily?"

"I haven't seen her. And I haven't asked. I couldn't. No one speaks English except Medicine Bear and Many Horses. Many Horses—"

"Left," he interrupted.

"Yes. Then Medicine Bear wouldn't let me back in the tepee with you."

"Why?"

Again, she looked away.

"What did they do to you?"

"It wasn't what they did." She sighed. "It was what I did. What *we* did. In the sinkhole. I thought . . ." Her cheeks flushed again. "I thought it was merely my . . ." She paused, coughed, bit her lip. "Monthly," she whispered.

That would explain why Medicine Bear had not allowed her back in his tepee or wanted Luke to enter this one if he was still unwell. The old man might have learned from white doctors, but he still kept many of the old ways. Menstruating women slept at the women's lodge. They took care never to touch a pot or a plate or a weapon or shield of a warrior, as this would ensure his death in the next battle. They could not enter any tepee that contained a medicine bundle, nor come into contact with someone who was ill.

While her condition might explain Medicine Bear's behavior, it did not explain hers. She wasn't a child. She'd had monthlies before. What was it about this one that had left her so wan and shaky? Why would she not meet his eyes? What did it have to do with the sinkhole?

"You *thought* it was your monthly," he said. "But it wasn't?"

"There was more blood than there should have been. More than there ever was before. And the pain—" Her voice broke, and he took her hand.

"I hurt you," he said. Why couldn't he remember?

"What?" Her eyes met his at last, wide, shocked. "No!"

"But—"

"No." Her hand tightened on his. "You didn't hurt me. Not in the slightest. Far from it."

"You said there was pain and blood."

"It was so soon. I'm not sure. But I've never been this ill before and—"

He yanked his hand from hers. "What are you saying?"

Her gaze lowered. "I might have had a miscarriage."

Reality and dreams shimmered again—together, apart, together. Like them. But that couldn't be right. It couldn't be true. He wouldn't. He hadn't.

Had he?

"I'm sorry—" she began.

"*You're* sorry?"

She sat up, clutching the blanket to her chin. She seemed so small, so frail. He wanted to take her in his arms. But, apparently, he'd already done that.

"It was my fault," she said. "I thought you knew, but you . . . didn't."

"Knew," he repeated. He seemed to be repeating a lot of things. Words. Mistakes. History.

"I thought you knew it was me. That you . . . But you thought I was . . ." She ducked her head, and her shimmering blond hair, tangled, sweaty but still so pretty, covered her flaming face. "Her," she whispered.

"God," he muttered, and tried to shove his fingers through his own hair. Instead he scraped his stubbly scalp with his too-long fingernails.

"I should have known," she continued. "A man like you would never touch a woman like me."

He blinked. "Huh?"

"You're so . . ." She waved her hand at his head.

"Crazy?" he suggested.

"You're no crazier than I am."

Did that mean yes or no?

"Pretty," she said when he continued to blink at her like an idiot. "You're so beautiful and I'm so . . . not."

"You think I wouldn't touch you because I'm prettier than you?" He rubbed his head. Now who was crazy?

"Well, when you say it like that—"

He dropped his hand. "When anyone says it at all, it's the most foolish thing I ever heard."

"I was there in Rogue when you ran from me and went straight to a whore."

He'd forgotten about that. Why couldn't she?

"You think I left you and went to her because I didn't care for how you looked?"

She shrugged, her fragile bones shifting seductively beneath her smooth bare shoulder. "I'm pale and small in a world full of wide-open spaces and color."

"What does that *mean*?"

"You're so beautiful you blind me."

"You're blind all right," he muttered, but she ignored him.

"You're tall and strong. Your skin is golden and your hair is . . ."

"Gone."

"You had hair women would kill for."

"There were plenty of men out here who would have been happy to kill me for it."

"Shh," she murmured. "I close my eyes." She did. "And I see you the way you were in the hills."

Insane? he wanted to ask, but she'd already shushed him, and in truth, the expression on her face, something in her voice made him swallow a sudden aching dryness in his throat.

"All gold and red and smooth."

He choked. Her eyes snapped open. "I know I'm not pretty or buxom. I was never very good at"—she waved her hand again, this time between the two of them—"man-woman things. My husband called me *kalt wie eis*."

He tried to decipher what that meant and gave up.

"Cheyenne and Sioux I know. German . . ." He spread his hands.

"Cold as ice," she translated.

Luke's fingers curled into fists. How dare the fool say something like that about the mother of his child?

Luke stilled. If not for an accident of nature, she would have been the mother of *his* child. That he had been unaware of his actions in the sinkhole, had thought himself dreaming, did not excuse what he had done. In fact, it only condemned him more. When the wind continued to whisper even after he left his hills, he should have returned to them. But he'd been too captivated by her, by the way he felt whenever she looked at him, by the image of himself that he saw in her eyes. And all the while the image she'd held of herself had been this.

"You are *not* cold, Rose."

"You don't remember what I was."

"I remember your kiss in Rogue, and it was far from cold. If your husband weren't already dead, I'd want to kill him." She winced. "What's wrong? Are you in pain? Should I get Medicine Bear?"

She looked away. "My husband isn't dead."

"You said he was."

"I said he was gone. He went back East."

"Without you?"

"I refused to go without Lily. He refused to stay for any reason. The attack broke him. We lost everything. He couldn't sleep. He was . . . afraid."

"So were you."

"I was more afraid of never seeing Lily again than I was of . . ."

"The Cheyenne."

"Anything," she corrected, meeting his gaze again. "Nothing could be more horrible than losing my child."

"You're right," he whispered.

"I said we could go after her. He said we could have other children. That Lily was as good as dead once she was with the Indians. That even if I found her he

wouldn't want her back. That she was dead to him."
Rose lifted her chin. "So he became dead to me."

"I'd like to make him dead to everyone," Luke muttered.

Just the thought of how Rose had been betrayed by the one person in the world who should have been protecting her made Luke's teeth clench. By riding away from his wife when she needed him the most, her husband had shattered his vows so completely they no longer existed. The army shot deserters. Abandoning those who depended on you was the worst kind of betrayal. Luke should know.

He contemplated her face. A lot of men—most men— would not want their wives back after the Indians had known them. Perhaps that was at the root of Varner's departure more than any fear of the hostiles.

"Did he divorce you?"

"Not that I know of." She didn't seem concerned.

"Did you divorce him?"

"Death is better than a divorce."

"He isn't dead."

She sniffed. "Prove it."

God, she was magnificent.

"The Dog Men hurt you," he said.

"I fought them."

What women wouldn't? "The reason I left you in that room in Rogue was that I didn't want to be too rough with you. I knew I shouldn't touch you. But whenever you touched me, whenever you *touch* me, all I want to do is . . ."

"What?" she whispered.

He tightened his lips. The violent pulse of his desire would only frighten her as much now as it would have then, perhaps more.

She set her hand on his arm. "Tell me. Please. I need to understand. What do you want to do when we touch?"

His gaze fixed on her fingers—both soft and rough— so pale against his darker arm. "I want to bury myself inside you, over and over, again and again until you—" He bit off the word.

What was wrong with him? He'd taken her in the mud. He'd gotten her with child, and he truly didn't remember. He was as much of an animal as the animals that had hurt her, yet he'd been about to say he wanted to make her scream.

"I'm sorry," he said. "You were taken against your will and I—"

"I wanted everything that happened between us, Luke. If there's blame to be had, it's mine. You had no will. You thought I was her. I took advantage. I didn't mean to, I—"

"I wasn't talking about me. I meant them. The Dog Men."

"You think the Dog Men . . ." She grimaced. "No! They pushed me, kicked me, slapped me. They never . . ." She just shook her head. "And neither did you. Why would you think that?"

"I rode with the Dog Men. I know what they do. Conquer the enemy. Kill the men, take the women—in one way or another—steal the children. It isn't pretty. It isn't nice. They're at war."

"Did you . . . ?" she began.

"No! I tried to make them see that behaving that way only encouraged the same behavior in retaliation. Some agreed."

"Some didn't."

But apparently some of those who did had been those who'd attacked her.

Relief flooded him. She hadn't been raped. Not by them. Not by him. Not by anyone. Hit, pushed, kicked, nearly scalped, terrorized, and impregnated.

But not raped.

"I thought they would." Her fingers tightened a bit. "Expected it really. The place was on fire. I had no idea where Jakob was, if he was alive or dead. Then one of them shouted and they all got on their horses and left. With Lily."

"They were looking for a child; they found one and left." Unusual, but not unheard of.

"Luke?" Her thumb rubbed the inside of his arm.

He shifted closer; he couldn't help it.

"You showed me what it could be like between a man and a woman. I had never . . ." She swallowed and lifted her gaze. "With you I discovered I wasn't cold. With you I felt for the first time everything I'd always wanted to."

"He didn't know you. He couldn't have and ever have thought you cold."

Her lips curved. "He *didn't* know me, and I didn't know him. I answered an advertisement."

"You were a heart-and-hand woman?" She nodded, and Luke realized how little he truly knew of her though he'd felt as if he knew everything.

"In Boston I was a spinster," she continued. "In Kansas I was a wife."

He'd deduced she was a Yankee, but Boston had always seemed Yankee-er than most. "There are farms in Boston?"

"No. Why?"

"You lived on a farm in Kansas."

"Jakob was a farmer."

"You left everyone, everything, you knew to become a stranger's wife, a *farmer's* wife, when you'd never lived on a farm?"

"Yes."

"And you say you aren't brave."

"I'm not."

"Farming is hard, Rose, even for women who were born to it. I lived on one until the war. I had four brothers and a sister and it was still backbreaking. My parents were old, tired, crushed by the land and the work. If they'd been stronger, they might have survived the war."

She rubbed her thumb along his wrist again, and he forgot everything but her.

"I was sickly all my life. The damp, the cold, I coughed all the time. But here my cough went away. My chest didn't hurt. I had color in my face." Her lips curved. "Not a lot but more than I'd ever had before. Coming west made me strong. It gave me life. Jakob gave me life. He gave me Lily."

Luke meant to give her Lily, too. And everything else that he could. He touched her face. "You are *not* cold."

Her lips lifted just a little—both sweet and sad. "You don't remember."

He was starting to. Every time he touched her, another recollection tumbled free. He'd believed those seductive flickers were secret dreams, lustful hopes, but now he knew that they were real, and he wanted to wallow in them. He wanted to wallow in her.

"You were beautiful," he said, wrapping his fingers around the back of her neck when she tried to pull away. He held her still with his hand and his gaze. "You tasted like rain, like the earth. The lightning turned your skin the shade of the moon. You looked so deliciously cool, and I was so damn hot. But I started to shiver and you . . ." Her eyes went wide, and though he knew them to be light, they seemed very dark. He tugged her closer until his lips hovered a breath from hers. "You made me stop."

"Yes," she agreed.

He kissed her. What else could he do? She was everything he adored—her eyes were blue sky, her hair the sun, her skin like the moon, her lips warm as the summer earth, soft and sweet. Where she'd once smelled of lilies, she now smelled like new grass, like life and heat and hope. He lost track of his thoughts; he lost track of himself while surrounded by her.

The blanket fell down. Her breasts brushed his chest, and his body responded as it had back then. The last bit of sense that he had—that voice telling him he couldn't, he shouldn't—fled. It didn't help that she was making soft sounds of pleasure, sounds he could feel against the palm of his hand, while his fingertips pressed against the back of her neck, her hair tickling his wrist, her nipples tickling his—

"I am glad you have come to an understanding."

Their eyes snapped open. Luke released Rose as she snatched the blanket and pulled it to her chin.

Medicine Bear stood just outside the entrance, holding the flap up so he could beam in at them as if they had done something very clever. Several other Cheyenne who had been passing by, or pretending to be, peered in, too. Luke cursed and scooted in front of Rose.

"The wedding will take place as soon as she is able to leave the women's lodge," the old man said.

Luke muttered, "Hell," at the same time Rose asked, "What wedding?"

"Yours." Medicine Bear remained outside the door. It wouldn't do for a healer to step foot inside the same structure as a woman who bled. An odd and foolish behavior for a man such as he, but Luke knew better than to try to convince him of it. Medicine Bear was an intriguing, and infuriating, blend of two worlds.

"I can't—" Rose began, and Luke set his hand on hers.

"Shh," he murmured. She cast him a surprised glance, but she shushed.

Medicine Bear's smile faded, and his eyes narrowed. "You cannot think that you can give her your child and not your name."

He hadn't thought of it at all, but he should have known the Cheyenne would have. The *tsitsistas* prized chastity in their women. To violate a virgin meant death. For an unmarried woman to lie with a man not her husband meant banishment. But Rose was not Cheyenne, and despite everything, neither was Luke.

"Tell me you would never do such a thing, Ve'ho'e Mestaa'e."

Considering what else he had done . . .

"I'm surprised you're surprised," he muttered, and Medicine Bear blew air through his nose like a bull buffalo ready to charge.

"How can you be certain there was a child?" Rose asked. She hadn't remained silent for very long.

"I am certain," Medicine Bear said.

"You haven't set foot in the same tepee since I—" She broke off. "You know nothing."

"I know that the first thing Ve'ho'e Mestaa'e said when he awoke was your name."

Rose glanced at Luke.

"I know that you called for him in your sleep."

Her eyes lowered.

"I know that neither one of you denied that there might be a child, that such a possibility was possible. And because of that, he will do the right thing. It is what he does."

Luke hadn't done the right thing in so long he wasn't certain he could recognize it anymore.

"I am not—" Rose began, and he shushed her again. She made an irritated sound and cast him a glare.

"Ma'heonenahkohe," Luke said. "I would speak with you outside."

"What is there that you would say to me outside that you would not say in front of your intended?"

It wasn't what he wouldn't say; it was what he didn't want *Rose* to say. She didn't want to marry him, and he could understand that. Not only was he a killer; he was a coward and a crazy man. Because he had made her come when no other man had, she was dazzled. But she wasn't dumb. Lust was one thing; life was another. She would refuse. Trouble would ensue.

After casting her a quelling glance, he joined Medicine Bear outside.

"You shame her," the old man murmured. "You shame yourself."

Telling the elder that he had believed he was making love to a ghost would not remove the shame. Only marriage could do that. There was nothing he could do that would change Medicine Bear's mind. He would say no, except for one thing. They had come to retrieve Lily. It would be difficult enough to do that at all. It would be impossible if the Cheyenne considered Rose unfit. And,

just like in the white world, she would be the one marked
as such by their behavior, not him.

Rose wanted to follow Luke and Medicine Bear from
the tepee, but she was naked beneath the blanket and
still bleeding. The old woman who had been caring for
her replaced the woven grass mat beneath her with a
fresh one every few hours, which was less often than she
had replaced them at first, but Rose still couldn't get up
and leave.

Well, she could, but she wasn't going to. Instead she
strained her ears, trying to listen to what they were saying. All she heard were murmurs that could be Cheyenne, English, both, or neither one.

Rose wasn't going to marry the young man no matter
what the old one said. If she'd ever been expecting, and
she wasn't certain of that, she wasn't any longer. There
was no need. Even if the horror on Luke's face at the
mention of marriage hadn't doused any happiness that
might have bloomed on hers from his kiss.

After a time, the door flap lifted. Luke didn't look
any happier coming in than he'd appeared going out.
She opened her mouth; he shook his head, letting the
flap fall behind him. He crossed the short distance and
sank to the ground at her side. She hadn't realized she'd
reached for his hand until their fingers tangled.

"We're going to have to do this if you want to get Lily
back."

"He made our getting married a condition in the
return of my own child?"

Until he set his other hand over her lips, she hadn't
realized her voice had risen above a whisper. "He doesn't
know about her yet. No one does. They can't until we're
married." He dropped his hand. "The Cheyenne have
very definite ideas about how women should behave."

Annoyance flashed, along with a bright flare of fear,
causing her to speak more sharply and bluntly than she
ever had before. "Are you saying that they won't give

me back my little girl if they think I behaved like a whore?"

He winced. "It was my fault, but—"

She held up her hand. "It isn't any different here than it would be back . . ." She'd been about to say "back home" but then she remembered she had no idea where home was anymore.

Boston? The thought of returning there with Lily made her feel as cold inside as Jakob had said she was. Her parents had not completely approved of her marriage to a stranger, and she doubted they'd be any happier about her returning home with a child and no husband. They would never turn her away, but there was a reason she'd left. In the East she'd been a ghost of the woman she was now. She could not go back to being that woman again.

What about the farm? There was nothing left for her there. There was nothing *left* there. Even if there had been, she didn't think she could. Luke was right. She wasn't a farm wife. She'd tried. She'd learned. She'd done what was necessary. But she didn't want to do it again, and she couldn't do it alone.

Where *was* she going to go once she had her child again? What place could they call home? Part of her couldn't believe she'd never considered the questions before, but she had been so intent on finding Lily. And now . . . the only place that felt like home was him.

"It would be the same anywhere," she finished. Odd that those considered savages had the same ideas of morality as those who considered themselves civilized.

In truth if the civilized discovered she had wallowed naked in the mud with a renegade, not only would they call her a whore, but they'd make sure she became one.

No one would give her a chance to become anything else.

CHAPTER 20

For the next week, Rose did little but lie about on the woven mat and stare through the smoke hole at the sky. Even though she hadn't known of the child, she still wasn't sure she believed there'd *been* a child, she missed the child. Or perhaps she just missed *a* child. She still didn't have Lily, and her arms felt as empty as her womb.

She asked for Luke often, in ever-louder and more strident tones, until at last Medicine Bear reappeared outside the entrance.

"Is he all right?" When the old man hesitated, she snapped, "Is he alive?"

"Of course."

She let out a breath. Many Horses had not returned and taken his vengeance.

"Why isn't he here? Why haven't I seen him?" Had he changed his mind about marrying her? Why did she care? It wouldn't be a real marriage, and they both knew it.

"He will not see you until the ceremony. It is our way."

"But he . . . I . . . we—"

"It is because he, you, together . . ." He waved his hand at the lodge. "That you will be married. So you will not see each other until you are."

Did the old man think the two of them would be unable to keep their hands, their lips, their bodies separate? Rose's cheeks, and everything else, heated. He was probably right, and considering what had happened the last time they'd touched—

"We should sleep apart," she blurted.

"Until the wedding, yes. Then you will sleep together, and you will not sleep. This is part of the marriage. Words bind, but bodies bind more deeply."

She had an image of her and Luke's bodies binding—deeply. "I can't."

"You will. He will. And you need not worry that you will make a child too soon. This will not happen. Not yet."

That *had* been at least one of her worries.

"You aren't a prophet."

"I am a doctor."

"How will you stop it?"

She wouldn't drink a concoction, the origins of which she did not know. She would not use some apparatus, or wear a bag of bones or any of the other slightly scandalous remedies she had heard whispered in drawing rooms across Boston as well as one-room cabins on the prairie. Regardless of location, women spoke of such things when the men weren't there to hear.

"I will do nothing. There is a time for such things, and yours is not now."

He sounded like a prophet again. She didn't trust that any more than she trusted any of the other whispers she had heard. Her distrust must have shown—she really needed to learn how to control her face—because he continued even though she hadn't said a word.

"A woman's time arrives each month. Women who do more than sleep with their husbands directly following this do not become with child."

"You're certain?"

"I have studied, watched, listened, learned. I am certain."

As every woman was different—hair, eyes, skin, bodies—she didn't think the same principals applied to every one. However, she wanted to sleep with Luke. She wanted to do more than sleep while he knew her, saw her, touched *her*.

Just once.

Luke spent the week before his wedding searching for Lily.

He knew the Cheyenne well enough to understand that any questions about a captive would be seen as an accusation and denied. But if Lily was here, she would be among the children. All he had to do was look.

However, the children avoided him as if he were a monster. As his name was *White Ghost* he wasn't surprised. The white men were to be both feared and hated, and for the Cheyenne, ghosts were troublesome. They recognized two kinds. *Mestaa'e* meant a spirit not of a person, one who was rarely seen, only felt or heard. The remnants of those recently dead were referred to as *si'yuhk*, and while they whistled and tapped for attention, they eventually went to *Seyan*, the place of the dead where Heammawihio welcomed them into the sun.

But a *mestaa'e* never went away.

If his being named a frightening, never-ending white man spirit weren't enough, when Luke approached the herd of children for a third or fourth time and they scattered, he heard one shout, *"Hoimaha,"* and he knew he would never get close enough to talk to them.

A *hoimaha* came from a land far to the north, beyond where any of the *tsitsistas* had ever gone. There the sky was shrouded with clouds so thick the sun never shone through. The *hoimaha* appeared as a white man. When he arrived the sun fled, and winter spread across the land.

Trust the children to see the truth. Wherever Luke walked, darkness followed. Whomever he touched soon became very cold. He should not marry Rose, but he would. He must. Hell, he wanted to.

Luke stopped haunting the children. If there were

one with hair the shade of the sun, he would have seen her.

The Dog Men had ridden off—to join Many Horses or perhaps to raid on their own. No one knew. He asked those who remained if there were rumors of captives with other Cheyenne bands. If people didn't duck away before he ever came near, he was ignored. The only one who spoke to him, who looked at him, was Medicine Bear.

"I heard of a golden-haired girl who was stolen by Dog Men."

"Black Kettle ordered that we would take captives no more."

Luke's gaze narrowed. Black Kettle had been dead for years. The old man was hedging, which made Luke suspect that he knew something. "Are people listening to him any better now that he's dead than they did when he was alive?"

The elder spread his hand to indicate the camp through which they walked. "Do you see her?"

"I didn't say she was here."

Medicine Bear grunted. "Why do you ask me this?"

"Captives cause trouble."

"You certainly did," Medicine Bear muttered. "Who told you of this child?"

"I spoke with the Sioux." Not a lie. He had spoken with them, just not of this.

"And they told you the Dog Men stole a child." He didn't wait for Luke to answer, which was good. Luke wasn't sure he could have. "There was a time the Dog Men were one band, but that time is no longer."

"I know," Luke murmured. "And I am sorry."

The days he'd spent with the soldier band had been some of the best of his life. He missed them.

"You should talk to Many Horses."

Luke snorted. That always went so well.

Medicine Bear's gaze flicked to Luke's, then away. "Though the Dog Men do not ride as one, they are still Dog Men."

There were very few of their kind left, and because of that those who were left would know of the existence of others. If a golden-haired child had been stolen, the man who had once led the Cheyenne's greatest soldier band would have heard of it. But would Luke be able to learn the truth from Many Horses before the warrior killed him? He would have to try.

"You have no horses," Medicine Bear said.

Luke blinked at the sudden change in subject. "I have one."

Medicine Bear's lip curled. "Your messenger will be embarrassed, as will your father and hers."

When a boy wished to marry a girl, he sent with a messenger as many horses as he could afford to the lodge of her father.

"I have no messenger," Luke said. "No father."

"That does not mean we can dispense with ceremony. I will leave your horse outside the women's lodge."

"Rose has no father to accept the gift."

If this were a true Cheyenne engagement, they would have courted for nearly five years. The horses would stand in front of the lodge for a day and a night, then be accepted or returned. After that, the wedding would take place before the moon had risen twice.

"Carrying your child was acceptance enough."

"Then why bother dragging my horse from your tepee to hers?"

"Because that is the way these things are done."

The old woman woke Rose at dawn. As she handed her a simple, unadorned deerskin dress and worn moccasins, Rose did not think today was any different from the day before. Perhaps Luke, or someone else, had decided there would be no marriage.

That shouldn't upset her as much as it did. This wedding was a ceremony that would mean nothing to anyone but the Cheyenne.

She dressed and stepped into the sun; Luke's horse

butted her in the chest. Behind him stood a dozen more horses, each led by a Cheyenne woman.

She was urged to mount Luke's animal, which wasn't easy since it wore no saddle, but she managed with a bit of help from the ancient woman who had been her only companion all week. Once astride, she had to clutch the mane—there was no bridle, no reins, either—as they walked toward Medicine Bear's lodge. The Cheyenne women followed with their horses. Rose assumed the procession was part of the ceremony, but there was no one she could ask.

As they arrived, the old fellow scurried outside, spreading a blanket onto the ground. Rose's horse stopped next to it.

"Step on nothing but that." Medicine Bear pointed at the blanket. Rose complied. "Sit," he ordered, and she did. He lifted a hand and four young men separated from a group that had gathered. They lifted the corners of the blanket, and Rose as well.

"You may not step over the threshold," Medicine Bear said.

"Why?"

"It is not done."

The carrying of the bride across the threshold was the end of the wedding in her world, not the beginning. But then nothing about this wedding was like any other.

Inside the tepee, the men lowered the blanket to the ground and left. The women poured in, chattering in Cheyenne. They urged her to the back of the lodge, where they stripped off the old clothes and dressed her in new.

Her wedding dress was the shade of butter and just as soft. Beads of many colors sparkled across the bodice and the hem; the moccasins were the same. They brushed her hair, stroking and murmuring their praise, then fashioned the length into two braids on either side of her head and fastened beaded, feathered wrappings to the ends.

They held ornaments to her ears, but there was no way to hang them. When they produced a needle, she refused. She'd had needles piercing her head enough. Instead they secured the hammered silver coins to her hair. Silver bands were placed about her arms and neck. Then the old woman painted her face.

One of the younger girls entered, and Rose caught a glimpse of the crowd gathering outside. They had seated themselves in a semicircle facing the entrance and appeared to be eating.

The girl brought Rose food, cut into tiny pieces. No one would let her touch it, instead lifting the meat to her lips and holding it there until she ate it. When the food was gone, the old woman lifted the flap.

"Luke," Rose whispered. He was so beautiful he made her eyes water.

His clothes and moccasins were the same shade as her own with similar beading, his trousers fringed like the bottom of her dress. Silver coins hung from his ears, a bone necklace across his chest. A headdress fell to his hips, the feathers rippling in the wind. His face had been painted as well, the slashes of black and white reminding her of the day he'd saved her from the Pawnee. She had been so frightened then, but now she only noticed how the paint made his eyes shine a brighter blue.

Those eyes, the reddish cast to his eyebrows, and the lengthening stubble on his head should have made the Cheyenne clothing appear wrong somehow. Instead he wore the clothes, the ornaments, the headdress as if he'd worn them all his life—as if they were his. Perhaps they were.

He held out a hand. She put hers into it and left the tepee. Together they stood before Medicine Bear, who began to speak in Cheyenne. The only words she understood were White Ghost and her own name.

"*Ánováóó'o,*" Luke whispered, and when she turned her gaze to him he translated. "The girl is beautiful."

She wasn't, and in these clothes, with the beads and the paint and jewelry, she must appear like a child playing dress-up. She wished she had something else to wear, but her saddlebags were long since lost, along with her saddle. The riding skirt and shirt she'd been wearing had been little better than bloody rags in any case.

The ceremony continued in Cheyenne, and Rose's mind wandered. Her first wedding had been so different. When she'd stepped off the train in Kansas, Jakob had been waiting, his face flushed pink with heat and nerves. She had seen his disappointment at the sight of her. Had he expected the most beautiful girl in Boston would come west to marry a stranger?

He could have walked away. He could have sent her back. Instead he'd lifted his chin, squared his already square shoulders, and greeted her in heavily accented English. Then he had led her to the hotel, where she'd stood on one side of a screen while she changed from her dusty traveling garments into the navy blue wedding dress she'd brought from home. On the other side he changed into a clean shirt and slicked back his pale hair.

The wedding had taken place before a judge, in a clapboard building next to the hotel. At least it had been in English. Even so, this wedding felt more real than the last, despite the fact that it wasn't.

Notwithstanding their attire of blankets and feathers, the crowd was reminiscent of the audience at many of the weddings she had attended in the past; they were quiet and attentive in the same way. Medicine Bear seemed more a priest than a judge did, and lent the ceremony a reverence associated with sacred vows.

Being married beneath the sky, as the sun shone and the wind stirred, seemed a lot closer to God than doing so in a clapboard courtroom. And if she had to be honest, Luke was a lot closer to the groom she'd dreamed of, even in his Cheyenne clothing, than Jakob had ever been.

"*Náhtse.*"

The old woman stood at Rose's side. She released a flurry of Cheyenne and swept out her hand, indicating a new lodge, which now stood behind that of Medicine Bear. Rose hadn't noticed it earlier. Perhaps it had been put up while she was being dressed and painted.

"Daughter," Luke translated. "There is your lodge. It is your home. Go and live in it."

"Daughter?"

"Those words should be said by your mother just as the horse would have been brought to your tepee by my father. Since we have no family, substitutes were found."

"All right," she said, oddly touched that Medicine Bear and his wife had filled the void. "Now what?"

"We go in."

"All of us?"

Luke laughed, and his hand tightened around hers, even as his gaze warmed her more than the sun. "Just you and I."

They walked toward the dwelling. She cast a glance over her shoulder. "Why are they watching?"

"We have to go inside. Only then are we completely married."

"Just by going in?"

"No," he said again.

"But it's daytime."

"So?"

The wind seemed to imitate the rustle of clothing being removed, the whisper of blankets against skin. She had never, ever, touched a man in anything but darkness. She was both shocked at the idea and desperately, hopelessly intrigued.

She had stroked Luke everywhere, but the promise of seeing him while she did so fascinated her. Until she realized that he would see her, too. She stopped several paces from the lodge. "I don't know if I can."

He tucked the hand he still held into his elbow, then patted it. "You don't have to."

"But the marriage isn't a marriage until we do."

"The marriage isn't a marriage anyway, Rose."

She ducked her head, horrified that tears pricked her eyes. He had done this to help her. Nothing more. She'd known that and still she had . . . what? Hoped? Dreamed? Yearned? Why should this marriage be any different from her last?

Luke tugged on her arm. Rose began to move again. She wanted to get away from the expectant gazes, too. He lifted the flap. She stepped inside. He followed and let go the flap. Cheers arose.

"To the Cheyenne," he said, "we're married."

"Not yet."

"No man and woman who consented to a marriage and then entered their lodge would come out without . . ." He spread his hands.

"No one will know."

"No," he agreed, his gaze on her face. The sun trickled through the smoke hole above them, spreading light and warmth all around.

Luke had married once for love. Rose wondered how that might be. Had his heart fluttered like a dragonfly beneath his skin? Had it been hard to breathe, hard to talk, hard to think? She rubbed the heel of her hand between her breasts as her heart fluttered faster than any dragonfly she'd ever seen.

"Why did you touch me that night?" he asked.

"I . . ." She dropped her arm. "What?"

"I thought you were her. But you knew it was me."

"Yes," she agreed. "You were . . ."

Exquisite. That glow of his skin in the moonlight.

Strong. The bulge of his muscles, the thrust of his hips.

Sweet. His soft lips, his gentle tongue.

She had wanted him, and he had wanted only someone else.

"Scared," she said.

"I'm always scared."

"You have a strange way of showing it. You run straight at death."

He met her gaze again. "I run *toward* death. There's a difference."

"You could stop."

"Running? Or being scared?"

"Yes."

His lips curved. "Maybe you could show me how."

She crossed the distance between them, stopping when she was so close the fringe of her dress brushed the fringe of his pants. "Are you scared now?" she asked.

His smile faded. "Terrified."

She touched him. What choice did she have?

CHAPTER 21

Rose set her palm on Luke's chest, rattling the hair pipe necklace made of bone that Medicine Bear had placed on him. He reached up to stop the sound, which reminded him too much of death—as if he needed reminding—and she caught his hand.

"Luke," she whispered, and he was lost.

Or maybe he was found. He had found her; she had found him. They had found each other and this place, these people. The only thing they hadn't yet found was what they'd come searching for—her daughter. A problem for another day.

She used her free hand to touch his face. He barely felt it. He was captured by all he saw in her eyes. The marriage wasn't real, but the lust he felt for her was, and his body still hummed with that need. He might have satisfied it once, but while he'd begun to remember, he didn't remember all of it and he didn't think he remembered any of it quite right.

She'd said he was the first man, the only man, who had brought her pleasure. He wanted to be that man again.

Her gaze searched his. For what, he didn't know. He set his hand on her hip, rubbed a thumb over her belly. "Are you all right?"

She blushed but she didn't look away. "Medicine Bear said I was well. That I wouldn't . . ." Her lips tightened.

"Hurt?"

"Conceive."

He lifted his hands, stepped back. He hadn't thought of that. *Fool!* How selfish could one man be?

She followed his retreat, reaching for him, catching him, pulling him close. And weakling that he was, he let her.

"How can you know?" he asked.

"He knows. I trust him." She laid her cheek to his chest. "And you."

She seemed like a child in those braids, that dress. And like a child she trusted him.

"We don't—" he began, and she lifted her head, peering into his face, waiting. "We don't have to."

She kissed him, and suddenly he had to.

Her mouth was warm and soft, open, welcoming, sweet, like a spring-fed pond. He dived in. Her hands at his waist tightened. He shoved his into her hair, but with the braids his big fingers stuck, pulled, and she flinched. "Sorry," he whispered against her mouth.

"Never," she answered, but she shuddered.

Was she afraid? Her eyes were closed, her lips open and wet. Her tongue darted out as if to taste, and those eyes opened just a bit. "Don't," she said.

"Sorry," he repeated.

"Stop," she continued. "Don't stop."

"I frightened you."

"You tickled me." She took one of the feathers from his headdress and rubbed it between her thumb and finger. "I could trace this along your arm and see how you like it."

His flesh prickled. His body hardened. He shoved the headdress off his head, tossed his necklace on top so neither would distract them. "Later." He lifted her into his arms. He'd forgotten how small she was. Her courage was so very large.

The lodge had been fashioned for this moment, the ground resplendent with thick grass mats, blankets, and furs. Water skins hung from the center pole, food awaited them in bowls near the fire pit. They could remain within for days if they wished. No one would dare disturb them.

He laid her on the blankets, began to follow her down, but she lifted a hand. He held his breath, but she didn't turn away. Instead she sat up and tugged the fur wrappings from the ends of her braids; then she tugged out the braids, as well as the ornaments fastened there. How could such a simple act make him yearn? Where Rose was concerned, what didn't make him yearn?

She combed her fingers through her hair. But the memory of the braids remained in the waves that traversed the length. She shook her head, and the tresses flared around her like rippling sunbeams. A strand settled against her neck. He wanted to brush it away with his finger. He wanted to lick where it had been with his tongue.

"Your turn," she said.

He lifted his hand to his grizzled head, frowned. "I already took off my headdress."

She lifted an eyebrow, then removed a silver bracelet and tossed it over her shoulder.

He wanted to tear off her dress—see, taste, touch everything that lay beneath. He'd dreamed of her body—both in the night and in the light. Now he knew that those dreams had been memories. But they were hazy, founded in darkness and dread, covered in mud, chilled by the rain. She was right to make this a game, lighten the mood, slow down his urge. He needed to be as gentle with her this time as he could not remember being the last. He removed an earring.

"Put it back," she said

The slim sliver of silver swayed as he held the item between two fingers. "Why?"

"I've been imagining you wearing nothing but those ever since I saw them."

He put it back and removed a moccasin instead. She did the same. He wanted to see more than her feet, though they were nice feet. He could think of only one way to move this a little faster. Luke pulled off his shirt.

Her breath caught. He glanced down, saw his scars— both old and new—and stood straighter. Scars were the medals of a man. He had earned them with blood and sweat and the last traces of his courage.

"Come here," she whispered.

He went to his knees, and she reached out, brushing her fingers along the ridges that marked him. "These are from the Sun Dance?"

"The Cheyenne call it the Medicine Lodge. We dance around the lodge pole until we are free." Only when a novitiate pulled away from the wooden skewer attached on one end through his skin and on the other to the pole could he say he had succeeded. "The Sioux call it the Sun Dance."

"Isn't it the same thing?"

He shrugged, and her fingers slid from his scars to his nipples. They went as hard as those scars. She stroked them in exactly the same way. "They marked you."

She stroked his scars again. Thank God. His nipples were singing. "I marked me. I swore a pledge. I fulfilled my promise."

"So you could belong?"

Had that been the reason? He couldn't recall. Would he have been able to remember if she weren't petting him, caressing every hard part and making it harder?

"Only a Cheyenne can take part in the ceremony of the Medicine Lodge." At her frown, he continued. "To do so I already belonged."

"What pledge did you swear? What promise did you fulfill?"

"The Medicine Lodge is a sacrifice. All religions make them."

"Not in blood and pain."

"You need to read the Bible again."

"Men," she muttered in the same way his wife had always said, *"Hetanesêstse!"*

Then she leaned forward and pressed her mouth to all the places her fingers had touched, and he forgot about his wife. Every time she lifted her lips, he had to clench his hands to keep from yanking her back, urging her closer, pressing her lower. When she placed her open mouth over his navel, then dipped her tongue inside, he nearly lost the fight. Glancing down and seeing her head inches from the bulge in his pants didn't help.

He set his palms on her shoulders. At her questioning glance he managed, "Your turn."

She straightened. They were both on their knees; her head came to the center of his chest. "Not yet," she said, and leaned forward, lips pursed to take his nipple between them.

His body shouted, *Yes!* His mouth said, "No."

She let out an exasperated huff, which puffed across his skin. He ground his teeth. She reached for her necklace.

He stayed her hand, tangling his fingers with hers. "I want to see you in just that."

She ducked her head, and her hair swirled over her face. He pushed it back out. "What's wrong?"

"I only have the dress."

"All right." He didn't understand.

"You have pants."

"Ah." Though it was her turn, not his, he got to his feet and removed them, along with his final moccasin. At this point, he'd do whatever he had to.

When he stood naked before her, she reached out to trace a long, jagged scar on his thigh. He ground his teeth again.

"Cheyenne?" she asked. He shook his head. "Pawnee?" Another shake. He couldn't seem to manage speech, or much thought, while she touched him. "Some other tribe?" Her forehead creased. "Who else rides in Kansas? Kansa? Comanche?"

"It was a *Savane*."

She frowned.

"It's what the Cheyenne call other tribes. Those who aren't from here." Her confusion made him continue, although who cared? Right now certainly not him. "The displaced tribes. From the East."

"Weren't they brought to the reservations in Indian Territory?"

"Just because they were brought doesn't mean they stayed." But he hadn't seen a *Savane* in years. He hadn't seen anything but soon-to-be ghosts.

"A *Savane* did this, too?" She touched his knee with the thumb of her free hand. He shook his head. "Yankee?" She ran her thumb from knee to—

He grabbed her wrist, held it away until his head cleared. "Moze," he said.

She glanced up. "Mosby?"

"No." If Mosby had cut him, he would be dead.

"You said Moze once. I thought—"

"When did I say Moze?"

"When we were in the sinkhole."

Other images of the pit tumbled through his mind. Where once any memories would have been of darkness and terror, being trapped, being imprisoned, waiting to die, now they seemed only to be of her.

He let go of her wrist to cup her face. "If you take off that dress, I'll tell you about Moze."

Her eyelashes swept down to hide her eyes. She reached for the hem, which pooled around her knees, and yanked it off in a rush—like pulling free a bandage stuck to a no-longer-bleeding wound. Best to do it fast or one might never do it at all.

She lifted her lashes. He fell back to his knees. *"Ánováóó'o,"* he breathed.

"The girl is *not* beautiful. The girl is plain on a good day."

"Then today is the best of days." He reached for her, and the tip of her small, but lovely and perfect, breast brushed against his palm. Her breath hissed in; so did his.

She glanced down and away. "Y-y-you said you'd tell me about Moze if I took off my dress."

He fingered the necklace that lay between her breasts, brushing her skin just a bit. "I didn't say I'd tell you now."

"But—"

Did she believe he could think, speak, breathe when she knelt so close wearing nothing but a necklace?

"Later," he managed, and drew her down on the buffalo robes. Her creamy skin glowed like starlight against them. He had to touch it to see if it was as soft as it appeared. He moved slowly. She was like a new fawn in the high grass—all big eyes and quivering flesh.

"Hush," he whispered, and cupped one breast, then ran his palm down her ribs and waist, to her hip. She wasn't as soft as she appeared.

She was softer.

Silver lines traced her flank—the remnants of her child. He ran his thumb over them, then leaned in to taste. Gooseflesh rose beneath his lips. He sat back, his gaze caught again on her breasts. Her nipples hardened; his mouth watered. His head lowered once more.

She tasted like heat and sun and life. He suckled, drawing from her a moan.

"Please," she whispered, and he lifted his head. But her eyes were closed, her head thrown back. His breath puffed across her damp skin and, if possible, her already tight nipples tightened further. The very idea of how hard and tight and ripe they would feel against his lips made him hard and tight and ripe, too.

He flicked both tips with his tongue, and her hands, flat against the furs, clenched. He became distracted by the matching silver lines on each breast. He traced them as well.

"Don't." Her eyes had opened; her hands were still clenched. "Don't look at me."

"I can't stop."

"Please," she whispered, and lifted her hands, laying them over her breasts. "I have marks."

He blinked, frowned, then pulled away her hands, laid them at her sides, patted them gently—a wordless request to keep them there.

"These?" He again traced the silver paths across her

breasts—with his finger this time—then her hips, found a few at her waist, a few more on her thighs, and did the same.

"Stop."

"No." He pressed his mouth to the longest line. "You've seen my scars. Do they make me ugly to you?"

A crease appeared between her eyebrows. "You're the most beautiful man I've ever seen."

Since she hadn't seen very many, perhaps. "Do the marks repulse you?"

"Nothing about you repulses me."

"Why would anything about you repulse me? These"—he traced the lines on first one breast and then another—"are the medals of woman. Forged in pain and blood and sweat." He took her hand and laid it over the scar above his heart. "Like mine."

Her eyes widened slightly, very blue in her now flushed face. "I never thought of them like that."

No doubt because she'd been told to think of them as something else. Rage nearly overwhelmed him once more. He pushed it back. Right now he should think only of her.

"There's a reason women bear the children, Rose. It's the only way mankind will survive. If men had to do it, there'd be one child to every family."

Her lips curved. She was no longer stiff and unyielding, but had relaxed bit by bit as he continued to stroke her. She traced his Medicine Lodge marks. "After this, childbirth would be simple."

"Childbirth is never simple."

He'd seen it, heard it, too, many times. How did any woman ever go through it twice? His mother had done so six times.

No way in hell.

"It's a miracle," he said. "You are a miracle."

"You don't have to flatter me, Luke. I'm already naked in your arms."

And he was discussing childbirth. Did he want her to run screaming? Or did he just want her to scream?

He took her lips and tasted joy. It had been so long, his mouth watered at the flavor. Her hands, which had clenched in the robes, now clenched on him—his biceps, his shoulders, his neck. She held him captive; he didn't mind. It wasn't as if he hadn't been a captive before. And while he'd thought that had been the beginning of his end, in truth it had been only the beginning.

Could today be a beginning, too?

He had failed at many things. He had failed at most everything. But one thing he had never failed at was this.

He kissed Rose until her hands loosened, caressing now instead of capturing. She ran her thumb along his ear, played with his earring. The brush of the cool silver along his neck made him shiver. Her smile taunted his lips, so his lips taunted her.

He nibbled her jaw, licked the hollow of her throat, teased her nipples, and suckled her stomach. She stroked his head. He tickled her thighs, waited for them to clamp shut, and caught his breath when instead they opened. Tempted, he leaned forward, and the heel of her hand pressed against his forehead.

"What are you doing?"

He stifled a groan. Would she thwart him at every turn? "I said we'd use the feathers later."

"You aren't using a feather."

"Close your eyes," he said. She narrowed them instead. "I won't hurt you."

"Of course not." She sounded offended that he would even say the words, and her eyes closed. He flicked the bud between her legs with his tongue.

"Still not feathers," she managed.

"Do you care?"

Her head thrashed against the furs. He took that for a no.

And he did it again.

CHAPTER 22

Rose held very still. Terrified Luke would stop, terrified he wouldn't. Mortified that she didn't want him to. What he was doing to her was so far beyond the realm of her experience she didn't know what to do except—

She cried out as her body tightened. Her legs came together. He was still between them, and she nearly boxed his ears. He set his palms on her thighs, his big, hard hands curling around them, making her feel so small. With him she didn't mind. He was not the kind of man to use his strength against her. He would never look down on her in thought or deed. He believed she was beautiful because to Luke everything beautiful was within.

His thumbs traced the quivering muscles of her legs, even as his tongue continued to stroke between them. Her body tightened more; she hadn't thought it could. A storm gathered on the horizon, whirling, bubbling; thunder lay beneath. He slid upward and came into her with a single, deep thrust that filled her, completed her, intrigued her. He groaned, the sound tingling against her chest and mouth, then rolling over her skin like that thunder. She nipped his lip, arched her hips, reached for his, and pulled him back in. They repeated the thrust and tug, their own secret give-and-take, until he stilled, lifted his head. Her eyes opened, and she found herself captured by the expression in his.

"Rose?" he whispered.

"Yes," she answered, and touched his face. The beat of his heart fluttered against her palm. His breath caught; his back arched, pressing him more fully within. The rhythm in his blood called to her. Her breath caught, too; her back arched. Surprise, wonder, and heat filled his eyes as, together, they came apart. She could have sworn she heard ice cracking, glass shattering, thunder booming. Or maybe it was just her heart.

When the tremors faded, he pressed his cheek to hers. One of them was damp. She didn't know which. She didn't care. Beneath the shroud of night, there had been no need for words. But in the sun she felt an uncommon urge to speak. "I've never—" she began.

He lifted his head, cocked an eyebrow. "You did today."

Her cheeks warmed. He kissed her and everything else warmed, too. "Don't be embarrassed. It's a gift."

"Thank you," she said, and he laughed.

"A gift for me. Thank *you*."

"I . . . what?"

He rolled to the side, but he lay next to her, hip to hip, and he tangled their fingers together, rubbing his thumb along hers. "A woman's pleasure is a man's gift."

"Is that what the Cheyenne say?"

"It's what men should say. Any fool can take his own satisfaction. For most, a hand is good enough." He lifted his, curved the fingers as if he were holding—

"Oh!" Her face heated again as he jerked his wrist back and forth.

"To give a woman pleasure, to make her gasp and moan, takes time and talent."

"I wasn't going to say I'd never . . ." She waved her free hand between them. "I was going to say I've never been naked in the daylight." Even when she'd bathed, she'd always worn her shift.

"Why?"

"Naked is for the dark."

"Only if you let it be."

The sun tumbled through the smoke hole, warm and gold and inviting. She stretched her arms straight up, enjoying the brush of the fur at her back, the heat of his leg at her side, the glow of the daylight on her face.

"God, Rose!" Her eyes jerked to his. He sat up, staring at her in wonder. "If you could see yourself, lying in the sun . . . worshipping it, or maybe . . . maybe it's worshipping you . . . you'd know that naked should never, *ever* be kept in the dark." She started to sit up, too, and he set his hand on her shoulder. "Please don't move."

She didn't want to. She patted the fur at her side. "Lie with me."

Once the dual meaning of those words would have made her blush, not that she would ever have said them to anyone. But she could say anything to him.

Together they contemplated the smoke hole, watching spring white clouds trace across the brilliant blue sky. She felt more at peace than she ever had in her life. How could that be? Her child was still missing, perhaps dead, perhaps—

Desperately she closed off those thoughts, reaching again for that peace, searching for some way, any way, to bring it back.

"You were going to tell me about Moze," she said.

"What do you know so far?"

"He isn't Mosby."

"No one is. But Moze . . ."

She waited to hear what Moze was, *who* he was, but Luke's voice trailed off and when she glanced at him, he was scowling. "Is he dead?" she asked.

"I don't know."

He'd said he didn't know if his sister was dead, either, which made her wonder . . . "Is Moze your sister's husband?"

"No." His frown deepened. "I don't think so. Maybe."

"Which is it?"

"Moze tried to kiss Annabeth once when we were kids. She broke his nose."

Rose liked his sister more and more with every tale she heard.

"Then probably not married," she allowed. That he didn't know what had happened to his family, his friend, and didn't seem to care disturbed her. How could he not wonder? Why hadn't he found out? Were there worse terrors in his past than prison, the pit, the Cheyenne, the wind and the ghosts, and the hills that she hadn't yet discovered?

"Moze lived on the next farm," Luke continued. "He came to live with us after his mother died. My brothers were . . . brothers. They picked on me. Once Moze was there, we were two. I wasn't so alone."

"Not alone is good." She took his hand. He seemed to need it. "Then what happened?"

"The goddamn war."

A very accurate description.

"I was good on a horse, so I rode with Mosby."

"You didn't learn your horsemanship from the Cheyenne?"

"Some, but I wouldn't have survived long with them in the first place if I wasn't already hell on a horse."

Hell on a horse, another very accurate description.

Of the Cheyenne.

"What was Moze good at?"

"Sneaky bastard," Luke muttered, though the words sounded admiring more than annoyed. "With Moze, you never knew he was coming until he was right there. Other times you'd see him, then blink, and he'd be gone. You asked how I got this?" His hand brushed the scar on his knee. "One night I crept out of the house. I was going to meet a . . ." He slid a glance her way.

She lifted an eyebrow. "Woman?"

"I was thirteen."

"Girl." Rose couldn't be jealous of that, yet somehow she was. She wanted him to be hers alone from the beginning. But he couldn't be, any more than she could be his.

Then or now.

"I should have known Moze would hear me. He heard everything. I snuck out, crept across the yard, around the barn, was climbing a fence, and suddenly he said, 'Where you goin'?' from right behind me. I fell. There was a nail that hadn't been pounded all the way in and . . ." He made a sharp, upward gesture and she flinched. "I never did meet that girl."

"Sorry," she said, and she was sorry for his pain. But she was also just a bit glad that he'd never met that girl. "If hell on a horse led to Mosby," she continued, "sneaky and quiet led to . . . ?" She waited, but Luke merely shrugged once more. "North of the Mason-Dixon, folks like that worked for Pinkerton. Was he a spy?"

Luke let out a long breath; she caught herself staring at the incredible flatness of his belly, remembering what it had felt like beneath her fingers, and had to close her eyes just an instant so she would stop.

"He brought me word of every one of my brothers' deaths, my parents' as well. That he did, that he could, that he knew was suspicious."

"You never asked?"

"He wouldn't tell. He was stubborn to the point of foolish. Loyal, too."

Sounded like a spy to her. Not that she knew any.

"I hope he survived the war," Luke said.

"A man like that? I'm sure he did."

"I doubt I'll ever know."

"You could try to find him."

"That would be a miracle."

"Then maybe he'll find you."

Time passed. More food and fresh water sat just inside the entrance, appearing while they slept, no matter when that might be.

They slept whenever they tired—in the light and the dark. They didn't sleep in the light or the dark as well. They talked and laughed, a few times Rose cried—a few times Luke wanted to. He had never shared so much of himself, so much of his past with anyone. He hadn't thought he could. But with Rose he wanted to. She had ghosts of her own that spoke to her, too. Perhaps not on the wind, but in the night. When she thrashed and murmured and called her daughter's name, he held her and she quieted.

Her words about Moze made him wonder. If his friend had known the fate of Luke's brothers during the war, wouldn't he have discovered Luke's fate as well? At the least he had to know that Luke had gone west. When Luke didn't return as he was supposed to, Moze would have tried to find him. That he hadn't yet was troubling. The man had always had a knack for showing up out of nowhere when he was least expected.

Luke remembered the times in the past few weeks when he'd felt as if they were being followed, being watched. He'd thought it was his imagination, or insanity, but maybe it had been Moze.

And that thought was as crazy as Luke was. Moze wouldn't have followed; he'd have found. If there'd been anyone on their tail, the Dog Men would have known. Just look what they'd done to the Pawnee scouts. Did that mean Moze was dead?

Rose stirred and he pressed his lips to her hair, pulled her closer, murmured nonsense until she quieted. What would she do—what would he do—when they left the tepee and returned to the world? Once Rose found Lily—*if* she found Lily—she would . . .

Luke had no more idea of what she would do than what he would do. He'd thought coming back to the Cheyenne would be his end, and he'd wanted that. Badly. Instead coming here felt more like a beginning, and death no longer appealed. Not when there was a possibility of life.

With her.

Luke laid his cheek atop Rose's golden, tousled head. The marriage wasn't real. Even if she wasn't already married—though he considered Jakob Varner's desertion a statement of divorce, no one else would—a Cheyenne ceremony would not be recognized in the white world. Considering all that Rose had seen, all that she'd heard about him, he wouldn't blame her for taking any way out that she had. Certainly she enjoyed his body, how he made her feel, but why would she want to be tied to him forever?

He was the White Ghost—a prophet to the Cheyenne first because he'd lied and then because he'd gone insane. Though he hadn't heard ghosts lately, he never knew when he might hear them again. He hadn't enjoyed gainful employment since before he'd gone to prison.

Prison. He gave a derisive snort. Hell, what woman *wouldn't* want to be his wife?

Rose's fingers on his chest moved, scraping, stroking, arousing. He waited for her to wake, to throw her leg across his, to ride him as the sun tumbled down her skin like a waterfall. He would trace the beams with his fingertips, then his tongue. They would begin this day as they had the last, as he wished they could begin every one. Instead she quieted, going lax, her breath puffing against him to the beat of their hearts.

One thing at a time, he thought as he drifted toward sleep, too. They still had to find Lily. Soon they would leave the tepee, and he would question everyone about the child. He would make them answer. Someone had to know something, and he wouldn't stop until he knew it, too.

If necessary he would question Many Horses and the rest of the Dog Men upon their return. He hoped he'd have time. Within moments of his arrival, the Dog Man would hear of Luke's marriage. As a crazy man could not take part in such a ceremony, Many Horses' next act would be to bring Luke another lance. And this time Luke would have to accept it. He didn't want to kill his old friend, and lately he wanted his old friend to kill him even less. Best to find Lily and get gone before he had to decide.

Thoughts of Many Horses, lances, challenges, death were probably not the best course for someone like him while in that state of half sleep. The next thing he knew, someone mumbled a jumble of Cheyenne and English, and as he opened his eyes he realized that someone was him.

He was pressed to the back wall of the tepee. Sweating. Shaking. Both on fire and ice cold. In his hand he held a knife so tightly his fingers ached; his knuckles were white.

"Shh. I won't hurt you."

He lifted his gaze from the blade to Rose, who knelt just out of swiping range. His eyes flicked to the knife— no blood—to her—not a scratch beyond the one on her forehead.

He opened his fingers. The hilt stuck to his palm. He had to shake his hand to get it to fall. The blade stuck into the ground with a soft *thunk*. He began to shake harder at the thought that he might have stuck it into her.

"What did I do?" he whispered.

"You had a dream. It happens to everyone."

"Not like it happens to me."

"You're fine."

Luke flicked her another glance. "I don't care about me."

"I'm fine, too."

"What did I say?" He couldn't even remember what he'd been dreaming.

"Nothing I haven't heard before." At his suspicious expression she threw up her hands. As she was naked, the gesture made her breasts jiggle. She didn't notice, or care. Right now neither did he. "War, army, Mosby, prison, Indian fighter, Dog Man, prophet, wife, child, crazy, White Ghost. Anything else?"

She was right. She had heard it all.

"Why are you still here?"

"Where would I go?"

"Away from me. I sound dangerous."

"You are dangerous, which is why I'm still here." She let out an exasperated huff, grabbed his hand, and tugged him back to the furs, where she made him sit and she did, too. "I'd be dead if it weren't for you, Luke." She brushed his cheek with her fingers. "If it weren't for you, I'd want to be."

He frowned. What did that mean?

"Come here." She pulled him into her arms. "Last time you dreamed, I sang to you like I used to sing to Lily."

"I *am* worse than a child," he muttered.

"Hush," she said, just the way his mother used to, and then she sang the song his mother had sung, too. "Hush a bye, don't you cry."

Had he cried? He thought so.

"Go to sleep, my baby."

"I remember," he said. The song, the words, the feeling he had when his mother, and now Rose, sang to him and made everything else—the night, the day, the pain, the fear, and the memories—fade.

Except, instead of fading, he thought of the sinkhole, heard the patter of the rain, the rumble of thunder; he saw the flare of the lightning, caught the scent of the mud. Then the warmth of a woman, her scent, surrounded him; that soft, gentle voice calmed him.

"When you wake, you shall have all the pretty horses." She hummed a bit as if she couldn't remember what came next, then ended with "Blacks and bays, dapples and grays. All the pretty horses."

Silence descended. He felt almost tranquil. She seemed to be as well. When she'd first drawn him into her arms, despite her claims that she was fine, she'd been anything but. Stiff, tense, she'd held him as if she'd never held anyone before and didn't want to. But she'd done it, because that was what Rose did. Whatever she had to, no matter how scared she was, no matter how much it might hurt.

He'd had a knife in his hand—God alone knew why—yet she hadn't run. Not Rose. She'd approached him, spoken softly, brought him back from wherever he'd gone. Then she'd taken him against her and sung to him like a child.

Beneath his cheek, her heart leaped even as her breath caught and her hands went from gentle to tight. He lifted his head slowly, afraid she was having a memory lapse of her own, returned to the past, frozen as she'd been with the Pawnee. But while her face was as white as his namesake, she wasn't looking at him but over his shoulder toward the entrance.

He sat up and her arms fell limply to her sides. He turned, just as a tiny body shot past. He reached out to grab it, but his fingers closed on nothing.

"Ayasha?" he whispered, and his voice, his hands, his everything shook. The world shimmered—now, then, real, imagined, dead, alive.

He blinked several times and saw the truth. Though the girl's clothes were Cheyenne—deerskin dress, leggings, moccasins—her skin was white and her hair had gone silver from the kiss of the sun.

Luke snatched a blanket and wrapped it around his hips as he got to his feet. The child hung tightly to Rose's neck, chattering in Cheyenne, a flow of words all jumbled together. But there was one Luke could make out because she said it over and over—first loudly in a shout of joy, then more softly as she released Rose to pat at her cheeks with chubby, filthy hands.

"Nahko'eehe!"

"What is she saying?" Rose whispered. The eyes she lifted to Luke's brimmed with tears.

"My mother."

CHAPTER 23

Joy flooded Rose at the sight of her daughter—alive and well—but she couldn't understand a word the child said until Luke translated.

My mother.

Lily no longer smelled the way that Rose remembered— like sunshine and spring grass. Instead she caught the distinct odor of horse.

The hands that patted her cheeks were rough and hard, not the sweet, soft baby palms of memory. Lily's face was pale, but not the way it had been when Rose had made certain her child always wore a bonnet, and her hair, which had once been the same summer-sun shade as Rose's own, now shone moon-silver instead. The ends of her braids were wrapped in fur, a long silver ornament hung from the crown of her head, and tiny silver discs hung from her ears. Who had dared to put holes in her baby?

"Where have you been?" Rose asked.

Lily stopped patting, her tiny hands still held on either side of Rose's face as her head tilted and her lips pursed. She said several words in Cheyenne, her frown deepening when Rose did not respond.

"She says she has been with her father."

Rose started so badly Lily patted her again. "That's not possible. Wait." Luke had translated Lily's answer to a query that had been in English. "She understood my question?"

"She answered it."

"Not in the language I asked it."

"She may remember some English, just not enough to speak it." He held up a hand. "I understood Cheyenne long before I could converse."

"She spoke English at one time."

"She was two. She didn't speak much."

Her child had been quite precocious. She'd spoken plenty. She spoke plenty now. Too bad it all sounded like gibberish.

"She hasn't been in camp," Rose said. "One of us would have seen her." Rose lifted a strand of shimmering silver hair and rubbed it between her fingers. "She would have shone like a candle in the night."

Luke didn't answer. Instead he stood, stiff and ready, his gaze on the tepee entrance, as if waiting for an imminent attack. She hadn't seen him that nervous since Many Horses had—

"Hell," she muttered as everything fell into place.

Voices rose outside the tepee. Shadows flitted on the other side of the skin wall. Luke snatched a blanket from their bed and draped it over Rose's shoulders an instant before the flap whipped upward and Many Horses stepped in. His gaze went to Lily, now sitting in Rose's lap, playing with the ends of her hair just as she always used to. His habitual scowl deepened.

"Neho'eehe," Lily said.

"My father," Luke murmured. Rose had already deduced that for herself.

"Nahko'eehe." Lily patted Rose's cheek again.

Many Horses growled. Rose put her arms around the child. She did not want Lily to be afraid. But her daughter did not cringe beneath the man's fury. She was no doubt accustomed to it. That she was not fearful of him showed she had not been the brunt of his anger. The knowledge soothed Rose just a little.

"I knew you would bring pain and suffering." Many Horses glared at Luke. "It is what you do."

"The Dog Men brought it first," Luke said. "Lily is Rose's daughter."

"The white man sent my daughter to *He'amo'ome*. It is only right that the white man give me another."

"The Dog Men took her," Rose said. "There was no giving involved. Now I'm taking her back."

"Rose—" Luke began.

"He can't deny she's mine."

The Dog Man's gaze flicked between Rose and Lily. Before his expression went stony, she saw a hint of pain.

"Ve'ho'e," Many Horses spat. "I found you chained in a soldier's wagon. I released you. But all along it was a trap for me. Like the spider, you spun your web and caught me in it."

"You took Rose on your horse so that I would follow, and you could kill me. Who set the trap and who was caught?"

"Just because Éše'he Ôhvó'komaestse looks like your woman, it does not make her the child of your woman."

"Well, she certainly doesn't look like you," Rose retorted.

"She sounds like me."

"What does Éše'he Ôhvó'komaestse mean?"

Many Horses pursed his lips and did not answer.

"White Moon," Luke said.

"Her name is Lily." Lily giggled and patted Rose's face again, then chattered on in Cheyenne.

"Not anymore," Many Horses muttered.

"Why are you here?" Luke asked.

"I returned and learned you had married."

"Why would you care?" Rose asked.

"A married man cannot be crazy," Luke said.

It took Rose a second to make the connection. "He came to kill you." She stiffened. "And brought Lily along to watch?"

"She followed me. When we came near, she heard—" Many Horses broke off.

"She heard the song I sang to her when she was a baby," Rose said. "She remembered and ran to me."

"Memory doesn't make you her mother."

"I don't need to be *made* her mother; I am her mother. She *called* me *my mother*."

"In Cheyenne."

"That doesn't matter."

He went to the entrance and shouted, *"Nâhtse'eme!"* Moments later the woman who had spat in Luke's face upon their arrival ducked inside.

"Nahko'eehe!" Lily shouted.

Many Horses lifted an eyebrow; the gaze he turned on Rose was triumphant.

"You can't just ride around stealing children," Rose snapped.

"I didn't."

"I'm sure you have at one time or another."

He shrugged. "She was given to me as a gift."

"She's a child, not a shiny new toy."

Many Horses murmured to his wife. After scowling in Rose's direction, the woman left.

"I suppose I should be thankful you didn't kill her," Rose muttered.

Luke stood to the side but remained close enough to step in if she goaded the Dog Man to violence. From the way the man's hands clenched, she was close.

"I do not kill children. I leave that to your army."

Even if Many Horses hadn't killed children—and she didn't believe that—the Dog Men had. In war, innocents died, and the battle between the whites and the Cheyenne was definitely war.

"I'm sorry about your daughter," Rose said. "But stealing mine won't bring her back." And it only set Lily in the path of danger. Who was to say Custer, or any other out-for-glory officer, wouldn't order a repeat of the Washita? It wasn't as if he'd been reprimanded for it. He'd probably been promoted.

"Éše'he Ôhvó'komaestse brought my wife back."

At the sound of her Cheyenne name, a smile wreathed Lily's face. Rose gathered her daughter closer, but Lily pushed away, tumbling off her lap and landing on her feet. Hurrying across the tepee, she threw her arms around Many Horses' knees, then stared up at him in adoration. He set a large, dark hand on her small, pale head and murmured, "Éše'he Ôhvó'komaestse."

"Her name is Lily," Rose repeated.

This time the child looked over her shoulder and grinned at Rose, who thought her heart might break. All she'd wanted, all she'd thought of, worked toward, lived for was finding her daughter. Though she'd been told that captives often came back changed, she'd thought that would mean stoic silence, perhaps nightmares. It had never occurred to her that when she found Lily she might be more Cheyenne than white.

"She doesn't remember her life before," Many Horses said.

"I think she does."

"What are you going to do? Dress her in white man's clothes, drag her to a town, shove her in a white man's school? She no longer understands the white man's words."

"Convenient," Rose murmured. "You know them. You could have spoken them with her."

"How do you think she learned Cheyenne so quickly?"

"How did she forget English so fast?"

"She wants to be like the other children."

"She'll want to be like the white children, too," Rose said, but she wasn't so sure.

A white child who'd lived with the Indians, who spoke Cheyenne, was not going to be welcomed in a white school. She wasn't going to be welcomed anywhere unless Rose could help her remember who she'd been. Could she? How would she if Lily couldn't understand her?

She glanced at Luke. He could help her. *Would* he help her? To do so he would have to return to the white world where he was not only scorned but wanted. Although if Éše'he Ôhvó'komaestse, daughter of a Dog

Man, could again become Lily Varner, couldn't Ve'ho'e Mestaa'e become Luke Phelan?

Only if he wanted to.

Medicine Bear lifted the flap. "The entire village is waiting outside, afraid there will be a fight."

"Tell them not to worry," Luke said. "We won't fight."

"They are not worried that you will fight," the old man said. "They are worried they will be unable to see it if you continue to stand in here." When no one moved or spoke, he stepped inside and let the flap fall closed.

Lily let go of Many Horses' legs and scurried back to Rose. The old man took one look at the two of them together and sighed. The gaze he turned on Luke was heavy with disappointment. "You did not return for our people."

Luke didn't answer.

"The woman probably gave him money to bring her to us." Many Horses curled his lip.

Rose *had* offered Luke anything he wanted, though they'd never settled on what that might be. She would have given him money if she'd had any to give.

"There is more between them than money," Medicine Bear said. "There was a child."

Rose stifled a wince. The child had been made with the memory of a dead woman and not her. She felt both horrible about its loss and badly about its existing at all.

"What happened between them on the way to us is not our concern," Many Horses said. "What happens as she leaves is."

"I came here to get my child back. I'm not leaving without her," Rose said.

"And Ve'ho'e Mestaa'e?" Medicine Bear asked.

"He spun a web," Many Horses said. "He placed himself where he knew I would find him. He pretended to be crazy so I would not kill him."

"He doesn't pretend," Rose insisted. "The spirits still walk and talk in his dreams."

"Rose, I don't need—"

"Quiet," she snapped, and Medicine Bear choked, then began to cough.

He coughed for a good long while, holding up his hand to keep everyone else from speaking. When he stopped, he fixed each of them with a warning glance. "The men will step from the tepee to speak."

"She's my . . ." Rose began, but they were already outside.

Luke followed Medicine Bear and Many Horses into the sun. He'd lost track of time in the tepee, sleeping when tired, eating when hungry, loving whenever they wanted to. He might have been inside with Rose for two days, maybe three. Perhaps four?

For all he knew that sun could be setting and not rising, or vice versa. Especially since he'd woken naked in a corner talking to ghosts and then listened to Rose sing to him like his dead mother.

He could not show weakness; he had to be strong. Just because they'd found Lily didn't mean they could leave with Lily. To the Cheyenne, possession meant everything.

A single sweep of Medicine Bear's arm and the crowd dispersed. Many Horses' wife stood in front of their tepee, unpacking their horses. But her gaze—both frightened and furious—kept flicking to them.

"Lily belongs to Rose," Luke said.

Medicine Bear set a gnarled finger to his lips and then beckoned. They followed him to the river where nothing could hear them but the floating chunks of ice atop the water. In contrast to the brilliant spring grass, the brisk wind carried the remnants of a winter chill.

"That child was stolen," Medicine Bear said.

"You merely had to glance at Éše'he Ôhvó'komaestse to know she was stolen from someone," Many Horses muttered. "That was never a secret."

"You deny she belongs to the wife of Ve'ho'e Mestaa'e?"

"The wife of Ve'ho'e Mestaa'e is dead."

"A man may have more than one wife," Medicine Bear said. "I myself have had many."

"He does not deserve a new wife when he has not paid for the last one."

"I will pay for them both," Luke said.

Interest lightened Many Horses' gaze. "How?"

"You have always wanted my life."

"Not always," Many Horses admitted. "Once I would have given mine for yours."

Luke bowed his head. "And I would have done the same."

"Those days are as dead as Kiwidinok and all the others."

Luke wasn't certain if those days were dead for him. Would he still give his life for Many Horses? Maybe. But he would definitely give it for Rose.

"Life for life." Luke repeated the first words Many Horses had said to him. "I will stay if you let them go."

Many Horses inclined his head. "The circle is complete."

Luke had come to the Cheyenne in the same way he would leave them—a slave, a prisoner, a sacrifice. It was fitting.

"Your wife will not accept this, Haestôhe'hame," Medicine Bear said. "The child has become hers."

"She has others."

Luke and the old fellow exchanged glances. Neither one of them would want to be Many Horses once his wife discovered that he had given Lily away, even if he'd given her back to her first mother. But the Dog Man's thirst for vengeance still overshadowed his sense.

"Your wife will not accept this, either, Ve'ho'e Mestaa'e," Medicine Bear murmured.

"She came here for her daughter."

"She came here with you."

"She will have to leave without me," he said, though he knew the old man was right. Rose wouldn't like it. He was going to have to think of a way to make her go before she understood why she was being allowed to. "I need some time."

Many Horses' lip curled. "So you can flee?"

"If I meant to flee, I never would have come."

"You shouldn't have."

"He has wanted to die since they did," Medicine Bear said. "He came back so that you could have your vengeance, and he could have what he believes he deserves." The old man held up his hand. "You will give him the time he needs to prepare." Medicine Bear turned and walked away.

"If you disappear . . ." Many Horses began, low enough so the holy man could not hear.

"You'll find me," Luke finished in a voice as tired as his soul.

"No," he corrected. "I will find her."

Though Rose wanted to listen to what the men were discussing, she was afraid that if she went outside, if *they* did, Lily would run to the woman she had also called *my mother* and Rose would never get her back. So she remained in the tepee.

Lily chattered in Cheyenne, not seeming to notice or care that Rose did not respond. To keep her occupied Rose began to chant "patty-cake," which had once been Lily's favorite game. Rose made the motions in the air until, after staring at Rose for several wide-eyed seconds, her daughter began to play, too.

She didn't want to let Lily out of her sight ever again. Not that the child had been out of her sight when she was stolen. Rose had seen the whole damn thing. She'd continued to see it every night, every day, ever since.

The flap lifted. Luke stepped in, a bundle of what was obviously white women's clothing in his hands. "For you and Lily."

Rose let out a rush of breath. If they were both being given white clothing, they were both being allowed to leave.

The blanket Luke had left in was gone, replaced by buckskin trousers and shirt. Without his earrings, armband, and necklace he appeared to be any white man on the plains. He'd found a pair of boots—cavalry boots from their appearance, knee high and black. Perhaps they were even his. They seemed to fit well enough.

"Where were you?" she asked. "I was worried."

His smile only emphasized the return of the darkness to his eyes. "Where did you think I'd go?"

"Into a grave if Many Horses has his way."

Luke glanced upward and Rose did, too. She glimpsed both the sky and a few birds through the smoke hole. She lowered her gaze as he did.

"He won't hurt me," Luke said.

"Are you—" She nearly said *crazy* and stopped herself. From the twitch of his lips he heard the word anyway. "All right?" she finished.

"We came to an understanding." He held up the bundle, then sat and placed it next to her.

Rose had continued to play patty-cake, though she'd stopped saying the words. She realized Lily was murmuring in Cheyenne, to the rhythm of their hands. "Is she . . . ?"

He nodded. "Patty-cake, patty-cake in Cheyenne. Or as close as she can get with the words they have." His face softened, and he ran a hand over Lily's hair.

The child stopped playing the game long enough to pat Luke's knee as if to comfort him. She said something to him that was obviously not *patty-cake*. He covered her tiny hand with his larger one. "She thanks the husband of her mother for bringing you to her."

"About that." Rose swallowed. "You don't have to worry that I'll hold you to the marriage once we're back in a town."

"Rose—" he began.

"I'm still married to him, so I can't be married to you." Just saying those words made her want to sob, but she wouldn't. Not here. Not now. Not in front of him.

Luke had married her only to fulfill his promise, and while that made him heroic, it didn't make him a husband. It didn't mean he loved her. He only loved the dead.

Luke stood and walked out of the tepee. Rose couldn't blame him. She hadn't meant to lie. But she hadn't wanted to tell the truth. She hadn't wanted to do a lot of things, but she had. She should have told him about her past long before now.

Luke stepped back inside holding a stick.

"I'd prefer if you didn't beat me in front of Lily."

He cast her a disgusted glance and handed her the wood. She had to stop playing patty-cake to take it. Lily kept playing with the air.

"Throw that to the other side of the tepee," he ordered.

"Why?"

"It's a Cheyenne divorce."

"You don't have to divorce me. We were never married."

"I'm not divorcing you. You're divorcing him."

"By throwing a stick?" Sounded too good to be true.

"Say, 'This stick is my husband. I throw him away.'"

"This stick is my husband." She considered Luke and then added, "Jakob Varner. I throw him away." She threw the stick so hard it bounced off the skin wall and nearly hit her in the face.

Lily jumped to her feet, laughing, took the stick, and started throwing it against the wall, picking it up, and throwing it again.

"I enjoyed that," Rose said.

"He's a bastard."

"He is," she agreed.

"When you get back you should divorce him again."

Hope lifted her heart. Might he want to marry her for real? Then she heard his words: *When* you *get back . . .* not *when* we *get back.*

"You're not coming."

"I can't."

Panic made her speak too fast, all her desperate words

tumbling from her mouth. "The White Ghost is wanted, not Luke Phelan."

"They're the same."

"Are they? When you did the things that you're wanted for, you weren't yourself. You didn't know—" Her voice broke. He'd done many things when he wasn't himself, when he didn't know. What he'd done had led to this.

Their marriage wasn't about love or even the promise of a future. It was merely the chance to fulfill a vow. She glanced at Lily. And now it was done.

"The Cheyenne are fighting for their way of life," he said. "They need me. I can help."

"Many Horses wants to kill you."

"He wants a lot of things that he can't have." Luke's eyes brushed over Lily and came back to Rose. "You said you'd do anything for her."

"I will."

"Then go. Before they change their minds."

He was right. "When?"

"I'll come back after dark with a horse and supplies. I'll lead you out of camp."

"That doesn't sound like I'm being let go. That sounds like I'm escaping."

"There's no escaping a Cheyenne camp."

"Then what—"

"The mother." He tried to shove his fingers through hair that still wasn't long enough. "She isn't going to want to let her child go any more than you would."

"Lily isn't her child."

"Tell that to her."

Rose remembered the fury in the eyes of the woman Lily had called *nahko'eehe*, my mother. That woman would fight for the child she'd named White Moon. And while Rose would fight, too, she wouldn't risk losing.

Chapter 24

Entertaining a three-year-old, even if it was Rose's own beloved and recently returned three-year-old, inside for an entire day was not for the faint of heart. Attempting to stuff a Cheyenne child into a dress and shoes wasn't, either.

Rose had redressed Lily three times. She'd cajole the girl into the garment and make a game of buttoning the bodice, then turn away for an instant only to discover the dress on the floor again. When Luke at last ducked into the tepee, his hands full of hats, Rose's patience was sorely frayed.

Lily immediately reached for the cavalry hat. She set it on her head, giggling when the brim slid past her nose. She began to play with it, lifting, lowering, tilting, then tossing the thing into the air.

"Are you ready?" he asked, his gaze on Lily's bare feet.

"Yes."

Luke picked up the child's shoes, lifting an eyebrow.

"Be thankful she left the dress on this time."

Lily scratched her stomach and yanked on the collar of the garment, but at least she didn't start unbuttoning again.

"She's not used to it." Luke held out a yellow bonnet to her child.

Had he remembered that yellow was the color Lily liked most? Did Lily? The idea that he had remembered, that he had searched through a pile of clothing for that one brightly shaded item for her daughter, made Rose's throat tighten.

Lily snatched the hat from Luke's fingers, but she didn't put it on.

"She screamed when I tried to remove her earrings and the ornaments in her hair," Rose said. So the items remained exactly where they'd been.

"The bonnet will cover them."

Together they watched Lily thread the strings of the poke bonnet through her braid like another ornament. She frowned as the rest of the material lay limply against her chest, then tugged the hat free and tossed it on the ground.

"I have a feeling the bonnet is going to go the way of the shoes," Rose murmured.

Luke spoke to the child in Cheyenne. Lily's lower lip jutted out, and she stomped on the bonnet as she shook her head. Her earrings clattered and the silver hair plate attached to her braid jingled. She looked adorable, though Rose doubted anyone but her would think so.

"I said she needed to wear a hat in the sun and shoes on a horse." Luke's lips quirked. "She disagreed."

Lily chattered for a few seconds; Luke answered before translating for Rose. "She asked where she was going. I said she would live with her white mother again for a time." Lily tossed the cavalry hat again. "She didn't seem to mind."

Rose hadn't even considered what she would tell her daughter about leaving. She'd been too intent *on* leaving.

"She also asked about her white father. I said he was gone."

"Good enough." Rose would have to decide if she wanted to let Jakob know that she'd found their daughter. "Why did you tell her she would live with me for a time?"

"If I said forever, I don't think she'd like it. The less noise when leaving, the better."

"Won't she want to say good-bye to her . . ." Rose wasn't sure what to call the *other mother*.

"Let's go before she thinks of it."

"Lily." The child lifted her gaze. Rose opened her arms; Lily dropped the blue hat and came into them. Rose lifted her daughter onto her hip. Certainly she could walk, but Rose didn't want to give her the opportunity to run.

Luke retrieved the bonnet, brushed off the tiny, dusty footprint, then bent to snatch up the cavalry hat. He set the latter on Rose's head and stuffed the former into one of the shoes.

Outside, all was quiet and very dark. Clouds danced over the moon; a late spring chill shrouded the air. Their cotton dresses were more suited for summer, but they would have to make do until Rose could buy them something else. Nevertheless, they couldn't ride all night like this. She stepped back toward the tepee, and Luke grasped her arm.

"Blankets," she said.

"On the horse. Along with food and water." He led her out of camp, Lily in her arms.

Rose's gaze went to the trees on the bluff, then to the swaying grass all around. "Will they let us go?"

"When Medicine Bear speaks, everyone listens."

She hoped so. Not just for herself and Lily's sake, but Luke's. It would be a lot harder to leave, nearly impossible—though she would; she had to—if she didn't know that Medicine Bear would be here with him.

A solitary horse waited on the prairie, the bridle, saddle, and packs attesting to its army origin.

"Will they think I stole it?" Rose ran her hand over the U.S. Army brands on both the shoulder and the thigh.

"Not if you have a good explanation." Luke rubbed the animal's nose.

"Care to give me one?"

"Less is better. Half-truths are more believable than absolute untruths."

Rose considered for a moment. "My farm was attacked. We found the horse loose on the prairie."

"Probably good enough to keep a lone woman with a child from being hanged for a horse thief."

He took Lily from her, swinging the child onto the horse. Lily murmured to the animal as she combed her fingers through its mane.

"Head east," Luke continued. "There's a train station in the next town. I'm not sure of its name, but you should be there by morning. From there, the train goes through Rogue." Her eyes widened. "I doubt anyone who might get on will recognize you now that you're with a child and not me."

"I doubt they'd recognize you, either." She lifted a hand toward his shorn head.

He snatched her wrist before she could touch him. "I'm not going with you, Rose. I can't."

"I know."

He released her, and she had to curl her fingers inward until the nails bit into her palm to keep herself from reaching for him again.

"If someone does recognize me they'll want to know why I'm with a child and not you."

"Tell them I'm dead. That usually makes people stop asking."

It certainly made Rose stop.

The wind whispered through the grass, rattled the branches of the trees, made her wish things she had no business wishing.

Luke yanked free two ugly army blankets. He cloaked Lily in one and handed the other to Rose. She drew the rough material around her shoulders, then stepped toward the horse, expecting Luke to move. He didn't. Their toes touched, and every breath he took echoed her own. She lifted her eyes, her lips forming his name.

His mouth took hers, both harsh and sweet. He drew her onto her toes, then off her feet. Cast adrift, she wrapped her arms around his neck and held on.

He tasted of tears, or maybe she did. The breeze felt icy on her cheeks. She wanted to crawl right inside him and never let go.

He stilled, his mouth hovering just above hers, their breath mingling, their bodies pressed together in the night, causing her to remember every instance they had been pressed together before.

"Luke?" Hope and need and joy lit her voice. How could he kiss her like that and then send her away?

The next thing she knew she was flying through the air, landing on the horse, snatching for a handhold, finding it, even as her daughter leaned against her, tiny hands grasping Rose's skirt. Rose had all she could do to grab the reins as the horse trotted off. She curved her arms around Lily to keep her steady, though the child appeared in no need of help.

Rose glanced over her shoulder, but all she saw were the trees, the grass, and the riverbank falling away into nothing.

Like her heart.

"Shouldn't have done that," Luke muttered, lips still burning from hers.

He hadn't kissed Rose like a man who didn't love her. He'd kissed her like a man who desperately did. Had she tasted that truth? The way she'd said his name—confusion and wonder and hope—she'd definitely tasted something.

If she turned around, if she came back, if she saw his face she would know. If she touched him he would be unable to stop himself from touching her. And he would not be able to let her go twice.

Run, said the wind, then blew hard against his back. Thus far the wind had almost always been right, so Luke ran. He reached the tepee. Their tepee. The instant he stepped inside he felt something, but he saw nothing. "Kiwidinok?"

No answer.

"Ayahsa?"

The same.

The tepee smelled like sun and wind and rain. Like Rose. Loneliness washed over him so deep he went dizzy with it. He'd thought he felt alone while in the Smoky Hills, his only companion insanity and the wind, but he had never known loneliness like this because he had not then known her. He would miss Rose until the day that he died. Lucky for him that was probably tomorrow.

The darkness shifted. He waited, barely breathing, but saw nothing more. Imagination or the wind? Was there a difference?

He couldn't stay here. The place was too lonely, too empty, or perhaps it was just too full of memories of her. He turned and bounced off a very solid, very large body. He looked up, up, up, but it was too dark to see a face.

"Ye're comin' with me."

Though he didn't know the voice, he was more curious than alarmed. "I can't." Rose's safety depended on him staying and dying.

"Didn't ask." The giant bent as if he would throw Luke over his shoulder.

Luke stepped back, though there was nowhere to go. "Who are you?" The man had spoken English; the accent had been . . . He wasn't sure. Not Southern, not quite Northern, either, but definitely not Cheyenne, as if there might be a Cheyenne this large that Luke had never noticed before. "How did you get into camp?"

Warriors lurked in the trees and the grass. Other tepees surrounded this tepee. A man of this size—hell, of any size—should not be able to sneak about without being seen.

"What do you want?" Luke asked.

"You."

Understanding dawned. A bounty hunter, and a very, very good one.

Luke feinted to one side, then fast in the other direction. Instead of falling for the dodge, the guy snatched Luke's arm. Luke swung. Before his fist could connect with the giant's jaw, the giant's fist connected with his.

A town appeared on the horizon with the sun.

Lily had fallen asleep soon after they'd left the Cheyenne, which gave Rose time to plan what she would do once they reached civilization. At least it kept her from thinking of him.

The streets were quiet. At the first saloon, Rose stopped the horse in the shadow of the building, dismounted, tugged a still-sleepy child into her arms, and set her down. Lily stood docilely, leaning against Rose's leg as Rose riffled the saddlebags, taking stock.

She'd been concerned she would need to sell the horse so they would have the funds to buy train tickets, and it wasn't an easy matter to sell an animal bearing an army brand. But she found money in the bags—she refused to consider where the Cheyenne had gotten that, either—and she thought it would be enough to get them away from here.

It would have to be.

After looping the horse's reins over a hitching post, she sailed the cavalry hat into the alley, withdrew the rifle from the saddle—she wished she could sell the saddle, but it was obviously army issue, too—then stuffed the blankets into the saddlebag, tossed them over her shoulder, took Lily's hand, and walked away. She'd leave the horse and the rest for someone to find, maybe give back to the army. It didn't matter to her. At the rail station she held on to a few greenbacks and used the rest to buy fare as far as they could go.

"Chicago," the ticket agent said, his gaze drawn to the sun sparking off Lily's earrings. Considering the way the sun sparked off his bald head, he shouldn't be so fascinated. "Can't say as I've ever seen a . . ." His dry lips pursed as Lily's silver hair ornament jangled in a sudden, unfortunate wind. "White child?" His forehead creased as he studied the shimmering hair and bare, sun-darkened feet; then he nodded as if answering his own question. "A white child with Injun earrings."

"They're not Indian earrings."

"What are they?"

"Hers." Rose snatched the tickets and hurried away.

Rose considered using the last of the money to buy new clothes, then decided they would make do with what they had. Until she could convince Lily to give up the Cheyenne ornaments for shoes and a bonnet, she could dress her in starched ruffles and folks would still stare.

Instead they boarded the train. The fewer eyes on Lily, the better. Even though the child had slept on the horse, the rest had clearly not been adequate, because as soon as they sat Lily climbed onto her lap and her head fell against Rose's chest. Within moments, Lily's breathing evened out and her body went lax and heavy. Rose took the opportunity to put shoes on her feet. The train car floor was filthy. Then she set her cheek atop the child's hair and the next thing she knew, the train jerked and began to move.

Their car was filled with men, women, children. No one paid them any mind. The town—she never had learned its name—already lay behind them. The prairie flew backward with dizzying speed.

A short while later Lily stirred, rubbing her eyes. When she lowered her hands, she pressed her nose to the window. *"Nahko'eehe!"* Lily pointed as Cheyenne spilled from her mouth. After *my mother* Rose didn't understand a word of it.

Rose smiled and nodded, though as time went on, her smile froze. It faded altogether when she realized that the longer she went without answering, the louder Lily's voice became. And people were beginning to stare.

She pressed her lips to Lily's brow. The child's hair brushed her nose, and she sneezed. Lily responded with a word that did not sound remotely like *gesundheit*.

Rose set her hand on her daughter's head, then whispered into her ear, "Shh. We need to be quiet, little one."

Little One. Rose had heard that phrase before.

"Ayasha," she murmured. Lily's head tilted. "Shh."

Rose braced herself for another spate of extremely loud Cheyenne. Instead the child lifted her finger to her lips as her eyebrows rose. Thank God, Lily seemed to remember a few things from the white world. Or perhaps the sound and the gesture for shushing were universal.

As her daughter was three and accustomed to spending her days running beneath the sun, the silence didn't last. Within a half hour, Lily struggled to be free of Rose's arms and made her dissatisfaction with her confinement known in the tone and volume of her words even if Rose could not understand the words themselves.

Desperate, Rose instigated patty-cake, which kept Lily happy until they reached Rogue. As the train slowed, several passengers gathered their things. Rose peered out the window, hoping no one would get on who recognized her. She had enough to worry about. Several of the folks who'd remained on the train continued to give them unfriendly looks.

When they pulled out of the station, the only person who had gotten on was a priest. He nodded to her as he went past. She'd no doubt been staring. She'd seen priests before. She was from Boston and Catholic. However, she had never—ever—seen one like him.

Instead of a cassock, he wore black trousers and a black shirt with a notch at the front to reveal his white collar. Spurs clanked on his dusty boots, and he'd thrown equally dusty saddlebags over his shoulder. But it wasn't his attire that drew her gaze. Had she ever seen a priest with wavy golden hair, eyes the shade of spring leaves, and a face so lovely the bump in his nose went unnoticed until the second, or perhaps the third, glance? That bump and his unshaven jaw were the only imperfections that kept him from being downright pretty. If not for the white collar, and his lack of weapons, Rose might have thought him an outlaw come to rob the train. What man who looked like that became a priest?

Rose set her hand on her rifle. She would keep an eye on him.

Unfortunately she only had two eyes and she needed both of them, as well as more hands than she possessed, for Lily. Her daughter could not sit still. She escaped Rose's hold and ran up and down the aisle shouting in Cheyenne. Rose managed to entice her back to their seat with the promise of food.

The man sitting right behind them leaned over. "What's that she's talkin'?"

"French."

"What's that she's eatin'?"

As Rose had eaten the flat cake before, she knew it was called pemmican—a mixture of pounded berries, equally pounded buffalo meat, and tallow—which was dried in the summer sun and then served all winter.

"Pain," she said, twisting the French word for bread to sound very French indeed, even as she prayed this fellow did not know the language. Her own vocabulary, courtesy of her mother, was confined to food and colors. She might even be able to count to ten if she tried.

"What you just said did sound like French, but what the little 'un is spoutin' sure don't. And them thar earrings must be Injun."

"Nahko'eehe?" Lily held out her tiny hand for more.

"That sounds Injun, too," he said.

"It isn't."

"All we've got is yer word fer that. How we supposed to know the savages won't come after this train searchin' fer a child y' done stole from 'em?"

"What Indian has hair like this?" Rose lifted a braid.

"And eyes like that?" She tilted Lily's face toward the man. The child smiled and babbled more Cheyenne.

"She don't sound white and she don't look quite white, neither. Mebe she's a half-breed."

"She's a child," Rose said. "My child."

"You don't look French."

"What does French look like?"

"Aha!" The man poked a finger at her face, narrowly missing her nose. "Then you ain't French."

"My husband was."

"What's his name?"

Rose's mind went blank. "N-none of your business" was all she could manage.

"You and yer half-breed need to get off this train."

"We will not!"

"Next stop y' will, or I'll throw y' off. I'm not gettin' scalped . . ." His gaze lit on her scar, and his scowl deepened. " 'Cause of y'all."

"Enough."

The priest stood in the aisle next to Rose. Lily babbled at him, and he gave her a quick smile before facing the man behind them. His smile faded. "The child is speaking French."

A bald-faced lie. Rose waited for him to go up in flames. Or, perhaps, she would.

"But—" the man began.

"You doubt my word?" The holy man lifted an eyebrow, the movement more menace than inquiry.

"N-no, sir."

"Father."

"No, Father."

"Take my place." The priest flicked his fingers toward the seat he had vacated near the rear of the car.

The fellow blinked slightly protruding eyes. "Sir? I mean, Father?"

"Less trouble if you sit there while they sit here." He tilted his head as the fool continued to gape at him. "I can smack your knuckles with a stick if you want. That usually makes folks behave, if they aren't inclined to right away."

"I . . . uh . . . no, s—Father." The man gathered his things and fled. The priest slid into the vacated seat.

"Thank you." Rose fought a nearly insurmountable urge to squirm and then confess every sin she'd ever committed, and a few she hadn't. Lily set her arms on the back of the seat and began to talk to the man as if they were old friends.

He leaned forward and lowered his voice so no one but Rose could hear him over the rhythmic thump of the train. "What is she saying?" he asked.

"I thought you understood French."

The man raised his eyebrow again. Again Rose fought the continued desire to tell him everything. Although did she really need to fight it?

Lily patted Rose's hand. *"Nahko'eehe."*

"That means my mother," Rose said.

"And the rest?"

Rose shrugged. She couldn't lie to a priest. She didn't even want to try.

"Why did you lie?" she asked. "About the French."

"He annoyed me."

"I didn't think priests were allowed to be annoyed."

He snorted—another thing she didn't think priests were allowed to do.

"Neho'eehe!" Lily shouted, and pounded on the window.

Rose was so interested in the priest who lied and snorted and admitted to being annoyed that she, at first, didn't hear the slight difference in the word—*neho'eehe* and not *nahko'eehe*. When she did, she turned toward the window so fast her neck cracked.

The Dog Men had nearly caught up to the train.

CHAPTER 25

Luke woke with a horrible headache. It wasn't the first time.

He opened his eyes. What he saw flashed by in a jumble—prairie grass, pounding horses' hooves, belly, chest. The sight made him so dizzy and sick he closed his eyes again. Once he did, he realized why. Everything was upside down.

He was upside down.

He'd been tossed over a horse, head hanging on one side of the saddle, legs on the other, ropes bound him in place. Considering the sun on the grass, he'd been that way for hours. His head ached not only from the blood pulsing there, but the punch to his jaw. His stomach hurt the same. Saddles weren't exactly feather ticks.

" 'Bout time you woke."

Luke's eyes opened again. Another glimpse of the swaying upside-down world and he shut them. But before he did, he saw the giant riding a horse beside him, and leading his own mount by the reins. "Let me up."

If Luke could get upright, he would be off. The bounty hunter might be very good at his job, but there was no white man alive who could ride as well as Luke Phelan.

"You do seem a mite uncomfortable."

Their mounts stopped. A saddle creaked. Grass swished in Luke's direction. Huge boots appeared beneath his nose and he felt the ropes holding him being tugged on. The world spun even more sickeningly as he was lifted by his belt and set on his feet next to the horse. He collapsed to the ground and waited for everything to stop swimming. Then he looked up, and up some more, until he, at last, saw the face of his captor.

Dark hair, gray eyes, early twenties.

"Never saw you before in my life," Luke muttered. He'd have remembered the huge scar on the man's forehead if nothing else.

The fellow spread hands as massive as the rest of him. "Why would ya?"

True enough. Every bounty hunter who'd come after the White Ghost in the past was dead.

Luke tried to get to his feet and fell back down. The man pulled him upright with one hand. Luke took a step toward his horse. If he could get on while his captor was still off, he'd have an even better chance of escaping.

He eyed the guns around the man's hips. He'd dodged bullets before. It was one of the things the Dog Men did best.

A sudden tug on one wrist made Luke still. He frowned at the rope looped over the area where both ropes and chains had been before. He raised his untethered hand to touch the rope, see if it was real, remove it if he could, and that hand was wrapped in rope, then tugged next to the first.

"Ya can't think I'm gonna let ya get on that horse and ride away. I'm no fool."

The giant picked up Luke as easily as he'd lifted him down and plopped him into the saddle. He tied the end of the rope to the horn so tightly that Luke, with his wrists bound together, would have a helluva time picking it apart.

Luke eyed the reins, which trailed on the ground. He doubted he could lean over far enough to seize them with his teeth, but that didn't mean he wasn't going to try. He had to get back to camp before Many Horses discovered him gone. The Dog Man had been very clear about what he would do if that happened.

Before Luke could kick his horse into motion, his

captor took a single broad step and snatched the reins. He was far too quick for his size and, despite his seeming youth, appeared to have done this many times before.

"Who are you?" Luke asked.

"Mikhail Romanov."

He did not sound like a Mikhail or a Romanov. He sounded like a slightly slow-witted farm boy. Too bad he didn't act like one.

"Where are you taking me?"

"Freedom."

Was the man tormenting him? Luke had never felt less free in his life.

"I done told ya she was an Injun brat!"

Rose ignored the insult, her gaze on the approaching Dog Men. From here she couldn't tell if one of them was Many Horses. Every face was painted; each wore a many-feathered headdress. She was still fairly certain they were the Dog Men from the Cheyenne camp she'd just left.

"Toss her out." The annoying man reached for Lily; Rose reached for her rifle.

"Don't," the priest murmured, and the fellow froze.

The Father had produced a Colt—must have been in the saddlebags—and trained it on the fellow's chest. The grip was as worn as his boots; from the way he held it he knew how to use it. He became less priestly by the second.

"Sit," he ordered. "I'd prefer to use my bullets on them and not you, but I could be persuaded."

The man sat.

"You know how to use that?" The Father indicated the rifle. Rose nodded. "Then do." He smacked the butt of his pistol against his window and then hers. Glass shattered, mostly outward. The rest she brushed from her seat onto the floor, thankful that she'd managed to put Lily's shoes on her feet while she'd been asleep, and miracle of miracles, the child had left them on. She tossed one of the army blankets over the mess anyway, just to be sure.

Rose stood with one knee on the seat to steady herself, as well as keep Lily behind her. The girl continued to chatter in Cheyenne, occasionally using a word that Rose recognized—*my father, my mother, horse,* or perhaps *Many Horses.*

The Dog Men rode east with the train. Rose sighted down the barrel at the lead warrior, then pulled the trigger. Every one of the Cheyenne disappeared on the far side of their horses. When no more shots were fired, they pulled themselves back up.

"Keep shooting." The priest fired several times himself. Some of the other passengers broke windows and began to shoot, too. The Dog Men disappeared again, but not one of them fell. Lily laughed and clapped as if she were watching a traveling show.

"What are they doing?" Rose asked.

"Tormenting us. Even if you didn't have to be an army-caliber sniper to hit a moving target from a moving train, if someone is good enough, or lucky . . ." He fired another, useless, shot. "They're using a sling to drop out of sight."

"Why shoot at all if we can't hit them?"

"Keeps them back. If they get close enough, they'll jump on the train."

"Why don't we *not shoot* until they get close enough *to* shoot?" Rose asked.

"That many riders so near and we won't be able to get all of them. Some will board. Those ponies are better than most, but they won't be able to outlast a train. Eventually they'll tire." He fired again. "If we can keep them back long enough, we'll leave them behind."

"You've done this before," she said.

"I've done everything before," he muttered.

An odd statement for a priest, but then he was an odd priest.

The train jerked. Rose's shot went wide. Not that any of them had been near. They began to slow. Instead of riding closer, the Cheyenne sped ahead, disappearing from view.

The Father leaned out the window, peering after them. As he pulled himself back in, he mumbled curses no priest should know, let alone use. "They've piled brush and rocks on the tracks. Until someone gets out and clears it, we aren't going anywhere."

"Who's gonna get out with them savages around?" The man whom the Father had ousted from his seat scowled. "We're all gonna die here." He jabbed a finger at Lily. She wrinkled her nose and jabbed her finger back at him. "Cuzza her!"

"Come out!"

Everyone's gaze returned to the prairie where a painted, feathered Dog Man sat astride his war pony. Rose recognized the voice, even without the perfect English.

"How does he know the language?" someone whispered.

Rose opened her mouth, then shut it once more. It didn't matter.

"Neho'eehe!" Lily shouted again.

"His child?" the priest asked.

"No," Rose answered. He crooked a golden eyebrow. "I swear, Father."

"Do not make me come for you," Many Horses continued.

She hadn't noticed she'd set down the rifle until the priest picked it up. She placed her hand on the barrel. "Don't shoot him. He's the leader of the Dog Men. They *will* kill you." She let her gaze wander over everyone in the car. "All of you."

She returned her attention to Many Horses. "He isn't here!" Why on earth did he think that Luke was?

"I did not come for Ve'ho'e Mestaa'e. I came for you."

"That doesn't make sense." Rose could understand

the Dog Man coming after Luke or Lily but not after her.

"She expects a savage to make sense," the annoying man muttered.

"Shut up," the Father ordered.

The fellow blinked and did.

"He promised me his life for the life of Éše'he Ôhvó'komaestse."

"Oh," Rose whispered as everything suddenly made sense. She had wondered why the Dog Man, who'd seemed to care for Lily—his wife certainly did—had agreed to let the child go. Now she knew. Luke had promised to give him what he wanted. Which meant that Luke was dead.

Her head went light; Rose had to sit down or fall down. She slumped in the seat, but she couldn't seem to catch her breath.

"Ma'am?" The priest set a hand on her shoulder. "What's the matter?"

She shook her head, but that only made the world spin faster. He shoved her between the shoulders until her forehead met her knees. "Breathe," he ordered in the same voice he'd previously used for *shut up*. She breathed.

"Nahko'eehe?" Lily's tiny hands patted Rose's hair, her neck, the sides of her face.

She looked up. The world shimmered but didn't shift. Her daughter appeared ready to cry. Rose forced a smile that seemed to scare Lily even more, so she stopped. "I'm all right." She kissed Lily's nose, and while the child's expression remained concerned, her tears receded.

"Come out!" Many Horses shouted again.

"Why?" Rose returned. "He gave you what you wanted."

"He gave me nothing. I told him what I would do to you if he disappeared."

Slowly Rose stood. "He isn't dead?"

"If he was dead, woman, why would I be here?"

"He would never leave if he promised to stay."

"Yet he is gone. And the life he owes me is now yours."

The priest lifted the rifle. Rose pressed it back down. There was something missing from this tale. "How did you find me?"

"I followed the tracks of the army horse to the town and watched you get on the train."

"Why didn't you follow his tracks?"

"There weren't any."

Rose frowned. "If he left, there would be tracks." Although she doubted the Cheyenne would fail to notice a man who was still in camp.

"He is Ve'ho'e Mestaa'e."

"That doesn't mean he can disappear."

"Perhaps it does."

Rose rubbed between her eyes. This wasn't the first time talking with Many Horses had given her a headache. She dropped her hand and met the gaze of the priest. "My name is Rose Varner. This is Lily. Her father is Jakob. He's in St. Louis." Or at least that was where he'd said he was going. He had family in the city that owned a bakery, or maybe a brewery. If he'd actually gone there, or stayed there, was anyone's guess. She hadn't cared enough to find out.

The man opened his mouth and she shook her head. "No time to explain." She could tell by the way Many Horses' pony had begun to prance that the Dog Man's patience was nearly out. "You'll have to convince Jakob to take her."

"*Convince* him?"

"He won't want to. He—" She sighed as she accepted the truth. "Never mind." Rose lifted Lily onto her hip and stepped into the aisle. "She'll be better off with the Cheyenne."

The Father set a hand on her arm. "He's going to kill you."

"I know. But he won't kill her."

"You're sure of that?"

"Absolutely."

"I still can't let you go."

"If you don't, everyone on this train is going to die."

"You're sure of that?" he repeated.

She glanced at Many Horses. "Absolutely."

"Send her out," the annoying man said, and murmurs of agreement rose from the rest of the passengers.

"I don't—" the priest began, but she hurried past and while he snatched at her skirt, he couldn't hold her. She glanced back at the sound of scuffles. Several of the men had grabbed the Father's arms to keep him from following.

Rose reached for the door that led to the platform between the cars.

A town appeared on the horizon at dusk. Mikhail rode straight for it.

They had stopped twice since that morning so Luke's captor could hold a water skin to his lips and then Luke's. Despite the nighttime chill, the day had heated considerably. What water they drank, they sweated out through their skin and neither felt the slightest need to relieve himself. Mikhail didn't offer food. Why bother to feed a dead man?

Luke had tried to explain that he had to return to the Cheyenne, that a woman would die if he wasn't there.

"You's comin' back with me. Ain't nothin' you can say that's gonna stop me."

He considered telling the man that the Cheyenne would kill Luke as soon as he returned, so he would die just as surely as if the bounty hunter returned him for hanging. But he didn't get the impression that Mikhail was in this for justice. What bounty hunter was? They wanted the money, and the money was in town.

At the outskirts of the settlement stood a weathered board that read WELCOME TO FREEDOM.

Luke started to laugh.

Folks on the street stared—either because Luke couldn't stop laughing, or because of the sight of his shaved head, or maybe even the size of Mikhail.

Mikhail reined in beneath the SHERRIF sign. As he climbed off the horse, Luke kept his gaze on the door, wondering if the lawman would come out or if Mikhail would have to drag Luke in. But instead of heading for the sheriff's office, Mikhail headed for the door beneath a marker that proclaimed DOCTER. Luke could definitely get a job here painting signs. Before the fellow reached it, a woman burst out.

"Mikey," she began. The big man growled. "I mean, Mikhail, did you—?"

Her gaze went past the bounty hunter, and she stopped so quickly her skirts swirled wildly around her feet. "Oh my God," she whispered.

Luke couldn't believe his eyes. "Annabeth?"

CHAPTER 26

As Rose's fingertips touched the door, Lily suddenly stiffened, throwing her arms around Rose's neck and burying her face there, too.

"What's wrong?" Rose asked.

In answer, the child trembled, her breath hitching in terror. A chill wind blew through the broken windows, trailing the silver ornament in Lily's hair across Rose's face. On that wind, she could have sworn she heard the trill of a bugle. She peered out the window on the opposite side of the train from the Dog Men. Cavalry swarmed in their direction.

"I will find you," Many Horses shouted, and Rose turned her head to the left. "There is no place on this earth where you can hide."

His horse leaped into a gallop as he led the Dog Men across the prairie, the horse soldiers in pursuit. Rose had no idea what to do except sit down. She really needed to.

The priest appeared at her side. He reached for Lily, but the child clung to Rose like moss to a tree, and she shook like that tree in the middle of a twister.

"Hush, sweetheart." Rose kissed her daughter's hair. "The soldiers are gone."

"Told ya she weren't normal! What white child is afraid of the gol-danged army?"

One that had seen, or at least heard, what the army had done to those she loved.

Rose returned to her seat. Lily continued to cling and shiver.

"Where did the soldiers come from?" Rose asked.

"The Cheyenne have been attacking the trains so often in this area that the army has started stationing troops along the route," the Father said. "Could be that someone in town saw those Indians watching and got suspicious."

Although Rose had a difficult time believing that the Dog Men would allow themselves to be seen, there was no other explanation for the sudden appearance of the army.

"Woo-hoo!" shouted one of the passengers, his face pressed to the window. "Look at 'em run! They's gonna be sorry they was ever born."

The priest's lips tightened. "Those fools will be lucky if they aren't drawn into an ambush."

"Like the Fetterman Massacre," Rose murmured.

"You'd think that after losing so many men the army would be more cautious."

Though the incident had taken place in Dakota Territory nearly five years past, the loss of close to one hundred men was not something easily forgotten. At least by the settlers. From the army's behavior, they'd not only forgotten but hadn't learned a damn thing.

According to reports, a small Cheyenne party had come close to Fort Kearny, taunting the soldiers. The army had ridden in pursuit and run directly into a force of three thousand warriors just over a ridge. Not one of the soldiers survived.

"Same thing happened at Julesburg and Fort Rankin," the Father continued. "The very next year."

The train jerked and began to move again. The engineers must have leaped off and removed the brush from the tracks as soon as the cavalry appeared.

"Why did the Cheyenne come for you?" the Father asked.

"That's a long story."

"I've got plenty of time."

Rose stared out the window. Without the glass, dust

blew in like rain. "My daughter was taken by the Dog Men."

"And you got her back?"

"I had help. There's a man the Cheyenne call Ve'ho'e Mestaa'e." Rose had to swallow before she continued. Just saying the name made her want to cry. "The White Ghost."

The priest went so still he barely breathed. "The White Ghost with Hair of Fire?"

"You've heard of him."

"I—" He lowered his head, took a breath, then lifted it again. "I've been searching for Luke since I lost him."

Her heart took one shocked, hard thud. No one but Rose—and maybe Many Horses—knew that the White Ghost and Luke Phelan were the same man. She peered at him more closely. "Who *are* you?"

"Moses Farquhar."

"Moze . . . ?"

His lips tilted downward but he nodded.

"Luke . . . he didn't tell me you were a priest; he thought you were—"

Farquhar gave one sharp shake of his head.

Luke had suspected his childhood friend was a spy. Considering the collar, Moze was certainly up to something.

"What are you two whisperin' about?" the annoying fellow asked.

"She's giving me her confession," Moze said, gaze still on hers. "A little respect, please." The man subsided.

Lily seemed to have fallen asleep, though she muttered and shuddered now and again. Rose rubbed her back and held her close.

"How did you end up on the same train as me?" Rose asked.

"I don't know you. I was in Rogue because I'd heard tell that the White Ghost was there. But he wasn't, and I have places to be."

"I thought I convinced the people there that Luke wasn't who they thought he was."

"Every tale of the White Ghost—real or imagined— finds its way to me."

"Who do you work for?"

He shook his head.

"Luke told me what you did during the war."

He frowned. "I never told him anything."

"He isn't stupid." She eyed his collar again. "Neither am I. How would a mere priest hear every tale of the White Ghost?"

Moze sighed, then glanced over his shoulder. No one was paying them any mind anymore, so he faced her, leaned in close, and whispered, "I work for Pinkerton."

Which made Moze a detective and not a spy—at least now—though Rose thought the two might be one and the same in a lot of ways.

"The White Ghost was in the Smoky Hills," Rose said.

"Your point?"

"If I could find him, why couldn't you?"

"At first the tales just spoke of a ghost in the hills. Could have been anyone or no one at all. Could have been anywhere. Then I was . . . " He indicated his collar. "Occupied. By the time the stories got more specific, and I was finally able to follow the leads, he wasn't in the Smoky Hills anymore."

Because he'd left there with her. "Sorry."

"Where is he now?"

"Back with the Cheyenne." She paused. "Or he was. But he wouldn't leave. Not when he knew Many Horses would come after me."

"If he stayed he's dead."

"I know," Rose whispered. The idea of Luke dying for her, for Lily, made her dizzy and sick. "But he pledged his life, and he would never run away. Courage matters. To Luke, it's the only thing that does." She rubbed her forehead, trying to think. "Many Horses said there were no tracks. That Luke vanished without a trace. But that's impossible."

"Maybe not."

Surprised, Rose dropped her hand. Moze contemplated the rapidly moving landscape through the open window.

"We have to get off this train," he murmured.

"Luke!"

His sister leaped off the porch, bypassing the stairs in one bound, then rushing across the distance between them. She stopped when she saw he was tied to the saddle. "What the hell is this?"

"He didn't wanna come," Mikhail said. "Had to toss him over my shoulder and make 'im."

"You know this guy?" Luke asked.

"Of course, he's—" Annabeth's lips tightened. "Mikhail, cut him loose, then take the horses to the stable, please."

"Sure 'nuff."

The large man produced an equally large knife, sliced Luke's bonds, yanked him from the horse before Luke could even attempt to get off himself, and deposited him in front of his sister, then led their mounts away.

"Who is that?" Luke asked. "No, wait . . . why are you here? I thought you were dead. What is going on?"

She jumped into his arms. He caught her; he had to.

"I thought you were dead, too," she whispered.

He hugged her back. So many years since he'd seen her, so many things had changed. She had changed, but she was still his big sister and he loved her. Finding her alive after all this time . . . he never wanted to let her go.

A movement in the doorway she'd just come through made Luke lift his head, though he kept his arms around Annabeth. A tall, slim man with dark hair and gray eyes stood beneath the DOCTER sign. Luke had seen those eyes before.

On the giant.

"Hello," Luke said, releasing his sister and meeting the man's gaze.

"Ethan!" She spun. "It's Luke! He's alive. He's here. Mikey found him."

Ethan glanced down the street where Mikey—or was it Mikhail?—could still be seen leading the horses. A brief sadness flickered over his face before he returned his attention to them. He came down the stairs, put one arm around Annabeth's shoulders, and extended the other. "I'm glad to finally meet you."

Luke frowned at the hand offered to him, then at the arm around his sister. "Who are you?"

"Ethan Walsh."

"Doctor?" Luke lifted his chin to indicate the sign.

"I am."

"And Annabeth is your nurse?" She'd always been good at it. Considering the Phelan brothers, she'd had to be.

"Yes." Dr. Walsh lowered the hand Luke had never taken back to his side. "As well as my wife."

"Wife." Luke's gaze flicked to Annabeth's. "Since when?"

"Just after the war."

Considering the doctor's Yankee accent, there was a story to that, but it would have to wait. "Can I exchange my horse for a fresh one at the stable? I have to go."

"Go? We just found you!" Annabeth exclaimed.

"Was I lost?"

"I've been looking for you since Rectortown," Annabeth said. Dr. Walsh shifted uneasily, and she set a hand on his arm. "Not now."

"Listen," Luke said. "Your . . ." He considered Ethan's eyes again. "Brother?"

"Yes."

"Mikey? Mikhail?" Luke frowned. "He said his name was Romanov, not Walsh."

"He was hurt in the war." Walsh lifted his finger to a scar on his forehead, which was in a similar place, but not as prominent as the one on the other man's head. "He doesn't remember me. It's best just to call him Mikhail. Calling him Mikey only annoys him, and you do not want to see him annoyed."

Considering the size of the man, Luke had to agree.

"He's not a bounty hunter?"

"Bounty hunter?" Annabeth repeated. "Are you in trouble?"

"No."

"Liar." Annabeth's blue eyes narrowed. "I know trouble when I see it."

"You sound like Ma."

"Thank you. Now, why would a bounty hunter have any reason to drag you into town? And what in hell happened to your hair?"

"Beth, we should bring your brother inside and feed him before you start an interrogation."

"Beth?" Luke asked.

She shrugged. "Yankee."

Yankees always shortened names. It was an odd practice.

"How long will we have to be married before you stop calling me that?"

Annabeth's lips twitched. "A lot longer than we have been."

"I can't stay," Luke said. "I wish I could but—"

"It's coming up dark," his sister interrupted. "You can't go now. Eat, sleep. Tell me what is so damn important that you have to leave when I only just found you."

"You didn't find me, Annie Beth Lou." Her eyes went moist as the nickname he and Moze had always tormented her with tripped off his tongue.

"Not for lack of trying," she said. When he opened his mouth to question that statement, she held up her hand. "First food. Drink."

The urge to return to the Cheyenne was so strong Luke could barely stay still. He shifted from one foot to the next and glanced west.

"I could have Mikhail tie you up again." Annabeth returned his glare. "You're only going to fall off any horse you get on. You need to rest."

Luke knew his sister well enough to know that she would follow through on her threat, and she was right about one thing. He needed some food in his belly or he wouldn't get far.

"I could eat," he said, then followed his sister and her husband into the house

An hour later, Luke sat at the kitchen table sopping up the last of his stew with a slightly dry biscuit. Annabeth had always been better at hunting than cooking, just as she'd been better at sewing flesh than sewing seams. The doctor didn't seem to mind. From the way he stared at Annabeth, it was clear he thought she'd hung the moon.

Luke was surprised he could eat, considering the news his sister had shared. He'd known his parents were dead, his brothers, too. But there'd always been hope the reports of at least one of the Phelan brothers' demises was false. That didn't seem to be the case. His turning up alive was, for Annabeth, as much of a miracle as her turning up the same way was for him.

His sister had led an interesting life during and after the war. Spying, lying, almost dying. Nearly all of it during her attempts to find him. In the end, Mikey—who had an uncanny ability to find anything or anyone—had gone off on his own in search of Luke.

"You shouldn't have risked so much," Luke said.

"You were all I had." She set her hand atop her husband's where it rested on the table. The doctor's fingers twined with hers. "Until Ethan."

"I wondered why they didn't shoot me." Luke shoved his empty plate back. Apparently Moze had arranged an exchange—Luke for the Union's greatest sniper—but the man brought to Richmond had not been Luke Phelan.

Surprise, surprise—the Yankees had lied.

"About that," the doctor began.

"Ethan."

"He needs to know."

"Does he? What good will it do?"

"Now you *have* to tell me," Luke said.

Annabeth's lips tightened. "I agreed to help find the Union spy at Chimborazo."

"You said."

"What I didn't say was that the spy was Ethan."

"You married a spy?"

"To be fair, he married one, too."

"Did you ever wonder how the Union knew about Mosby's meeting at Rectortown?" the doctor asked.

"You?"

"Me," Ethan agreed.

"Huh." Luke had spent a lot of time while in prison, and in the pit, considering what he would do if he ever met the man who'd put him there.

"He was trying to end the war sooner."

"Don't defend me," Walsh said quietly. "He went to prison because of what I did." The man considered Luke. "If you wanted to break my nose I'd understand."

After years of dreaming about killing the one who had betrayed him, Luke now found he had no such desire. Yes, his capture had led to prison. But prison had led to Kansas, which had led to the Cheyenne—his wife, his daughter, becoming part of a family, a tribe. Would he rather none of that had happened? That he'd never loved Kiwidinok, or known Ayasha, or ridden the plains with the Dog Men? During the times of great pain he'd thought so, but things had changed. He had changed. Because of Rose.

"It's"—he wasn't sure what to say; it wasn't all right, but it was—"over," he finished. "In the past. We should leave it there."

"You *could* punch him," Annabeth said. "But not in the nose." She drew a finger down its center. "I like his nose."

"I'm not going to punch your husband," Luke said. "Though if I ever see Moze again, I might punch him."

"Get in line," Walsh muttered.

"Recruiting you to be a spy and a detective." Luke looked at his sister. "What was he thinking?"

"I was good at it!"

From the stories she'd been telling him while he was eating, she had been a very good spy. After the war, Moze had joined the Pinkerton Detective Agency and enlisted Annabeth's help in catching one of the most dangerous outlaws in the West. Luke wasn't surprised she'd been good at the job, but he was surprised her husband had allowed it. Apparently there'd been some sort of trouble between them. They hadn't lived together for a time, and it was then that Annabeth's sojourn as a Pinkerton had occurred.

There was more to the story—much more—but Luke didn't have time to ask about it now. He needed to save Rose.

"I have to go, Annabeth. I'm sorry."

"What is so all-fired important?" she asked.

Quickly he explained about helping Rose rescue Lily. He left out a lot. He had to. If his sister knew that he'd pledged his life for the others, that he was returning to the Cheyenne to die, she really would have Mikhail tie him up.

"I said I'd stay with them awhile, try to help smooth over some rough spots with the army."

"How long is a while?" she asked. Luke shrugged, and her gaze narrowed. "I'm going with you."

"Oh, no, you're not," her husband began.

She cast him a glance. "After all I did to find him, you think I'm going to just let him ride off now?"

"No." Walsh let out a breath. "But why don't you send Mikhail?"

She threw up her hands. "Fine. I'll get him."

"Wait," Luke said. He felt as if he were on a runaway train. How was he going to stop this before he had an escort back to the Cheyenne? He didn't mind dying, but he wasn't going to be responsible for the death of anyone else—even the giant. "Where is Mikhail?"

"He stays at the stable," Ethan said. "Seeing me upsets him."

Annabeth had explained that, although Walsh had saved his brother's life after an injury at Castle Thunder Prison, the younger man's only memories were of excruciating pain, which he associated with Ethan. That was no doubt the root of the sadness in the doctor's eyes, but Luke hadn't asked. Some things were better left unvoiced. He had not told them about Ayasha and his wife, and considering his plans for the future, he never would. They'd endured enough pain of their own without adding his.

"You know . . ." Luke stretched, yawned, rubbed at his eyes. "You're right. I won't make it back without some rest. We can leave at first light."

His sister's gaze was suspicious, but she got to her feet. "You can sleep in the extra room upstairs."

Upstairs. She definitely didn't trust him.

Rose, Moze, and Lily got off the train in Ellsworth.

"How far to Freedom?" Rose asked, trying to keep pace with Moze's long steps.

He turned, scooping Lily into his arms without even breaking stride. "Twenty miles."

Rose cursed. Twenty miles on a horse could take all day depending on the terrain. With the sun already tumbling down, she doubted they'd be there before morning.

"We'll ride all night," he said. "I know the route."

"What if the Dog Men come back?"

"If they do they'll be chasing the train."

A long, low, mournful whistle signaled its departure. "What if they catch the train?"

"Doubtful," he said, and ducked into the stable.

He was unfamiliar with the Dog Men if he thought that was true, but there was nothing she could do. For now, she was going along with Moze. He believed Luke had been kidnapped by an acquaintance of his and taken to Freedom. That made more sense than anything else she'd considered.

According to Farquhar, this man—Mikhail—had been the Union's best scout. He could sneak up on anyone—even Indians, he'd done it before—and he could disappear without a trace. The latter she would have found hard to believe if Luke hadn't been gone.

The hosteller stumbled over his feet in his haste to provide the good Father with the best mounts for a ridiculously low price.

"I'm surprised he didn't make them a gift," Rose muttered as they left Ellsworth behind.

"Ellsworth is a rough town. I doubt he sees many priests."

"He didn't see one today."

"He doesn't know that."

"You didn't bless him or anything, did you?"

"What if I did?"

"Have you been marrying, burying, and blessing folks?"

"Only when I have to."

She was never quite sure if the man was serious or not. That he was Luke's best friend made her want to trust him. His disguise and his obvious penchant for lies told her she should not. However, if he could lead her to Luke, she would follow him anywhere.

The night passed in silence. Lily slept in her arms most of the time. The sky was clear and the moon was out, casting a silvery light over the plain. As the sun rose, Freedom darkened the horizon, and Rose urged her horse into a gallop. The movement woke Lily.

"Ai-eee!" the child shouted, clearly enjoying the wind in her hair.

They thundered into town—probably not the best idea as it caused folks to rush into the street. Rose expected the sheriff to appear when Moze reined up right in front of his office, but the door remained closed.

"There is no sheriff," Moze said.

Rose glanced at the sign, which was spelled wrong, though she doubted many people noticed.

"Well, there was, but he went out the window." Moze pointed at the second story of the building marked DOCTER. "I think he broke his neck."

What kind of town was this?

Moze dismounted, lifting a hand when several townsfolk greeted him as *Father* before reaching up to take Lily. The child went into his arms with ease. For some reason, she liked him. She began to babble, carrying on a conversation, pausing momentarily so Moze could nod. Lord only knew what he'd agreed to already.

The door of the doctor's office opened and a woman stepped out. Rose took one look at the color of her hair and murmured, "Annie Beth Lou."

The scowl she aimed in Moze's direction could have boiled oil.

"Wasn't me," he said.

Moze had explained quite a bit on the train—about Annabeth, her husband, their pasts—but he had not once called the woman by the name Luke had used in the sinkhole.

Annabeth's eyes narrowed on Lily's silver-gold hair, several shades lighter than the detective's but still similar.

"Wasn't me, either," he said.

Her gaze turned to Rose. "Are you Rose?"

"She is," Moze said.

"Good." Her lips curved. "He'll be glad to see you."

"He's still here?" Rose asked.

"Upstairs."

Rose rushed by Luke's sister without an invitation, ran through the waiting area, past a dark-haired man she assumed was Dr. Ethan Walsh, then pounded up the steps. The first room was empty. She burst into the second.

It was empty, too.

CHAPTER 27

Luke went out the window soon after Annabeth and the doctor came upstairs.

They closed their door. The bed creaked. Then it creaked more. Luke winced. That was his sister. But she was also a wife. At least the creaking made it easier for him to slip out. Not that they'd have heard him anyway. He wasn't called the White Ghost without reason.

If Annabeth thought a second-story room was going to keep him here, she was mistaken. Of course, the last time she'd seen him he hadn't yet become adept at hanging from the side of a galloping horse. After performing that feat, while being shot at, mind you, descending a building was simple enough.

The streets were deserted. Freedom wasn't Abilene or Ellsworth—wild cattle towns with their share of trouble. There *were* six saloons and a whorehouse. But while the buildings were lit up like sunrise and music, laughter, and smoke tumbled out a few open windows, no people did. The amusements resided inside.

Luke didn't want to go to the stable. Mikhail was there, and despite the man's not knowing his own name, he wasn't a fool. But Luke wouldn't get far without a horse.

He paused in the shadows of the sheriff's office, peering toward the barnlike structure. The doorway gaped black and endless, no sign of the stable boy or Mikhail, but as he hadn't seen, heard, or felt Mikhail in the Cheyenne camp he remained understandably skeptical of the man's absence now. If Mikhail caught him again, Luke would never get another chance to leave. And he had to. He might already be too late.

A raucous hoot erupted from the saloon nearest the prairie. The golden squares of light thrown by the windows were just enough to illuminate horse-shaped shadows. Luke slid along the buildings. Figuring the least dusty mount would also be the least tired, he removed the saddle and saddlebags—he was already stealing a horse; he wasn't going to take anything more than he had to—and led the animal far enough away from town that the sound of hoofbeats would not reach back in.

He rode hard throughout that night. By midmorning, he reached the camp at the river. When he was still several hundred yards away, mounted warriors surrounded him. They knocked him from the horse, beat him around the head and shoulders with their coup sticks, the bravest among them using their hands.

For the Cheyenne, killing a foe was a good thing, as it reduced the size of an enemy force. But the truly courageous merely rode in close and touched their opponent with a stick, their hand, or a part of the body.

"*É-énêšévaenâhtséstove!*" Many Horses had arrived. He pointed toward camp. "*Nés-tsêhe'otseha.*"

Stop fighting! Bring him there.

They herded Luke like a steer.

At the edge of the circle of tepees Medicine Bear waited. "I am sorry," the old man said.

Luke frowned. What did he have to be sorry for?

"You have not changed." Many Horses remained atop his mount, staring down at Luke, triumph in his eyes. "You break every vow you make; you desert everyone who loves you. She died because of you."

Luke's skin prickled. "What have you done?"

The triumph in the Dog Man's eyes deepened. "Unlike you, Ve'ho'e Mestaa'e, I keep my promises."

"Is he still asleep?" Annabeth asked from the landing.

Rose spun. "He's gone."

"Gone? He can't be."

"You don't know Luke," Rose muttered.

Annabeth pushed past her and into the bedroom. When her gaze lit on the bed—never been slept in—she thundered down the stairs, then stood in the hall as if she wasn't sure what to do next.

"What's wrong?" her husband asked.

"He's gone, dammit."

"He said he was leaving at first light. Though you'd think he would say good-bye."

"He never slept in that bed. He snuck out last night."

"Last night. This morning. What's the difference?"

"The sneaking. He wouldn't have if he didn't have something to hide."

Moze stepped inside with Lily just as Rose descended to the foyer. He nodded at the man who stood next to Annabeth. "Doctor."

The doctor narrowed his eyes.

"Ethan," Annabeth warned. "Behave."

The two did not get on, and considering what Moze had told Rose about their history, she could understand why.

"Nahko'eehe?" Lily held out her arms to Rose.

"Is that Cheyenne?" Annabeth asked.

"Yes." Rose set her daughter on her hip. "Where's the livery?"

"Down the street," Dr. Ethan said. "Next to the haberdashery."

"Thank you."

"Hold on," Annabeth said. "How in hell did you turn up here?" Her gaze flicked to the Pinkerton priest. "With him?"

"Long story," Rose said. "Moze knows it." Or at least the part of it that she wanted anyone else to know. "I need a fresh horse."

Rose took a step toward the door, and her way was blocked by the giant who had ducked to enter.

"Mikhail." Annabeth's lips tightened. "Hell."

Rose had also heard about Mikhail, once known as Mikey, from Moze. Poor man, to lose himself, forget his past. Then again, maybe forgetting the past wasn't the worst thing. It might have helped Luke to heal.

"What's wrong, Missus Annabeth?"

Moze inched back, and the movement drew Mikhail's attention. One look at Moze and a growl rumbled in Mikhail's chest. Apparently he didn't care for the detective any more than the doctor did.

"My brother's gone. I'd hoped you were with him."

"I'm right here, missus."

"You were in the stable all night?"

"Yes'm, and no one took a horse. Your brother couldn't go nowheres without one." His forehead scrunched; his scar lifted in one large lump. Though both had been caused by bullets, his was much worse than the one on his brother's forehead. "There was a fella came in early to buy a mount complainin' that his had been stolen. Ain't no sheriff." He spread his hands. "So he told me and the stable man all about it."

"Luke stole a horse?" Annabeth murmured. "Why?"

"He knew he'd never get past Mikhail," Ethan said.

"What's so important that he had to risk a hanging for a damn horse?" Annabeth snapped.

"He's trying to save me," Rose said. "It's what he does." She headed for the door. "But this time, I'm going to save him."

As Rose and Lily headed for the livery, folks on the street stepped out of their way. Though no one said anything, they did stop and stare, then whisper among themselves. Rose couldn't blame them. Her hair was a tangle. Her clothes fit so badly they were obviously not her own. She'd tossed the cavalry hat to avoid the attention it would bring, which only meant the scar from her near scalping was visible. Probably always would be. Lily's constant, obviously Indian chatter, her earrings, the silver ornament in her moon-bright braids, and her bare, dirty feet—she'd kicked her shoes off somewhere between Ellsworth and Freedom—made the child a curiosity.

Rose passed by the telegraph office, paused, turned back, and went in, where she composed a wire to Jakob Varner in St. Louis.

Lily alive.

That was all. Jakob deserved nothing more. Hell, he didn't even deserve that much, but Rose sent it anyway.

She exchanged the horse she'd ridden in on for a fresh one. Hoping to replenish their water and food, she made her way back to Annabeth's just as a wagon driven by a man dressed in black, right down to his gloves, pulled up in front of the building labeled DOCTER. At his side sat a woman, in her arms a baby. The man jumped lightly to the ground, hurried around to the other side, and accepted the child into one arm, then used the other to lift the woman down.

"Droo-ziya!" he called out. "We are here!"

The woman lifted a hand to his face. His profile was nothing short of beautiful, and his smile was the same. She kissed him—right there on the street—as if she meant it, and memory flickered. She was the woman who'd helped Rose save Luke in Rogue.

"Hey!" Rose hurried forward, reaching the couple just as the others spilled out of the doorway.

"Alexi!" Mikhail shouted, clapping the black-clad fellow on the shoulder.

"Hello." The green-eyed woman smiled. "Who's this?" She took Lily's hand and shook it, causing the child to laugh, then babble Lord knows what in response.

"Her name is Lily," Rose said.

"Éše'he Ôhvó'komaestse," the child announced.

"Or White Moon," Rose allowed. "I'm Rose Varner."

"We meet properly at last. I'm Catey Romanov. And this . . ." She drew back the blanket to reveal a tiny face surrounded by ink black hair and stunning blue eyes that contemplated Rose solemnly. "Is Willemina." She kissed the child's brow. "But since she's awful little for a mouthful like Willemina Romanov, we call her Billy."

"Lily and Billy," Rose murmured.

"They're going to be best friends."

Rose had liked the woman in Rogue. She liked her even more now.

"Why are you here?" she asked. It was odd to say the least.

"We've brought Billy to meet the Walshes."

"She can't be more than a couple weeks old." The last time Rose had seen Catey—less than a month past—she'd been huge with child.

"My wife is exceptional in all that she does." Alexi joined them. "She gave birth with the ease of a . . ." He lifted an eyebrow. "Cat."

His wife lifted her own eyebrows. "Compare me to an animal again and I will hurt you."

He set his gloved hand on his black shirt. "You wound me."

Catey rolled her eyes. "Always the showman. He can't help himself." She looked around, frowned. "Where's the man you called your husband?"

"Moze?" Annabeth asked.

"Again, not me."

"You must be Farquhar." Catey's frown deepened as her gaze fell on the detective's priestly collar. "Her *husband* had the same shade of hair as Ethan's wife, which is why Alexi contacted you. So why are you here and not in Rogue?"

"Maybe everyone should come inside," Annabeth said. "Those of us who don't know one another can meet at last." She nodded to Catey. "Those of us who've met before can explain to the rest how." She moved her gaze from Catey to Rose. "And I'd like to know why neither you nor my brother mentioned that you were married."

"She pretended," Catey said. "To save him. There was a mob."

"Isn't there always?" Alexi murmured.

"My head hurts," Annabeth said.

Catey's lips twitched. "My husband often has that effect."

Annabeth went into the house. Everyone followed, not noticing that Rose did not. She set Lily on the new horse. She had just climbed up behind her when the telegraph operator arrived.

"There was an answer to your wire." He handed her a piece of paper and hurried away.

Rose glanced at it with little enthusiasm. There was nothing Jakob would say that would interest her. Or so she'd thought.

Jakob Varner died of smallpox six months past.

"Huh," she said.

"Where are you going?" Moze asked.

Rose lifted her gaze. Everyone was gathered on the porch. They all stared at her. She slipped the paper into her pocket. "Where do you think?"

"I'll come with you."

"The Cheyenne won't like that."

"From what I saw of them, they don't like much."

"If there is a possibility of trouble, we will all go," Alexi said. "Except for you." He pointed at his wife. "And you." He lowered his finger to his daughter.

"I'm the best shot here!" Catey protested.

"Are not," Mikhail muttered.

"Well, maybe not. But I'm still better than the rest. And you're talking about riding into a Cheyenne camp."

"Not just Cheyenne," Moze said. "Dog Soldiers."

"Sheesh." Catey threw up one arm. "You need me."

"Be that as it may," her husband drawled, "you aren't going."

"I—"

"Baby," he said.

"Darling," she snapped.

Alexi sighed. "I did not mean it as an endearment,

moya zhizn', I meant . . ." He waved at the child sleeping in her arms.

Catey glanced down at her daughter, frowning as if she'd forgotten she was there. "Oh."

"Yes, oh. I would stay with her, but I lack the necessary . . ." He let his gaze drop to her breasts. "Equipment."

Catey muttered several words that were also not endearments.

"Why is everyone in such an all-fired hurry?" Annabeth asked. "Luke sneaks out in the night. Rose barely dismounts before she's off again."

"They're going to kill him," Rose said.

Annabeth blinked. "Excuse me?"

Rose glanced at Moze. "You tell them. I'm leaving."

"Wait!" Annabeth blurted.

"No." Rose lifted the reins. "If you want to follow, I'm sure Mikhail can find me as easily as he found Luke."

"Weren't *easy*," Mikhail said, "but ye're right."

They caught up to Rose before midday. As she'd forgotten to replenish her supplies, Rose was glad to see them. Catey and Billy were the only ones absent, which was understandable.

When they stopped to water the horses later that day, Alexi Romanov dismounted beside Rose. "You should have stayed with your wife and daughter," she said.

He cast her a quick glance. "My wife and daughter will be fine."

"No doubt," Rose agreed. "But you aren't related to me, or to Luke. Why leave your family to help us?"

His gaze touched on Ethan, then Mikhail. "Family isn't always about blood."

He was right.

Lily let loose a spate of Cheyenne. Alexi smiled as if he'd understood, then murmured a few words in what sounded like the same language. The child giggled in delight and practically dived into his arms.

"You speak Cheyenne?" Rose asked as he settled Lily onto his hip.

"He speaks everything." Ethan joined them. "I have no idea how."

Alexi shrugged. "I've always been good with languages."

"What is she saying?"

"I don't understand all of it." He tilted his head, listening. "The water tastes good. The night has stars. She would like to have many horses."

Rose didn't think the last sentence was quite right.

When they got back on their mounts, Lily clung to Alexi as if he were her long-lost uncle. "We will ride together and converse."

"Women love him," Annabeth said.

"It is my curse," he agreed.

"Catey doesn't mind?"

"She knows my heart belongs only to her and one other." He considered Lily. "Perhaps two others."

By the time the tops of the trees on the riverbank that shaded the camp appeared on the horizon, Alexi was fairly fluent in Cheyenne. Maybe it would help.

The Dog Men who approached did not wear war bonnets. Their horses did not wear war bridles. None of them were painted. The sentries would have seen Rose and her companions coming for miles, so she took the absence of those things as a good sign. However, the warriors seemed agitated. They rode in circles around the new arrivals, whooping and hooting, urging them toward camp as if they were in a desperate hurry.

Rose would have been concerned if Lily, still riding with Alexi, hadn't clapped and called out to them happily. However, Many Horses was not among them.

"What is she saying?" Rose shouted as they cantered toward the ridge.

"Hello," Alexi answered. "Their names perhaps? Something about her father."

Lily no doubt wondered where in hell Many Horses was, too.

They didn't have long to wait for their answer. The instant they reached camp, Rose saw the man, lance in hand, glaring at a bruised and bleeding Luke Phelan.

CHAPTER 28

L uke!"
He was hearing ghosts again. He shouldn't be surprised. Every time someone he loved died because of him, the wind whispered. Except he hadn't heard the wind since . . .

Luke tried to remember, couldn't. He *had* been hit in the head a few times. A cut over his eye was bleeding. He couldn't see very well. Those injuries might explain why he heard Rose; he saw her, too.

He blinked, rubbed at his good eye, but she was still there. Not only was she there, but so were a lot of other people. Maybe he was already dead. Except that would mean his sister, her husband, his brother, Lily, and two strangely familiar looking men, one who resembled his childhood best friend, Moses Farquhar—both dressed in black—were dead, too.

Luke staggered, nearly fell, and Rose cried his name again, leaping off her horse and running in his direction. One of the Dog Men snatched her around the waist and lifted her kicking and shouting from the ground. Luke growled and started for them.

No one touched her like that. No one.

A lance stuck in the ground right where he had just been.

"Stand still," Many Horses ordered.

"No." Luke kept walking.

The Dog Man tackled him, and they fell to the dirt,

rolling, punching, snarling. Luke was tempted to bite. Until now he had not fought back. He hadn't planned to.

"I cannot stop this fight," Medicine Bear had told him that morning. "You promised not to disappear."

Luke said nothing. No one would believe that a white man had snuck into the camp, kidnapped the White Ghost, then left again with no trace that he had ever been there. Luke wouldn't believe it himself if he hadn't been the one taken.

He was tired of excuses. He was tired of everything, especially breathing. Many Horses deserved his revenge, and without Rose to live for, Luke would gladly let him have it.

It was Many Horses' own fault that he had decided to torture Luke rather than kill him outright. He should have learned the folly of that the last time they'd battled. Again, he'd kept Luke alive long enough that the gods, or maybe just God, had shown Luke the truth. Many Horses had lied. Rose was alive. And suddenly Luke wanted very much to live, too.

Somehow, with all the rolling and jostling, Many Horses ended up straddling Luke's chest. He wrapped his hands around Luke's throat. "Because of you, she died."

Luke tossed Many Horses over his head, just the way he'd always tossed James whenever his brother had tried to throttle him. Many Horses landed on his back—hard—and lay there stunned just long enough for Luke to draw the knife he hadn't planned on using and press it to the Dog Man's throat. "If you mean to kill someone, kill him. Don't talk."

Luke's wrist twitched, and blood trickled down. He had to give the Dog Man credit; he never flinched. He wouldn't.

"Why did you say Rose was dead?" Luke demanded.

"I wanted you to suffer."

Luke considered the man who had once been his

friend. He should probably kill him. Rose would never be safe if he didn't.

Lily's sweet, clear voice rang through the silence. Both Luke and Many Horses froze as the exceedingly handsome man in black, who Luke now recognized as the gambler from Rogue—he had no idea what *he* was doing here—translated, "Why do my fathers fight?"

"Fathers?" Annabeth murmured.

"Family isn't always about blood," Rose said.

"Neho'eehe!" Lily cried.

"Yes?" Luke and Many Horses answered together. Their eyes met. Luke lifted the knife, got to his feet, then held out his free hand to the Dog Man. Many Horses pretended not to see as he got to his feet without help.

Lily barreled toward them like a runaway carriage. She wrapped her left arm around Luke's knee and her right around the Dog Man's.

"Neho'eehe," she whispered.

Luke set his hand on her head. Many Horses set his on her shoulder.

"Éše'he Ôhvó'komaestse!" another voice called.

Lily released the men and ran toward Ominotago, the Dog Man's wife.

Concerned that Lily's joy at the sight of her "other mother" would hurt Rose, Luke glanced her way, but she wasn't looking at Lily. She was looking at him. The next thing he knew they were in each other's arms.

"I thought you were dead," he murmured, at the same time Rose said, "I was afraid I'd be too late."

She leaned back. "God, you're a mess."

"I love you, too."

Her eyes widened. "You . . . what?"

"Love you."

She stepped away. "You love your dead wife."

"Always," he agreed. "But she's gone."

"Is she?" Her gaze sharpened. "Really?"

"I might hear her voice sometimes, but that doesn't make her any less gone."

"You don't have to love me just because you had to marry me."

"Just because I had to doesn't mean I didn't want to."

"Had to?" his sister asked.

Luke lifted his gaze. The rest of the contingent had surrounded them. The man in the priest's collar didn't just resemble Moze—he *was* Moze. Talk about showing up when he was least expected.

"Annabeth told me you were a Pinkerton. She didn't mention you were a priest."

"He's not," Annabeth said. "He's up to something. Don't bother to ask. He won't tell."

Moze slapped Luke on the shoulder. Luke winced. Many Horses had done a lot more than slap the same place. "I'm glad you're okay."

Luke thought, at last, he was.

"Tell me why you *had* to marry," Annabeth repeated. "And why you didn't bother to mention it to me when I saw you."

"At the time, we didn't think it was legal," Rose said.

"A Cheyenne marriage?" Moze's brow furrowed. "In what world would that be legal?"

"When I said those vows, I meant them." Luke held Rose's gaze. "I wished they were legal. I still do."

"The Jesus man could marry you now." Medicine Bear had joined the circle.

Annabeth shot Moze a glare. "Don't you dare!"

"I wouldn't."

"We don't need a priest." Rose cast Moze a look, too. "Not even a real one."

Luke didn't blame Rose for not loving him. Why would she? The first time they met he'd tried to kill her. Half the time they'd spent together he'd been babbling crazy. She'd nearly been scalped; she'd been captured by both the army and the Cheyenne. He'd made love to her thinking she was another woman. She'd lost a child while he'd been insensible. Certainly she'd come here to save his life, but that didn't mean she wanted to share the rest of it with him.

"I understand," he said.

"I don't think you do." She reached into her pocket, pulled out a crumpled piece of paper, and held it out to him. Curious, he took it.

Jakob Varner died of smallpox six months past.

Luke lifted his gaze. "You weren't married."

"I was, just not when we were."

"You didn't know that."

"No."

"You thought it wasn't real."

"It was always *real*, Luke. I just didn't think it was legal."

"It isn't," Moze murmured.

"Shut up," everyone said.

Luke took a step toward Rose; she took one toward him. Then he was kissing her, and she was kissing him back. He never wanted to stop, probably wouldn't have if tiny hands hadn't patted his knee.

"My father? My mother?"

Rose drew back, eyes wide. "Was that English?"

"Mama!" Lily shouted, and pushed them apart so she could get in between.

"Definitely English," Luke agreed.

Rose turned to the gambler from Rogue who, for some inexplicable reason—perhaps tied to why in hell he was here—understood Cheyenne. "You taught her?"

"Reminded her. She already knew."

"Who the hell are you?" Luke asked.

"You don't remember me?"

"Of course I do." His voice was sharp and it shouldn't be. There were many things he didn't remember, and equally as many that made no sense. For instance . . . "Why are you with them?"

"We should have that discussion on the way home," Annabeth said.

"Home?" Luke repeated. The only home he'd known for too long had been here.

"Freedom."

"I . . ." He looked at Rose.

She looked at Lily, then at the Cheyenne. "If you want to stay, we'll stay."

"No!" Annabeth said. "I can't lose you again."

Luke took his sister's hands. They were cold, and they trembled a bit. "If you know where I am, Annie Beth Lou, how can I be lost?"

Her eyes filled. "They took you and they hurt you."

"They accepted me, and they loved me."

"They just tried to kill you."

"Not they. Many Horses."

"Won't he try again?"

Luke glanced around for the Dog Man, but he wasn't there. "I don't think so."

"You don't *think*?" Annabeth threw up her arms. "You have a wife now, a child. You need to be more certain than that."

"I am." He had won the battle with Many Horses. The Dog Man would not dare to fight him again. At least over Kiwidinok.

While he doubted they would ever be as close as they'd been—they probably wouldn't even be friends—Luke thought they would be able to coexist, if not for the sake of the Cheyenne, at least for the sake of Lily.

His sister sighed, then hugged him and went back to her husband's side. Luke turned to Rose—a woman who'd once been terrified of Indians, and now had offered to live with the Cheyenne. For him. "You're sure?"

"I am," Rose said, and she did seem sure. She lifted Lily onto her hip. "How can I take her away from her mother?"

"You're her mother."

She turned her gaze to Lily's other mother, who watched them with a familiar, terrified expression. "So is she."

They wouldn't be able to stay forever. The Cheyenne way was dying. They couldn't still be here when it did. But for a while they could help. He could heal. So could she.

"When we were on the train and in town, people stared, pointed, whispered. I don't think Lily will be accepted. At least not until she's older and understands why."

"Probably not," he agreed. He wasn't certain he'd be accepted, either. Wasn't certain he wanted to be. But he'd go back for Rose, if she needed to. "You're not afraid anymore?"

"I'm afraid all the time."

"You're the bravest person I've ever known."

"Only when I'm with you." She took his hand. "With you, I can face anything." Her gaze wandered over the village. "I know you still love Kiwidinok and Ayasha."

"They're dead, Rose."

"That doesn't mean you can't love them."

"You don't want me to stop?"

"Can you?"

He should be honest. She deserved that. And so much more. "No."

"I'm so glad."

She laid her palm on his right cheek. Lily, who'd been glancing back and forth between the two of them, leaned forward and set her palm on his left. He stood framed between them and knew at last that he had come home.

"If you've loved them this long," Rose said, "imagine how long you're going to love us."

EPILOGUE

Freedom, Kansas
One year later

Lily stood at the window of the doctor's office. "When will she come, Mama? When?"

As predicted, Lily and Billy had become best friends. Or as best of friends as a one-year-old could make. Whenever Billy saw Lily she had gurgled and smiled and reached out with long-fingered, clever hands. Her first word had been *Papa*, her second *Mama*, but her third had definitely been *Lily*.

"There they are!" Lily shrieked, and ran onto the porch.

"She seems to have remembered English," Annabeth said.

"She has," Rose agreed. Her daughter chattered often, and well, in both languages.

They joined Lily on the porch as Alexi pulled the wagon to a stop. He helped his daughter to the ground. She started to toddle toward the steps, and he swept her up and set her next to Rose before turning to lift Catey down. The three women contemplated one another's newly rounded bellies.

"Autumn?" Annabeth asked.

"Close enough," Rose agreed. Catey just nodded.

They followed the children into the house, Lily

holding Billy's hand and helping her walk as they spoke in a mixture of English, Cheyenne, and baby talk.

Alexi drove toward the stable. Ethan was at one of the neighboring farms delivering a baby. In the past Annabeth would have gone with him, but the instant he'd discovered his wife was with child, he'd refused to allow her near a horse, even one attached to a buckboard.

"If he had his way I'd stay in bed until my water broke," Annabeth had muttered.

Considering that they had lost a child before, Rose understood his caution. But that didn't make it any easier for a woman like Annabeth to bear. She was used to being busy and helping others.

Instead of his wife, Ethan had taken his brother-in-law along. Not that Luke knew anything about birthing babies, but it gave him something to do. His having something to do was one of the reasons they were in Freedom.

Though they'd enjoyed a nearly idyllic year with the Cheyenne, times were changing fast. The tribes were being pushed onto the reservation, and many of them were pushing back.

Buffalo hunters had begun to destroy as many buffalo as they could find, leaving the Comanche, the Cheyenne, the Kiowa, and many others both confused over the senseless slaughter and desperate for food. Desperation and warriors were not a good combination. There had been several attacks and the army was massing a force. It wouldn't be long before something terrible happened.

Again.

Luke had tried to convince the Dog Men to surrender, but that was like convincing a river to run uphill. Though he and Many Horses had managed to live in the same village, the man took the opposite position from Luke in every argument. Many Horses wanted to head north and join the Cheyenne and Sioux who had been given a reservation in Montana, along with hunting lands and the sacred Black Hills. However, white people were invading those hills, cutting down timber and building towns, and the government wasn't stopping them.

"Sooner or later," Luke said, "all hell's gonna break loose."

So instead of joining the friends they'd made as they headed north, Luke, Rose, and Lily had come to visit their friends to the east. The promise of Billy, along with assurances that they would visit Many Horses and his wife, had kept Lily from crying too much.

"Wouldn't it be nice if we could all be together for the births?" Annabeth asked.

"Nice?" Catey asked. "Or loud?"

"I don't mean the actual births. That would be . . ."

"Frightening," Rose finished at the same time Annabeth said, "damn near impossible. Unless there's a storm." She shrugged. "Storms seem to send everyone into labor at once. Dogs, cats, cattle, people."

"If Luke gets the job—"

"He'll get it," Annabeth interrupted.

Freedom still didn't have a sheriff, and they were really starting to need one. The town had continued to grow. More people, more problems.

"How can you be so sure?" Rose handed Lily her rag doll, which Lily promptly handed to Billy, and she, in turn, promptly stuck the head into her mouth.

Annabeth rubbed her stomach and smiled. "Ethan's in charge of the hiring."

"That'll be two of us in town," Rose said. Unfortunately she didn't see how Alexi and Catey could ever move to Freedom. The gambling hall they owned in Rogue was turning far too much of a profit to close.

"About that . . ." Catey began, just as Alexi stepped into the room.

"The deal is done, *mi corazon.*"

"What does that mean?" Annabeth asked.

"My heart," Catey said.

"Not that." Annabeth waved the translation away, her gaze sharp on Alexi. "What have you done? Don't make my brother arrest you the instant he becomes sheriff."

"Your brother is the new sheriff?" His lips curved. "How convenient."

Annabeth's eyes narrowed, and he held up a hand.

"Do not worry, *mon amie*. I will do nothing in Freedom to cause trouble."

"In Freedom," Rose repeated, and he winked.

"I have bought the Jayhawker."

"That's the least profitable saloon in town," Annabeth said.

"Not for long," Catey murmured.

"I think I will rename it Cat's Hideaway."

Once upon a time, Catey had been known as Cat O'Banyon, bounty hunter. The story was as interesting as both Catey and Alexi themselves.

"Like hell," his wife said.

"We will discuss."

"What about your place in Rogue?" Rose asked.

"Mikhail will manage it."

A shuffling sound had them all glancing toward the door. Ethan and Luke had returned. Each had put on needed weight. Luke's hair had grown nearly to his shoulders once more. Every time he threatened to cut it, Rose threatened to bury every scissors and knife that they owned.

"Is he up to that?" Ethan asked.

"He's better," Catey said. "I doubt he'll ever be who he was, but he isn't so angry and he hasn't tried to strangle anyone since the last time Moze showed up."

"Can't hardly blame him," Ethan muttered.

A lot of history lay between the Pinkerton agent and everyone in the room. Not much of it was good. Moze was always up to something, and he didn't much care how he succeeded.

Rose wasn't sure how he and Luke had become friends. Although maybe, as was the case with all who'd lived through that war, times had changed them. Moses Farquhar was most likely a far different man now from the one he had been then. Same as every one of the men surrounding her now, as well as the women.

"This is good," Alexi said. "It feels right. Families should be together, *oui*?"

"Oui," his wife agreed.

"We," Luke said, and laid his hand on Rose's stomach.

"Wheee!" Billy shouted, and everyone laughed.

Friends. Family. Freedom.

What more could they ask for?

CHEYENNE GLOSSARY

ameohtsé: go
anováóó'o: The girl is beautiful.
Ayasha: Little One
e-énêšévaenâhtséstove: They stopped fighting.
ema'o: red
Éše'he Ôhvó'komaestse: White Moon
Haestôhe'hame: Many Horses
Heammawihio: the Wise One Above, the creator
He'amo'ome: above world
heehe'e: yes
he'eo'o: women
Heova'ehe: Yellow Hair (Custer)
Hestôsanestôtse: renewing of the earth (Medicine Lodge
  ceremony)
hetanesêstse: men
hetómestôtse: This is true.
hohnohka: contrary
hoimaha: a spirit from the north that brings winter to
  the land, appears as a white man
Hotametaneo'o: Dog Men
hotoao'o: buffalo
hova'âhane: no
Kiwidinok: Of the Wind
ma'e-ve'ho'e: red white man
Ma'heonenahkohe: Medicine Bear
mestaa'e: spirit not of a person
motšéške: knife

nahko'eehe: my mother
náhtse: daughter
nâhtse'eme: wife
Nana'tose: I am cold.
Ná-néehove: I am the one.
neho'eehe: my father
Né-néevá'eve: Who are you?
Nés-tsêhe'otseha: Bring them here.
Netonêševehe: What is your name?
nóxa'e: wait
Ominotago: Beautiful Voice
oo'estseahe: shaved head, baldy
Savane: other tribes, not from the plains
Seyan: the place of the dead
si'yuhk: spirit of a person recently dead
tsitsistas: our people (what the Cheyenne call themselves)
ve'ho'e: spider
Ve'ho'e Mestaa'e: White Man Ghost

SIOUX GLOSSARY

ha: yes
hoka hey: generic call to action, similar to "come on!"
le mita pila: my thanks
Nake nula waun welo: I am ready for whatever comes.
Paha Sapa: the Black Hills
wicasa wakan: holy man, prophet
witcko tko ke: crazy
wi-wanyang-wa-c'i-pi: Sun Dance

Read on for a sneak peek at
Lori Austin's next historical romance,
coming soon from Signet Eclipse.

A man of your reputation would be most welcome in Montana. If you are in need of employment, please come to my ranch north of Little Falls.

"What is that? Out there, *mon ami*?"

Matthew Mackay—once Lieutenant Mackay, U.S. Army, turned Major Mackay, Army of the Confederacy, become just Matt: wounded, vanquished, dismissed wanderer—looked up from his letter to find Lucien Duvier pointing a long, elegant, indolent finger at the horizon.

His voice as lazy as his movements, nevertheless, Lucien was not a man to be trifled with. A gambler by trade, a Creole by manner and perhaps by birth, too—Matt was never quite certain with Lucien what was real and what was not—the man had survived the same war as Matt through guile instead of gun.

Matt's intercession in a New Orleans saloon scuffle had saved Lucien's life, or so the man insisted. Matt had always believed Lucien would have talked his way out of his troubles. He could talk his way out of hell itself. But in a world where everyone had lost someone if not everyone, where it was dangerous to travel alone, particularly if your voice hinted of Mississippi or New Orleans, they found themselves better off together than apart.

So it had been just the two of them, headed west, until—

"Whatever that is, it ain't movin'."

—until Matt had found the grubby, feral, obviously half-breed boy starving alone on the streets of Fort Worth.

The age of Alejandro Chavez was as unknown to Matt

and Lucien as it was to Alejandro himself. Matt figured the kid at about fourteen, though in Alejandro's eyes sometimes he caught glimpses of a man even older than Matt's own thirty-two years. Alejandro was an orphan— his mama a Mexican peasant girl, his papa a member of one of the raiding tribes north of the border. That was all Alejandro knew about his past, or at least all he was willing to share.

Tucking the letter from his prospective employer, Edward Hoyt, back into his saddlebag, Matt peered out over the Badlands. A more apt name for a place had never been invented. Stark and silent, the dry grass and brown ridges seemed to spread into eternity.

Matt had decided to head straight through the center in hopes of avoiding some of the Indian problems occurring both east and west of here. Not that the Sioux didn't have every right to have a bug in their bonnet over the gold fields that had been stolen out from under them, but Matt didn't think any war parties would ask his thoughts on the matter before killing him and those he rode with.

The men halted their mounts at the top of a ridge and stared at the three white specks—one large, two small— in the distance. A thin line of smoke drifted toward the unbelievably blue, impossibly wide Montana sky. And Matt knew what he would find down there at the heart of the Badlands.

Death, destruction, and despair. If he'd been a superstitious man, he'd believe they'd followed him all the way from home.

"I'll go and see what happened," Alejandro said.

"Like hell," Matt growled.

Lucien sighed. "Must we go down there at all? It would be so much easier to keep heading the way we have been, no?"

"No," Alejandro and Matt answered.

"I don't suppose I could wait here, and you would regale me with the tale of your adventure upon your return?"

Alejandro snorted. Matt just clucked to his horse and headed down the slope.

"I did not think so," Lucien muttered. But he followed, as did Alejandro.

Nearly six months together had bonded them as close as any family. Or at least Matt thought they resembled a family. He wasn't sure; he'd never had one. Neither had the others. Perhaps that was why they got on so well.

Since the end of the war, times had been hard all over. Harder still for an ex-Confederate officer with a nasty limp and few marketable skills beyond his ability with a gun. Matt had managed to keep a roof over his head, clothes on his back, and food in his mouth by working odd jobs—an embarrassment for a soldier who had once been responsible for hundreds of men and valuable weaponry.

Sometimes Alejandro worked alongside him, but more often than not, especially in Texas, the sight of the child made folks snarl "breed" and kick him out the door.

Lucien had managed to earn a bit in card games here and there. When he ran short, there was always a woman who welcomed him into her bed for as many days as he chose to stay there. The man possessed not only the lazy grace of an aristocrat and the clever fingers of a gambler, but the smooth tongue of a con artist and the dark, albeit handsome face of an angel fallen.

However, in a country that had endured four years of civil war only to be left conquered, depleted, and leaderless, most folks had little to lose in, and even less enthusiasm for, the games of pleasure or chance, which were Lucien's stock and trade.

Therefore when Matt received the offer to manage a cattle ranch in Montana Territory for the son of a man both Matt and his father had served with, not only Matt had packed his meager belongings and headed north, but his friends had, too.

Montana promised vast opportunity for farmers, ranchers, and miners—the latter prime pickings for someone like Lucien. The gambler had been rubbing his hands and talking of little but gold and silver the entire trip.

As they reached the bottom of the slope and headed across a short rocky area, the white specks loomed larger and larger, becoming a covered wagon and—

A French curse erupted from Lucien. Matt didn't know much French, but with Lucien around he was beginning to catch on to a little. Mostly the curse words, which had a certain flair all their own.

"*Merde!* Look what they have done to these people. Savages." He glanced at Alejandro. "No offense, *enfant.*"

Alejandro muttered a phrase in Spanish, which when translated turned out to be a physical impossibility, then moved off. The two behaved like brothers sometimes, children most times, and Matt felt on occasion as if he were the only adult in their small, ragtag group.

Lucien raised his gaze to the sky. "No buzzards and the fire's still hot."

Scanning the area, Matt saw nothing, no one. Which no doubt meant there were fifty Sioux warriors over the next rise. He drew his gun.

Lucien held up a staying hand. Matt frowned at the motion and the man. But Lucien jerked his head in the direction of the boy.

Alejandro stood at the edge of the small campsite, staring west into the seemingly endless expanse of the Badlands—listening, watching, waiting. His black hair, which seemed to be forever too long no matter how many times Matt hacked at it with a bowie knife, fluttered in the smoke-scented breeze.

"They are gone," he murmured.

Matt glanced at Lucien, but the other man shrugged without even meeting Matt's gaze as he continued to watch Alejandro. Though the boy had never known his father, never spent a day living as an Indian, sometimes he was downright spooky anyway.

Matt holstered his gun and climbed from his horse.

He knew better than to come down on his bad leg. But since walking involved both legs, and he was determined to continue with that activity despite all predictions to the contrary, he gritted his teeth and took a step.

Agony spliced along his hip, into his belly, then shot straight through his chest, halting his breath, before seeming to settle in his brain screaming. He refused to give the pain power by flinching, refused to acknowledge weakness by grimacing. He'd endured the same and worse since the minée ball had shattered his hip.

He was lucky to be alive. Lucky to have his leg. Lucky he was so all-fired stubborn he'd refused to believe for an instant that he would never walk again.

Matt took another step, ignored the lesser but still abominable pain. Funny, he didn't feel lucky.

He continued to hitch along, his stride becoming quicker, smoother as he worked out the stiffness. But no matter how far he walked, no matter how stubborn he was, he would never walk correctly again.

Matt stood above the two bodies. These folks would never breathe again. Perhaps lucky was all in the way a person looked at things.

Lucien appeared at his side. "What were they doing out here alone?"

Matt's gaze skipped from the bodies, to the wagon, to the ground, glancing off the single set of tracks coming in from the east, and ending with the churned-up grass and dirt left by a multitude of ponies that had raced off to the west. The settlers *had* been alone—and very, very foolish.

"We'll never know," he said.

Lucien's sigh was as sad as Matt had ever heard from the man. "I'll see if there's a shovel."

Matt nodded. Lucien might find a shovel, but he'd never use one. Any activity that might cause a callus on his hand or a bead of sweat on his brow would not be one that Lucien Duvier participated in.

Alejandro had no such qualms. The boy worked harder

than anyone Matt had ever known—almost as if he needed to prove something, though to whom Matt wasn't sure.

The dead folks hadn't even made it out of their bedrolls before the Indians sent them to a better place. Or at least Matt hoped there was a better place than this and someone watching over. But all he had seen, all he had done, made him uncertain of anything but the fact that hell resided here on earth more often than not.

Bending, ignoring the pain from the movement, he wrapped the young man and young woman in their blankets. The sun fell rapidly toward the western horizon. Though he'd hoped to continue on and perhaps leave behind this still and forbidding land tonight, or tomorrow at the latest, by the time the pilgrims were buried he and the others would do best to camp here.

He didn't like it, but things could be worse.

As if in answer to that thought, a chill wind shrieked out of the north. Smoke hit Matt in the face, acrid and near blinding. Snowflakes swirled about his head.

"Dammit, it's September," he muttered. "What next?"

And somewhere nearby a baby began to cry.

Alejandro Chavez sensed things that others did not. He'd learned to hide the ability, as it usually earned him a slap if not a kick, a punch if not a beating.

But during the short time he'd spent with Matt and Lucien, he'd discovered it was all right to listen to the whispers of the wind, the voices of the trees, and that tiny, prickly sensation along the back of his neck, beneath the heated curtain of his hair, that told him they were not alone.

While Lucien and Matt spoke quietly over the bodies of the fallen, Alejandro shifted his shoulders to ease the itch, then closed his eyes and opened his heart. He sensed no evil beyond the rocks, no death awaiting them in the grass, but someone was here. Someone he couldn't see. Was it perhaps the souls of the departed still hovering, waiting for their guide into the Great Beyond?

Alejandro stiffened at a tiny scratch, a precious hint of sound from . . . He opened his eyes and slowly turned toward . . . the wagon.

A single glance at Matt and Lucien found the elder wrapping the bodies in blankets while the other strolled off toward a pile of belongings the raiders must have tossed through before departing.

Alejandro shook his head. Lucien always moved as if he had an eternity to get wherever he desired, and when Alejandro ran he would sigh as if Alejandro's energy tired him just by watching.

But Matt . . . Matt always smiled gently, even when Alejandro ran too fast for Matt to keep up on his bad leg, and told him to be a kid for a while longer. Alejandro wasn't sure how; he'd never been a kid, but he was sure that he'd do anything just for Matt's smile.

Another slight squeak from the wagon and he started in that direction. He wished he had a gun, but Matt had put an end to that idea with a single frown. Alejandro did, however, have a knife in his belt, and to keep Matt—heck, even Lucien—safe, he would use it without a qualm.

Though Matt insisted Alejandro was too young for a weapon, in truth Alejandro had done many things that would earn Matt's frown and perhaps those two words Alejandro feared above all others.

Go away.

He paused a few feet from the smoking wagon. Most likely the sounds he had heard were only the lick of flames along one side or the drift of the breeze against a loose bit of canvas. Alejandro wished he could convince himself of that, but he knew better. Something lived inside that wagon.

An animal would have run off at their approach, or, if mad, attacked. A human—be he friend or foe—would have shown himself by now. So what could be hiding just out of sight?

Alejandro should call Matt and tell him what he felt. But what if he was wrong and there was nothing? What if he was right and Matt was hurt? The latter thought caused him to take the last few steps quickly, on feet as silent as those of his ancestors, before bounding into the wagon, knife clasped in his hand.

No one was there.

The Indians had dumped a lot outside, leaving the inside mostly empty. There was only one place to hide.

Alejandro tightened his grip on the knife and threw open the top of a large, vaulted chest. Nothing leaped out. Instead the clothes inside wiggled.

Heart pounding in his throat, Alejandro held the knife aloft with one hand and tossed a dress the color of Badlands grass out of the way with his other hand. The knife, already descending toward what he pictured was a snake or worse, clattered to the floor.

The sharp sound made the wide blue eyes of the baby girl open even wider. Her mouth, which had been making a sucking motion when he first saw her, now opened into an O. She drew in a breath and her face darkened.

"Uh-oh," Alejandro muttered.

The howl she emitted was louder than any Indian war cry and caused a chill to race down his back, even as his pounding heart seemed to stop. Without thought, he snatched her up. Then he wasn't sure what to do with her.

She was heavier than she looked, and warm and wet. She smelled, and she squirmed, and she screeched. So when Lucien bounded into the wagon faster than Alejandro had ever seen him do anything and shouted, "What in hell—?" he shoved her into the man's arms.

Startled, Lucien nearly dropped her. She screamed louder, the shade of her face deepening from red to purple. Terrified, ears ringing, breath coming so fast he could not think, Alejandro prepared to flee the wagon. Only to be brought up short as Matt climbed inside, too.

"Lucien, what—?"

The gambler practically tossed the baby into Matt's arms. Matt had no choice but to catch her. He held the child out in front of him like a rotten sack of apples. She smelled a whole lot worse, even if she did look a mite better. With her pale face, golden curls, eyes the shade of a mountain sky, Alejandro's first thought had been—*pretty*.

She didn't look so pretty anymore.

"What is this?" Matt demanded, nose wrinkling in distaste.

"*Une bebe.* Are you blind *and* deaf?"

"None of your lip, Lucien. Where did she come from?"

"Ask the boy. He made the creature cry, then tossed it at me."

Alejandro's mouth fell open. "No, I— What I mean is, she— Well, I did come in here, but—"

"Never mind." Matt's gaze ran over the wagon's interior, glanced off Lucien and Alejandro, then settled on the baby once more. "She's obviously the only survivor." He sighed. "We can't just leave her here."

"We can't take her across the Badlands howling as if we were sticking pins in her, either," Lucien grumbled. "Do something."

"What?"

"I don't know. Jiggle her." Lucien raised his voice above the din. "Wash her. Feed her. Hug her. Something."

"*Hug* her?"

"She's a female, isn't she?" Lucien shrugged. "When they cry, you hug them, no?"

"I have no idea," Matt muttered.

"It has always worked for me."

"Good, then you hug her." Matt pushed the baby at Lucien, but the man backed away.

"Not me. I will make camp."

"Yellow belly," Matt accused.

Unrepentant, Lucien grinned. "*That* would be me." He jumped from the wagon and disappeared.

Matt slid a glance toward Alejandro. "Not me," Alejandro said quickly. She might be cute, but she was loud, and she was smelly. He wasn't hugging *that*. "Uh-uh. No, sir!"

The baby continued to wail. Matt scowled, shrugged, shifted. "Well, I guess it wouldn't hurt to try. If anyone knows how to handle females, it would be Lucien and not me."

The comment made Alejandro frown. Come to think of it, he had never seen Matt with a woman. Lucien, *sí. Mucho.* Matt, *nunca.*

He shook his head at the stray Spanish thoughts. When he was tired, sick, or scared, he often reverted to the language of his mother. But he'd learned, just as he'd learned to keep his odd feelings about things to himself, never to speak "Mex talk" in front of others or risk more of the usual slaps and scorn.

But Alejandro forgot about the curious fact involving Matt and women as his friend took a deep breath and pulled the child to his chest. "Hush," he whispered. "I'm here."

And she stopped. Just like that.

Matt and Alejandro blinked at each other, then tensed, waiting for a louder, more horrific complaint to follow. Instead all she did was whimper in between the sharp hitches of her breath. Matt shifted, and she gave a sharp, coughing sob, then grabbed onto his shirt with one tiny fist.

Matt was a big man—tall, broad, strong despite the limp—but holding a baby against his chest only made him seem bigger, broader, and stronger. Alejandro understood why the little girl had stopped crying and clung. From the moment he'd seen Matt looming over him in that dark, damp, lonely alleyway in Fort Worth, from the instant he'd heard Matt's deep, soothing Mississippi drawl, he'd known he was safe—even though he had no idea what safe was.

Alejandro could not tear his gaze away from the picture the two of them made. Matt's face, tanned and lined from the elements, only served to make her pale, smooth cheek appear sweeter and younger. His golden hair would have matched hers, except for the silver streaks playing hide-and-seek among the strands. For the first time in as long as he could recall, Alejandro wondered if this world wasn't such a terrible place to be.

"Appears Duvier was right."

Alejandro lifted his gaze from the sunshine shade of the child's curls to Matt's face. He raised an eyebrow, tried to look arrogant in case Matt had seen him go soft. If Alejandro wanted to ride with these men, he could not behave like a little boy.

"For a change," he said, sneering.

Matt rolled his eyes as he often did whenever Lucien and Alejandro squabbled like children. When he did that, Alejandro almost felt like one of them.

"How about you bury those folks while Lucien sets up camp, hmm? Appears as if I've just drawn cleaning and feeding duty."

"What does it eat?" Alejandro blurted.

"*It* is a baby." Matt's sigh was long and heartfelt. "And I have no idea."

Matt stretched out on his bedroll and tried without success to get the baby back to sleep. The slightest noise woke her from a sound slumber, and out in the wilds of Montana the noises were much more than slight.

He'd lost track of how many days since they'd found her. At least the snow had stopped after dropping a few flakes on the dirt brown earth. Matt didn't want to think about how difficult it would have been to carry on through a freak autumn snowstorm.

They'd continued to travel northwest but a lot more slowly since one of them had to carry her. She'd taken a dislike to Lucien, probably because he held her so clumsily. For a man as smooth as molasses, Matt couldn't quite figure how he bobbled the baby so much. Unless, of course, he did so on purpose to avoid his turn. Matt wouldn't put it past him.

At any rate, she slowed them down because she had to eat, drink, be cleaned up every other minute, and at night . . .

Matt froze as she hiccuped against his chest. But she didn't start to cry, thank God, so he relaxed—a little.

At night she kept some of them, if not all of them, awake so that they could barely roll out of their beds come sunrise.

Tucking her closer to his side, Matt began to hum. Sometimes that worked. But if he stopped too soon, or got up and left her when she wasn't completely asleep, she shrieked. In truth, she shrieked a hell of a lot. Why, then, did he like her so much?

Matt glanced behind him at Lucien and Alejandro. They were asleep. They couldn't see him reach out a large, rough finger. She clasped on and stuffed it into her mouth. Pretty much everything within grabbing range went into her mouth. Matt had learned that the hard way with grass. He'd spent a good thirty minutes picking a baby handful out of her screaming mouth. That stuff sure could stick to a tongue like a burr.

She had a few teeth, and he'd discovered if he soaked crackers in water, she swallowed the food like a starving baby bird. The child ate more than Alejandro, it seemed. Drank more, too, which only resulted in other disgusting pastimes that Matt appeared to be completely in charge of.

She was a smelly, loud pain in his behind. And Matt wondered what he had done for amusement before she'd turned up. She laughed at everything, when she wasn't crying over nothing, and the soft wonder on her face at each new experience made them new to him as well.

Alejandro thought she was pretty cute, and played with her whenever he thought no one was watching. But Lucien, too easily amused in Matt's opinion, could not be coaxed to smile in her presence. Matt wasn't sure why, and he didn't ask.

There were certain things the three of them did not discuss, and their pasts were one of those things. Such rules forced them to look forward instead of back—or at least that's what they all chose to believe.

The child gave a sweet, baby sigh and her eyes drooped. Matt kept on humming. He must have drifted off, and the little one, too, because the next time he opened his eyes, the sun was full up and the baby was gone.

He shot to his feet, his gaze darting around their camp. The sight of her in Alejandro's lap, playing with his long hair, allowed Matt to exhale his pent-up, panicked breath.

"Why didn't you wake me?" He poured himself a cup of coffee.

Lucien gazed sourly into the fire. "You wouldn't be woken. Even the creature screaming in your ear and pulling on your nose did not cause a quiver."

Matt frowned. He didn't like the sound of that. She couldn't walk, or even crawl well, but she'd been known to roll pretty damn fast. What if she'd rolled into the fire while he lay snoring? His heart stuttered, then thundered at the thought.

But what could he do? Tie one end of a string to her leg and the other to his hand so she couldn't get away? Maybe that wasn't a bad idea.

"Ma! Ma!" The little girl held out her arms to Matt.

"Mama?" Lucien exclaimed. "Why is it calling you Mama?"

"I think she's trying to say Matt." Touched, he lifted the child into his arms, where she promptly latched on to his shirt collar with her mouth.

"What are we going to name her?" Alejandro asked.

"We will name her nothing, *enfant*. We *aren't* keeping her."

Lucien looked as tired as Matt felt. The man did not do well when his routine was interrupted. Since the baby had joined them, their routine was shot to hell and gone.

Matt narrowed his eyes on the gambler. "We've kept you."

"I don't drool."

"Sometimes you do," Alejandro offered. "When you're

sleeping you drool a little, and when you're drunk, even worse."

"I don't recall asking for your opinion."

Matt jumped in before the two could escalate their exchange into a full-blown squabble. "Well, we can't keep calling her 'baby' and 'it' and 'the child' all the time."

Matt wasn't even going to bring up Lucien's unfortunate habit of calling her "the creature."

"Why not? The creature doesn't know any better."

Matt stifled a sigh. Maybe he should bring it up.

Before he could, Alejandro blurted, "I have been calling her *Corazon*."

"Whatever for?"

Matt shot Lucien a quelling glare. Sometimes the man's disdain for everything was too much to bear.

Alejandro stared at his feet. "*Mi madre* called me *mi corazon* when I was small." The boy peered up at Matt, and that look was back—the one that made Alejandro appear as old as those hills in the distance. "I remember very little of her, but I do remember that. It means 'my heart.' The words always made me feel special."

Matt smiled. "It's a very nice name."

"It's not a name—it's a Mexican body part," Lucien mumbled.

Alejandro's eyes narrowed, his lips thinned, and his fingers curled into fists.

"What if we call her Cora?" Matt said quickly.

The baby lifted her head and grinned at him. "Ma!" she shouted.

And Cora she became.